Raspberries and Vinegar

A Farm Fresh Romance

Book 1

Valerie Comer

ISBN: 0993831338
ISBN-13: 978-0993831331

This is a work of fiction set in a redrawn northern Idaho. Any resemblance to real events or to actual persons, living or dead, is coincidental.

First edition, Choose Now Publishing, 2013
Second edition, GreenWords Media, 2014

Printed in the United States of America

Endorsements

"A spunky heroine on a mission kicks off Comer's series, making for a sweet read with touches of humor and a hint of tang that tugs at the heart."
~Lynette Sowell, award-winning author of the ECPA best seller, *Christmas at Barncastle Inn*

"The best things in life are the ones you can't buy, including the beauty of nature and the power of love. *Raspberries and Vinegar* demonstrates both the pleasures and challenges of sustainable living with warmth and humor. A vivid portrait of the simple life!"
~Nancy Sleeth, author of *Almost Amish: One Woman's Quest for a Slower, Simpler, More Sustainable Life*

"Valerie Comer has created a truly unique concept with her Farm Fresh Romance series, and Jo Shaw is a corker of a heroine to start the stories rolling. She's sharp, smart mouthed, and sure to win your heart. What can you expect from feisty Jo and her stubborn, handsome neighbor? Fireworks!"
~Trish Perry, co-author of *The Midwife's Legacy*

"*Raspberries and Vinegar* is a humorous and heart touching read. Comer brings real issues to light, with her passion for local sustainable food and family shining in a perfect summer read. You'll find yourself ready to sip on a raspberry and vinegar drink after delighting in this fresh farm read. And yes, Comer shares the recipe right here in the book!"
~Melissa K. Norris, author of *Pioneering Today: Faith and Home the Old-Fashioned Way*

"Valerie Comer has created a unique concept with her Farm Fresh Romance series, sandwiching the importance of local grown food between Jo Shaw and her handsome neighbor who doesn't get Jo's passion. A romance sure to feed you."
~Diana Lesire Brandmeyer, author of *Mind of Her Own, A Bride's Dilemma in Friendship, Tennessee,* and *We're Not Blended We're Pureed.*

Dedication

Dear Jim,
Thank you for believing in me and
supporting my dream every step of the way.
~ all my love always, Val

For Rick and Nancy Hawreschuk,
Whose misadventures with Guillain-Barré Syndrome
I passed off to an unsuspecting character.
Thank you for demonstrating your faith in God
even through hard times.
You two are my heroes.

Books by Valerie Comer

Farm Fresh Romance Novels

Raspberries and Vinegar
Wild Mint Tea
Sweetened with Honey (November 2014)

Christmas Romance Novella Duo

Snowflake Tiara (September 2014)

Fantasy Novel

Majai's Fury

Acknowledgements

It takes a village to write, critique, and prepare a novel for publishing. I'm so thankful for the inhabitants of my village.

Thanks to my girls, Hanna and Jen, for being the inspiration for this story. Both of you have way more raspberry and way less vinegar than Jo. Thank you for raising my granddaughters on real food—local when possible.

Thank you, Margaret and Maripat. You've been beside me on this journey longer than anyone. Your friendship, inspiration, and critiques have made all the difference.

Nicole, you've taken your "life goal" of getting your critique partner published to a whole new level. Without you, *Raspberries and Vinegar* would not have seen the light of day. Thank you for everything.

Angela—friend, mentor, editor. Your friendship means so much to me. I'm delighted God brought you into my life.

To the many fans who read, enjoyed, and reviewed *Rainbow's End*: your excitement and encouragement gave me a shot in the arm when I needed it most. Thanks.

And to Jesus. Thank you for giving me abundant life and the stories to explore it in so many ways. Isaiah 55:8 is true in my life: *"For my thoughts are not your thoughts, neither are your ways my ways," declares the* LORD. *"As the heavens are higher than the earth, so are my ways higher than your ways and my thoughts than your thoughts."*

Winner

Raspberries and Vinegar: A Farm Fresh Romance is the winner of The Word Award 2014 for best in contemporary romance.

The Word Guild is an organization that seeks to impact Canadian culture through the words of writers, editors, and speakers with a Christian worldview.

Chapter 1

Josephine Shaw gritted her teeth as she jerked the harvest-gold range forward on worn linoleum. There it was again. That incessant scratching could only be from one source. Mice. Of course the old trailer would have the despicable creatures. It'd been vacant for how long? The beam of her flashlight found half a dozen naked newborns sheltered in a nest of insulation and wood chips. A full-grown rodent shot through the gap she'd created and scuttled right over her foot. Jo gasped, nearly dropping the light as she jerked back.

Her roommate, Sierra Riehl, shrieked and danced a fierce jig designed, Jo presumed, to fend off an attacking two-inch-high army.

"Whoa! You're going to go right through." A distinct possibility, given the spongy feel to the old trailer's floor.

Sierra's gaze tried to capture every inch of space at once, but at least her feet slowed their tempo. "Th-the mouse…"

Jo tried to get her own heart rate under control. "Long gone."

At least, Jo would be if she were in his shoes. If mice wore shoes. Which they didn't.

"Are you sure?"

What was she, some kind of fortuneteller? Oh, wait. There was still the nest, and somebody would have to deal with it. Didn't look like Sierra was up for the job. Never mind, Jo could do this herself. "Um. You might not want to look."

Sierra dug purple manicured fingernails into Jo's arm, her blue eyes wide. "Why? What's back there?"

"You don't want to know." Jo steered her friend into the living room, empty but for the musty shag carpet. "Just look out the window for a minute. Admire the view. Dream about all the things we're going to do here at Green Acres. Think about the straw-bale house we're going to build." She pointed across the snow-flattened yellow grass to the building site. "Right over there." Pouring the foundation couldn't come fast enough. Even spending one night in this disgusting, moldy trailer would be more than ample. Bad enough without the mice, but *with* them?

Jo shuddered. They weren't going to get the best of her. She grabbed a dustpan, shoved it hard under the nest and gagged at the stench of feces she'd disturbed. Choking down her bile, she hurried to the door, wrenched it open, and flung the dustpan's contents…

…right at a set of chest buttons. Scraps of insulation clung to a shearling-lined suede coat right at Jo's eye level.

Jo froze. What had she done? "Sorry," she gasped. Her eyes jerked up. For an instant she focused on the shocked brown eyes of a tall guy with a closely cropped beard and mustache. Dark blond hair curled from beneath his tweed newsboy cap. His hand, poised to knock, dropped to his side.

At the same instant, the sound of frantic clawing pulled Jo's attention down to a Border collie puppy nearly yanking the leash from his master's hand as he surged at the slug-like blobs. Jo stooped and swept the wiggling mice from the wood-planked porch with her dustpan. "No! You don't want to eat those."

The dog rewarded her with two paws on her shoulders and a slurp up her cheek, nearly knocking her over.

Jo stifled a giggle then remembered the guy. The totally hunky man she'd just baptized with rodents.

Oh, no. She could use a do-over of this meeting.

He cleared his throat and shortened the leash. "Domino, sit." The pup almost got his rump to touch the boards, but his wagging tail threatened to topple him.

Apparently Jo was stuck with *this* introduction. She took a deep breath, straightened, and reached out her hand. "Hi. Sorry about that. I'm Josephine Shaw."

The guy stared down.

What had she done now? Jo followed his gaze to the dustpan she clenched in her outstretched hand. It dropped from nerveless fingers and clattered against the boards. The pup pounced on it.

Jo closed her eyes, breathed a quick prayer, and wiped her hand on her overalls. Ideal garb for cleaning out an old, filthy trailer, but not so perfect for meeting the cutest guy she'd seen in a while. She summoned a smile and looked up at him again. "Let's try that again. I'm Josephine Shaw, and I'm really sorry I threw mice at you."

A sparkle gleamed in his eyes. "I'm sorry you did, too. Zachary Nemesek, from next door."

"Is someone at the door?" Sierra's footsteps padded up behind Jo. "Oh!"

It was over before it had even begun. Not that it was Sierra's fault. She was so sparkly and confident guys practically tripped over their own big feet to get her attention.

"Sierra, I'd like you to meet our neigh—"

His hand shot past Jo's shoulder. "Zachary Nemesek. My friends call me Zach."

Friends. He hadn't said that to Jo. "Zachary, thi—"

"Hi, I'm Sierra Riehl." Sierra's hand lingered in his longer than necessary as the two locked gazes.

Jo's smile froze solid on her face. Yep. Over. Stifling a sigh, she stepped aside. As usual.

"Nemesek? You must be related to the folks we bought the land from." A dimple punctuated Sierra's smile as she flipped long blond hair over her shoulder.

"My parents handled the sale for my aging grandmother."

Somehow Sierra had managed to avoid any dirt smudges on her designer jeans and lavender top. Jo glanced down at her striped t-shirt peeking out from the overalls. She hadn't been so lucky. And it wasn't just the mouse nest, either. Her gaze dropped to the adorable puppy, still tugging at his snug collar. Mutts of various sizes and colors had been her constant playful companions on her grandparents' farm when she was small. This pup was no mongrel, but his silky ears begged for a scratch. She crouched down.

"Oh, this is Domino."

"That suits him, all black and white." Jo was a big fan of black and white. How comforting when things simply were what they were. Nuances made things messy.

Zachary chuckled. "My folks raise and train Border collies as working dogs. Or, at least, they used to."

Sierra nudged Jo. "I met the Nemeseks when I signed the papers a couple months ago. They're wonderful people, and I bet they'll be great neighbors."

"I didn't have the privilege of seeing the land before we signed." Jo glanced at Zach. "Our other friend, Claire, and I couldn't get away from Seattle just then, so Sierra sent the paperwork to us by courier."

"I hope seeing it in person wasn't too big a disappointment."

What was that supposed to mean? This was all but heaven. Forty acres, mostly flat, at the end of a public road. How many logging trucks could possibly go by in a day from up the mountain? No, this was a perfect place to make a stand and show the world what three women on a mission could do.

Jo scratched the puppy's ears once more and stood. Time to get back in the game. Not that it would do any good after this disastrous beginning.

"I'm sorry the trailer is such a mess," Zach said. "My dad got really sick a few days ago and was sent to Kootenai Health Center in Coeur d'Alene. I know Mom promised to have things ready for you, but she's spent every minute with Dad."

"I wondered," said Sierra. "I told her at the time we'd take the place as is, but she seemed adamant she'd get it cleaned."

Jo frowned. "Is your dad going to be okay?"

His brown eyes clouded over and a muscle twitched in his cheek. "I sure hope so. I think they caught it in time."

Sounded serious. "Any diagnosis?"

"Guillain-Barré Syndrome. I don't suppose you've heard of that."

Guillain-*what?* Jo opened her mouth to ask, but Sierra beat her to words, reaching out and touching Zach's arm. "Oh, that's dreadful. They got him on immunoglobulins quickly, I hope?" She turned to Jo. "It's an auto-immune disorder that can actually be quite serious. Affects the peripheral nervous system."

Zach's eyebrows shot up as he focused on Sierra. "Yes. Someone you know had it?"

Sierra shrugged, her blond locks swishing over her shoulder. "I studied it in school. My major was holistic medicine."

A smile creased Zach's face then froze. "Holistic?"

"Herbal and natural remedies."

The smile faded as his eyes narrowed. "New Age, then."

His pup whined. Did he feel the chill in the air, too?

Jo bit back a grin of her own. "No, actually. We're Christians. Holistic simply means looking at the whole system and treating it as a unit."

"I understand the definition."

And apparently didn't approve. So be it.

Zach shifted his weight. "Anyway, like I was saying, I'm sorry the place isn't cleaned out for you. Mom's still in the city and won't be back for a few days, but I can give you a hand if you like." His gaze rested on Sierra. "It's the least I can do."

Gag. Made Jo want to take his offer and make suggestions about its disposition.

Not surprisingly, Sierra's eyes lit up. "That'd be great. We're expecting the moving truck in a couple of hours or so. We've got buckets and cleaning supplies along."

"But no hot water." Zach peered past them. "Dad turned off the tank and drained it when my grandmother moved out." He took half a step forward.

Jo crossed her arms. "I already got it, thanks."

He pulled his head back and really saw her for the first time since Sierra had come to the door. "*You* turned it on?"

"It's not that hard."

"Oh. Well, then…"

Speechless. Guys couldn't seem to handle a competent female.

Sierra's hand found its way back to his sleeve, purple nail polish gleaming against brown suede. "We could really use help with the mice, though. Jo found this nest…"

Jo bit the insides of her cheeks to keep from laughing.

"We met." Zach didn't manage to hold back his chuckle.

Sierra frowned. "Pardon?"

"We met, the nest and I." Zach brushed the remains of it from his coat.

For the first time, Sierra looked down past the edge of the wooden landing. She gasped and stumbled back.

Zach's eyes twinkled.

Jo couldn't take her gaze off him. So cute and with a sense of humor as well.

"Oh, my! I didn't even see them there." Sierra pressed a hand over her heart.

Not that Jo had a chance to snag a guy like Zach with Sierra on the loose. She took a deep breath. Time to shut down this fiasco. "At any rate, we have a lot of work to do. Thanks so much for stopping by. It was nice to meet you."

Zach looked from Jo to Sierra and back again. "My offer was sincere. However, I'm thinking I should go home and get some traps first. Anything else I can bring? Window cleaner? Vacuum?"

Oh, the guy was actually willing to get his hands dirty, not just gaze adoringly at Sierra? "Traps would be great. We've got everything else covered."

He nodded. "I'll put the mutt in his run and be back in a few. Domino, heel." Once off the steps, Zach stretched into a brisk stride, the pup trotting at his side.

"Now that is one hot-looking male specimen." Sierra's hands rested on her curvy hips.

As though Jo didn't have eyes.

o0o

Zach dropped his rag into the bucket and settled onto his heels. Who'd have guessed this much dirt could accumulate in only two years? But he'd promised his mother he'd help out—in fact, that he'd do whatever he could to alleviate her worries about the farm so she could focus on Dad.

Handy for them he hadn't landed a permanent job since his graduation from veterinary college. Zach cringed at the memory of his former boss refusing to extend his temporary work assignment, telling Zach he was looking for someone more compatible with the over-all business. Subtext: someone who would please his spoiled-rotten daughter. Well, Zach had tried, but there were games he would not play.

Not that he appreciated what the farm offered, either. But today was a bright spot, hanging out with a cute, shapely blonde. Sierra didn't seem conscious of her beauty like Yvette. That disaster ought to have made him wary of women. It didn't matter, though. He wouldn't be around long enough to get serious about Sierra, or anyone else, whether they threw mice at him or not.

Jo's backbreaking work detail gave him the munchies. Zach stood and grabbed his pack. "Anyone want some chips?" He pulled a bag out, ripped open the top, and extended it to Sierra, who shook her head. He turned to Jo.

Her forehead creased in a frown. "We have apples and carrot sticks in the cooler, thanks."

Seriously? "Sounds too healthy for a guy like me." Zach poured a few chips into his palm and tossed them in his mouth.

Jo's eyes narrowed. "You'd rather eat junk food made by some multi-national corporation? Not this gal."

"Breakfast of champions." She was kind of cute, all perturbed like that. Some strands of her thick brown hair had pulled free of her tight braid and now frizzled around her head. She looked a bit less intimidating without a dustpan in her hands.

"There's no redeeming value for your body or for the local economy in that stuff."

Never mind about the less intimidating. She was like those whackos he'd been avoiding at college for the past eight years. "I'm sure it provides jobs for someone somewhere. Just doing my part." He inhaled a couple more handfuls then pulled a pop bottle from his pack and swallowed a deep glug. No point in offering that with his germs all over it. Like either would accept.

He glanced up to catch a scowl pass between the two females. Whatever. If Sierra turned out to be as much a health food nut as Jo, no loss. Fewer entanglements meant a quicker getaway after Dad's recovery.

A cell phone rang. Zach's hand automatically reached for his pocket before Sierra's voice interrupted him.

"Hey, bro. Where you guys at?"

She'd said something earlier about her dad and brother bringing a U-Haul with furniture.

Jo, scrubbing out a kitchen drawer, paused and cocked an eyebrow at her friend.

"You'll be here in ten minutes? Good enough. See you." Sierra slid the phone into her pocket.

Not a chance the cleaning detail would be ready that quickly, even if they made some serious moves. Zach tossed the pop bottle toward his pack and reached for the bucket and rag. He'd do what he could.

Jo opened the under-sink cupboard door, gasped, and slammed it shut. "Okay. Apparently there are more of them." Her voice sounded rather pinched.

"More mice?" A chance to be indispensable—while not getting rodents thrown at him. Good deal. Zach leaned over, opened the door and peered in. This litter seemed older than the previous one. "Where's that dustpan?"

Jo shot him a look somewhere between disgust and gratitude and handed it to him.

Zach jammed the pan underneath the mice and lifted it out of the cupboard. One of the nestlings fell off and landed with its feet scrabbling in the air.

Sierra screamed and flung her scrub brush, missing the mouse by half a room. She stared at it, eyes wide.

He paused with his hand on the doorknob and grinned, unable to help himself. "It's just a baby, Sierra. I'll come back for it after I've dumped these."

"Just?" Her voice caught.

Jo peeled a strip of paper towel off the roll by the window. "I've got it." Her nose wrinkled as she gathered up the squirming mass in at least a triple layer and rushed past him through the open door. "Ick." She threw it, paper towel and all, onto the previous pile.

"Way to go." Zach couldn't resist a dig. "But really, no screaming? No jumping on a chair?"

Amusement flickered in her eyes. "Sierra screams enough for

both of us, and there's a distinct shortage of chairs until the truck gets unloaded."

Unexpected response. Or was it? Not much seemed to rattle that little spitfire. Zach tossed the dustpan's contents. "I'll clean up out here when we know we're done."

"Thank you," Sierra managed to say. "But surely that's the end of them?"

Zach turned aside to hide his grin. If only it were that easy.

Jo laughed out loud. "I hate to break it to you, but baby mice generally have parents. Possibly aunts, uncles, and cousins as well. Getting rid of a nest isn't the same thing as being *done*."

Sierra's eyes grew wide. "But they're so dirty."

Jo knelt beside the cupboard again. "Did we forget to post a sign asking them to wipe their feet on the mat as they came in?"

"Uncalled for, Josephine."

Zach choked on a chuckle. At least having these gals for neighbors would provide a bit of diversion while he was home.

Chapter 2

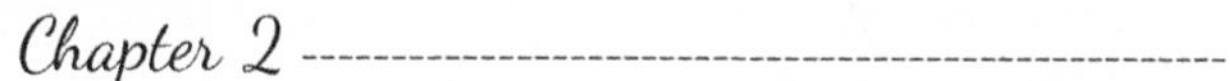

Jo patted the long braid wrapped around her head and took a deep breath. The folks in the first few rooms of Galena Hills Care Facility had been too deep in their dementia to notice a visit from the newly hired nutritionist. Too bad their generation once welcomed enriched pre-packaged foods as though delivered straight from the hand of God. Most old people wouldn't be such a mess if they'd eaten healthier. Probably too late to make a difference, but Jo couldn't squelch the desire to try.

She straightened her back, pasted on a smile, and consulted her clipboard. Ellie, at the front desk, had barely glanced up from her solitaire game to inform Jo that the resident of Room 224 lived in the present, at least some days. She tapped the door and nudged it open. "Hello, Mrs. Humbert?"

An old woman, white hair floating around her face halo-like, sat in her wheelchair by a small table. A man swiveled at the intrusion from his seat facing the window.

Jo caught her breath. *Zach?*

"Please come in, my dear." The old lady peered at her through rheumy eyes. "Do I know you?"

Jo closed the space. She could block Zach from her thoughts. This was her job. She took the soft white hand in hers. "I'm

Josephine Shaw, the facility's new nutritionist, and I'm here to talk to you about food."

Zach chuckled. "Be careful, Grandma. She'll toss your stash of candies in the garbage."

Thanks a lot, buster. Jo shot a glare at Zach. Just her luck he felt the need to interfere on his grandmother's behalf.

Jo turned her back on him and tried for a light tone. "Unless you have any free-trade organic dark chocolate in there. That stuff is hard for me to resist."

Mrs. Humbert's poufy hair shimmered as she shook her head. "Now that's something I don't have, but John can pick some up for us if you like." She patted Jo's hand. "Then I can bribe you to be nice to me."

John? Jo shot a questioning look at Zach, but he just lifted a shoulder and shook his head. She squeezed the old lady's hand. "I don't need bribing." Not with anyone who needed help, and the fact this was Zach's grandmother clinched the deal. "It's my job to make sure you're getting the best possible nutrition, though, so let's keep those empty calorie snacks at a minimum, shall we?"

Zach laughed.

If it hadn't been directed at her, Jo might have enjoyed the deep, full sound. But no. It was at her expense. She gritted her teeth and swiveled to face him. "May I ask what's so funny?"

He waved a hand. "Really, does it matter? Why make big changes? Let these folks enjoy the remainder of their days and eat what they like. It's not like a diet modification is going to make that much of a difference."

She narrowed her eyes. "It's my job. I've been hired to improve the menu."

Zach leaned back in the chair and ran his gaze down and up her. Not, sadly, in a romantic way. More like an intimidation attempt.

Well, she wouldn't stand for it. Jo parked her hands on her hips and the clipboard clattered to the floor.

He grinned and snatched it before she could react.

Why did she always seem to forget what she had in her hands when he was nearby? Heat crept up her neck and across her cheeks as she retrieved her board from his grasp. She stared at it, trying to remember what questions she'd meant to ask Mrs. Humbert, but Zach's face seemed to swim upon the paper.

He leaned forward and cupped his hand over his grandmother's. "Maybe I should introduce you. Grandma, Miss Shaw is one of the people who bought your farm from Mom and Dad."

Oh! This was *that* grandmother? Of course. Jo should have realized.

The old woman shook her head, a slight frown marring her face.

"That's okay, Mrs. Humbert." No need to perplex the woman. Jo patted her shoulder. "Just call me Jo. I'll come back and talk to you later, when you don't have company." And when Zach couldn't interrupt with his own ideas of how Jo should do her job.

Or just plain distract her.

"That will be nice, my dear. I'd love to visit."

Jo turned for the door but froze at Zach's chuckle. "Let me know if you're being deprived of treats, Grandma. I'll sneak you some."

She was going to have to keep an eye on him. Too bad that would be a pleasure.

o0o

"Have you met the girls next door yet?" Mom pushed up the sleeves of her blue sweater as she glanced out the kitchen window toward Grandma's old trailer. She turned on the faucet and waited as water streamed into the kettle.

Met them? Talk about an understatement. "Two of them."

He assumed the third resident had arrived by now, but he was in no hurry to meet her, thank you. Zach stretched his legs under the retro chrome table, thankful his mother was home from nearly a week at Dad's bedside. Worry pressed her slight shoulders down, and her graying hair looked overdue for a trim.

Mom turned to face him. "How about Sierra? She's the one who came to sign the papers a couple of months ago. She's a pretty girl."

Cute and curvy. "Yep. She's got a good scream to her."

"Scream? Why would that be?"

He couldn't resist. "Perhaps because the place was full of mice?"

"I'm so sorry about that." Red tinged her cheeks. "But there's a chance for you to be a knight in shining armor to a group of young ladies. You can take them some traps—"

"Done."

"—and remove the carcasses for them. There's not a woman alive who wouldn't appreciate that kind of help."

She obviously hadn't met Josephine Shaw, though Jo hadn't turned him down precisely. "Didn't you know how bad the trailer was?"

"Zachary John. I've had nothing but your father's health on my mind for the past ten days. Thank God they figured out what was wrong with him and got him on that medicine in time, but he's been very sick. It'll be a long haul to recovery." She shook her head. "I do feel bad I let cleaning the trailer slip, though. Maybe I'll take a casserole over in apology."

"Just make sure it's healthy, or they'll send it right back with you." Second thought, that would be okay. Then he could enjoy it himself.

A frown marred Mom's forehead. "Right. They're on a health food kick over there. Sierra checked the zoning about opening an event destination for sustainable living before making an offer."

"Sustainable living? What's that supposed to mean?"

Mom parked the kettle on the range and turned it on. "I guess they're environmentalists of some sort. One thing is they're planning to grow their own food."

Another good reason to stay clear, as if he needed more. "You might want to watch out, though. Josephine Shaw is the new nutritionist at Galena Hills. I met her there when I was visiting Grandma yesterday. Sounds like she plans to shake up the menu." Probably everything else, too, by the glint in her eye.

Mom's face brightened. "That can only be good. The food there is abysmal. It's bland and tastes like so much straw."

Zach parked his elbows on the table. "She's checking out all the residents' snack drawers. I don't trust her. When I helped them clean the trailer she spouted at me about eating chips and drinking pop and —"

Mom laughed. "No more than I've said to you for years, Zachary John. I told you they'd rot your teeth out one day."

"Yeah, well. According to her, the whole earth will collapse on account of my food choices." And she'd looked so earnest saying so.

"The whole earth? I suppose I can't expect her to care about your teeth." Mom sat at the table across from Zach. "So, tell me. Is she as pretty as Sierra?"

Zach stifled a groan. When would she let up trying to find him a wife? "Not looking for anyone right now, remember? Not here, not anywhere."

"But you're twenty-seven. We had two children when your father was your age."

Yeah, he'd heard the story a dozen times. But look where that had landed his folks. Four offspring and always too broke to go on vacation or fix up the house. The kitchen still sported old painted cabinets and metal-rimmed countertops with no space for a dishwasher.

"You're not getting any younger. Now that you've got your veterinary degree…"

Zach sucked in a deep breath. How many times had they had this discussion? "I need a job first."

"I'm sorry, Zachary. I just want to see you settled. Happy." The kettle whistled, and Mom rose to fix the tea.

Time for a subject change. "What did the doctor have to say about Dad's condition? Give me the details."

Mom's shoulders slumped. She set two ceramic mugs on the table and sank back into her chair, burying her face in her hands. "He's weak as a baby. He can't even stand up without support."

"I'm sorry." Zach reached over and gently pulled her hands away from her face. He rubbed his thumbs along her palms. "I'm sure they're doing all they can for him. What happens next?"

She tugged loose and reached for a tissue. "Physical therapy. Weeks. Maybe even longer."

Weeks he could handle, probably. More than that? "I see. Long-term prognosis?"

"Most…victims…resume normal life within a year."

Victims. *Ouch.* "A year? That's a long time. How will you manage the farm with Dad out of commission?" So much for changing the subject.

Mom blew her nose. "I haven't talked to him about it. He's too busy trying to keep his head up as it is. But I thank God you were able to come home at all. Maybe you'll stay and help out as long as it's needed?"

As he suspected. Obviously it was time to clear the air. "Right now I can't promise a year. I can give you a few weeks, maybe more, depending on the job situation. Remember, I have quite a few résumés out. Someone is sure to call soon." If they could balance his receipt of the president's award with the fact that he didn't have a recommendation from his last employer. That smarted.

"I'm trusting God you'll do what's right."

Zach clenched his fingers against his knee to stop the jittering. "I'm supposed to put my future on hold?"

She bit her quivering lip. "I wasn't thinking of it as on hold. More that God could provide what you need right here in Galena Landing."

His mother knew this wasn't what he wanted. How could she pray against her own son? Zach didn't have much of an in with God these days. Of course, it was entirely possible He wouldn't answer her prayer anyway. Didn't He have bigger things to worry about than this little farm so far north in Idaho they nearly bumped the Canadian border?

Zach pushed his mug of tea aside. "How about praying for one of my sisters to move back here?"

Mom twisted the tissue into knots. "You loved the farm so much when you were a boy. And your sisters are already seeking God in everything they do." She sighed. "I wouldn't say no to Cindy and Tom bringing the grandkids closer. You know I miss being a part of their life. But God called them to a vital ministry in Denver."

"And I'm not doing anything important because I'm not a youth pastor? Or teaching ESL in Thailand?"

"Oh, Zachary. That's not what I meant at all." She dabbed her face with the tissue. "Don't put words in my mouth."

What other meaning could there be?

"I'm sorry, son. How about I just pray for you and ask God to do what He wants with your life? I'll try not to plant ideas of my own, though He certainly knows my mother heart."

Zach pushed his chair back. "Fair enough. I can't say I'd mind having God on my side." Once that had been his normal life.

"Then you'll come to church with me in the morning?"

She had him cornered.

Chapter 3

"Really? This town has no farmers' market?" Jo leaned against the counter of Nature's Pantry in downtown Galena Landing. "Why?"

The owner, Gabe Rubachuk, shrugged. "Someone tried starting one a few years ago, but it didn't last. Nobody quite knew what to do with it."

"What do you mean, *do with it*? People sell their garden excess to people who don't have any, or they purposefully plant in order to sell." Didn't seem that hard to her. When she'd met Gabe and his wife Bethany at church the day before, she'd assumed they'd make great allies. After all, they were about her age and owned a health food store. Somehow, though, Gabe didn't seem to have caught Jo's vision.

"Yeah, well. There was some of that going on, but not much. The sellers didn't come regularly, and then the few people who were counting on fresh vegetables couldn't get any." Gabe bit his lip and stared at the far corner of the store before looking back at Jo through his intense brown eyes. "It should have worked, but it didn't. The final straw was when the town council took notice and figured the vendors should have a business license."

She could feel her eyes bugging out. "Every single one of

them?"

"Yeah. Rules, you know." He tugged at the cuffs of his university sweatshirt.

"But that's ridiculous. If they're members of the farmers' market association, then one set of annual dues covers all that."

He frowned. "What association?"

Jo waved her hands, taking in the whole musty herb-smelling store, the whole town, maybe the whole world. "Did they ask anyone from somewhere else how to set things up? A place with a thriving market?"

"I don't know." He pulled back. "Look, Josephine, it was while I was away at college. I'm not up on the details."

There she went again, pushing people until they got defensive. She had to learn to stop that. "Any other ideas of how I can source fresh local food? Not only for my roommates and I, but also for Galena Hills Care Facility. I'm working there part-time. I don't want those poor old people to keep having to eat produce with all the nutrition drained out of it from so long on a truck."

Gabe scowled. "I carry a line of organic canned vegetables."

Did she dare tell him that barely touched her hopes? "I'll keep it in mind, but they probably don't come in number ten-sized cans. How about bulk frozen?" That would be a bit closer to the real thing.

"I'll ask my mother-in-law about volume orders. She used to own this store."

Jo nodded. "That'd be great as a stop-gap, but we'd really like to hook into whatever is going on with food from the area." She leaned forward. "My roommates and I were thinking of organizing a little festival later in summer, seeing what our neighbors and friends could bring that they'd grown themselves." Assuming they'd made any friends by then. "We won't have a lot ourselves, other than from the garden we'll put in and fruit already growing on the farm. Looks like lots of raspberries, at least. Do you and your wife plant a garden?"

A small grin played about his lips. "No, we live in the apartment above the store so we don't have any land. And besides, Bethany is pregnant."

"All the more reason to have good fresh food."

He shook his head, the grin mostly intact. "You don't give up, do you?"

Jo's grandfather used to call her a little Chihuahua. Yap and grit in a pint-sized package. She tried a deprecating smile. "Not often, no. Sorry if I come on too strong. I'm just really passionate about knowing where my food comes from, the closer to home the better."

Gabe waved a hand around the store with its wooden shelving and a few metal racks. "Not much here that's local. I buy from the same suppliers every other health food store does in the Pacific Northwest."

"That could change. Have you ever thought of putting a produce cooler in here? You could sell vegetables and fruit. Meat, even."

"Super One Foods has everything most people want." Gabe shook his head, grimacing. "I've got some loyal customers, but most don't want to pay extra for organics. I do best on the vitamins and supplements. Or I used to."

"See, that's the thing. Just because something is organic doesn't make it better."

By the look on his face, she'd lost him. She tried again. "Most of the organic companies are mega-businesses, like regular grocery store brands. They may not use the same types of chemicals, but they're still raping the land. It's called agribusiness."

"It's called free market." Gabe placed both hands on the counter and leaned toward her. "I can buy some of these organic brands, like the pasta, cheaper now than a few years ago. It's all about price, and I'm just a little guy. It's hard to compete with the big grocery chains."

That wasn't the point. "You sound about ready to give up."

Gabe glanced toward the door and lowered his voice. "Look, we bought this business from Bethany's mother three years ago. Since then, Super One has put in an entire aisle of organic food and expanded their vitamin selection. I honestly don't know how long I can keep this place running."

Jo vowed to buy as much from Nature's Pantry as she could, even if it meant canned vegetables. "So what are you doing? Just letting it slide? Or are you fighting back?"

He closed his eyes for a second and rubbed his hands across his face. "I don't know. If I could bail without losing my shirt, I probably would. But Galena Landing means everything to us. This is where we want to raise our kids."

"Does Bethany work in here with you?"

"We can't afford that." Gabe's eyes softened. "She's a nurse. Commutes to the hospital in Wynnton. It's nearly an hour's drive each way, and the twelve-hour shifts are killing her. She can hardly wait for maternity leave, but it's still a long way off."

Jo used to dream of marriage and babies herself. She and her friends had all but given up. They'd stopped looking when the Mr. Rights didn't materialize during college. Instead, they'd chosen to pour their energy into creating the kind of world they wanted to live in. Didn't mean Sierra didn't turn the head of every guy who saw her. Didn't mean Jo didn't crave the kind of love Gabe obviously had for his wife and unborn child.

"That's a brutal commute." It probably wouldn't be polite to ask about the efficiency rating on Bethany's car. Claire would kick her shin if she'd been there and Jo asked a question like that. Jo forced herself to focus. "So you're saying you're going to fight."

His brown eyes bored into Jo's and he took a deep breath. "By default." He laid his hands palm-up on the tile counter. "But how?"

She couldn't help grinning, but the bell jangled as someone

came into the store. Gabe glanced past Jo and his face brightened.

Jo backed away from the counter to let his new customer in. "It was nice meeting you. We'll talk again another time."

"Nemesek!"

"Rubachuk!"

A clenched fist flashed past Jo's shoulder and thumped into Gabe's.

She tensed, her traitorous heart zipping at full speed. Zachary.

"Hey, man. What's up?" Gabe had clearly moved on.

Jo turned and pasted a smile on her face. "Hello, Zach."

"Jo! Hi there."

He wasn't really looking at her but at Gabe. She could take a hint. She shouldn't even think twice about him. They had nothing in common. Not really. But her heart didn't understand there was no point doing somersaults in his presence.

o0o

Zach stepped aside as Jo turned toward the door. She sure seemed in a hurry to leave. He hadn't meant to break into her conversation with Gabe. "Have you been stealing candy from old ladies lately?" he called after her.

She froze, her back to him. "Pardon me?"

"Aw, you heard me." He glanced at Gabe. "That's what she does, man. Goes around that nursing home and makes the old people feel bad for stashing peppermints and gingersnaps."

Gabe looked uncertainly from one to the other. "Not the way I heard it. She was looking for organic veggies a few minutes ago."

Jo swung back, glaring at Zach. "That's how you see my job?" Her face flushed a becoming shade of red.

Why hadn't he noticed before that she was no taller than his armpit? She was kind of cute, all frazzled. This time she looked like a normal human being clad in jeans and a sleek-fitting fleece jacket, not grungy from cleaning and not formal for work. That green was a nice color on her.

She tapped her foot. "Is it?"

He angled his head. "I was just teasing. I'm sure you have everyone's best interests in mind. Don't worry, I'll just keep bringing her more."

Now if only he could read the expression on her face as she opened and closed her mouth a couple times. But no go. She swiveled and hoofed it out the door.

Gabe's voice came out in a drawl. "Pretty little gal, isn't she?"

"Not that I'm looking. She's just a fun one to hassle." Zach watched through the window as Jo mounted a bike and rode off.

"You're well rid of Yvette, you know. She wasn't worthy of you."

Trust Gabe to get right to the point, taking all the fun out of tormenting Jo. "That's not the way I heard it."

"Who you going to believe, me or her? You've known me since we were yay high." Gabe measured off the height of his store counter. "You only knew Yvette for few months."

"Should've been long enough."

Gabe chuckled. "You're talking to the wrong guy. I knew Bethany for ten years before I popped the question."

Zach couldn't help grinning. "Not true. I think you proposed when you were twelve."

"Fourteen." Gabe hooted and slapped the counter. "But that wasn't asking. I told her."

"Semantics."

"Hey, I'm sorry things didn't work out with Yvette." Gabe straightened a pile of business cards. "But I'm also relieved. She wasn't the right girl for you."

"So it turned out." He still couldn't believe she'd been sleeping around while professing devotion to him. And he'd been dumb enough to ask her to marry him.

His buddy chewed on his lip and restacked brochures on the counter. Finally he looked up. "I've been praying for you."

Zach took a deep breath. "Well, I could use some divine intervention. I don't know what I'm going to do. I took that temp position with the assumption of something permanent at the other end."

Gabe grimaced. "So your job's gone."

"You guessed it. Not only that, but Jeff already spread the word around that I'm not reliable."

"Jeff. Who's that, Yvette's dad?"

Zach nodded. "I can't believe he said that. I met Yvette through him, not the other way around. He couldn't find a thing to quibble about my work. She lied to him."

"About what, man?"

Zach glared. "Said I'd come on to her. Pushed her to have sex."

Shock glittered in Gabe's eyes.

Zach reared back. "I just said she lied. She was getting back at me for not going all the way like she wanted. Where's the trust, Rubachuk? We made a pact. Remember? Back in high school. Girls were supposed to value that."

"God does."

Yeah, and Bethany had. Zach heard the censure in his buddy's voice. "That too. Look, I messed up, okay? She was a fun date. I respected her." He looked in Gabe's eyes.

Pity.

Man, he didn't want to see that. "How was I supposed to know I was temporary entertainment for her? Some kind of game?"

"You want the truth?"

Not that Gabe could shed any light. He'd only met Yvette once.

"Did you ever bring her home to meet your folks? Did you ever take her to church?"

Zach's breath whooshed out. Seemed Gabe didn't need to know Yvette. He only needed to know Zach. "She's a city girl." Maybe Gabe wouldn't notice he was only addressing one of the aspects. Sort of.

"Meaning? You're ashamed of your folks?"

"Hey!"

"Well, what then?" Gabe's face softened. "I wasn't trying to pry. Honest. I just want my buddy back."

Zach took a deep breath. "I couldn't see her walking around the farm in her short skirt and high heels. I couldn't see her sitting in my mother's decrepit kitchen drinking black coffee. She's a mochaccino kind of girl." He couldn't imagine her in overalls like Josephine. Now that was a girl who could dress up or down to suit any occasion. He ran his fingers through his hair and glanced at Gabe. "I did ask her. Once. I promise."

Gabe studied Zach's face. "I'm worried about you."

Something heavy sank in Zach's gut. "How so?"

"I get the feeling you're drifting, hoping something will snag you and reel you in. You might need to get a bit more proactive, man. Ask God what He wants of you, then go out and get it."

"I'm not drifting. I don't have a job, but I've got résumés at a bunch of clinics in Spokane and Coeur d'Alene. Something will surface soon."

Gabe's gaze pierced Zach. "You've been praying about it? Sure you're on track with what God wants?"

"Look, the Almighty is sort of ignoring me right now, okay? Praying is like talking to a brick wall. Not much point."

Gabe shook his head. "Not so. When did you last spend time on your knees for more than two minutes?"

"Um." It had been awhile, hadn't it? "I've been busy."

"So don't go saying God's ignoring you, okay? You have to do your part to keep the pipeline open."

When had Gabe started to sound like Zach's mother?

Gabe shifted his weight. "Something I don't get, man. Once

upon a time you wanted to come back to this valley and be a farm vet. Now you're in an all-fired hurry to get away, but why? There's no job, no girl."

Did he really need to spell it out? "Security. Everybody I know in this town is barely scraping by. Are you making anything on this place?" He paused a moment, but Gabe didn't answer. Zach had nailed it. "My parents never had anything for extras. No trips to Disneyland, no new cars, nothing. My dad can't even earn enough money farming to make ends meet. No, he had to go work for Leask, and look where that landed him. All but paralyzed. It's not the life I want."

"So it's the big bucks you're after."

Zach threw his hands in the air. "You make it sound so wrong! Don't try to tell me you wouldn't like more cash than you're getting out of this store. You've got a baby on the way. Don't you worry about how you're going to cover that kid's basic needs?"

Pain sprang into Gabe's eyes.

Zach hadn't meant to hurt his best friend. "Look, you know there's more to life than this town, this valley. Your parents are in Romania. They need people with good jobs and a few spare bucks to help support that mission orphanage. I can help. Yeah, Mom organized her quilting league to make quilts and ship them over, but those kids need more than blankets."

Gabe leaned over the counter. "If that's what God is calling you to do, go for it. Just make sure. Because I know He's looking after my needs here, as well as the Romanian orphans."

Right. Trust Gabe to bring it back around to God.

Chapter 4

"So much for that little maneuver." Sierra dumped her purse on the farmhouse table and flopped dramatically into a chair around the corner from Claire. "Town hall doesn't care. I asked if anything was being planned for Earth Day and the receptionist looked at me like I'd sprouted wings and a pig's snout."

At the stove, Jo gave the wok full of vegetables a quick stir with her spatula. "Yeah, Galena Landing doesn't seem that environmentally aware." Or food aware. An open bag of butterscotch candies lay on Zach's grandmother's side table today. Need Jo wonder where those came from? "It's not surprising there's no farmers' market with this atmosphere."

"But we're here now." Claire shot a glare at Sierra. "Without as much research having gone into the area as I would have liked, I might add." She shoved the papers she'd been working on into a stack.

"Hey! This farm was a great deal. Tell me how it isn't perfect."

Claire raised her hands, all prepared to count off fingers. "The trailer—"

"Now, don't blame me just because my dad found the place." Sierra surged to her feet. "I didn't make you sign the papers. We were all looking for farms out west. Just because you were both too far away and too busy to make a trip doesn't mean I'll take the blame for everything. Yeah, the trailer is junk. So what? We all knew it was temporary, anyway. What about our plan for a communal house and some smaller outbuildings? One little summer of living in a dump too much for you?"

Whoa. Somebody felt a little defensive. Jo sighed. "Sierra has a point. Other places in our price range might've had similar issues."

Claire snorted.

Peacemaking. A rather new role for Jo. "So forget the town. Let's focus on the church."

"Why would they be any different?" Claire thumped her papers, aligning them. "Still people."

"It's the Christians who should care." Jo added diced tofu to the wok and reduced the heat. "Our bodies being temples of God and all."

"They say that's only spiritual. You've heard all their arguments." Claire shrugged. "Well, we can try. Don't say I didn't warn you when they shoot the plan down."

Sierra dropped back into her chair. "Jo's right. We have to start somewhere, and the folks at the church seemed pretty friendly. There was a good age range, too. Some of those folks must have farms and gardens."

Jo leaned against the cupboard beside the range.

"I'd hoped the town had some things in place." Claire scraped her short fingernail along a crack in the wooden table. "I did look up farmers' markets before I signed the papers. They have a website. It hadn't been updated in a while and looked kind of tired, but I assumed people were too busy *doing* the market to worry about online stuff." She looked up. "I take food very seriously. In Paris we started every day at the markets, and what we found dictated the menu for the day. The restaurant in Seattle followed the same model. Here, there's just a Super One."

Sierra opened her mouth, but Claire's raised hand cautioned her. "And Nature's Pantry, but come on. Organic canned vegetables when we're used to fresh? It's a huge challenge."

"All good points." Sierra tapped French-manicured nails against the tabletop, her eyes narrowing. "Does that mean you want out?"

"I don't know." Claire swallowed hard. "I'm leery. I want to be settled so badly, to have a home, *land* that I can sink myself into." She glanced up between her lashes. "I'm afraid."

Claire craved stability more than anyone Jo knew, and that was saying a lot. Jo's chain had been yanked from one direction to the next as a kid, too. Away from the grandparents, who offered her and her mom stability, to Brad's "paradise" in California. If only he wasn't such a liar. If only Mom hadn't totally fallen for the money he dangled.

"I understand, Claire. I'm scared, too." Jo cleared her throat. "This is our first major act as grownups. We're done with school. We have an education and a career path chosen. But these forty acres represent the stage our lives will play out on. It's big." She focused on Claire. "I say we're home. There are negatives. There will be downsides everywhere we go. It's the way of life."

"It's cool here." Sierra leaned back. "This place is growing on me. The building site is as close to perfect for what we need as possible in this universe. Our original sketches for the retreat center work perfectly and the building permits should be through any day."

The smell of scorching food wafted to Jo's nostrils. Oh, great. She swung around, turned the element down a smidge, and added a splash of organic vegetable broth. Would that be enough to salvage supper?

Sierra's voice went on. "I say we can make a real difference here. Isn't that more important than being somewhere where it's already all in place and we just contribute a bit? This is kind of like being missionaries."

Claire inhaled, gathering steam no doubt, but a knock at the door forestalled her reply.

"Hello, anyone home?" a woman's voice called out.

Jo glanced up as Sierra reached behind her to open the door.

A middle-aged woman with short graying hair stood on the landing. Smiling, she held out a casserole dish. "Hi, I'm Rosemary from next door. I just wanted to come welcome you to the neighborhood."

Next door? That meant…

"Rosemary." Sierra surged to her feet before sweeping a bow in welcome. "Do come in. I'm Sierra. We met a few months ago."

That meant she was Zach's mother.

The woman smiled. "Of course I remember you."

Because no one ever forgot Sierra. Man, woman, or child. Especially man.

"This is Claire Halford," Sierra went on. "She's a French-trained chef. Know anyone who's hiring?"

Claire got to her feet. "Pleased to meet you."

Laugh lines crinkled around Rosemary's eyes. "In Galena Landing? There aren't many restaurants. Maybe you should open another one."

"I'm thinking of it."

"And this is Josephine Shaw. She's just started as nutritionist at the nursing home."

Rosemary's brown eyes, so much like Zach's, met Jo's. "So you're the young lady I've been hearing about."

Uh oh. Jo's smile froze. What was that supposed to mean? From Zach—or his grandmother?

Sierra broke in smoothly. "Only good things, I hope."

"Of course." Rosemary glanced down at the dish in her hands. "I'd meant to get here earlier with this, but the puppy got loose and I had to go looking for him. If you've already got supper for tonight, you can just reheat it tomorrow."

Jo found her tongue. "Thank you so much. You shouldn't have." She fumbled behind her to turn down the burner a little further. Hopefully no one noticed the lingering acrid aroma.

"Oh, it's the least I could do." Rosemary passed off the dish to Claire, who brought it over to the stove and set it down. "I'd made a promise to have the trailer cleaned and ready for you, and I feel so badly I wasn't able to do it. I wasn't even here to welcome you."

Claire handed the oven pads back to Rosemary. "I hope your husband is feeling better."

Rosemary's jaw clenched. "A bit, thank you."

Sierra shrieked and all but elbowed Rosemary out of the way as she leaped at a kitchen chair, sending it skittering across the floor. She jittered on one foot, pointing at the floor beside the range.

Jo swiveled, sure of what she'd see, wishing Rosemary didn't have to stand witness.

A little gray mouse nibbled the peanut butter on the wooden trap's copper catch. Though not fond of gore, Jo couldn't tear her gaze away as the rodent enjoyed his snack. Any instant now he'd make a wrong move and *snap*, that would be the end of him. She or Claire would haul the trap outside, dump him behind the pole barn, and re-set it for the next victim.

Only nothing happened. He pretty much licked the catch clean, sat on his little haunches for a few seconds, staring at them, then scuttled away, right over top of the trap.

Which still didn't snap.

Rosemary's voice broke the stunned silence. "Well, then. Zachary mentioned you had mouse troubles, but I never dreamt they'd be as brazen as this. You girls need a cat."

Jo shook her head. "Nice idea, but I'm allergic."

A high-pitched beep filled the air. Of course. The smoke alarm.

Not only allergic, but incompetent.

o0o

The salesman parked the galvanized metal box onto the counter at the hardware store. "It's basic. You put some bait in here, and the mice come in the tunnel. They can't get back out."

Jo eyed the large trap with distaste. "I'm not keen on the idea of emptying out live mice."

He shrugged. "You don't have to. Just leave them in there and they'll die eventually." A wicked grin spread across his face. "Or eat each other."

Jo's stomach rolled over. "Eww."

"I'm serious. Probably half a dozen or more will fit before it's full. Then just have a bucket of water outside and dump the contents into it. That way, if there's anyone still wiggling, they'll drown."

Not her preferred way of doing business. "That doesn't sound…humane."

He patted the box. "Well, your choice. There's always poison."

"No." Just the thought made Jo recoil. "That's not happening."

"Then I guess you're out of options. Mice, ten points. You and your, ahem…" The guy's eyes gleamed. "*Partners*, zero."

She should have known someone would start a rumor like that. Jo's eyes pierced his. "We're not lesbians, if that's what you're hinting at. We're friends who happen to want to own property and couldn't afford it on our own."

"You deny it like it's a bad thing."

"I deny it like it's not true, actually." She stared him down until he fumbled with the display on the counter.

"Well, then. Keep doing what you're doing. It doesn't matter to me."

Jo drew a deep breath. Keep doing what they were doing,

indeed. She'd assume he meant the mice. Trouble being, it wasn't working. The reek of mouse feces permeated the whole trailer no matter how much they scrubbed and trapped.

Claire had bought tubs to store the non-perishable food in, though plastic was totally against their mandate. How much less eco-friendly could they get? No, they needed their food secure, but poison wasn't the answer.

Jo eyed the live trap and slapped her wallet onto the counter. "I'll take it."

o0o

Sierra pocketed the car keys in the church parking lot. "Ready?"

Claire nodded, and Jo lifted her lime green portfolio in silent acknowledgment. A sharp breeze reminded her that even though it was late April, winter hadn't completely given up. She shivered, both from the chill and from the thought of making a public presentation tonight. She'd approached one of the elders on Sunday, and he'd agreed to give her a few minutes. Now she was stuck doing it, when Sierra would have been a far better choice.

The parking lot was over half full. Jo's gaze skimmed the vehicles, wishing she knew what Zach drove. He wasn't likely to be here, of course. He was only a visitor to town.

Too bad, on so many levels.

The foyer was empty, but light streamed up the stairway. The girls proceeded down and into the fireside room packed with church members of varying ages. The chairman of the board, Mr. Graysen, called the meeting to order and, after dealing with official business, called Jo forward.

She laid her portfolio on the lectern. Definitely not made for her height, but it wasn't adjustable. Jo could barely peer over the top. Grr. They wouldn't take her seriously.

"Oops, sorry, Josephine." Mr. Graysen got a small footstool from the lounge area in the corner. "Does this help?"

Jo eyed it. Wobbly looking. Mindful of everyone watching, she carefully stepped up and hoped it would hold together.

"Hi." She looked out over the group, recognizing a few of them from the three Sundays they'd been in attendance. Gabe Rubachuk sat in the back row with an empty seat beside him. Bethany probably had to work. "I'd like to introduce myself and my friends and roommates. I'm Josephine Shaw, and I have a degree in nutrition. Sierra Riehl has studied natural medicines. Claire Halford is a chef, and she's looking for work." As Jo called out her friends' names, they waved to the group. "We've moved to Galena Landing to build ourselves a sustainable future, doing our part to take care of the earth God created, as He asked us."

A few people shifted uncomfortably in their seats and murmured with their neighbors.

"There's a lot of talk on the news these days about global warming, and whether or not it's a hoax. It doesn't matter which side of the fence you sit on. Our world is in trouble, and God's people, who were given the mandate to care for it, are often at the front of the pack, leading it downhill."

Claire caught Jo's eye and gave her head a slight shake.

Right. She was getting wound up and not pinpointing the current cause. Accusing these people wouldn't win them over. Baby steps.

"Sometimes we don't know what to do to make a difference. Each of us is only one person out of billions. Well, today's Earth Day. And here's one small suggestion for change."

Jo nodded at Mr. Graysen, and the stool wobbled. She grabbed at the lectern to steady herself. "I'd like to suggest that as many of us as possible grow a garden over the next few months, and that we plan to share a feast of bounty at the end of summer. My friends and I are hoping to host a completely locally grown-and-cooked meal as an example of what we can all do to make the world a better place if we work together."

The whispers and the nudges grew.

Mr. Graysen stepped to Jo's side. "When Ms. Shaw approached the church board with her idea, it seemed as strange to us as it does to you. But we prayed about the decision and believe that it would be a good thing for our church to align with." He looked down at Jo—even though she was standing on a stool at least eight inches high—and smiled. "My wife and I will plant potatoes to contribute to this dinner."

Jo flashed him a bright smile. "We need folks to sign up to grow a few turkeys, if anyone has raised poultry before and would like to take this on. Also a variety of salads, vegetables, and desserts are listed on sign-up sheets at the back. Just talk to one of us if you have questions on what you can grow and bring."

A few folks nodded, while others seemed baffled.

"We'll be happy to answer any questions after the meeting." Jo held the lectern and stepped off the stool, which swayed dangerously.

Mr. Graysen caught her elbow and assisted her descent. Face aflame, Jo made her way back to the girls.

"That concludes our meeting for tonight."

"Don't we have to vote on that food thing?" a man's voice from the room's fringes called out.

Jo couldn't catch who said it.

"No." Mr. Graysen shook his head. "It's not an official function, rather a sanctioned one. You may participate or not as you choose."

"I'm always good for a church dinner, but I don't know why I can't bring a deli platter from Costco. I don't have time to mess with this garden stuff. My business requires all my attention."

This time Jo could see the speaker, who leaned forward earnestly. She slipped into her chair and nudged Sierra. "Who is he?"

Sierra shrugged and shook her head.

"I'm sorry to hear that, Mr. Leask. I'm sure those of us in attendance will enjoy a very tasty meal."

Whoa. Good one, Mr. Graysen.

"I, for one, think it's a wonderful idea."

Jo swung her head but couldn't see the female speaker. Being short was annoying. The voice sounded familiar, though.

Claire nudged Jo and whispered, "Rosemary Nemesek."

Oh! Zachary's mother. Jo hadn't even noticed her in the room. Of course, they'd only met the once.

"It will help us keep our focus on God's mercies, and that's never a bad thing. We have much to be thankful for every day."

There was a rustling as Rosemary rose to her feet, and Jo could just make her out through the crowd.

"You all know Steve was diagnosed with Guillain-Barré Syndrome. We're not sure yet what caused it." She looked in the direction of the disgruntled man then went on. "We're so thankful that the doctors diagnosed him in time to get him on the right medication quickly. It's going to be a long haul until he's back on his feet, but I think he'll get there." She turned toward the back where Jo and her friends sat in a row. "I'd considered not putting in a garden this year. Too much stress and effort. But thank you, girls, for reminding me of what's important."

There was a sort of snort from Mr. Leask's side of the room.

Rosemary caught Jo's eye. "Hope and thankfulness are good reasons to grow a few things this season."

o0o

"Can I get you to hook the rotovator to the tractor and till the garden patch over the weekend, Zachary?" His mother hung her spring jacket on the hook behind the kitchen door.

"Um, sure." Zach came through the archway from the living room with Domino padding at his side. "I thought you'd decided not to plant a garden this year." And furthermore, how had this thought come to her from the church quarterly meeting? Didn't they usually decide who was on the Sunday school committee and other similarly riveting topics?

Mom filled the kettle from the faucet, turned it on, and sat down at the kitchen table. "Well, the girls next door got me thinking."

Zach had been thinking about them, too, though trying not to. Sierra was cute, but he didn't trust himself after Yvette. Pretty girls were trouble, plain and simple.

With a start he realized his mother was still talking. "Sorry, Mom. What was that?"

"Josephine—you know, the tiny one—challenged the church to plan ahead for an all locally grown dinner later this summer. I think it's a great idea."

Zach pulled his eyebrows together and sank onto a red vinyl-covered chair. "All local dinner? What do you mean?"

The kettle whistled and Mom got up. "Want some tea?"

"Sure."

She started the tea steeping then leaned against the counter. "Just that all the food would be grown or raised by the people having dinner together."

Domino parked himself in front of her, head cocked expectantly.

Mom grinned and pulled a treat out of the cupboard. After Domino spun three times, she gave it to him. Domino padded over to Zach.

"Sounds strange. Even the meat?" Zach reached down and played with Domino's ears. The pup pressed against Zach's ankle and chewed his biscuit.

Mom nodded. "The Donaldsons used to raise chickens. Jean said they'd fix their old henhouse and fence if someone else wanted to go with them on the cost of raising the birds. I think she got a few volunteers."

Zach settled back in his chair. "I didn't think vegetarians ate poultry."

"Vegetarians? Whom are you talking about?" Mom peeked

into the teapot.

"Well, the neighbors, aren't they? I thought you said they were back-to-the-land environmentalists."

She put the tea ball in the sink and reached for the sugar bowl. "That's not the same thing as vegetarian."

Since when?

Mom lifted the lid off the chipped sugar bowl. "We don't grow sugar around here."

Zach gave his head a shake. Talk about switching topics. "Um. Sugar. That's from cane or beets, right?"

"Good thing I didn't sign up for a dessert." Mom spooned some into her mug and passed Zach his plain. "I'm not sure how they're handling that."

Zach took a sip. "Honey, I suppose. Anyone around here have hives?"

Mom sat back on her chair. "Now that I don't really know. Somebody may. There are so many things I've stopped thinking about."

He waited, certain that her statement was the prelude to deeper insights. But the only sound was the ticking of the clock over the sink. Domino rolled over, looking for a belly scratch.

Mom's spoon rattled in her mug. "My parents always had a big garden and raised a few chickens. We had eggs and milk off the farm and our own beef. Mom baked bread every week."

"It was a lot of work for them." By the looks of his grandmother, it had worn her right out.

His mom looked surprised. "But they enjoyed it. We didn't buy much at the grocery store. Flour and yeast, sugar. Some treats here and there."

Meaning they'd eaten the same thing week after week. Life in general had certainly improved with the advent of Tex-Mex seasoning packets and boxed mac and cheese. Zach nearly lived off the stuff in college. How could he have survived if he'd had to grow his own food or even cook it from scratch?

Mom sighed. "Simpler times, when families worked together and stayed together. There wasn't this rat race our society has gotten into the past few decades."

"What would Grandma say now? I'm sure she's plenty thankful for all the amenities in her old age." At least if the nutritionist didn't hassle her too much about little indulgences.

"I guess when you're her age, those comforts are a help."

"I bet she doesn't miss her old wringer washing machine, or hauling buckets of water from the pump. Don't forget it wasn't all sunshine and roses."

"No, you're right. Some of it was hard."

He pressed his advantage. "Things have changed. Now city life is the simple way. All a person needs is a good education, a good job. Basically enough money to buy what they want. How much simpler can it be than eating out every night? Not only do I not have to grow my own food, I don't have to cook it or clean up behind myself." Zach grinned. "As far as I'm concerned, that's progress."

Mom bit her lip. "Easier in some ways."

"More people live in cities than on farms. You get a bunch of people in one place and the conveniences build up. Cindy's kids have swimming lessons year round at an indoor pool. We never had that here when I was a kid. Or the museums and concerts and malls." He eyed his mother. "It's called culture. What's wrong with it?"

She traced the design on her mug. "Nothing, when you put it that way. But it doesn't mean the old way is wrong, either. It's just different. More connected to nature and the seasons."

Zach laughed. "And I, for one, don't miss scraping out sheep pens during winter blizzards."

"All animals get sick at the worst of times. Cats and dogs, too, not just farm stock."

"But people keep their pets in nice warm houses. I'm not likely to have to brave the elements to care for an ailing cat, though the city streets can get quite nasty in the winter, too."

Mom jerked to her feet. "Fine, you win. The city is better than the country. Working with pets is better than farm animals. Junk food is better than fresh vegetables. All I'm asking is that, while you're here, you prepare the garden patch for me. I'll take care of it from there." She dumped the remains of her tea down the drain and rinsed the cup, her shoulders shaking.

Whoa. "Look, Mom. I'm sorry. I wasn't trying to be contentious. I just wanted to explain."

She turned to look at him, tears quivering at the corners of her eyes. "You used to love it here as much as I do. I hoped you'd feel the pull again when you were back for a bit. Well, apparently I was wrong." She swept from the room.

Zach stared after her then dropped his gaze to the puppy at his feet. Domino grinned up at him, tongue hanging out. Zach patted the pup's head. "She's just worried about Dad, about their future, isn't she, Domino? That's stress speaking."

Wasn't it?

Chapter 5

"Don't you all have something better to do than watch me?" Claire wiped sweat off her forehead with the back of a gloved hand, leaving a smear of dirt. Good thing she had a clue about mechanical stuff, because Jo sure didn't. Claire had scrounged up a rototiller in working condition at an auction, but running it looked to be crazy slow going.

Sierra and Jo looked at each other. They'd kept busy all morning pruning out the old raspberry canes. Claire was only on the third length of the berry beds, with three more rows to go. To say nothing of the herb garden. And the overgrown vegetable plot. And adding soil amendments for all those and tilling them in, too.

Jo had offered to spell Claire but the handles came almost to her shoulders.

"Never mind." Claire struggled to turn the tiller around at the end of the row.

Jo shook her head. "This isn't going to work." *News flash.*

Claire grunted. "Steve Nemesek might've told Sierra he'd be happy to help us, but he's in the hospital. Not much help there." She lined the tiller up for its return trip.

"Ah, but he has a son." Sierra hip-checked Jo. "I bet Zach

can drive his dad's tractor."

Trust Sierra to bring the guy up. She was just looking for an excuse to see him again. But hey, two could play that game. "Good idea. I'll go ask him."

"I'm not needed here. I'll come with you." Sierra peeled off her gloves and smacked them together. Clumped dirt flew off.

Jo tried to douse the flare of resentment that shot through her. "Sure, let's go."

"You might want to comb your hair."

Jo had thought of doing just that, but not anymore. "Not trying to impress anyone." She shrugged. "It's a work day. I look like I've been working. It's all good."

Sierra's mouth twisted slightly. Sure *she'd* want to look her best. Give her five minutes and she'd outshine Jo by a huge magnitude. But right now, Jo didn't think Sierra looked any cuter than her. Not with the dirt smudged on Sierra's forehead and cheeks. Jo probably had some, too. "Ready?"

They headed down the driveway. After a minute, Sierra said, "So what's up with you?"

"With me?"

"Yeah. You seem rather eager to go find Zach."

"It was your idea." Jo kicked at a rock. "I thought we wanted to get the garden ready today."

Sierra sighed. "Nothing more?"

"No, why would there be?" Just because every guy she'd met in the past five years had barely given her a glance before falling hard for Sierra? No reason.

"It's not like we need to compete, you know. He's a nice guy, but he's not staying."

"Yeah. I know." Unless he fell in love and changed his mind. Even then it would probably be Sierra he went for. Maybe Jo should encourage her. It wasn't likely she'd ever find a guy who loved her until Sierra was happily married and out-like-a-watermelon pregnant. Even then, she'd probably be one of those that glowed. No doubt Jo would throw up for nine months and look like a bloated shrew.

Good grief. Where were these thoughts even coming from? *Please, Lord, don't let this come between us.*

Sierra bumped Jo's shoulder. "So you're saying you're attracted to him?"

"I didn't say that." Jo blew a deep breath to release her envy.

"You're not denying it, either."

Jo stopped in the middle of the road. "Look, it doesn't matter. Like you said, he's back to urban life the minute he's free to leave. I'm not interested in moving off to the city, even a small one like Coeur d'Alene. Are you?"

Sierra laughed. "Nope. But you never know with the right guy. We need to be open to God's leading. Step-by-step, right?"

Yeah, step-by-step. Walking down this road was like walking to her doom.

o0o

"Where'd Domino go?" Zach set the wheelbarrow handles down and turned to his mom, who was on her knees in a flowerbed.

She settled onto her heels and brushed hair off her forehead with the back of a gloved hand. "He was here a minute ago. I got after him for digging. Thought he was with you."

Zach groaned and whistled for the pup. Sadie and Old Pete loped around the corner of the house and dropped beside Mom.

"Good dogs." She ruffled their ears. Old Pete closed his eyes, sighing in delight. "That pup is the runningest collie we've had on the place. He disappears every time I turn my back."

"Domino!" No happy yelp greeted him, and no flash of black and white appeared between the trees or outbuildings. The stupid dog. Why couldn't he be content hanging around when they were outside working in the yard? Domino was only locked in his run when no one was home and even then managed to get out. Otherwise he was with Zach or Mom, often in the house, but he had plenty of exercise, too.

"Like people," Mom mused. "Always wanting what he doesn't have."

Zach shot her an irritated look. True, he didn't like the farm any more than Domino did, but at least he announced when he was leaving and kept in touch when he was gone, unlike the mutt.

"*Domino!*" he bellowed. Here he'd thought he was making such great progress with the pup. He'd been a wee bit proud Domino responded better to him than Mom, being as she was the expert. Probably wasn't a good idea to foster the relationship, though. He couldn't take a dog that size with him to the city. Soon enough the spring farm work would be done and he'd be free to pursue his own life, even if Dad wasn't quite ready to come home yet. By the time the hay needed cutting later in June, Dad should be up for the task. Zach hoped.

Zach opened his mouth to call again, but thought he heard something. Voices. He cocked his head. Women's voices and laughter. Coming closer.

Great, he needed somebody witnessing his failure at keeping the dog under control. To say nothing of his grungy farm clothes, now covered with dirt and manure on the knees of his oldest jeans. Doubtless he smelled a treat.

What did it matter? Nothing. The women he'd meet in the city would be sophisticated and never have to see him looking like a farm boy.

The voices came closer, and Jo and Sierra came around the corner of the house, Domino prancing beside them.

Zach focused on the pup, trying to squelch his flare of frustration. "Domino, come."

The dog stopped and stared at him just long enough for Zach's ire to surge. He took a step closer ready to grab the collie by his scruffy neck and clarify who was boss. Domino bounded the remaining few steps.

"Sit."

The pup's bottom sank to the ground for an instant.

"Stay."

Domino flopped over onto his back, twisting and grinning at Zach. This wasn't precisely sitting, but Zach figured he'd made enough of a scene already. Domino was due for some detention time for his escapade. "I apologize. He vanished a few minutes ago. I'm sorry he bothered you and you had to return him again." He looked into Jo's brown eyes, but it was Sierra who responded.

"He wasn't a problem. Jo and I were on our way over to ask a favor and he ambushed us at the end of your driveway. I don't think he'd been off your property."

Some sort of consolation, at least.

Jo knelt beside Domino, who squirmed over onto his belly like a beached seal. "He's a great pup." She scratched between his eyes and down his nose until Dom dissolved in a quivering puddle. "Aren't you?" she all but crooned.

Zach didn't precisely want a nose scratch, but he could relate to the bliss on the dog's face. He glanced at Sierra.

Her mouth twitched when their gazes met, and a lively spark of humor danced in her blue eyes.

Zach's mom clambered to her feet. "Good to see you girls. Would you like a glass of juice and some cookies? Come, sit on the veranda and visit a few minutes."

"We really shouldn't," said Jo at the same time Sierra said, "Sounds lovely, thanks." Jo shot her friend a look, but Sierra ignored it.

"I'll just be a moment." Mom headed to the back door then turned and called for Domino. He leaped up, nearly knocking Jo over. Zach's reflexes kicked in and he caught her before she landed rear first on the ground. Domino bounded into the house and the screen door smacked shut behind him.

Jo pulled herself away as soon as she'd regained her balance.

"Thanks." But she didn't look up at him.

"Not every day a girl falls for me." Zach nearly slapped his hand over his mouth.

Sierra chuckled. "Clever." She elbowed Jo. "You okay?"

"Yeah, fine."

Now why had her face turned so red? She couldn't be—nah. No way would a little gal like her find a guy like him of more than passing interest.

Time to get back in focus. "You had something you wanted to ask?"

"Here we go!" Mom pushed the screen door open with her elbow and carried out a wooden tray with red liquid sparkling in tall glasses. "Come on up to the veranda and make yourselves comfortable." The screen door slammed against Domino's nose and he whined, sinking to his belly inside the door. Mom set the tray on the side table.

He'd find out soon enough what the girls had meant to ask. Zach motioned toward the steps. "After you."

Jo and Sierra went up and sat together on the quilt-draped porch swing. Zach picked up the tray and offered the contents to the girls first, then to his mother before taking the final glass and a handful of cookies to a wicker chair.

Apparently even apple-and-carrot girls ate homemade cookies.

"Mm, this is delicious. What kind of juice is it?" Ice cubes clinked in the glass as Jo turned it.

"We call it raspberry vinegar." Mom took a sip herself. "I learned how to make it years ago from an old neighbor who lived to be over a hundred before he passed on. Quite simple, and a way to stretch a summer treat year round."

"Vinegar?" Sierra frowned and peered into her glass. "I wouldn't have thought you could just drink it."

"That's all it is. Raspberries fermented in vinegar, with sugar added. Makes a concentrate that keeps well when canned into quart jars."

"It's really refreshing. I suppose a person could use honey?" Jo gave the swing a little push with her foot.

"I don't see why not."

Right. Yet sometimes Jo seemed so normal. He needed to remember to keep his distance. "You said you'd come over to ask a favor?"

This time Sierra spoke up but her gaze met Mom's. "When we signed papers on the land, Steve mentioned he'd be willing to till up a garden spot for us." She held up a hand. "Now, I know he's sick, and I hope he's feeling better soon, but I was wondering if you knew someone else who could help out? It's rather a large area for our little hand tiller."

Nice of her not to put Zach straight on the spot, but the question was clear enough all the same.

Mom glanced his way. "Yes, I remember the conversation now that you mention it. I'm so sorry, but it completely blanked out of my brain when Zach and I were talking the other night about the spring work here. He's hooking the rotovator up to the tractor and getting my patch prepared later today."

Were they going to talk around him the whole time? Zach couldn't stand it. "Sure, I can do it for you this afternoon." Might as well go the extra mile. "While I have the machinery going, would you like me to bring over some rotted sheep manure and old hay to work into the garden plot? I'll be hauling some for ours, too." He jutted his chin toward the dirt patch.

Jo's face lit up and she looked right at him. "Oh, that'd be great. What will we owe you?" She had gorgeous eyes, all brown and sparkly.

"Oh, Zach wouldn't dream of charging," Mom broke in smoothly. "It's the neighborly thing to do. We have no shortage of either commodity."

"But the diesel..." Jo glanced from his mom to Zach.

"The tractor doesn't use as much as you'd think." Zach

shrugged. "Don't worry about it."

"We'll accept those terms on one condition." Sierra leaned forward on the swing. "Stay and have supper with us."

Did he look like someone who liked tofu? He cast a helpless look at Mom, who smiled warmly at Sierra. "That's a lovely idea. Not that Zach can't cook for himself, of course, but I'm going over to my friend Jean's this evening."

She was? Zach frowned, trying to remember if she'd mentioned anything before. Then he realized Jo didn't look too happy, either, as she leaned over to Sierra and whispered something. That bugged him more than Mom's obvious matchmaking attempt. "Sure, I'd love to. Sounds like a plan." If they served him tofu, he could always raid the fridge for leftovers when he went back to the farmhouse.

o0o

"You're such a good puppy," Jo murmured as Domino squirmed on his back for another belly rub. She'd offered to keep the pup at Green Acres for the afternoon, away from the growling tractor.

Sierra sure had put the moves on, inviting Zach to dinner like that. The sensible side of Jo figured she might as well concede to her friend right now and forget about the guy next door. But there'd been something in his eyes, for a minute on the veranda. Jo might have a chance.

Maybe Sierra would burn supper or something, though that was usually Jo's department. She'd have to remember to send Rosemary's casserole dish back with Zach later this evening.

Domino wiggled, reminding Jo he was an ally. It was apparent Zach loved this dog more than a guy who was leaving the farm ought to, but that was a small thread holding Zach to this place.

She turned her back on the pup and grabbed another bucket of blueberry bushes. Why was she letting herself dream, even a little? It was a crazy idea to think Zach might come to care for her. If he did, how would he fit in at Green Acres? Jo couldn't imagine it.

"I can't believe Sierra invited Zach over." Claire rammed her spade deep into the freshly tilled blueberry bed, tilting it forward so Jo could drop a plant into place.

Domino pranced around them, trying to snatch the bushes.

"Me, neither. I guess she's being neighborly." No point in filling Claire in on the competition. She might want to join in. Ridiculous thought.

"She's going to desert us for some guy. I can see it already. She gets us out here to the edge of beyond, then falls in love and ditches us."

Thanks for the confidence. Jo straightened her back and stretched. "Thought you were a hundred percent in."

Claire shoved the spade into the dirt and reached for her water bottle, but a black-and-white nose intercepted. She pushed it aside before taking a swig. "Yeah, I'm in. I'm just not ready to think of any one of us being *out* practically before we've begun."

She had a point. This place was beginning to grow on Jo. Thoughts of feasting on sun-warmed raspberries later in the summer and vine-ripened tomatoes in the fall…man, her mouth was watering already. Sure it was going to be a lot of work, but blossoms on the plum and apple trees flaunted their fragrance while honeybees zoomed in and out gathering nectar and pollen. So worth every aching muscle.

Jo and Claire found a planting rhythm as the sun crept out from behind the clouds, warming their backs. The tractor grumbled around on the neighboring property.

"So the building permits are all in place?"

Claire nodded. "The inspector had some questions about the straw bales and the roof trusses, but he okayed everything in the end."

"Did Sierra's dad find enough solar panels at that auction?"

Even though Sierra didn't approve of her dad's truck driving job, all three girls basked in the knowledge that at least one set of parents were behind their operation and had co-signed on their mortgage.

"Almost." Claire moved to the next row. "We'll need a few more, but it's a good start."

The tractor grew louder then shifted gears and turned into the Green Acres driveway. Domino was off like a spooked rabbit, only headed *toward* the danger. Jo bellowed at him, but he was already so far away he didn't seem to hear at all.

"Hope Zach's watching out for that dog," said Claire.

Jo waved both arms frantically as she ran, hoping to catch Zach's attention before Domino dodged in front of the tractor. Zach yanked on the wheel and spun the tractor hard to the right. Jo held her breath, but the machine was more stable than she'd given it credit for.

Zach swerved left again and ground the equipment to a halt while Domino continued to dance around it.

Jo grabbed the pup's collar, yanking him off to the side. He whimpered.

Zach nodded and drove on past. The tractor bucket clanged as he dumped manure on the garden patch, backing the tractor inch by inch.

Domino whined at Jo's side as Zach turned the tractor and chugged back down the driveway. She kept a firm grip on the pup's collar and lifted a hand to wave at Zach as he passed.

He tipped his hat, an old straw one today.

Jo turned to watch him drive away, tall and straight on the old John Deere.

"Maybe it's not Sierra I ought to be worried about," Claire drawled from behind her.

Jo swung around. "Just making sure he's gone before letting Domino go." She released the pup. He immediately began to chase his tail round and round.

"Uh huh. That's what you'd like me to think." Her gleaming brown eyes met Jo's.

Even though Jo had to look nearly nine inches up at Claire, she put on her most innocent look. "Ready to get the rest of those bushes in?"

Claire snickered and grabbed the spade. "Sure. Any time."

Chapter 6

Zach tucked in his clean t-shirt and rapped lightly on the door of Grandma's old trailer. He'd rather think of her here than in the Galena Hills facility, but he had a sneaking suspicion this place would be so changed his mind could never get that picture back from his childhood. Barking sounded from within, then the door opened and Domino leaped out, colliding with Zach's belly. "Hey there. Domino, down."

Laughter reached Zach's ears as the pup bounced around him on the narrow landing.

Josephine. She'd taken time for a shower, too, by the looks of things. Her hair, still damp, had been pulled into a ponytail that swung way down her back when she turned to beckon him in. She'd changed into dark jeans and a mossy green top with a ruffled neckline.

The aroma of stew tickled his nose, and his forehead creased. Smelled like beef, not tofu. Not that he'd recognize tofu. He'd been raised a farm boy, suspicious of anything too weird. That concoction—

"Sierra's turn in the kitchen," Jo was saying. "Now if you want a *good* meal, you'll have to come back when Claire's cooking."

He noticed she didn't make any claims for her own.

The young woman who'd been working outside with Jo this afternoon came down the hallway, and he nodded at her. Taller than Jo or Sierra, and the only one of the trio with short hair, she assessed him from brown eyes.

Jo stepped closer. "Claire, have you met Zach yet? Zach, this is our roommate Claire."

"Pleased to meet you." Zach reached out and shook Claire's hand.

"Same." But she quickly looked away.

Not that it mattered. "Thanks for the invitation," he said to the group in general. "Smells good."

Sierra glanced over her shoulder at him from her spot by the stove. "Thanks."

"We appreciate all your hard work for us today." Jo knelt beside the bumbling puppy and soothed him. "Least we could do is feed you, especially with your mom out tonight." A twinkle appeared in her eye when she squinted up at him.

He felt a flush creep up his neck. "About that. I really do know how to cook." Would she consider opening a can or preparing packaged noodles cooking? "At least enough to get by."

Jo pointed Domino at a folded blanket behind the door and, to Zach's amazement, the pup wandered over and plopped down on it. Jo looked back at Zach and indicated a chair in front of the window. "Have a seat, if you like. I'm just going to wash up."

He edged behind the farmhouse table and slid into a sturdy wooden chair. Grandma's drop-leaf table had been much smaller, but that was far from the only change in the old trailer. The place looked a lot better than the day he'd helped Jo and Sierra clean it up. Was it really only a month or so ago?

Claire sat down across from him "This was your grandmother's home?"

Zach nodded. "She sold out in Spokane and bought this piece of land when my grandfather died. She lived here for more than twenty years, and my dad farmed it." So many memories. "I'd often sneak over after school for cookies and milk. Plus she kept band-aids for scraped knees on hand." He grinned. "I think she liked having me around. I had too many sisters and needed to get away sometimes." And yet here he sat with a room full of females and barely felt uncomfortable.

Jo came back into the kitchen. "Your grandmother is very sweet. Stopping by to see her is a highlight of my day."

He glanced over at her, but she turned away, her cheeks pink. Intriguing.

What time did her rounds take her to Grandma's room? He might have to visit more often. Maybe bring some dark chocolate. Not that he was considering a relationship, of course. Now *that* was a ridiculous thought. It meant weighing the pros and cons of city life, and he'd been all over that. He'd chosen.

Domino, sound asleep on his blanket, let out a snuffle.

Zach had chosen something that didn't include Border collies. Or fruit trees in bloom.

Jo drifted past him toward Sierra. "Need a hand?"

"Sure, if you'd like to get the biscuits out, that'd be great." Sierra lifted the cast iron Dutch oven and carried it to a trivet on the table.

Zach's stomach grumbled. Whatever Sierra had put in there—even if it turned out to be tofu—would be mighty tasty.

Jo popped open the oven and rescued a baking pan then deftly transferred them to a platter while Sierra dished up bowls of the stew.

The tantalizing aroma wafted closer. "Wow, you're spoiling me. You went all out here."

Sierra frowned at him. "All out? This is pretty basic. Even I can barely mess up stew." She passed a bowl to him.

He closed his eyes and inhaled the fragrance. All the right mixes of meat and vegetables and seasoning. Even Claire, no matter her reputation, could hardly improve on this. Or maybe it had been too long since Zach had spent hours working up an appetite in the sunshine.

A little clink and the aroma of baking powder biscuits joined the stew.

"Would you like to ask the blessing?"

Zach's eyes flew open and he focused on Sierra, who'd spoken. "Um. Sure." He closed his eyes again. Where to begin? How long had it been since he'd thanked God for anything? Couldn't announce that in front of these women, though. "Dear Lord, thank you for this good food and the hands that have prepared it. Please bless it in Jesus' name, amen."

"Amen," the women agreed.

When he looked up again, Jo passed him the biscuit platter and he helped himself to three. A dish of butter followed. Zach tucked into his meal, as tasty as it smelled. For a few minutes the only sound to be heard was the scraping of spoons in bowls.

Sierra turned to him. "Was your grandmother a quilter?"

What brought that on?

At his puzzled look, Sierra added, "Oh, I wondered if she was the one responsible for the quilt on your mom's swing. And the one airing on her clothesline."

Ah, those. "She did some, but mostly out of old clothes. My mom is really into it, though. She loves all the colors and designs and stuff."

Sierra beamed. "I've always wanted to take it up. Maybe now that we're living out in the country I'll have time. Think she'd be willing to teach me?"

A slight movement from Jo caught Zach's attention but, when he looked, her focus was on her food. He turned back to Sierra. "I don't see why not. She's part of a club that makes quilts for orphanages in Romania. You've met Gabe, at Nature's Pantry?"

Sierra nodded.

"His parents retired early and went over there as missionaries."

She leaned forward. "Oh, that is so cool! That would be even better than making them for myself or my family."

Claire laughed. "At least we wouldn't have to look at your early attempts."

Sierra scrunched up her face at her friend.

Zach leaned back, grinning. Who would have thought he'd enjoy talking about quilts around a meal with these women?

Jo pushed her half-eaten stew away.

Domino whimpered in his sleep. A light scratching sound on metal followed, and a wee thump.

Zach glanced up, trying to place it. No one else must have heard it, because they all seemed focused on their food.

Sierra set her glass of water down with unnecessary force.

Claire turned to him. "So, tell us about your job. I hear you're a veterinarian?"

"Yes, that's right. Just got my license to practice a few months ago."

The scratching turned into a scuffle. Domino cocked his head.

Zach frowned. "What's that sound?"

The pup whimpered, his gaze trained on the garbage can beside the stove.

The girls exchanged glances. "Sounds like we caught another mouse," Jo said at last.

He hadn't heard a snap. And dead mice didn't scratch.

"We got a live trap." She took a deep breath. "We weren't catching enough of them with the kind you brought over."

Enough of them? What on earth did *that* mean? "How many have you caught?"

She poked her spoon around her bowl. "We've…um…kind of lost track. Too many."

Claire snorted. "And yet not enough."

"Are they reproducing in here, or are more coming in from the fields?"

Jo spread her hands. "How would we know? We haven't found any more nests."

A good start, anyway. "Have you located their entry point, then?"

She looked at him blankly. "Um. Like where?"

"Around water pipes, maybe. Places like that."

She shook her head. "We haven't found any big gaps."

"It doesn't take much. They can squeeze through nearly anything." Surely the girls had done a thorough inspection.

"Claire stuffed some insulation around the pipes under the sink." Sierra poked a thumb in the direction of the counter.

"That won't stop them. They'll push right past fiberglass."

"Then what?" Jo leaned her elbows on the table. "We can't seem to get ahead of them."

"Steel wool works. Of course there's no insulating value to it, but they won't chew through the metal wires or push against it."

Claire raised her eyebrows. "Even if we block more from coming in, there are still a gazillion in here somewhere."

"You need a cat." Zach grinned. "Grandma had a fat old tom named George. He certainly kept pests under control."

Sierra poked her chin across the table. "Jo says she's allergic."

"Well, I am!"

Zach had another bite of stew. Nearly gone, to his regret. "A lot of people who think they're allergic can adapt to one they live with. How severe are your reactions?"

"I get stuffed up and sneezy." Jo narrowed her gaze at him.

Oops, looked like he'd touched a sensitive spot. "You could have tests done. If you wanted."

"We don't want a cat anyway." Claire shifted in her seat. "They get on the counters and stuff. I don't want cat hair in my food any more than I want mice around."

So much for Mom's idea of foisting off some of Mindy's

kittens. He pushed his bowl away slightly. "That was a great supper. Thanks."

"Oh, there's more if you're still hungry." Sierra reached for the ladle. "And then there's dessert."

How could he resist?

o0o

She'd hate Sierra if they weren't best friends. Quilting indeed. Jo had two left thumbs—she couldn't vie with that if she tried. Her color sense was limited to whether plants looked a healthy green.

No point in dreaming about Zach, anyway. A cute guy competent on the farm and respectful to his mother only went so far. He'd be headed back to the city soon enough, and Jo's life would go on the way she'd expected. Alone. Might as well keep it in mind.

When the meal ended and Claire began to clear off the table, Jo excused herself, grabbed her hoodie, and accompanied Domino outside. He ran circles around her while she made her way to the tire hanging from a branch of the elm across the yard.

Had Zach played on this swing as a child? Jo pushed off slightly with her feet, allowing the rope to twist the tire slowly.

In the distance, the sun sank toward the horizon and the waxing moon brightened overhead. The scent of freshly turned earth filled her nose as shadows stretched. An owl hooted up the hill, and another answered from down the valley. Domino zigzagged the ground, sniffing. She leaned over to scratch his silky ears when he came near.

Dear Lord, why? She'd thought she had come to terms with staying single. She didn't need a man, a husband to make her happy. She had God, her girlfriends, and a chunk of land to grow food and demonstrate living gently on the earth. The community house they'd soon start wasn't the end-all. Each of them had plans for a cozy home of their own to build nearby. They'd help each other and keep living in community. Someday they'd have guests and students, people who'd want to emulate their lifestyle. Folks they could teach. None of that required getting married. She simply hadn't planned on finding someone at this stage.

Besides, if Jo had to fall in love, why couldn't she be logical about her choice? God knew if she picked a mate, he'd need to feel as she did about His green earth. Someone who shared her values, her faith, her passions. She didn't have these things in common with Zachary Nemesek. There was little evidence of strong faith. Zach longed to return to the city. And as for passions…

He was falling for Sierra, like every other male on the planet. Jo was twenty-five years old and never been kissed by a guy who meant it. Unless she counted her grandfather.

The door to the trailer creaked open, revealing Zach silhouetted against the rectangle of light. Jo heard low voices and the door closed. He whistled for Domino and by some sort of instinct, Jo's hand tightened on the pup's collar. Domino whimpered.

Why had she held him? Juvenile move. She released him with a pat, and he shot off across the yard, only his white parts showing.

Jo twisted the tire swing, not wanting to strain her eyes as Zach and the pup walked down the driveway. Too dark to really see. Too pathetic to try. Tears burned in the back of her eyes. Stupid, stupid Josephine.

A warm, moist tongue licked her hand. She startled, clutching at the rope to prevent falling off the tire.

"Ah, that's where you are." Zach's voice was surprisingly close. "I figured Domino would lead me to you."

If he only knew. Jo hesitated, unsure of her voice, before rotating the tire back around. "Hey there."

Zach climbed on the picnic table and sat with his boots on

the plank seat, elbows on his knees. "Beautiful night." His face glowed slightly in the moonlight and his hair gleamed. It looked soft, like Domino's ears.

A flush crept up Jo's neck and onto her cheeks. Good thing the shadow of the elm protected her from his gaze. "Yes," she managed to say. "I love spring."

He tilted his head, but his eyes remained in shadow. Was he looking at her? She couldn't tell. "What about it appeals to you?"

"It's like a promise. Seeds planted. Anything can grow." Jo could have kicked herself. Nothing like playing with innuendo.

He sighed and tilted his head downward. In the outline of his posture Jo saw discouragement, not hope.

In a snap decision she stopped the tire swing and slid off. She climbed onto the picnic table, leaving plenty of space between them. "Spring doesn't offer promises to you?"

He shrugged. "It's been a rough few months. I'm not sure what I believe anymore."

His family had been through so much with his father's illness. "How so?" For a long moment, Jo didn't think he'd answer.

"I thought I had a permanent position lined up for after my graduation. It, um, fell through." He shifted on the table. "I'm headed into Coeur d'Alene later this week to follow up on some job leads with the hope my dad gets better soon."

Right. And it wasn't nice of her to pray to the contrary, but she could hardly help herself.

"That Guillain-Barré is a kicker." His voice was so low she barely made out the words.

Had he received more news, worse news? "He'll be okay, won't he?"

"Depends what you mean by okay. The immunoglobulins halted the progress of the disease, but he's not recovering quickly. It may be partly due to his age." Zach shook his head. "He'll be in physical therapy for a while. It may be months before he's well again. If ever."

A light breeze riffled through Jo's hair, causing her to shiver even in her hoodie. "Then it's a good thing for your folks that you were free to come home and help. God worked it out for them."

Zach snorted. "That was nice of Him."

He didn't sound convinced, and she could understand why. She only half-believed it herself. Wasn't it better to make a plan and pursue it to the finish line rather than wonder what secret meaning God had behind things?

"Sorry. I have trouble thanking God for messing up my dad's health and making me lose my job, so I could help Mom. Sounds like backward assistance."

Dear Lord, give me the words. "We often don't see the whole picture. God has reasons we can't understand." At least that's what everyone told her when things slid out of her clutching grasp.

Zach lifted his shoulder in a shrug. "I suppose. I was raised in the church. I've heard the lingo." He paused for a moment, scratching Domino, who had his front paws on the bench between their feet. "How about you? Are you a Christian from way back?"

Her? He wanted to know about *her*? "I went to Sunday School when I was a kid living with my grandparents. My mom and I moved to California when I was ten and she married Brad." Jo grimaced. "He wasn't much interested in church." Or anything that didn't look like tremendous short-term profit. Forgetting Brad would make her happy. "Meeting Sierra in college helped me find my way back to God." *Nice one, Josephine Lynn. He hadn't been talking about Sierra. Good of you to bring her up.*

"How'd you wind up buying a farm here in the north panhandle? It's not what I'd expect out of a group of beautiful young women."

It'd been awhile since anyone called her beautiful. Not when Sierra was around. "We believe God wants Christians to demonstrate living in respect for the Earth He created for us. Everyone's so interested in money and power." Like her mom and Brad. "The planet can't sustain all this commercialism for much longer. So few people know how to grow their own food and live simply on the land. We want to prove it can be done."

He chuckled, and her blood rose. How dare he.

"It's not all it's cracked up to be, Jo. Trust me. Look at my folks. Their house is practically falling apart around their heads. They've been farming forever and getting nowhere. Dad had to take a job off the farm to make ends meet. I never want to be as poor as them."

"We're not afraid of hard work, Zach. We know what we're up against. My grandparents farmed over the border in Canada. They taught me things worth having are worth fighting for." Jo slid off the picnic table and stood there, hugging herself, missing her grandparents. If only they'd still been there to go back to, but they'd died not long after her mom had hauled her away.

"Hey, no offense. I was just showing you the other side of the coin." He hopped off the table.

Conversation over.

Too bad he didn't share her values. He persisted in believing they—all three of them—were children that had no idea what they were in for. Well, he might be right and he might be wrong, but it didn't change things. They were staying anyway.

An owl hooted from straight up the elm, startling Jo. Domino went into a barking frenzy and she tried to step out of his way, only to trip over him. Strong hands held her up and didn't let go. She looked straight at the buttons on Zach's suede jacket as the warmth from his hands seeped through her sleeves. She trembled, and not from cold.

"Hey, you okay?" The moon cast a gentle glow on his face.

"Yeah, fine, thanks." If only she wasn't such a klutz around him. Jo pulled away, but he didn't let go. She looked up.

"Jo?" His gaze captured hers.

Her breath deserted her for an instant.

He gave her arms a little squeeze then released her. “Good night.”

Jo stumbled backward a step, but regained her balance before he needed to rescue her yet again. She couldn’t tear her eyes from his deep brown ones. “Good night, Zach.” Jo turned and hurried for the trailer door, trying already to remember how her words had sounded. Harsh…or desperate?

Chapter 7

The Hammond Pet Clinic waiting room was full of people and animals of all sizes, shapes, and species. Sure looked to Zach like Jeff could use another veterinarian, but the only emotion Zach could summon was relief it wasn't him. He picked his way between pet carriers and approached the reception desk.

Yvette peered up at him through artificially long eyelashes and swung her expensive platinum curls over her shoulder. "Daddy's busy."

He'd expected to feel more emotion—a sense of loss, maybe—at seeing her again. So not there. He kept his voice even. "I just need to see him for a minute. I'll wait and catch him between patients." He forced himself to keep holding her gaze.

"He doesn't want to talk to you. He gave you your pink slip. Remember? That means he's done."

The paper had legally terminated his employment at the Hammond Pet Clinic. Filled in by Yvette's hand, but signed by her father. Like Zach could forget. "I need a letter of reference from him." He'd done good work here for his temp position. Jeff Hammond had no reason to deny him a referral.

Yvette's gaze narrowed.

Except for personal reasons, of course. But other vets at other clinics wanted to know why Hammond had signed on a different vet after Zach had been there for nearly three months.

He didn't want to drag Yvette's name into it and risk getting sued. Besides, it would only prove how poor his own taste in women had been. Sure, she was beautiful. Enough money could make any girl gorgeous. He studied her now, and tried to remember what had once increased his heart rate.

He could walk around the desk, down the corridor, and find Jeff on his own. He'd worked here long enough to know his way around. Yvette had no muscles to speak of—she couldn't stop him. But a white-coated man came out of the hallway just as Zach gathered himself to follow through. A guy from Zach's class at the veterinary college. "Draper?"

"Hey, Nemesek. Fancy meeting you here." Garth Draper entered the reception area as Yvette stood to meet him. He pecked Yvette's cheek and squeezed her shoulder. "This guy giving you some trouble, sweetie?"

Zach expected to feel jealousy, but it didn't rise. Instead, relief grew into something near palpable. If he had a job, he could be thankful it wasn't here. Zach glanced at the waiting room behind him and lowered his voice. "Hey, Draper. Sorry to see she got you suckered in."

Yvette wrinkled her nose at him.

Draper chuckled. "Nice try, Nemesek." His fingers massaged Yvette's neck as he scanned the waiting room. "Who's next?"

Nothing remained for Zach at Hammond Pet Clinic. Jeff never went against his darling daughter, so there was no reason to think he'd have charitable thoughts for Zach now. Time to leave. He swiveled on his heel and strode toward the door. Yvette's chuckle came to his ears just before the door swooshed shut behind him.

Good thing he'd parked around the corner, out of sight of the clinic's windows. He rested his forehead on the Mustang's steering wheel for a long moment. How could he have been so stupid as to tangle his love life with his job? Why couldn't he have seen her for what she really was before he'd gotten in so deep?

She'd wanted him to sleep with her, but he'd meant the oath he'd sworn in high school. Some vestige of the honor he'd been brought up with gave him the courage to hold the line. Oh, he'd desired her all right, and believed she felt the same about him. Until the evening Zach remembered he'd left his cell phone at her apartment and discovered a man's jacket and boots in her entry. Bad enough, but the bedroom door had been closed and Yvette's breathless voice had told Zach to get lost.

That still stung.

Josephine's elfish face drifted into his mind and settled beside Yvette's. No comparison. There was nothing fake or manipulating about Jo. She was who she was. Refreshing, if a little blunt.

But he still needed a job, and sitting in Jeff Hammond's parking lot wasn't getting him one.

o0o

Jo read the email from her mother with growing dismay. Mom intended to visit, dragging Brad in her wake. Jo looked around the dingy trailer. It took no imagination to see the dilapidated, foul-smelling place through her mother's eyes. The whole structure was smaller than the suite Jo had in Brad's house as a teen. No way did she want Mom seeing this. Ever.

She couldn't possibly mean it, anyway. The only feasible reason she'd come would be to criticize. Jo had never done anything good enough for her mother and her current living conditions weren't likely to change Mom's opinion. As for Brad, he'd given Jo everything but the time of day. There wasn't a chance he'd started caring now.

Jo hit 'reply.' *It was great to hear from you.* A lie she hoped God would forgive. *Things are crazy hectic here this spring and we're not really settled in. Probably best if you wait until next year to come all the way out here, once our community house is up.* Not that Mom would expect to stay at the trailer. Even Brad's friends stayed in posh hotels when they visited California, though it was hard to imagine anyone with more room for guests. *Keep in touch. Love, Jo.*

The message seemed rather terse but she couldn't summon up the politeness to change a word of it. *Send.*

Hectic was an understatement, but today she found herself with a couple of hours alone on the farm. Planting the garden was out of the question as it had rained heavily during the night. Her chicken-fried rice wouldn't take long to fix once the girls were home.

What to do with her bonus day? Restless, Jo prowled over to the window and peered out. The sun bored a hole through the thick cloud cover. Jo needed some fresh air, a place to sit and read her Bible. A place to pray.

In minutes she trudged through the wet woods, wishing she had Domino at her side. The pup's only speed was hyper-bounce, but Jo enjoyed his company. He needed someone with more energy than Rosemary. Jo couldn't afford to buy him even if he was for sale, though. Pushing the thought of the pup and Zachary right out of her mind, she angled deeper into the trees along the creek. Jo hadn't had a lot of opportunity to explore along the hillside property line.

Numerous golden willows nestled in a hollow, thin branches littering the ground beneath them. A knotted rope dangling from above collided with Jo's head. It disappeared through a square hole in a wooden platform. Her pulse quickened. A tree house. She rolled a stump closer and managed a good grip on the rope, then hoisted herself up to the first solid branch.

Zach's childhood tree house. It had to be. She hesitated only an instant, then climbed the rest of the way up and through the hole.

Jo was in a space more than eight feet square with the willow's trunk taking up a fair bit of the middle. A rickety railing surrounded it and another knotted rope dangled from above.

She grinned, delighted, and took the challenge, clambering to the next level a dizzying height above the ground. Not that she could see the forest floor through all the drooping branches. This platform was a little smaller. She sat down, her back to the trunk, and closed her eyes.

The sweetness of willow sap mingled with the aroma of wet decaying leaves. Dampness saturated the air, and Jo shivered slightly. She tugged her Bible and notebook out of her jacket pocket and opened both, staring blankly while chewing on her pen cap.

The Earth is the Lord's, and everything in it. Here in the woods, far from any manmade sounds, Jo could easily believe in His control. People had a way of ruining nearly everything they touched. She knew she was doing what God wanted, raising awareness of the needs of the planet itself. And yet her mind would not stay on the passage she'd meant to read.

Zachary Nemesek interfered with her capacity to think. If only he were content to live a quiet life in the countryside. But no, he longed for the bright lights and the fast pace of the city. Galena Landing and its valley full of farms did not beckon him.

Jo's university years had provided enough sirens, car exhaust, and flashing neon lights for an entire lifetime. She couldn't go back. Not even for the love of a man. She took a deep breath. She was deluding herself anyway. He'd looked like he might kiss her—yeah, right—but gave her a friendly hug. Nothing romantic. Just the mark of a simple friendship that would soon be merely a memory.

There was no reason to think he was falling for her, but maybe he wasn't enchanted by Sierra either. That thought put everything on new ground.

No, it didn't. He was leaving as soon as he could get a new job and his dad was back on his feet. There was no new ground. Jo's own deepening roots into this farm provided the only reality. God had given her and her friends a mandate, and they intended to complete it.

That left no room for a city slicker like Zachary Nemesek.

Jo opened her eyes, and her gaze fell upon a rusty coffee can tucked into a crook of the willow. Curious, she reached out and tugged it free, then peeled off the plastic lid. A little spiral notebook and stubby pencil lay inside.

Telling herself it was none of her business did nothing to slow her reach for the notebook. She turned its pages and saw a boyish hand state a desire to alleviate suffering in this world. God made the animals, and they needed doctors, too. She thought of Domino, and Zach's obviously strong bond with the pup.

She flipped through the pages. Words in a more mature hand stated, *As God is my witness, I, Zachary John Nemesek, do hereby vow to reserve my body for my future spouse.*

Jo snapped the notebook shut. The images those words produced were way too personal. Had Zach kept that vow through the intervening years? If only his dream of doctoring animals could be fulfilled here.

She leaned back against the willow trunk and closed her eyes. In her dream, Zach worked beside her building a house, harvesting a garden, working the land. Kissing Jo.

Only a fantasy.

o0o

Zach poked his head around the open door in the rehabilitation unit. Four beds lined the ward. His father lay in a semi-reclining position next to the window, sagged back against his pillows. "Hey, Dad."

His mom glanced up from her seat beside the bed, and Dad's eyes opened at the sound of Zach's voice. "Hello yourself."

Mom gathered up her hand quilting and set it on the foot of the bed. "I'm going down to the cafeteria to get a cup of tea. Either of you want one?"

"Sure." Zach glanced at his dad, who nodded.

She leaned over the bed and kissed her husband. Zach winced as his dad's arms barely cleared the bed's surface in an attempt to return her embrace. This was the man he'd thought could cut his own hay in a couple months? Not likely.

Zach sank into the vacated chair. Outside the window, dreary gloom had settled over the city. Depressing view, but he didn't want to look at his father, either. Still, that's what he was here for. "How are you doing, Dad?"

"Been better."

"Yeah. Looks like. You get started on therapy today?"

Frustration welled in his dad's brown eyes. "Such as it was."

Zach leaned forward, elbows on his knees. "That good?"

"I don't know if I have it in me to combat this." Dad's gaze flicked to the door, then back to Zach. "Don't tell your mother I said that."

"You're a fighter. You can do it. There's a lot to live for."

Dad shook his head, his thinning hair rustling against the pillow. "I don't know. I can't do anything. They have to help me sit up and lie down. If you're here at mealtime, get ready to laugh. Getting a spoon to my mouth is hit or miss." He sighed. "Mostly miss."

Zach's gut clenched. "It'll get better. You just have to practice."

Dad's eyes closed. "It hurts."

It wasn't like his father to be a whiner. This was the man who'd told Zach to keep his chin up, that he could do anything he strove to do. Pain and discouragement had dragged a strong man down.

"Do they need to up your meds? I can talk to them."

"I don't know." Sadness lined his dad's face. "I'm glad you're there for your mother. I worry about her."

"She's doing fine. Keeping busy."

"You're a big help. Thanks."

Zach shrugged. "I found myself with time on my hands. No problem." Not how he really felt, but so be it. None of this was his dad's fault. Sometimes life just dealt a bad hand and a guy had to make the best of it.

"I keep telling myself God allowed all this for a reason." Dad took a deep breath. "I'm hanging onto that. The hospital chaplain has been in a few times to pray with me."

Zach said nothing. Easier not to incriminate himself that way.

"We're praying for you, son. I know you're in a difficult situation, but I'm so grateful for you. Thanks for tilling the gardens."

Zach nodded.

"Your mother said you were going by Jeff Hammond's clinic. How did that go?"

Like his dad didn't have enough to worry about without taking on Zach's future. But it was easier to talk about his sordid issues than Dad's. "I didn't get a chance to see him. It's a dead end."

"There are other clinics."

"And they ask for a referral from my previous employment, which Hammond won't give. Or so Yvette tells me. I screwed up big time, Dad." Felt good to get that off his chest.

"You should talk to Doc Taubin, maybe. Heard a rumor that he was looking for a temp so he could get his hip replacement surgery done. Not too many willing to come to a small town like Galena Landing."

And who could blame them? Zach thought of the vets he'd graduated with, an entire class full of young people high on city living and the big money rich patrons offered to keep their purebred pets content. Something tinged in his gut. Had it really come to this? "Yeah, I guess I could talk to him. Looks like you're not going to be back to full speed for a bit here."

His dad grimaced. "Not right away. No."

Mom came around the corner carrying a cardboard tray of

Styrofoam cups. Zach sprang up to take it from her. She smiled at him wanly. "Thanks, son."

They did need him. He'd have written the story a different way, for sure. But he couldn't walk away from his folks in this difficult time. Did God really have a reason for all this?

Chapter 8

"Hey, Rubachuk." Zach let the door of Nature's Pantry jingle shut behind him, then looked around the little shop. He couldn't see his buddy, though.

"Nemesek? Give me a hand, man." Gabe's voice came from the back corner. "Got a degree in engineering?"

Zach followed the voice between rows of tall shelving loaded with vitamins. He found Gabe squatting on the weathered plank floor with an array of bolts, nuts, screws and boards around him.

"Um, not in engineering, no. Why? Can't you follow simple directions?"

Gabe raked a hand through light brown hair, which looked messy enough this might not be the first time he'd pulled that move. Frustration lined his set jaw. "If these directions are simple, I'll eat my hat."

"Game on." Zach grinned and reached for the paper. "I hope you like the taste of canvas seasoned with sweat." He scanned the first page then glanced at the assortment of parts.

Gabe raised his eyebrows and sank onto the floor. "Oh, wise one, explain it all to me. Do I need to go get my hat?"

Okay, a page in Spanish, one in French, one in…something Asian. Chinese? Finally, back page, English. Zach held it up in triumph.

Gabe rolled his eyes. "Seriously. You think I didn't find the readable section?" He picked up the Allen wrench and a short plank. "I'm thinking these go on here, like this." He demonstrated, holding two boards together at right angles. "But there aren't the right number of bolts if that's true."

Zach knelt and examined the hardware. His buddy had made piles of like items. Zach chewed his lip and picked up the instructions, then flipped the page over. Blank.

"I take it my hat is safe?" A sardonic grin creased Gabe's face.

"Perhaps. What exactly are you trying to build here?"

"A rack for organic garden seeds. Isn't it obvious?"

Zach let out a laugh. "Not very, no. But I'm sure we can figure it out. How many long boards are there?" He set the instructions aside and laid out the parts in a way that made sense to him.

Gabe nodded. "So far so good. It's the hardware that's messing me up."

Zach test-fitted a piece. "Since when are you in the seed business?"

"Jo and Sierra talked me into giving it a try. They said all they could find at the feed store and the hardware store were big commercial brands, all full of herbicides and such."

"Huh? Who knew seeds came organic or not?" Dumb words. Jo would know.

Gabe shrugged and reached for a bolt. "Makes sense, when you think about it. I never had. I don't know how much clout those girls have in the community, being new and all, but they wanted to have access to organic seeds and said they'd make sure everyone knew I was carrying them. They even found me a few companies online and helped me to decide who to go with."

Zach rocked back on his heels. "Really now."

"What?" Gabe glanced over at him. "I'm putting an ad in the paper and a big sign in the window. Should be decent business. With some of the church folk supporting that local harvest dinner of Jo's, more people I know are planning to garden this year than ever before. Why shouldn't I jump on the band wagon?"

That crazy girl. She sure stuck her neck out in support of her cause. Didn't let her size bother her. Just like a yappy little dog with as much bite as bark, despite her small stature. Zach shook his head, trying not to grin.

"What? You think I'm crazy?"

Zach stared at Gabe. "Huh?"

"For going into seeds." Gabe frowned and waved his hand over the partially assembled rack on the floor. "For taking their advice."

"Oh. No, not at all. Just admiring their spunk." Not that putting the girls in plural would fool Gabe for a minute.

It didn't. Gabe guffawed as he sat back on his heels. "You're speaking of Josephine, of course. The word spunk in the dictionary should have her picture beside it."

Distract him. "What of Sierra? What word is her picture for?"

Gabe looked at him funny. "What's that got to do with anything? You don't have the hots for her, unless I'm way out of practice reading you. It's the little gal that has your attention."

The store was too brightly lit to hide the flush Zach felt creeping up his neck. He shrugged. Time to sidetrack Gabe, if it wasn't too late already. "She's interesting, but I'm not sticking around. Remember?"

"Ha! Not sure what God has to say about that, Nemesek. I'm thinking He's got other ideas. He's gone to a lot of trouble to orchestrate your life. You listening?"

Zach stared at Gabe. "It's just how things are right now, but it'll change."

"Right." Gabe fitted another bolt and tightened a shelf into the developing rack. "How's your dad doing? You were in Coeur d'Alene yesterday, weren't you?"

"Yeah." Zach leaned back on his heels. "He'll be in there for a long haul. They've started him on physical therapy, but he can't even get out of bed by himself."

Gabe whistled. "It's been, what, a couple weeks since he got sick?"

"Over a month now." Zach sucked in a deep breath. "I'm really worried about him. I don't see how he'll ever farm again, but Mom won't listen to me when I suggest they sell out. They're living in denial."

"Is that a family trait or something?"

"Hey now!" Zach lifted the electric drill and buzzed it in Gabe's direction.

His friend laughed. "Seriously. There's Doc Taubin needing a hand right here in Galena Landing and you're off trying to get a job elsewhere. Have you even stopped by?"

Zach swallowed hard. "That's what I came to tell you, actually. Talked to him this morning."

Gabe set the Allen wrench down and gave Zach his full attention. "And?"

"And I'm going to work with him a couple days a week until he gets the call for surgery. It'll give me a chance to get to know the practice some. Then I'll run the clinic until he's back on his feet."

Gabe's palm came up and Zach automatically high-fived it. "Way to go, Nemesek. I told you!"

"Doesn't mean I'm staying permanently. It just gives me a couple months or so while he and my dad recuperate. Then I'll be free again." Zach shrugged. "Besides, I need a solid referral, and Taubin can give me that."

"Tell yourself what you need to hear." Gabe winked. "God can work with it."

o0o

Mrs. Humbert patted Jo's hand. "There you are, my dear. I wondered when you'd come visit me again."

Jo perched on the edge of the bed and smiled at the elderly woman. "They lock me up in my office."

The narrow eyebrows pulled together.

Oops. The poor old lady only had a partial grasp on reality. "Oh, I didn't mean it that way. Just that I've been busy."

"But I have something for you." Mrs. Humbert struggled to a sitting position then reached over and fumbled in the drawer of her nightstand. "At least I think I do."

Something for her? Jo leaned forward, trying to guess.

"I'm sure it was in here somewhere." Mrs. Humbert shuffled several crumpled tissues around the drawer. "I'm sorry, dear."

Jo rounded the bed. "Do you need a hand? What am I looking for?" She peered into the cluttered enclosure and rested her hand on the old woman's shoulder.

"Zachary brought some. I don't think I ate any."

Jo's breath hitched. "Oh, what did he bring?" Probably some chips or something to mock her in front of his grandmother.

"That chocolate you said you liked."

"Really?" Jo stared at the woman. No way.

"Unless I imagined it." Mrs. Humbert turned to look at Jo, her blue eyes cloudy. "Maybe it happened a long time ago. They say I live in the past."

"It's okay, Mrs. Humbert." Jo sat next to her and wrapped her arm around the trembling shoulders. "I don't need anything. Don't worry."

"John brought me candy. I can't find that, either."

"Who's John?"

Mrs. Humbert peered at Jo. "Why, my sweetheart. Haven't you met?" She held her left hand out, displaying a set of classic wedding rings.

"That's a beautiful diamond." Jo touched the ring gently with her free hand, and the stone slid until it touched the neighboring finger. Mrs. Humbert's finger must once have been thicker. "He must have—must really love you." No point in insisting the man in question had been gone for twenty plus years. Apparently love—true love—endured beyond the grave.

"Yes." Mrs. Humbert twisted her hands together on her lap. "I don't know where he is, but he brought me candy in a heart."

If there was no box full of candy, there wasn't likely to be any organic dark chocolate, either. Jo stifled the twinge of disappointment. But could she do something about the heart box? Probably not. Valentine's Day was nearly three months past, so the odds of finding one of those candy boxes still on the shelves anywhere were pretty slim. What was she thinking? Those companies didn't put ecologically sound chocolate in them. It was just a gimmick…but a gimmick that would make an old lady happy.

"Grandma?"

Jo's head jerked up and she met Zach's gaze. She pulled her arm from around his grandmother's shoulder.

"John?" Mrs. Humbert struggled to get her feet under her. "You've come."

Zach crossed the space in two strides and knelt in front of the old woman. He shot Jo a look she interpreted as apologetic then took his grandmother's face between his hands. "It's Zachary, Grandma."

"Zachary?" Her fingers clutched at his.

Jo, not knowing where else to look, focused on Mrs. Humbert's profile as the old woman blinked several times.

"Rosemary's boy. Remember?" He was so tender with her.

Mrs. Humbert's voice sank to a whisper. "Y-yes. Not John."

Jo scooted over a little. She should probably leave Zach to deal with things here. This was about all the familial affection she could handle without either getting all teary-eyed herself or wishing Zach's hands cradled her own face.

"Don't go."

She paused halfway to her feet. Looked into Zach's pleading eyes.

"Unless you have to. I mean, to go back to work or something."

He actually wanted her to stay? Jo sank back onto the edge of the bed, lost in the brown eyes that met hers.

"Who are you?" Mrs. Humbert's voice had strengthened.

Jo turned to reassure the old lady, but Zach beat her to it. "This is Josephine, Grandma. Remember?"

It was easy to see she didn't. Not really. Jo focused back on Zach. "I should go. I'm sorry if I disturbed her. She was telling me about the candy hearts her husband used to give her."

By the look on his face, he had no clue what she was talking about. But then, he'd only been a little boy when his grandfather died. Jo rose. "I'll get back to my office now."

Zach clambered to his feet, his gaze guarded. "I suppose you told her the candy would rot her teeth or something."

"Of course not." Jo glared at him. "What do you think I am, some kind of tyrant?"

A slow grin spread across his face. "I wasn't sure. I think you're really just a softie under all that bristle."

A million emotions writhed and jumbled like living things in her head and heart. She backed up a step.

"John? Did you give that girl her special chocolate?"

Jo's cheeks burned as she stared at Zach. Not good. She turned and fled.

Zach's words followed her. "Not yet, Grandma. Don't worry, I'll find her some."

o0o

"Dratted mice!" Claire bellowed as she came down the trailer steps with a burlap sack in hand. "They've gotten into the seed potatoes."

Jo jumped off the tire swing and headed for her. "How bad is it?"

"Bad enough." She scowled. "A few have been gnawed to pieces, and most have at least a few bites out of them."

Jo peered into the bag. "Can't blame them for liking their potatoes organic."

Claire thrust the sack into Jo's hands. "I sure can."

"Fine then. Blame away. You ready to start planting?"

Claire let out a long sigh. "Do you really think it's worth it?"

"What, these potatoes? Yeah."

"Them." She waved an arm around. "All of it."

"You mean Green Acres? Definitely. Where's the spade?"

Claire grabbed it from where it had leaned against the trailer steps. While she was never as outgoing as the rest of them, today she looked dejected.

"You okay?"

She glanced at Jo then made a show of swinging the spade. "I'm probably just PMSing."

Jo followed her, hauling the potato bag to the garden plot.

Claire shoved the spade into the freshly turned soil and Jo cut a chunk off a potato with an eye on it and dropped it into the hole. They'd planted half a row before Jo was certain Claire wasn't going to say more without prodding. "So what's up? Besides hormones."

"I've never succeeded in anything in my life, so why should this be any different? I'll drag you all down with me."

Good grief. "You have so succeeded. You're a good chef."

"Who finally got a part-time job cooking in a small-town hotel kitchen." She stomped dirt over a seed potato.

"But that's probably the best job in your field in Galena Landing. You knew there weren't any five-star restaurants here." Jo wound a long potato eye around the chunk before planting it. "Seriously, Claire. You wanted to come. Didn't you?"

"Well, yeah. I want a place to sink some roots of my own."

"So you made a choice. I know that Michel dude wanted you to stay in Seattle. You were his rising star."

Claire shrugged, her back to Jo, as she dug another hole.

"You *were*."

"He only said that because I gave my notice. He was being nice."

Jo rolled her eyes, but of course Claire wasn't looking. "Right. 'Cause he tells everyone who leaves the restaurant that if they ever need a job or a reference to call him any time. At his home number. Didn't he even give you the right to use some of his recipes?"

No response.

"Claire?" Jo tossed a potato into the nearest hole and stomped the dirt back in. "What is really bothering you?"

Claire glanced over her shoulder, then turned away again and dug another hole. "I'm scared. Scared to let myself fall in love."

Jo's heart lurched. She should have known Claire would fall for Zachary. Jo was used to coming in second to Sierra, but it never occurred to her that Claire might be competition, too. *Oh, dear Lord, help me to be a good friend.*

"He's an awesome guy."

The words hadn't come out that loud, but Claire's head whipped around and her eyebrows pulled together. "Pardon?"

Jo bit her lip and met Claire's gaze. "I said he's an awesome guy."

"I heard what you said. What I didn't hear is what you meant."

Jo's turn to frown, not understanding. "Zach? You said you were afraid to fall in love."

Claire let out a shriek of laughter, slapping her hands to her knees while the spade dropped to the tilled ground. "You thought—" She gasped, and another peal erupted. "Oh man, Josephine Lynn Shaw. You have it worse than I thought."

Jo stiffened. "Have what worse than you thought?"

"You've fallen for our neighbor, and you have fallen hard."

Her mumble of protest fell on deaf ears because Claire was still killing herself laughing. Tears poured down Claire's face as she sank weakly into the dirt.

"Well, supposing I misunderstood you—"

Claire howled.

Jo chucked a seed potato at her friend. "I was trying to say *if* I misunderstood you, what on earth were you trying to say?"

"What I've fallen in love with," and Claire's eyes twinkled, "is this farm. Not a guy. Not even Zach Nemesek." She sobered quickly and pushed to her feet, finding the spade. "No more men for me. You know that." She tossed the potato back at Jo.

Claire had been engaged once, and it hadn't gone well. The guy hadn't really been willing to settle down and Claire hadn't been willing to spend the rest of her life living like a gypsy. No, Jo knew that a permanent home was more important to Claire than romance. It was to all three of them. They'd pledged it. "Why are you worried about the farm? We're making our payments, no problem."

"It's too good to be true. I can't relax. I keep waiting for the other boot to drop."

"Or the other mousetrap to snap?"

She mustered up a grin. "That, too."

"Claire, sweetie, Green Acres isn't a whim. You know that. We've all worked too hard to make this a reality. For like five years. We're on track with our plan."

"I know, but—"

"By Christmas we'll be into the new house." Jo waved at the staked-out area across the driveway from the garden. "We'll have more room and no mice. We'll settle in and it won't be quite as much work. You'll see."

Claire leaned on the shovel and stared at Jo. "You're one to talk, crawling around in the dirt dreaming of Zach."

Jo shoved a potato chunk into the ground with unnecessary

force.

"I mean it. You'll marry him and go off to the city, and Sierra will find somebody and do the same. I can't keep this place by myself, Jo."

"Not going to happen." Would Jo really be willing to leave the farm if Zach asked it of her? He wouldn't make her choose, would he? She shook her head, hard. Talk about getting ahead of things. But the gleam in his eye at the nursing home seemed to mean something.

Jo opened her mouth to respond but a flash of black-and-white caught both their attentions. Domino ducked under the barbed wire fence and into the garden. He leaped onto Jo, knocking her rear first into the dirt.

"Domino, down! Where'd you come from?" Jo knelt and gave the pup the loving he so strongly desired. A faint whir increased in volume.

Jo looked at Claire, eyebrows up.

Her expression was mirrored on Claire's face. "What's that sound?"

"Tractor." Jo strode over to the fence, the Border collie bouncing around her. She looked up the fence line and saw a John Deere chugging toward them, a faint plume coming out from behind it. She sniffed, and the air was filled with a thick sweetness that had nothing to do with spring flowers. Her ire rose. "He's spraying."

"But what?"

Jo barely heard Claire's words—or the machinery—through the clanging in her head. How could he? He knew they were trying to farm organically here, right alongside the Nemeseks' property. And unless Jo missed her guess—which wasn't possible—that stench was not from an organic source.

She pressed down on the middle wire, climbed through the fence and stood, arms akimbo, staring at the tractor grinding its way toward her, a man with a straw cowboy hat on his head instead of the usual newsboy cap. Didn't fool her. She still knew who it was.

Zachary Nemesek.

Traitor.

Chapter 9

Zach shifted on the tractor seat. The thing he'd always hated most about driving a farm rig was the twist in his back as he tried to keep an eye on the equipment behind and the furrow ahead. He'd be up for a lengthy hot shower later to undo the kinks.

His longing thoughts turned to the weight room, pool, and hot tub in his apartment building in Coeur d'Alene. Those jets would feel awesome tonight. He probably ought to give up his unit, though his mom used it sometimes when she was down visiting Dad for a few days. Who knew when he'd be back in the city? Not for a couple months, maybe more, depending on how quickly his dad and Wally Taubin recovered. The good vet must be pushing sixty by now. Zach racked his brain. Maybe more. He hadn't been all that young when Zach used to hang out at the clinic as a teen.

Might he be willing to take on a partner? Nah. That meant cows and horses and goats. It meant emergency calls to manure-studded barns. City pet practice paid better and kept humane hours, for the most part. And didn't stink as bad.

Zach glanced forward again, checking the fence line for the upcoming corner.

Someone stood not far in front of the tractor, both arms

waving frantically, with a dancing Border collie beside her. *Jo. Domino.* His heart lurched. Must be an emergency.

He shifted down and eased the brakes, hoping she'd know this machine didn't stop on a dime and would keep Domino out of his way this time. Where had the pup come from, anyway? The tractor ground to a halt, and he pulled the levers to seal the fertilizer injectors.

Jo stood with her feet firmly planted and her hands on her hips. The flash in her eyes didn't look like the panic that might come if one of her friends had been injured or something.

Couldn't be so bad, then. "Hi there, Jo! Beautiful day." He pulled out his water bottle and took a long swig.

No response.

Zach mopped his dripping forehead with his denim sleeve. He leaned both elbows on the steering wheel. "Is something wrong?"

One hand shot out and pointed behind him. "What do you think you are doing?"

Whoa. She'd bit every word off with precision. Zach glanced at the pressure tank. Was it leaking or something? No, it looked okay. He turned back to her with a frown. "Pardon me?"

"You're spraying the field with…with *poison.*"

Zach slid off the tractor and approached her, but she backed away, eyes flashing fire. She grabbed onto Domino's collar.

"It's not poison. It's fertilizer. Nitrogen, to be precise."

"Didn't you read the directions? You're supposed to be suited up to handle that stuff." She took a step closer. "Did it ever occur to you that if you should wear protection, and if there is a big danger sign on the tank, you shouldn't even be using it?"

"I suited to load the tank. I'm not stupid."

She narrowed her eyes. "You could've fooled me."

And he'd thought she might be something special. Not that he wanted her to be, but at least he'd found out before it was too late for his heart that she really was just as narrow-minded as his first impressions had been. She had no better grip on reality than his grandmother.

"Not only are you not suited, you aren't following appropriate procedures."

She'd lost him. Zach frowned. "What do you even know about it?"

"That?" Her hand shot out, pointing at the tank again. "Far too much. My stepfather uses every kind of commercial chemical there is to produce higher yield on his mega farm. I've smelled them all. And this one is rotten." She pursed her lips together, obviously biting back a further tirade.

Her whole face, flushed. Her eyes, flaming. Her hair, flying every which way out of the long braid that attempted to contain it. Her lips. Enticing.

He bent his head to hers and kissed those tantalizing lips. A shock ran through him at her passionate, welcoming response. He held her shoulders for a brief instant, then as the kiss intensified, slid his hands around her back and snugged her tight against him. Zach trembled as her arms rounded his waist, clutching him as completely as he held her. He gave himself over to the moment, reveling in the contact, in the tiny but powerful woman in his arms.

She pulled away all too soon, and Zach opened languid eyes just in time to see her hand flying at his face. He lurched back, but not quickly enough to avoid her open palm as it stung his cheek.

"How dare you!"

It took him a second. "Deny you kissed me back."

She couldn't. That kiss had been absolutely mutual, even though he'd started it. His lips still tingled. So did his cheek, but that was a different matter, nothing to do with the memory of her mouth under his. His gaze locked onto her lips. He wanted more in the worst way.

"Zach. A. Ry." She spit his name out in bite-sized pieces. "Stop it."

He didn't want to. But he'd better pay attention. This wasn't the time or the place to pursue the attraction that now lay out in the open. He had to woo her, but what would he do with her once he caught her?

A little voice reminded him he hated rural life—that he couldn't wait to be gone from Galena Landing. The voice also knew Jo wasn't going to join him in Coeur d'Alene. But none of it mattered. There was just now. The two of them. The future would work itself out.

The three of them. Jo squatted on the ground with her arms around Domino's neck, her face buried in his coat. Domino wiggled and tried to lick her face to no avail, then looked up at Zach with a happy smile and tail wag.

He never thought he'd be jealous of a dog.

Zach shifted from one foot to another as his thoughts slowed and came into some sort of alignment. "Jo? I'm sorry."

"Sorry for what?" Her voice was muffled in Domino's shoulder.

Not for kissing her. Not really. "For surprising you. For not asking."

She turned her face enough to peer at him. "What?"

Good, he'd startled her again. This time in a good way. He hoped. "Jo, if you want me to say I'm sorry for kissing you, I can say it. But I'd be lying."

Her face still flamed, and her gaze met his for only the briefest of instants before sliding away again.

He had to know. "Are you? Sorry we kissed?"

She buried her face in Domino's coat. Lucky dog.

o0o

Jo clutched Domino so tightly he whimpered, but letting go meant facing Zach.

The nerve of him. She didn't know which was worse, her body betraying her, or Zach kissing her in the first place. She'd responded like some desperate woman. Her first kiss, and it had caught her off guard and turned her knees to jelly.

He couldn't possibly love her. He'd only been trying to fluster her. Oh, wow. If that were the case, it had totally worked.

Jo gathered her courage and stood, careful to keep Domino between them. "Don't distract me. We were talking about your toxic rig here." She kept her trembling hands down and pointed with her chin.

Zach kept staring at her mouth. Finally his gaze rose to her eyes.

Jo did her best to regain the ire she'd had earlier, but he'd shaken her to the bottom of her size six boots. "Seriously, that stuff is dangerous."

Zach opened his mouth to protest, but Jo held up her hand. Pretty steady. Good. "One, you absolutely need to be suited up. It is toxic, regardless of what you think. Two, it's way too warm for the pressure tank today. The gas dissipates quickly at this temperature and sinks straight into the ground water." She took a deep breath.

He waited for her to continue. They were getting somewhere, then.

"And three, it's *our* drinking water you're affecting as well as yours. We all get our water from the same spring. Do you really want to be drinking poison?"

"I have goggles and gloves on the tractor, and I wore them when I adjusted the injectors."

Trying to redeem himself. "Good start. But how about just not using it in the first place?"

Zach frowned, drawing her attention to his close-cropped beard. It had prickled slightly while they kissed, but in a pleasant way. If only she believed he really meant it, she'd be happy to try all over again. She yanked her gaze back to his eyes.

Which danced as though he'd caught her out.

Maybe he had.

The heat hadn't ever left her face, so Jo doubted this new surge would add any telltale color to her cheeks. She raised her chin. Probably shouldn't have. That position would only make it easier for him to kiss her again.

She needed out of here in the worst way. Primal instinct churned in her gut, urging her to throw herself back in Zach's arms, to pull his face to hers and resume where they'd left off. She wanted to tangle her fingers in his thick curls, and trace his facial hair with her lips.

Jo backed up. Her environmental authority evaporated more every second she stood in Zach's presence. What was more important? Their water supply and the health of the land beneath their feet, or her desire to be fervently kissed? And why did her brain even hiccup over that question?

"Please, Zach." It was hard to keep her righteous indignation in place after that electrifying kiss. "All else aside, today's too warm. Go look up optimum conditions on the Internet. Or better yet, find some natural product to fertilize with. Like sheep manure." Of which they must have plenty, with all those woolly animals traipsing around their pastures.

He nodded slowly. Only to placate her? Maybe. Didn't matter, so long as he followed through.

"And much as I like Domino, take him home. He shouldn't be around that toxic sludge, either."

Zach's gaze dropped to the pup, wagging his tail at the mention of his name. Zach frowned. "Where'd he come from?"

Dumb question. "From your place, I assume? I certainly didn't come over and steal him."

His face flushed. "I didn't accuse you. But I left him in the run."

Jo hardened her will. "So he's opened the latch again." More likely Rosemary was home and had let him in the yard to play.

She turned away, still trembling from the confrontation. Or something else.

"Jo?" Zach's voice came out raspy then his hand rested on her forearm.

She stared at it for a long moment before turning slightly to face him. He was so close. Too close. Not close enough. She couldn't look up.

Zach cleared his throat. "Jo? You need to know. I didn't kiss you to stop you from yelling at me. Honest."

She studied his work boots and nodded slightly.

"I'm just…you're just…"

Scuffmarks lined his boots, proving their familiarity with farm work. Why didn't he finish his sentence?

"I'm sorry I acted in haste."

No way was Jo meeting his eyes. She had a fair idea what would happen if she did. She forced another nod.

"Jo?" Softer, now.

She held her breath.

"May I kiss you some more?"

Yes! Yes, yes, yes, YES. Please kiss me. Never stop. Jo clenched her fingernails into the palms of her hands until the pain began to bite. She could hardly blame the guy for his ignorance, shared with millions of other farmers. But that didn't excuse him. They'd never be compatible, not with an attitude like his. Slowly she found strength and straightened her posture, daring to meet his gaze for a brief instant.

Emotion flared in his brown eyes.

"No, Zach. That's best not repeated." Jo turned away and paced evenly to the barbed wire fence. Why didn't she feel his hands on her waist or shoulders, holding her back? Why did he let her walk away from him like this? Jo ducked between the wire strands and never looked back.

Chapter 10

Jo stalked past Claire—not daring to glance her way—up the steps, and into the trailer. She did not slam the door. She marched into the bathroom, locked the door, and leaned over the sink.

Her reflection stared back. The likeness of a woman who'd been kissed. She looked wild. Wisps of hair escaped down the length of her braid. Her face was blotchy and red, more from anger and embarrassment than the unseasonable early-May heat.

Jo put her hands to her cheeks and the reflection did the same. What had Zach seen in her? For the spark had been undeniable. That wasn't just a friendly peck between friends.

The door handle jiggled. "Jo? You okay?"

Couldn't answer that. Claire must've seen everything that happened. Maybe even heard the conversation over the tractor's idling. Jo tried to steady her voice. "I'll be out in a minute."

"That's not what I asked." Finally Claire sighed. After a moment her footsteps sounded down the corridor and Jo heard running water in the kitchen.

She turned back to the sink and splashed cold water on her

face, then undid her long plait and brushed out the mess. Rebraided it. Stared in the mirror some more. Stared at her lips, as Zach had seemed to do.

Why? Had it all been a ruse to shut her environmental mouth? But what of the other evening out by the picnic table? She hadn't been spouting off then, just staying away from his praise of Sierra's cooking and all the talk of womanly tasks such as quilting. Hiding. Lest her attraction to the man should show.

Hiding. Again. Claire didn't deserve this.

Jo unlocked the door and stepped out.

o0o

Zach watched Jo stomp across the field and climb through the fence. Watched Claire follow her into Grandma's old trailer. He shivered, suddenly chilled as though the sun had slipped behind a cloud. He even glanced up to check, but only blue sky resided above him.

Domino whined, recalling Zach to the present.

"C'mon, buddy. Let's go home, and I'll see how you got out this time." He'd leave the tractor here and come back for it when he'd decided what to do. Was Jo pulling his leg about the issue? He couldn't imagine it.

Gary Waterman had loaned him the ensemble, saying Dad's fields looked like they could use a boost. Zach followed Waterman's instructions, and the guy had been farming for long enough Zach hadn't thought to doubt him.

A few minutes later he unplugged the cable from his folks' desktop computer and attached it to his laptop. If he was going to stick around for a while, he should rig up a wireless router. Hard to believe he'd been home over a month now and hadn't fired up his MacBook once.

Domino flopped down in the corner, nose down but keeping

watch while Zach opened the fridge and poured a glass of raspberry vinegar. By the time he returned, his email home page had loaded. Twenty-eight unread. Would've been more if most of the guys from his graduating class weren't into texting. He clicked to review the list. Halfway down an unfamiliar name flagged his attention.

East Spokane Veterinary Clinic? Had he applied there?

Zach's heart sped up and his hand shook as he clicked on the email.

> *Dear Dr. Nemesek,*
>
> *Thank you for your application.*
>
> *We currently have a temporary opening for a qualified veterinarian that may turn into a permanent position for the right applicant. If interested, please contact our office by May 7. Interviews will be held the following week and the position begins Monday, May 17.*
>
> *Signed,*
>
> *Dr. Albert Warren, DVM, ABVP, ACVS*

May seventh? Zach's stomach plummeted. A bona fide job opening, right in the Spokane Valley, and he'd missed it? Why hadn't he been checking his email regularly? His cell number was on his résumé. Wouldn't they have left a message? He pulled his phone out of his pocket and checked. Nothing.

They were interviewing this week. Maybe it wasn't too late. What could it hurt to phone? He scanned the email for the number and punched it into his cell. Held his breath while it rang.

"East Spokane Veterinary Clinic, Corinne speaking. How may I help you?"

"This is Dr. Zachary Nemesek calling about the opening for a veterinarian. I received an email from your office."

"I recall seeing your name on the list, Dr. Nemesek, but the competition closed last Friday."

"I'm sorry. My father has been ill and I haven't kept up with my email. I'm wondering if there's any chance I can still get an interview." Zach held his breath. *Please, Corinne. Be nice and say yes.* There was a brief pause and Zach heard the tapping of keys. *Please. If there is a God, please.* Then he was put on hold and the music began.

Several minutes went by before he receptionist returned. "Dr. Warren was impressed with your résumé, Dr. Nemesek. If you can come in at eight tomorrow morning, he'll be happy to interview you."

Yes! "I can make that, no problem. Thank you very much. I'll see you in the morning."

"Thanks for phoning, Dr. Nemesek."

Zach rested both elbows on the table and sank his head into his hands. Wow. Talk about a close one. Thanks to Jo for sending him online today. Jo. The slap told him how she really felt. It would be best for both of them if he returned to the city. She'd find herself some tree-hugging hippie to kiss and he'd be back in the city he loved.

She'd get over him. Not that there had been a lot of sign she was *into* him to start with.

He'd get over her. Easier said than done.

When had he started thinking about her instead of Sierra? Or about nobody at all? At Galena Hills. Grandma had a soft spot for Jo, and it seemed mutual. He'd even picked up a package of organic chocolate, though he hadn't dropped it off yet.

Yikes. Eight in the morning. At least the clinic was near the interstate. He'd have to drive into Coeur d'Alene tonight. Good thing he hadn't given up his apartment yet. If he landed this job, he'd be able to keep it. If he didn't, he'd give his notice.

But he'd get it. Dr. Warren was disposed to like him, and Zach could make himself even more attractive when they spoke in person. Besides, he'd asked God for help and obviously God had granted his request.

He jogged out to the field, Domino at his heels, to bring the tractor and pressure tank into the pole shed. He'd deal with that later. Taking tomorrow off to check out this position was only one day. Then he'd have a few days to get things set up for Mom before Monday. She'd be happy for him, and he could come home weekends to do the fieldwork until Dad was back on his feet. It would all be good.

o0o

"I think Jo has something she'd like to share," Claire announced as the three girls sat at the supper table.

Jo shot her a nasty look and sighed. Oh, how she'd prefer to erase the scene with Zach from late this morning. But it had happened, the good and the bad. She glanced at Sierra. "Zach fertilized the pasture next to our garden this morning with some chemical junk."

Sierra set down her fork. "You're kidding. What happened?"

Way too much. Jo stared down at the delicious meal Claire had created and that she wasn't hungry for. "I confronted him."

"Good for you. He obviously needs some things explained to him. What did he say?"

Jo couldn't remember. Something disagreeable.

"He kissed her."

Thanks, Claire.

A sharp intake of breath from Sierra. "*What*? How did that happen? Did you kiss him back?

Answering that was too incriminating. She swallowed hard. "I slapped him."

"No way." Sierra's hand squeezed Jo's. "I thought you liked him?"

Jo lifted a shoulder. "Not really." *Liar.*

Claire leaned back in her chair and looked at Jo like she was an alien. Perhaps true. "That's not the way I heard it."

Jo glanced at Sierra, who stared back with questions in her eyes. Did she dare admit to Sierra—or to Claire—how confused she really felt inside? "He's okay. Or I thought he was."

"I'm sure—if you just explained things to him. I mean, did you have to smack him?"

Had she needed to? Jo pondered. It certainly seemed so at the time. "He caught me off guard."

"Sounds like it." Sierra sighed. "But wow, that's quite an opportunity for you."

Jo stiffened. "Meaning?"

"He's such a hot guy, a great catch."

"Who poisoned the field. Who hates living on the farm."

Sierra narrowed her gaze. "Guys are malleable. If he really loves you, he'll try to make you happy."

Malleable? Love? Yeah, right. "So you think I should just have ignored what he was doing? That a kiss should have made everything all right?"

"Well, not exactly. But you could have given it a bit of time to see what would happen, rather than belting him one."

He'd asked to kiss her again. Did Sierra think Jo should have let him? Welcomed him? Oh, she'd wanted to, but it hadn't seemed wise at the time.

Sierra tapped her fingers. "What happened then? Did he keep right on fertilizing?"

Had he? Jo didn't even know. She'd been too busy crying in the bathroom.

"No," Claire said. "He and the dog walked across the field to the farmhouse. About an hour later he came back and drove the rig away."

"See?" Sierra leaned closer. "You would have gotten the same results without violence. Honestly, Jo, what came over you? That's not how to win a guy over."

Jo jerked her chair back from the table and surged to her feet. "Sorry I haven't been keeping up with my romance lessons. Why do you care so much what I said or did?"

Sierra's big blue eyes stared up at Jo.

"Well, why do you? You got your own designs on Zach, or what?"

Sierra glanced at Claire, then back to Jo. "I didn't say that. I was leaving the field clear for you, but it doesn't look like you took advantage of it."

Jo pressed her hands against the table and leaned closer. "Thank you so much. I appreciate the condescension." She stalked off down the corridor.

"Nice one, Sierra," came Claire's voice.

"That's not how I meant it at all."

Oh yeah? What other way was there to take her words? Jo slammed her bedroom door.

o0o

Zach stacked extra bales for the sheep by the feeder. Had he forgotten anything that would ease the day for Mom tomorrow without him home? He grinned. Not that it was the first time she'd fed the stock since he'd gone off to college.

He spent a bit of time working with Old Pete, hoping Domino would catch on to the basic whistles and commands as Old Pete loped through his paces. Domino bounded beside his sire, seemingly oblivious to the reason for the older dog's actions. Zach sighed. It would take more of Mom's concentrated effort to teach the pup, but he'd be a good sheep dog once he'd outgrown his headstrong ways.

Mom's car pulled in the driveway and Domino zigzagged beside Zach on the way back to the house, his tongue lolling happily from the side of his mouth. Zach was going to miss that dog.

"Hey, Mom." He gave her a quick hug. "I'll just wash up."

When he returned to the kitchen a few minutes later, she had loaded plates of pasta on the table. Smelled awesome.

"So how was your day?" Mom asked after she'd said grace. "Did you get the pasture done?"

"Not entirely. Jo had some question about the fertilizer not being organic and harming the spring water." That wasn't the only question Jo brought to mind. Wow.

His mother frowned. "That's strange. Everyone around here uses it. I thought it was so good of Gary to loan you his rig, being as we've never been able to justify getting our own for the small amount of acreage."

"I'll read up on it some more before I keep going." Zach twisted his fork into the pasta. "I came into the house to look it up online, actually, and discovered I had an email from East Spokane Vet Clinic inviting me for an interview."

She glanced up. "Oh, that's great! They don't care that you don't have a recommendation from Hammond?"

"The receptionist never asked, and I didn't draw her attention to it." Zach took a deep breath. "Here's the thing, Mom. My interview is tomorrow morning, bright and early, so I'm leaving right after dinner tonight and staying in at the apartment. I stacked extra hay for you by the sheep feeder."

"So soon?" Her eyes clouded. "When does the position start?"

Zach met her gaze. "Monday."

"Oh." She looked down, jabbing her fork into the food. "I'd hoped it wouldn't come to this so quickly, but I know it's what you want. I'll try to be happy for you."

Zach's heart constricted. "I'll come home every weekend until Dad's ready to take the farm back on. The sheep will be out on pasture in the next week or two which will make things easier for you."

She took a deep breath. "I'd thought…I'd hoped you'd want to stay, after all. Mom said she thought you might be getting sweet on Jo."

"Like Grandma even knows which decade she's in." He'd never guessed his grandmother had that much insight left intact, but Jo wasn't a conflict his mother needed to know about. The farther he could get away from that girl, the better off he'd be. No reminders of his infatuation, his…his *lapse*, would be best. Jo wanted nothing to do with him, after all, though her lips had told a different story. Ah, that kiss…

"Zachary?"

Deep, steadying breath. "Nope. She's just as enviro-crazy as I thought at first." He forced a grin. "Definitely not a match made in heaven."

Mom studied his face, and Zach kept it carefully blank until she looked away. "What about Doc Taubin? Haven't you made some kind of deal with him?"

Drat, that's what he'd shoved to the back of his mind in his eagerness to get out of Galena Landing. "Last we talked, he didn't have a date for surgery yet. If I get this position, I'll just let him know he'll need to find someone else to fill in. I'm sure it won't be a problem."

She pushed her pasta away, half eaten. "Zachary, the timing on this doesn't seem all that good."

Funny. After that confrontation with Jo, it seemed perfect to him.

Mom pulled his gaze and held it for a long moment. "Nonetheless, I'm really proud of you. You've worked extremely hard, gotten topnotch grades, even got the president's award. I know this is what you've dreamt of. I have only one request."

Zach raised his eyebrows. "And that is?"

She reached over and squeezed his hand. "Your dad and I have tried to be an example. Tried to teach you to pray about decisions as they come up. I'm sure you want God's best for your life. All I ask is that you spend some time on your knees with God, asking for confirmation of His will for you."

His turn to poke at his plate. "God and I—we're not talking

so much these days."

"I know, son. He's right there, though, wanting that communication open again. Give Him a chance?"

He met her gaze. "I'll try."

Chapter 11

Jo lay in bed the next morning, listening to rain pound on the old trailer's metal roof, hoping it would hold up to the storm's barrage and not leak. She snuggled under the cozy duvet. Obviously no need to get up and get cracking. Soggy mornings didn't crack. They squished, and squishing wasn't good for planting gardens.

"Sure you don't want to go to Kalispell with Claire and me?" Sierra stuck her head around Jo's door, which had been left ajar. She obviously wasn't fooled by Jo's pretend-sleep. "It's not like you can plant the corn in this muck."

Jo sighed and rolled over. Spending the day with Sierra after their spat yesterday did not sound like the most fun, even though Sierra had apologized. "Tempting, but no." She sat up and stuffed her feet into tiger-face slippers.

"But we might find a source for herbs."

"I hope you do." In some ways she'd enjoy it, but they'd had rather a lot of togetherness since they moved in. An entire day alone on the farm sounded like bliss. Maybe she'd be able to get some distance from her aggravation with her best friend and her confusion about Zach.

"Bu—"

Something crashed in the kitchen. "That *does* it! I can't take it anymore," Claire yelled.

Sierra turned and ran down the hallway. "What happened?" Then she screeched.

Jo stuck her arms in the sleeves of her fluffy pink bathrobe and wrapped the tie around her waist. "Claire? Sierra?" She hurried down the corridor and into the kitchen.

A brazen mouse scampered across the window ledge behind the sink and disappeared behind the ceramic canisters at the back of the counter. Jo caught her breath.

Sierra's knuckles whitened as she gripped the back of a wooden chair, her eyes fixed on the spot.

Claire stood in the middle of the room, arms akimbo. "There were *three* of them! I just disinfected the counters so I could make breakfast and now I have to do it again." A shudder ran down her lean body. "That's it. Time for some action."

Sierra shot a questioning glance at Jo before refocusing on the countertop.

First things first. "Is the trap full again?"

"I emptied it yesterday. Four more." Claire took a deep breath. "If the steel wool is working, I'm afraid to think what it would be like otherwise." A mouse shot across the floor and disappeared behind the garbage can.

Claire kicked the corner of the live trap with her toe. Something scuffled.

Pretty serious when they'd caught so many that Sierra didn't shriek for every single one anymore. Jo didn't even want to add up the number. Her brain veered away from the knowledge.

"Wh-what kind of action are you thinking of?" asked Sierra. "I thought you said we'd tried everything."

"Everything humane." Claire pitched an oven mitt at the step-on garbage can, but the mouse didn't reappear.

Oh no. Jo could see where this was going next.

Sierra backed up a couple steps, dragging the chair with her.

"What do you mean?"

"We've tried snap traps. And the live trap. And steel wool around the pipes. They're still getting in somewhere." Claire retrieved her oven mitt.

Jo held up a hand. "I'm allergic to cats. Really. Hives and everything."

"I don't want a cat anyway." Claire tossed the mitt into the laundry hamper. "I'd still have to scrub counters all the time because you can never be sure the cat hasn't walked on them."

It would have been silent except for the little scratching noise from behind the garbage can.

Sierra cleared her throat. "Are there any other options?"

Claire's gaze met Jo's. "Just poison."

"Oh, we couldn't do that!" Sierra looked from one to the other. "Could we? I mean, that goes against everything we believe in."

"*Mice* go against everything we believe in," Claire said shortly.

They couldn't get into the new house soon enough, and the foundation wasn't even due to be poured until next week. Months and months of the trailer remained. Months and months of mice.

"I don't like the idea." Jo chewed her lip. "I really don't."

"I'm open to a better one. If you've got something up your sleeve, this would be a good time to mention it." Claire jerked open the cutlery drawer.

"I think—if that's what it takes." Sierra loosened her grip slightly. "I mean, if we don't have other choices."

Jo looked at Claire helplessly. She loathed giving in on something like this, their first major crossroads, but… "What would people think? I mean, we've made such a big deal about doing everything so eco-friendly."

The mouse scrambled across the floor and Claire lobbed a table knife at it. "We don't have to phone the newspaper and tell them." She missed, but only by an inch or two. The rodent scurried to safety behind the trap.

Yeah, but what if someone found out anyway? Jo hated to admit defeat. Sheer willpower ought to be enough. Um, and a little prayer. She'd prayed about the mice, too. At least as often as she'd cleaned out the trap. Maybe not often enough?

"Action, Jo. That's what we need." Claire grabbed another utensil from the drawer and readied it for the next mouse she saw.

Looked like every piece of cutlery they owned would bounce along the floor before long. Jo's turn to do dishes, too.

Sierra pushed the chair back into place. "So you want to buy poison? Is that what you're asking?"

Jo laughed. "It will never stay a secret in this town, I can promise you that. The guy who sold me the live trap already knew all about us." Or thought he did.

"I'm all over that." Claire shifted closer to the garbage can, fork at the ready. "I really hoped it wouldn't come to this, but I'm prepared. I got a few packages last time I was in Wynnton."

A sinking feeling settled in Jo's gut. But what else could they do? Claire was right. It wasn't healthy to keep living the way they were, and there seemed no end to the creatures. "What do the directions say?"

"Open the package and put it in a dry place where mice will find it."

The rodent made a run for it, and the fork clattered off the wall mere fractions of an inch away. The mouse disappeared. To have a heart attack, Jo hoped. Or to tell all his buddies how perilous it was in the kitchen.

"But…poison." Sierra stared at the corner the gray creature had ripped around. "We don't really want it in the kitchen, do we? Even though that's where they seem to hang out."

Claire retrieved the cutlery and dropped them into the sink. Soapy suds puffed up, releasing bleach vapor. "No, you're right. Not in the kitchen."

"Under the trailer?" Jo suggested. "I was going to go back under there with another box of steel wool today. Maybe I haven't packed it around the pipes and wires tightly enough."

Claire regarded her thoughtfully. "That's a good spot. Here, I'll just wipe off the counters again so we can make breakfast. I'll set the package on the landing outside before we leave. Sure you don't want to come along?"

Jo shook her head. "No thanks. But have a good time."

o0o

Zach strode across the hospital parking lot toward the physical therapy unit, still high on a great interview. Albert Warren was the nicest guy imaginable, the clinic immaculate and up to date. Corinne, thankfully, turned out to be a middle-aged mother of teenagers, so there was no danger of a repeat episode. What an awesome opportunity.

His cell phone jangled. Could they possibly have decided to hire him this quickly? But he didn't recognize the number on the display. "Zachary Nemesek here."

"Ah, Zach, my boy."

Zach's stomach fell. *Doc Taubin.* How was he going to tell the old guy? He made an effort to put some brightness in his voice, though his mood suddenly matched the weather. Somber. Dripping. "Hi there. How's it going?" *Please say they can't schedule the surgery any time soon.*

"I just heard back from my GP. Somebody had to cancel so they were able to move my hip replacement up to next week Monday. May seventeenth. Isn't that great news?"

Couldn't get much worse. "Wow, that's fast." Zach ducked under the overhang by the main entrance to get out of the drizzle.

"He knows I've been waiting a long time. Thanks so much for giving me this chance, Zach. Can you come in this afternoon and I'll start showing you around?"

Zach's brain raced. "Um, sorry. I'm in Coeur d'Alene. On my way up to see Dad right now, actually." Should he tell Doc Taubin about the possible job? Call Albert Warren back and ask for a delay? What?

"Well, tomorrow's soon enough. Greet your dad for me."

"Will do." Zach swiped the cell off and stared out at the gray rain glancing off the gray pavement in front of the gray building across the street. He'd screwed up, plain and simple. He never should have agreed to fill in for Doc Taubin, but it wasn't right to leave him in the lurch now. Maybe he should text some of his buddies and see if anyone wanted a stint as a farm vet. He mentally scanned his class yearbook. *Nah.* City kids, every one.

On the other hand, the position at East Spokane was absolutely perfect. What he'd always wanted. This would be the perfect time to seek guidance if he thought God was listening. Apparently He wasn't.

o0o

"The doctors suspect I contracted Guillain-Barré Syndrome from contaminated water at the feedlot."

Zach stretched his legs alongside his dad's bed. "I thought it wasn't traceable."

His dad shrugged. "They're not certain, but there's plenty to suggest a link with cattle farms. Most people can fight this bug, but apparently I'm one of a tiny percentage who get an auto-immune reaction."

"It's pretty strong stuff, I guess. How's PT going?"

Dad grimaced. "I feel like a baby learning to walk, only I'm not as resilient as they are. I've got a session in half an hour. Want to come watch your old man flounder?"

As if. It was hard enough seeing his strong father bedridden. "No, sorry. Have to get back to the farm. The field work calls."

"Your mother says you're going to fill in for Wally's hip

surgery. That's wonderful news, son."

"About that." Zach leaned forward, elbows on his knees. "I've got a little problem."

"Oh?"

"Yeah. See, I left a résumé at East Spokane Vet Clinic back before all this happened. They called me for an interview."

His dad frowned but said nothing.

Zach pushed ahead. "I just came from there. The head vet is a great guy and the clinic looks really well run. I'm almost certain he's going to offer me the job. Remember I got the president's award? Well, Doc Warren got it back in his day, too."

Dad sank back against his pillows, but his eyes searched Zach's face. "I see."

Hope lightened Zach's heart at the understanding expression. "I'm not sure how to tell Doc Taubin. If I get the job, that is."

"You do have a dilemma."

Zach nodded. God might not be talking, but Dad was. He leaned forward.

"What do you think you should do, son?"

Not questions. Answers. "I was hoping you could tell me that."

His dad shook his head. "You're twenty-seven years old, Zachary. You've been on your own for years. This is a decision you need to weigh carefully and prayerfully, not something I, or anyone else, can make for you."

"But…" Zach scanned his dad's face then looked down at the floor. Watched the toe of his shoe trace a pattern on the tiles. He took a deep breath. "I've made some really dumb choices the last while. I don't trust myself."

"You don't need to, son. You know that. Depend on God. He's reliable."

He should have known that would be Dad's answer. Not much help. Didn't Dad know how much this job meant to him?

"It's your decision."

He tried avoiding eye contact, but something in the soft, sad words snagged Zach's eyes and wouldn't let go. For a man who couldn't walk, Dad was very strong. Compassion flooded his father's eyes. Understanding. But also an unflinching knowledge of what was right.

Zach dragged his gaze away, focusing on his shoe scuffing the floor. He'd once held firm to what he knew was right, but it had become wearisome during his college years. Easier to run with the crowd, though he'd maintained a reputation for staying aloof and not participating.

He hadn't given in to Yvette. He wasn't such a horrible person.

What kind of recommendation was that? *Not a horrible person.* Was that how he wanted to be known? He took a long, shuddering breath. No. Dad was right. To respect himself, he had to do better. He had to *be* a good person. An honest man. A trustworthy man.

Was he willing to go all the way and become a God-centered man?

o0o

Jo couldn't get the passion of Zach's kiss out of her mind. Every instant not filled with something else—like spreading the mouse poison—had become a replay of the moment they'd shared. Over and over she sought a different way for it to end. For her not to have slapped him. For him not to have needed it. Sure, he said he hadn't kissed her to shut her up, but what else could it have been?

Stop it.

Nothing good could come of dwelling in that moment. She wasn't a teen to drool over the cute guy who'd finally noticed her. She was mature, a woman.

And what a man he was.

Yes, but a man who did not walk with God, who did not value rural life, or the works of God's hands.

Jo stared up at Zach's tree house through the mist. How had her feet carried her right to *this* golden willow? Had his dad helped his son build the fort? Had Gabe Rubachuk played here, too? She envisioned two young boys clambering around in the tree, swinging off the rope, pretending they were…what? Pirates? Cowboys?

The rope beckoned. She grasped it once more and hauled herself up on chilly strands shimmering with rain. When she stepped onto the slick planks, her feet shot out from under her. *Oh, noooo.* There was nothing to grab but the spindly railing, but as she rammed into it, it splintered in her hands.

The willow's branches did nothing to temper Jo's fall as she swept downward. When she hit the ground, everything went black.

o0o

Zachary pulled away from the curb at his Coeur d'Alene apartment. He drove down Sherman in the heart of downtown, quaint cafés and trendy businesses on either side. Even at this time of day, the city bustled. He passed the theater, its sign unanimated in the early afternoon.

Galena Landing's theater seats had lost their padding, but what did that matter? Movies didn't arrive in the valley until they'd been out everywhere else for a couple of months. Netflix was easier and faster.

Two different worlds. He'd chosen the city, but the other still tugged and wouldn't let go. What did he really want? Things that didn't go together, obviously. Convenience…and quiet hillsides. Enough money for comfort…and life in the country. Peace…and Jo. Polar opposites, in every case.

He turned onto Highway 95 and headed north, watching for

the first drive through. There'd been nothing worth scavenging in his fridge or cupboard, and it wasn't like he could get this much variety back home. He paused. Since when had he started thinking of the farm as home again? Scary thought.

The speaker crackled as Zach ordered two triple bacon cheeseburger meals with the works. He idled the car forward in line. Why hadn't Dad given him any solid advice? Something real and substantial—not merely a reminder to pray about things? If Zach could put words in his father's mouth, what would the words have been?

Dad would've said, "Son, you made a promise to Doc Taubin before you had this interview. An honorable man keeps his word."

So maybe Zach didn't want to hear Dad's counsel.

He paid the cashier, wedged waxed drink containers into cup holders, and accepted bags of greasy, salty heaven. He snatched a handful of blistering hot French fries and eased back into traffic.

And what was *God* going to say if Zach sincerely wanted an answer?

Oh, man. He didn't even want to go there. Asking for God's direction would get way more complicated. It wouldn't end with which job he should take. It wouldn't end with where he should live. It wouldn't even end with Jo and her enviro-crazy ways. God was going to want to meddle in every facet of Zach's life.

Once that had been acceptable. Desirable. But did he want to go back to it?

Enough thinking. Too much, even. Zach cranked his favorite radio station and reached for his first burger. Three hours to the farm.

Chapter 12

Jo awoke crumpled on the forest floor. Pangs of agony knifed through her left arm, nearly sending her back under the waves. She blinked, trying to focus on the rain slithering down the yellowed grasses inches from her nose.

Oh, the pain. She clenched her teeth and tried to shift off her arm. Broken. It had to be. Where else could such torture come from? Nauseous dizziness threatened to pull her under but she hung on, trying to take stock. Head? Pounding. Back? Brutal. Hands? Raw. Core temperature? Dropping. Water from the rain-soaked ground saturated her jeans and jacket. She had to get to safety.

So, she couldn't use her left hand to brace her body. Not a big deal. Jo rolled onto her right hip and pushed herself to sitting. Her head swam and blackness shoved at the edges of her consciousness. Bile shot up her throat. She choked it back, barely.

This wasn't going to work. Must be a concussion.

To get help required her cell phone. She had one, but where? Zipped into her jacket pocket. Thankfully, her right one. Jo struggled to pull it out, gritting her teeth at the fresh onslaught of agony that came from shifting her position. She slumped and closed her eyes, fingers wrapping around the cell, fighting for consciousness.

She could pass out again after she'd called for help. Not before. She wouldn't allow it. But who to call? Sierra and Claire were off to Montana for the day, too far away to help. 9-1-1, then. Jo lifted the device and pressed the phone button, then the three digits. Nothing. Of course. No signal here under the trees, up against the hillside. How many hours until her roommates got home? Would they have any idea where to find her when they did arrive, likely way after dark? She could die of exposure out here, but God wouldn't let that happen. Would He? He'd given her a job to do and she wasn't finished. She'd be okay. She just needed to stay strong.

Nothing to do but wait.

Maybe pray, too.

In everything give thanks.

Um, yeah. Easy to say. A broken arm would put her in a cast for at least six weeks. And then it would be atrophied and take more weeks to rebuild the muscle in it. By then the summer would be half over.

Jo had *plans.* So much to do. The garden, the house, visiting the families who'd agreed to grow vegetables for the local dinner. She had no time for this.

Be still and know that I am God.

She practiced that. Honest. At least fifteen minutes a day. She'd open her Bible, read a chapter, think about it a bit, and pray. It was like taking a coffee break in the middle of a workday. Rush, rush, rush. Quick, relax for a few minutes. Then go again.

Tears burned the backs of her eyelids.

oOo

Zach pulled into the driveway, but Mom's car wasn't there. Quilting bee night? He couldn't remember. Domino barked from the backyard, so Zach rounded the house to let the pup out of his run. For once he'd stayed put. Old Pete's tail thumped against the veranda planks as Zach went by. Not much ruffled the old dog anymore.

Domino, on the other hand, whined and leaped at the gate as Zach approached, then bounded out when the latch released. He ripped a couple circles around Zach then trotted toward the driveway, head high.

Zach laughed. "Hey, boy. You trying to tell me something?" One thing was certain, if he did get that job at East Spokane, he'd miss this pup something crazy. None of the dogs had wriggled this far under his skin since he'd been a little tyke, and Chig had been his constant companion.

Domino plopped down in a puddle to scratch his ear then turned his brown eyes on Zach. He jumped up and whimpered.

"Oh, all right, then. You've been locked up all day, is that it? You just want to get some exercise?"

Domino let out a sharp yelp.

"Just give me a minute to get my rain jacket and a hat. Sit, Domino. Stay." Zach jogged up the steps, over Old Pete, and into the house where he swapped outerwear. When he came out a minute later, the pup was gone.

"Domino!" Zach bellowed. "Come."

The pup barked from down the driveway.

Zach shook his head and pulled his hood up against the gusty rain. A cup of hot coffee would be most welcome when he got back into the house. Probably a shower. Definitely dry clothes. The things he did for the animals in his life.

By the time Zach got to the end of the drive, Domino had swung a left and was loping down the road. Zach grimaced. If the mutt thought it was a good day to visit Jo—after the fiasco yesterday—he was sadly mistaken. But he trotted on past Grandma's former driveway, hesitating only to piddle on some bushes along the ditch, and Zach breathed a sigh of relief.

So complicated. He didn't even want to think about Jo.

At the end of the pavement, Domino zigzagged into the forest.

Zach shoved his hands deep into his pockets and hunched against the splatter of water dumping off every branch he knocked. They were impossible to avoid. But the pup sniffed every bush and rolled in every hollow, so Zach just trudged behind, glancing up occasionally to see where Domino was leading him this time.

The pup barked in the distance, and Zach jerked his head up. How had Domino run so far away without him noticing? He whistled, but the pup didn't return, just increased the frenzy of his barking. Shadows lengthened as Zach increased his stride, following the auditory trail. He only hoped the pup hadn't cornered a porcupine or skunk, but surely the tempo of Domino's yelps would have amplified by now if that were the case.

Zach broke into a familiar small clearing a few minutes later. A dark lump lay unmoving at the foot of the golden willow that supported his childhood tree house.

o0o

A dog barked frantically.

A sloppy tongue wiped her cheek.

A warm nose burrowed in the crook of her neck, nudging insistently.

Consciousness was a slippery thing. Jo fought to gain it, but the agony of her arm pushed her back under. It was easier in that fuzzy place, where she was warm and happy and playing with a black and white puppy. But that pup seemed to be in reality, too. He insisted she pay attention to him here, where it was cold and wet and painful.

"Jo?"

A hand—Zach's?—brushed hair off her forehead. "Jo? Are

you okay? What happened?" The fingers slid down her cheek, pressed against the curve of her throat for a few seconds. "Thank God."

Jo struggled to open her eyes, but her heavy lids wouldn't cooperate. Something rustled, and then weight on her body pressed heat closer. A jacket, maybe.

"No cell coverage. Domino, lie down. Stay." Zach's voice came from a distance.

The dog's length stretched out tight against Jo. A slip of the tongue warmed her cheek for an instant, and she tried to smile. Footsteps crashed away through the forest then all lay silent.

Chapter 13

Whatever they'd given Jo for pain helped. Part of her knew she should hate lying immobilized on a crisp white bed, pressed against the pillows like she weighed two hundred pounds, but she was too exhausted to care.

When her eyes next drifted open, the room had dimmed. Still, there seemed to be someone at her bedside. She blinked, trying to focus.

Zachary?

"Jo, you're awake."

Even though much of today was missing from her head—gaps for the ambulance ride, the x-rays, and the surgery—she distinctly recalled yesterday. She and Zach hadn't parted on the best of terms.

A nurse bustled in, took Jo's vitals, gave her a sip of water, and adjusted the dials on her IV. "If you need anything, press the button." She moved on to the neighboring bed.

Jo couldn't avoid Zach any longer.

He looked so good in the semi-darkness of the hospital room. His dark hair was tousled as though he'd run his hands through it a few too many times and his eyes were lined with worry.

"You. It was you who found me."

"Domino, actually." He turned a Styrofoam coffee cup around in his hands.

Styrofoam. If she could summon up caring, that would bother her.

"I got home from Coeur d'Alene and he begged for a walk, even though it was rainy and cold."

"I'm glad."

His eyes traced her face, warming her. "Me, too. The exposure wasn't good for you. You were chilled right through."

"Sierra?"

"There was no one at the trailer. I got cell reception practically on your doorstep so I called the ambulance, but I don't know where your friends are."

Jo's brain tried to function. "Near Kalispell. An herb farm."

"What's her number? I'll call for you if you like." He pulled his cell out of his pocket, and Jo recited Sierra's number. A moment later he shook his head and put the device away. "She's out of the service area."

Jo closed her eyes. So many places with poor reception in the North Country. But Zach was here. A miracle, after the way she'd smacked him. She turned to look at him.

He set the coffee down and reached for her hand, the one that wasn't immobilized by pins and a cast.

Warmth from the contact trickled up her arm and she couldn't help gripping back, at least until her palm screamed in agony and she winced.

Zach pulled away, a hard line settling on his jaw. "Sorry."

"No." He needed to understand. Jo turned her hand so he could see the raw flesh. "Cedar splinters."

With gentleness, he slid his hand under hers, raising it slightly to get a closer look at the raw flesh. It hadn't warranted more than salve once they'd pulled out all the shards of wood.

"From the tree house railing?"

Jo nodded. Her cheeks felt as inflamed as her palm. Good

thing it was nearly dark in the room. She hadn't really planned to tell Zach she'd found his childhood hangout, but had that been her intention, she'd have chosen a different method.

"That deck is awfully slick when it's wet. I remember that." His eyes examined Jo's and he chewed on the inside of his lip. Was she imagining it, or had the color on his cheeks deepened, too? "Gabe and I built that the summer we were ten. We'd stop at Grandma's trailer and she'd give us homemade cookies to take up with us. We were the coolest kids around."

Somehow the image of a tow-headed Zach seemed endearing. "What kind of games did you play up there?"

He looked past Jo and grinned as he slid down memory lane. "Cowboys and Indians. Star Wars. Everything in between." He met her gaze and shrugged. "We had good imaginations."

Jo closed her eyes. "I always wanted a tree house." Grandpa had been going to build her one the summer Mom met Brad. Then they'd moved to California and the end of her universe. She'd never seen her grandfather alive again.

"You have one now." Zach's thumb rubbed the back of Jo's hand.

She'd forgotten he still held it. Probably she should pull away, but that would require more energy than she could muster as sleep tugged at her edges. "But it's yours."

There was a slight hesitation. "I bequeath it to you."

That nurse must have dialed up more sleep meds. Jo wanted to stay awake and talk to Zach here in the absence of...whatever they'd fought about yesterday. But inertia claimed her.

His whispered words were the last thing she heard before succumbing. "I'll be right here when you wake up."

o0o

Zach's stomach growled, but he couldn't bear to leave Jo's side. What if she woke up and he was gone? He couldn't break the promise he'd breathed to her. Not when he'd seen the slight smile that creased her face as she drifted off. He picked up the coffee and tossed back the cold dregs. *Bleh.*

He stretched then wandered over to the window. Wynnton's lights twinkled all around him, though not as many as he could see from his apartment in Coeur d'Alene. This town that lay between was the north county seat. He could be thankful Jo's condition wasn't deemed critical enough for her to be sent on to Coeur d'Alene, like his dad had been.

Dad. Mom. Jo's roommates. Zach glanced back at Jo, her lips parted in sleep. He had some phone calls to make, and he didn't want to wake her up doing it from here. Not that she'd likely hear him, but whatever.

He slipped out into the brightly lit corridor and nearly ran a nurse over.

"Zach?"

He jerked in surprise and took a closer look. "Bethany! You're on shift tonight?"

"Yes, just came on at seven." She shifted her clipboard and glanced at the closed door behind him. "You know Josephine Shaw?"

Zach nodded. "She and her friends bought my grandmother's land."

"Oh, that's right." Bethany cocked her head and grinned up at him. "So how come you're the one sitting here with her?" Bethany's elbow nudged his ribs. "You like her?"

Now this was the disadvantage of Jo's nurse being his childhood friend and the wife of his best pal. He tried for an easy grin. "I'll never tell."

She rolled her eyes and reached for the door, but Zach caught her hand. "Listen, I need to call her roommates, but what do I tell them? How long will she be kept in?"

Bethany checked her clipboard. "Well, they had to put a pin in her arm. If all goes well, she'll probably be released on Friday."

Zach ran his fingers through his hair.

"She's going to sleep for awhile now, Zach. Probably all night. It's the best way to promote healing."

"I promised I'd be here when she wakes up."

Bethany's mouth twitched, and Zach groaned silently. *Nice move, Nemesek.*

"Good thing I'm sworn to patient confidentiality." She tilted her head, her eyes twinkling. "But you're not a patient. Does Gabe know?"

He will now. Zach met her gaze and shook his head slowly, then realized he was admitting there was something to know. His stomach grumbled. Maybe he could blame his vulnerability on hunger.

Bethany frowned. "When did you last eat, Zachary?"

He scratched his head. His last meal had been on the road, hours ago. Even two triples couldn't hold him much longer.

She shook her head. "Honestly, Zach. Go get some food. Something real and healthy, not a junkburger."

Right, the girl was married to a guy who owned a health food store. "Probably nothing else is open this time of night."

"We're not in Galena Landing. There are places to eat around the clock. Zach, I mean it. She'll be fine."

"Check on her. I'll wait till you come out."

Bethany rolled her eyes and pushed open the door. Zach's gaze strayed to Bethany's small round bump of a belly. His best friends were having a baby. They were all settled down with a home and a business and starting a family.

And he was jealous. Oh, not of Bethany herself. A nice enough girl, but she'd always been Gabe's. When he thought of a home and a family, Jo elbowed her way to the front of his mind. Way ahead of Yvette. Whatever had he been thinking in Coeur d'Alene?

The door opened and Bethany slipped out. "Everything's all good. Go get some food and go home. Get a good night's sleep."

"I promised."

"Don't be ridiculous." Bethany swatted her clipboard in his direction. "She's not dying."

"I promised."

"Whatever. Pull a footstool up to that nasty uncomfortable chair, then. She'll be out all night."

And he needed to be at Doc Taubin's at eight. He'd have to leave Wynnton by seven. Six if he was going to swing by the farm and get a shower, and he suspected that would be wise. "Fair enough."

o0o

For a few seconds Jo didn't remember where she was. The dimly lit room reeked of antiseptic, unlike her musty room in the old trailer. A now-familiar ache throbbed dully in her left arm, and everything flooded back.

Including Zach. Jo turned her head. Sure enough, there he was, sleeping mostly upright in a rigid plastic chair. His head was angled to one side with his mouth open, and he snored gently.

Jo's pulse quickened at the sight of him and she closed her eyes again. Why had she fallen for this guy, of all the ones that walked the planet? There was no logic, but maybe she could just climb out the other end of this pit when Zach disappeared from her life and carry on. The future looked bleak. Gray. Just like the early morning twilight.

A low drone settled into the air, and Zach jerked upright, arms flailing as he came awake. He saw her looking at him and a slow smile crept across his face.

Jo's heart melted.

He pulled his cell out and thumbed it open. The hum stopped. He shoved the phone back in his pocket and reached for her hand.

Jo couldn't help placing hers in his, and his grin widened.

"How do you feel?"

"Like I got run over by a bus."

He squeezed her hand. "Good thing you didn't." His dark eyes examined her face.

She tried to pull her gaze away from his but couldn't. He looked so good. What a welcome sight to wake up to. "That chair can't have been all that comfortable."

Zach shook his head. "I said I'd be here."

He had. A guy who actually kept his promises? Ones made to her? Wow.

"But I do need to get going." He grimaced. "I'm doing some shifts with Doc Taubin and I need to be on duty at eight."

No clock in Jo's line of sight. "What time is it now?"

He didn't look. "Just after six. I'd set my alarm and only hoped you'd be awake before I had to go."

Ah. The hum she'd heard. "Thanks. Thanks for staying."

His eyes softened. "No problem. I'll be back this evening. I got through to Sierra last night and let her know you'd be in for a couple days. Is there anyone else I should call for you? Your parents?"

Jo turned away. "No."

Zach's thumb stroked the back of her hand.

She poured all her focus into savoring the sensation.

"You probably want to call them yourself. Your cell is on the nightstand there."

No point in trying to explain her mom and Brad to Zach. She shrugged.

Zach released her then stretched his hands over his head, his back cracking audibly. "Anything you want me to bring when I come back later? Toothbrush? Clothes? Call Sierra and get her to pack you a bag."

She glanced over to the nightstand. Yep, her cell was there.

Zach grinned, a bit lopsided, and poked his chin in its direction. "Call your mom. If she's anything like mine, she'll expect you to check in every day or two. Mothers seem to get worried easily."

She bit her lip. "She's not like yours." Jo could wish, though.

"Oh."

Jo met his gaze but didn't volunteer anything more.

Zach leaned over and brushed her forehead with his lips, his beard tickling.

She clutched at the sheet under her right hand in an effort not to grab his head and force him into a proper kiss. Good thing she resisted because the next sound was a soft chuckle. Zach's head pulled back.

A nurse appeared in Jo's line of sight. "Josephine? How are you this morning?" She moved closer, grinning, and her voice changed to a tease. "Good morning, Zach."

Jo looked from the mischievous nurse to Zach's face and back. Gabe's wife.

He closed his eyes and rubbed his forehead for a second, then straightened and turned. "Hi, Bethany."

Zach took two sideways steps toward the door. "Just heading home for the day. See you later, Jo." He edged past the nurse and disappeared.

Bethany chuckled. "Boy's got it bad."

Jo bit her lip. No way was she going to comment on that one.

"Anyway." Bethany tapped her clipboard. "I'm here for an assessment before I head off-shift. Your doctor will be in to see you shortly."

"You commute here every day?" An hour each way? What a lot of fuel.

"Yep. It's crazy, isn't it? At least the shifts are twelve hours long, and I only work four on, four off." She patted her belly. "Once baby comes I'll be taking maternity leave. I'm really looking forward to that."

"I bet. When's your due date?"

"Early August. Almost three months away still. But enough

about me." She reached for Jo's wrist and took her pulse.

Jo let Bethany complete her tasks. "Your husband's a great guy. Has he been selling many of the organic seeds from the new rack?"

Bethany's face clouded. "Not a lot. People want something for nothing. They don't know why they should pay more for seeds, even if it's pennies on the dollar."

"But…"

Bethany waved her hand. "Oh, you don't have to convince me. I grew up in the apartment above that little store, right where Gabe and I live now, but times are tougher. I wish Nature's Pantry had a larger market share so we could live off it. Then I wouldn't have to leave my baby to come back to work." She sighed deeply. "Well, enough about that. Anything can happen between now and then, right? It pays to be an optimist.

Chapter 14

Zach answered his ringing cell phone Friday morning as he prepared to leave for work at Landing Veterinary. "Zachary Nemesek here."

"Zachary! Just who I was looking for. This is Albert Warren."

Zach's gut twisted. The vet wouldn't call personally to tell him he *didn't* get the job, would he? "Hello."

"I'd like to offer you the position, Zach. It starts Monday. I know that doesn't give you a lot of time to arrange things, but hopefully long enough."

"I, um. I'm honored." Zach's mind raced. Some days he just hated being a guy with integrity. Today, for instance. All he wanted was to seize the opportunity. "About that."

"Yes?"

Zach took a deep breath. "There's a little problem."

He could nearly see the frown on the older man's face. "Like what?"

"I'd spoken to our local vet, Doc Taubin, about filling in temporarily. He's been looking into hip replacement surgery."

"I see. It's too bad you didn't mention this on Wednesday."

"I-he thought it might be a long waiting list. I thought he might be able to find someone else to cover his practice in the interim. But they pushed him to the head of the list, and his surgery is on Monday. I can't very well back out on him now." Though how he wanted to. Thoughts of Jo revived. *Aack*. He didn't know what he wanted.

"I see."

"It seemed like a good idea last week." Zach stared out the window at a tree. "I told you about my dad. I figured I could just come back to the farm on weekends to help out until he's back on his feet. He's still in therapy so it's hard to know how long it will be. At the time I spoke with Doc Taubin, I thought I might as well get two birds with one stone and fill in my time back home to good purpose."

"I do wish we'd had this conversation the other day."

"I'm sorry, sir. I honestly thought I'd be able to cancel on Doc Taubin and it wouldn't be a problem, but then he got a surgery date, and it's just a few days away. I can't—I can't make promises and not keep them. I've given my word." How many times over the years had his dad reminded him that a man's word was his bond? "I need to stay in Galena Landing for the next six to eight weeks, between the vet's recovery and my dad's. The time line is just a guess, at the moment."

Albert Warren sighed. "I could only wish the loyalty was for my benefit. You really came out ahead during the interview process with your topnotch grades. I hate to move on to the next prospect."

An odd mixture of joy and grief bubbled up. Where one clinic saw his credentials and not his lack of a reference, surely he could find another when the time was right. But, oh, how badly he'd wanted this exact job. "I'm honored, sir."

"Listen, why don't you keep my number on file? Give me a call when you're free, and I'll see what I can do. I need a man like you on my team."

Zach was certain the ringing in his ears kept him from hearing correctly. Was Albert Warren actually offering to hold the job open for him? "I don't know what to say."

The older man chuckled. "This isn't quite a promise, Zach. I do need someone right away, but if the new hire doesn't work out or another position opens, I'd like to reconsider you."

"Wow. I can't thank you enough."

Zach ended the call and stared at his phone for a long moment. He'd put things in God's hands. Reluctantly, fighting every inch of the way, but he'd done it. Was he truly to be rewarded with another crack at the job of his dreams?

Suddenly the day ahead, accompanying Wally Taubin on farm visits, didn't look so bad.

o0o

"Hey, girlfriend!"

Jo jerked awake from a doze as Sierra breezed into her hospital room. Oh, good. Sierra and Claire had had car trouble on the way home from Kalispell the other day and Jo had been worried their Golf wouldn't be fixed in time to pick her up. Trust Sierra not to call to confirm one way or the other.

Jo struggled to her feet. Her arm throbbed even around the pain meds they'd dosed her with before clearing her to go home. Thankfully the girls had sent clean clothes with Zach yesterday, yoga pants and a tank top along with Claire's poncho. It might be a bit chilly out there dressed in that garb so early in spring, but getting her cast through a regular sleeve wouldn't be possible.

"Hi yourself!" As Jo reached out to give her best friend a hug she noticed someone stood behind Sierra. Zach.

Jo's heart melted just a little more. He'd come, too, unable to stay away from her even for one day. His eyes crinkled when he grinned at Jo and nodded.

"Do you have your stuff packed? Zach offered to give me a ride today. Well, give *us* a ride." Sierra reached for Jo's bag, but Zach beat her to it. "The wrong parts came for the car so we're still waiting. And Wynnton is a bit too far from home for cycling."

"To say nothing of me being unable to right now." Oh, man. How would she get to and from work? How would she even function until this cast came off? So many things she needed to do this spring. Just thinking about it could give her a headache to match the throb in her arm.

"That, too. Come on. Let's get you discharged. Zach will bring the car around." Sierra walked beside Jo, chattering away as they headed for the nursing station.

A few minutes later a nurse wheeled Jo to the car.

That chafed. Jo wasn't an invalid to need that kind of babying. Even worse, Sierra opened the door, folded the seat forward, and swept her hand.

Jo was being banished to the back? With Sierra beside Zach? That didn't seem right, somehow, but what could she do about it without making a scene in front of the nurse? She was probably reading something into the situation that didn't exist. She clambered in, and Sierra reached past to tuck a large cushion under her cast. Then she slid into the front seat.

Zach dropped the overnight bag into the trunk then rounded the car and got into the driver's seat. He glanced over his shoulder at her. "Need a hand with the seatbelt?"

"No, I can manage." Barely. Thanks anyway.

"Sorry we were a little late," Sierra said as the car pulled out onto the town's main street. "I needed a couple of things from the hardware store so we stopped off there first. Didn't think you'd want to get dragged up one aisle and down the other in your condition."

Her condition indeed. "You could have called."

Sierra twisted in the front seat. "I tried, but it went straight to voice mail."

Oh drat. Jo had kept her phone turned off in her room unless making a call herself so as not to have the jangle disturb the others in her ward. Turning it back on instead of grousing at Sierra might have been a good idea. She opened her voice mail and found two messages. One from Sierra—no point in listening to it now—and one from her mother. And because today had quickly degenerated into the kind of day where salt got poured into sore spots, Jo tapped "message."

"Josephine darling. This is your mother. You may remember me." Yay, sarcasm. One of Mom's finest traits. "I must not have made it clear in the email that Brad has a business meeting in Spokane next week and that's why I'm coming to see you. We're not making a special trip, so it can't be canceled. Don't worry. I'll get a hotel. See you soon."

Jo stared at the device as she slowly reached for the button to power it down. Her mother. Just what she needed.

"See, told you I'd tried!" Sierra stuck out her tongue.

Jo leaned her head back and closed her eyes. "Yeah. Sorry." She should tell Sierra about her mom's call, but that would mean airing her dirty laundry in front of Zach. Not ready to go there yet.

"You okay?" Concern trickled through Sierra's voice. "You look kind of pale."

Why would she be fine? Not likely. Jo lifted a shoulder to shrug and winced from the pain.

"You just get a little nap in, then. It's only an hour home. Maybe less with Zach driving."

Jo opened her eyes just in time to see a little grin pass between Sierra and Zach.

"Who, me?" asked Zach.

Sierra laughed and patted his arm.

Jo shut her eyes tight against burning tears that wanted out. Over-reacting. She had to be. No way would Sierra be flirting with Zach. Didn't her friend know how hard Jo had fallen for him? Oh, what did it matter? Sierra oozed the kind of charm guys went for. Always had.

Zach laughed at something Sierra said, and Jo tried to harden her heart against him. Had she imagined everything that had happened the past few days? He'd been so attentive, so…adorable. She'd convinced herself she'd finally snagged the man of her dreams. Okay, he wasn't quite Mr. Perfect, but probably no one was. If he loved her enough—dare she think of love this soon?—he'd be willing to make some changes. He only lacked some knowledge about environmental things. Once he was informed, he'd come around in a heartbeat. Like with the field chemicals. Because he loved her.

So she'd thought.

Or maybe he just put up with her for Sierra's sake. But that didn't make sense. As though there was logic to be had with how much her arm hurt.

Sierra's giggle blended with Zach's chuckle.

Nice they found something funny in the front seat.

o0o

His grandmother's door stood ajar. "Hey, Grandma." Zach poked his head around the corner. "Brought you a treat!"

She lay on her side facing the window, barely stirring at his announcement.

Zach strode in and set the bag of take-out burgers and fries on the side table. "Sorry, did I wake you?"

"Always dozing off." She struggled to sit up, and Zach steadied her as she swung her legs over the edge of the bed. "There's nothing much else to do."

"This will break up your day a little, then." In fact, he could barely wait to rip into his own part of the meal. The salt-laden aroma had tantalized his nose the whole way to Galena Hills. Grandma liked hers with bacon, mushrooms, and cheese, same as he did, so they'd been bonding over these delights for years. "It had been a while since I brought you lunch, Grandma. Want some?"

"Zachary?" Her cloudy eyes examined his face.

"It's me, Grandma. Let me help you to the table." He got her upright and wobbling toward her wheelchair.

"Sometimes you remind me of my John. Did you know him?"

Here they went again. "I met him a long time ago." Zach settled her in the seat, unwrapped a burger, and placed it in front of her. Then he squeezed the contents of a ketchup packet onto the edge of the wrapper and tipped a few French fries out beside it. Smelled like heaven.

"You should thank the Lord for this." Grandma bowed her head.

He hesitated before covering her pale hand with his own then said a quick grace. "Enjoy your treat, Grandma. Sorry it's cold." But not as chilly as her hand.

She sucked ketchup off a fry and redipped it. "Mmm."

Zach took a big bite of his burger, wishing he could break through and communicate with her the way they'd used to. It was painful watching her grow so distant. Maybe another reason it was easier to remain in Coeur d'Alene, where he didn't have to watch.

His grandmother turned over the top half of the bun, picked up a cheese-embalmed piece of bacon, dipped it in the ketchup, and licked it off.

Zach hid his grin behind another bite of his own. It was like watching a child eat. Like the child she was becoming once again.

A light tap sounded on the door, and Zach glanced up to see Jo's smiling face fade to agitation. She took a step into the room, cradling a clipboard against her cast. "I see you're here to undermine all the progress I've been making. Don't you think that much fat and sodium are excessive?" Her pen rat-a-tatted against the board. She didn't look all that happy to see him, considering their closeness in the hospital. She'd seemed rather quiet on the drive home, but he'd chalked that up to being tired and the pain meds. He'd decided not to be a nuisance and bother her over the weekend. Besides, he didn't want Sierra getting ideas. Not now when he was falling for Jo, anyway.

Best not to think about that. "It's not like she eats one of these every day."

Her eyes narrowed. "Do *you*?"

He shrugged and dipped a few fries into the ketchup. "Only when I go past the drive through on the highway." Zach winked and popped the fries into his mouth.

The expression on her face turned even more hostile, though he wouldn't have thought it possible. What was her problem? The girl needed to learn to live a little.

Jo marched around the foot of the bed and leaned over Grandma's shoulder. "Here, Mrs. Humbert. Let me take that away. If you're hungry, I'll bring you some yogurt and berries. Doesn't that sound yummy?" Jo started folding the wrapper up over the burger one-handed, but Grandma's hand was in the way.

"I want some more of this, please." Grandma turned her face up at Jo, confusion clouding her features.

Jo smiled at Grandma, but persisted in trying to move her hand.

Zach snaked out his own and caught Jo's wrist. "Leave her."

She glared at him. "I'm just doing my job."

"No, you're not. You're harassing an old lady. I brought her something I know she likes, and I'd thank you for leaving her to enjoy it in peace."

"It's bad for her. Don't you value her health?"

Grandma snuck another piece of bacon to her mouth, and Jo didn't seem to notice. Zach tried to squelch the humor from his eyes before looking back at Jo. "I value all of her. More than you do. She's very important to me."

Jo yanked her arm out of Zach's grasp as though she just noticed he held it. "Didn't she teach you to be upright and ethical?"

Zach leaned back in his chair, matching her stare. "What's that supposed to mean?" He reached for more fries, just to infuriate her.

"Do you know how those cows are treated?" She pointed at the burger.

He swallowed the bite. "What cows?"

"The ones they make the burgers out of. The chickens they make nuggets out of."

"Jo, they're animals. They're grown to become food." He reached for more.

"They have feelings, too. You're a vet. You know when an animal is in pain."

Great. A bleeding heart. "I had beef at your house." Though he'd suspected all he'd get was tofu.

"That's different."

Nice try. "How so?"

"We only buy meat that's been ethically raised. We're not going to support the feed lots and slaughter houses that feed animals their own waste and animal byproducts and newspapers and…other things herbivores were never meant to eat." Jo's hands clenched tight on her clipboard and her chin stuck a bit in the air. Tears welled on the tips of her eyelashes—her very long eyelashes. She tightened her lips, looking like a pouty little kid.

Why put himself through this? Zach took another bite of his burger before he said something he'd regret. Only…what was to regret? Any fantasies he'd been harboring about this, this *woman*, this high-and-mighty environmentalist, had been nothing but idiocy on his part. He should have known. Should've seen the warning signs. What had she done to really welcome him? Nothing. She'd only tried to change him every chance she got. "So, let me get this straight. You're taking already prepared food from an old lady? Because of some dream ethic?"

"It's not a dream. It's my life. The way I've chosen to live it."

Zach took a long pull on his cola and hardened his emotions. "The way you're trying to force it on others, you mean. What if it's not how I envision my future?"

For an instant a vulnerable child shone from Jo's eyes. Then the flame returned. "Then—"

He surged to his feet. "You know what's wrong with you? You think you're the only one that's right. You think that if people don't do or believe the way you do, then they're evil. Maybe God is even reserving a special place in hell for people who are environmental rebels. Well, you know what?" Oh, man, where was his mouth going? His brain wasn't even keeping up. "Life is more than black and white. So you don't like my food choices. Does that mean any recycling I do has no value? Nothing I do to help people or animals? What about your garden? I helped with that, didn't I? Wasn't that a good deed?"

Jo's eyes widened, and her lips parted.

He should kiss her.

Zach pulled back. *No way. Not going there again. Ever.*

He shoved the last of the burger in his mouth, stuffed the remainder of the fries into the brown bag, and rolled down the top.

"Zach, I—"

"Never mind. I know where I stand. I'm not good enough for you. Never have been, never will be."

Jo shot a wild glance at the feast still spread out in front of Grandma then back at him. He locked gazes with her, daring her to make another attempt to deny Grandma her treat.

"I'll be back later." She pivoted and headed for the door.

"Who is that young lady, John? Is she married? She'd make someone a nice wife."

Time held still and Jo's shoes seemed glued to the floor for an instant before she launched out of the room.

o0o

Jo slammed her office door and sank down on her swivel chair. She pressed her forehead against the cold metal desk. The pounding in her head and heart might outdo her arm. She should've taken the care home's offer of a few more days off to recuperate. Then she wouldn't have witnessed that disgusting junk food. Wouldn't have had to fight with Zach over it.

Was that really how he saw her? As some sort of self-righteous agenda-driven prig? Her own words replayed in her mind. Sure, she'd only said what she believed, but somehow it didn't sound so appealing the second, third, or fourth time she rewound it.

Still, what kind of steward of God's nature would she be if she abandoned it all for the love of a man? As though she could get *that* back. No, he'd go running off to find solace in Sierra, who at least managed to keep her tongue in her head instead of spouting off in public.

Congratulations, Josephine.

Her heart ached. That one kiss had held so much promise, even if she'd been angry with him at the time. Back then he'd wanted to please her. He'd been gentle and pleasant company every time he'd visited the hospital. Had she judged him wrongly?

The stench of greasy, salty fries and a congealing burger still roiled her stomach. No, there was no potential with Zachary Nemesek. Any guy worth planning a future with needed to see the true Josephine Shaw and like her anyway. Love her. Value her. That probably meant she'd be single forever. So be it. At least she'd be true to her calling. She'd been perfectly content before Zach showed up, and she would be again.

The sooner she moved on, the better. She'd get on with life, doing what she knew God had placed her on this Earth to accomplish.

But empty.

Chapter 15

"Hey, Nemesek!"

Zach looked up to see Gabe filling the door of Landing Vet Clinic a few days later. "Hey man."

Gabe glanced around the waiting room as he moved toward the desk. "You busy? I haven't seen you in a while."

Because Zach hadn't felt like talking to anyone. He'd never have guessed that his innards would still be twisted over that fight with Jo.

The waiting room was empty. After all, the sign said they'd closed ten minutes ago, so it wasn't like he could pretend he had much more to do. "Tidying up here so everything is ready for morning."

"I'll wait for you. Want to go out to The Sizzling Skillet for dinner? Best grub in town."

No, he did *not* want to, but Gabe was nothing if not persistent. If he didn't connect with Zach tonight, his friend wouldn't let up until he had. Zach sighed. "I might be a while."

"No problem." Gabe plopped down in one of the chairs and grabbed a magazine from the end table. "I've got nowhere else to be."

"Bethany must be at work."

Gabe grinned. "Yep. She doesn't get off until seven, and won't be home until eight."

"Yeah, I saw her the other day."

"So she said." Gabe held Zach's gaze for a few seconds, then brandished the magazine. "Take as long as you need. Doc Taubin has the best reading material in town, so I'm sure I'll be fine."

A grin forced its way around Zach's reluctance. "Oh, yeah. Everything on that table has been published in the last decade, I think."

Gabe peered into the magazine and flipped a few pages. "Shh. I'm just getting into it here."

Zach shook his head and a laugh bubbled out. "Never mind. Let's go. I'll come back later and finish up." Not that there was really anything that needed doing.

"You sure?"

"Yeah. Come on."

The Sizzling Skillet's dining room was less than half full. The waitress led Zach and Gabe to a table near the window and handed over menus.

"Is Claire cooking tonight?" Gabe asked.

The waitress shook her head. "No, she works the weekends. But some of the menu items are ones she's introduced. Can I get you anything to drink while you decide?"

Both men ordered coffee and she hurried away to greet someone else.

"Too bad." Gabe opened the menu. "Claire's really shaken up the restaurant fare in this town. She's one of the gals that lives next door to you, isn't she?"

Like Gabe didn't know the answer to that. "Yes."

"Right." Gabe scanned the menu and his eyes lit up. "Oh, that looks like one of hers. What are you having?"

Zach shrugged. Nothing had tasted good since before that stupid burger and fries. "The special, I guess."

Gabe leaned back in his chair. "So what's up with you? Didn't see you in church."

"I wasn't there."

His buddy grinned. "Yeah, I noticed. That's why I mentioned it."

The waitress returned with two cups of coffee, and they placed their orders. Zach wrapped his hands around his mug. Sniffed the pleasant caffeinated aroma. Tonight he could blame his lack of sleep on caffeine. Lovely. More time to replay the argument with Jo and wonder what he'd been expected to say to make things better.

Gabe lifted his mug. "So?"

The childish response surged. "So what?"

"Hey man, don't mess with me. I'm not giving up. You might as well spill. What's going on? Bethany said you'd been to Wynnton to see Jo when she was in the hospital and you looked pretty happy. Now you look like you swallowed acid."

Felt like it, too. Zach sipped the coffee, trying to find words. Any words. "Yeah, well, it was a dumb idea."

"What was?"

Zach shrugged.

"Are you going to make me guess? It's about Jo, isn't it? You've fallen for her. Hard, by the looks of thi—"

"No."

Gabe laughed. "Oh, man, that was way too fast. So…two options. One, she can't stand you, or two, she kind of liked you back, you had a fight, and *now* she can't stand you."

Zach met Gabe's gaze. "Yeah. I'm a horrid guy. What can I say? I wear some kind of female repellant."

"Don't even go talking about Yvette and Jo in the same breath. Two separate women. Two separate issues."

Right. Yet all roads led to Rome.

"You don't believe me?" Gabe leaned over the table. "Yvette was using you, Zach. She wanted a party boy on her arm, and when you wouldn't play her way, she dumped you. Tell me how Josephine Shaw is like that."

"The same but different."

"Huh?" Gabe pulled back.

"Not a party girl, no. But just as determined to mold me into the image of what she wants. I'm not having it, Gabe. Not going there. I'm my own man."

"Tell me what happened."

Zach took a deep breath. "She's a strange girl. I can't figure her out and half the time I don't want to."

"And the rest of the time?"

"I mean, it could never work. She's an environmentalist snob. I'd never be able to do anything right. She *wants* to live on a farm. I don't have a future here."

The waitress set their plates down and went away.

Zach stared at the roast beef, mashed potatoes and gravy, and the limp, pale broccoli. Uninspiring.

"You mean you don't *want* a future here." Gabe ground pepper over his meal, some sort of strange-looking layered thing, like lasagna only not.

"It's a dead-end town. There's nothing to do."

"Cause you're the life of the party? Come on, man. That's the teenager in you talking. I remember craving all the glitzy stuff, too."

Zach parked his elbows on the table and leveled a glare at his best friend. "So you're calling me immature."

Gabe looked up and the lines on his face softened. "No, Nemesek, I'm calling you a seeker."

Whatever he meant by that. But Zach could feel a little something warm trickling into the cold, dry cracks of his life.

"Man, not everyone can live in Galena Landing. If everyone found its charms, it would be the biggest city on earth." Gabe forked in a mouthful.

"Did you say *charms*?"

Gabe swallowed and grinned. "Sure did. The peace, the quiet. The lake at sunrise. Wind in the trees. Deer grazing in people's yards. We're connected to nature here, Zach. Connected to God."

Zach set his fork down and stared at Gabe. "You're saying a person can't be connected to God in the city? Totally disagree with you, man."

"Not what I said. I was talking about you, not the city. Remember when we were kids? How many times did we talk God stuff in our bedrooms or family rooms?"

Um, almost never?

Gabe nodded, reading the expression on Zach's face. "No, our most serious conversations took place in the tree house or while hiking in the mountains. That's where we connect, both of us. Not in buildings or busy places."

Zach focused on cutting a piece of roast beef. Gabe had a point there. Other than youth group meetings, it had all been out in nature.

"There's two things missing in your life, man." Gabe leaned closer. "The peace of God for one. The lack thereof is written all over your face."

He'd had that serenity, growing up. Even as a teenager. He'd felt close to God back then. Read his Bible, prayed, sang worship songs, even shared his faith around the high school. Why did it all feel so hollow now? He met Gabe's gaze. "And number two?"

Gabe flashed him a wicked grin. "The love of a good woman."

o0o

It was still dark outside when Jo's cell phone rang. She'd been awake half the night, unable to get comfortable, unable to free her mind of Zach. But it wouldn't be him calling this early. Or ever. She groped around the bedside table for the phone and slid the bar to accept the call. "Hello?"

"Hello, Josephine."

Her mother. Jo sank against the pillow. *No.* Was today the day? "Hi, Mom."

"I haven't heard back from you. Our flight leaves in half an hour and I wanted to make sure you remembered we were coming."

"I, uh, broke my arm a few days ago. Had to have surgery to put my elbow back together. I'm in a cast for the next month or two. It's not exactly a good time for a visit." Not that there ever was.

Mom clucked her tongue. "Sounds like you need your mother more than ever. Listen, I'll get Brad to bring me to your place this afternoon. He has meetings in Spokane tomorrow and Friday. Our return flight is Sunday afternoon, so he can join us on Saturday and we'll spend a day all together like a family. Won't that be nice?"

Nice was *so* not the word. Panic was more like it. "Mom, you can't stay here."

"Nonsense. It sounds like I'm needed."

"I'm serious. I told you, we live in a dinky little trailer with three tiny bedrooms. Mine is barely big enough for a twin bed. We don't have room for guests."

"But…"

Jo visualized her processing that. Her mom wasn't used to failing in her objectives. Once she set her teeth in something, she won. That's how she landed Brad, after all.

"I'm sorry, Mom. I told you this wasn't a good time."

"But I've already bought my ticket. We're boarding in just a few minutes."

And that was Jo's problem how?

"I'll just stay in a hotel nearby, then. You can bring me out to your place for the day. You can still drive, can't you?"

Just like a terrier. Her teeth had sunk in and she wasn't letting go. "My whole arm is immobilized, Mom. From bicep to fingers.

We have a stick shift. No, I can't drive."

"I'll get a rental."

Please, dear God, give me patience. "Galena Landing doesn't have a car rental place. It's a very small town. A village."

Pause. "It does have a good hotel, doesn't it? A Marriott or something similar?"

It was to laugh. "No Marriott. Only one hotel, and it's called The Landing Pad."

"The Landing Pad?" Mom echoed weakly.

"Yes."

Jo heard a loudspeaker crackle in the background.

"They're loading first class. I'll call you from Spokane when we arrive."

"Okay. Bye, Mom." Jo pressed the button to end the call and a rustle from the doorway caught her attention.

Sierra, leaning against the doorjamb, cleared her throat. "So. Your mother is coming."

Was God punishing Jo for something? First the fall from the tree house, breaking her arm, then the fight with Zach, then the competition with Sierra. Now her mother. She needed a hole to crawl inside. And die. She took a deep breath. "Yep."

"I wish your folks were as cool as mine."

Jo had yearned for that herself, many times. Sierra was the only one she knew with some sort of normal family. Too bad it hadn't made her friend more understanding. Enough. She'd do her best to set aside the jealousy over Sierra's ease with Zach.

"Speaking of which, I had an email from my dad," Sierra continued.

Jo swung her legs over the edge of the bed. "Oh?"

"He and Jacob will be here the fifteenth for two whole weeks. We'll get the straw bales up." She retreated to the hallway as Jo advanced toward her.

Two strong guys would go a long way to raising the walls on the new house, even if they knew as little about straw bale building as the girls did. Sierra's dad had renovated their Portland house, though, and her little brother had helped. They were in good hands.

"Where are they staying?" called Claire from the kitchen.

"Oh, Dad's bringing the motor home."

Jo followed Sierra down the hallway. Sierra's dad and brother had helped the girls move, and it would be great to see them again. They had such an easy relationship.

Unlike her and her mom. Never mind Brad.

Chapter 16

"The GPS unit doesn't know where Thompson Road is, Josephine. How are we supposed to find you?"

Jo bit hard on her tongue. Mom made it sound like Jo had blanked the navigation system's memory on purpose. "I could give you directions."

"Well, please do. Brad needs to get back to Spokane tonight. We don't have all day."

"What are you going to drive while you're here? I told you there isn't a rental place in Galena Landing."

"Nonsense. Don't you still have that little hatchback? I'll drive it."

Deep breath. "I don't own a car, Mom. I sold it before we moved out here. The girls and I share a car, and it's not available."

"What?" There was static then her voice became muffled. "Brad! She doesn't have a car anymore."

Jo heard her stepfather curse. How she had missed the two of them.

Mom spoke to Jo again. "Well, we'll deal with that when we get there. We're on Highway 95 at some park by the lake. Lakeside Park. How original."

"Do you want to stop off at the hotel and freshen up first?"

Maybe she'd hate the place so much she'd leave again with Brad.

"No, I told you. Brad has to get back to Spokane. Which road do we take from here? I'll stay on the line while we drive."

Jo sighed and rattled off the first stage of directions. She had no more than five minutes before the grand arrival, but in that amount of time she heard all about how Brad's son's ex was suing the family. Served Earl right. He was a jerk.

Jo counted the seconds since she'd told them to turn at the last intersection.

Her mother's monologue ended with a sharp intake of breath.

Right on time.

"Oh my word. Josephine. You can't mean you live in that…that…"

Her mother, at a loss for words? Couldn't remember when that had happened last. "The old dumpy trailer? Yep, that's us." Jo couldn't resist. "We got a really good deal on it."

"And it's a mud driveway." Mom disconnected the call.

Nothing else to say? Not likely. She was saving it up.

Jo peered out the window as a gray Lexus sedan turned into the pot-holey driveway and inched forward. Her stepfather obviously meant to keep the rental's muffler intact. *Good call, Brad.*

Claire appeared by Jo's shoulder. "They're here, I see."

Brilliant observation. "Yeah."

"God must have brought them here for a reason. We're praying for you."

Guilt knifed through Jo's heart and tears flooded her eyes. "Do you really think so?"

"Jo, you know so. You asked us all to pray for your mom and Brad years ago. And we have been. I know you have some bitterness still—"

Now that was an understatement.

"—but I think God brought them here so you could make things right with them."

In the absence of a true parking spot, Brad pulled the Lexus in alongside the old Golf. Brad waved his hands and then slammed one down on the steering wheel. Jo's mother looked like she was yelling back at him.

Delightful. Everyone was in a great mood to start. That would make things go even smoother. And they had yet to slog through the mud to the trailer steps.

Mom got out of the car and rounded the back of it, her gaze on the ground. When she came into Jo's line of vision wearing a narrow lavender skirt with matching jacket—and teetering on impossibly tall heels—Jo understood why. Those pumps were no match for the muck created by a week's worth of rain.

Claire's hand squeezed Jo's shoulder. "Wow, I thought your mom had lived in the country before. She's sure not dressed for it."

A giggle tried to bubble up, but in reality, Jo's mom would be only that much more commanding because of the added difficulty when she finally got into the trailer. "Oh, yeah. She grew up on a farm across the border in Canada."

"In other words, she should have known better."

Brad exited the car in a dark gray suit, complete with a tie. Those polished black oxfords would need to stop at a shoeshine stand before his fancy schmancy hotel would let him in.

Jo sighed. "They both should have guessed. And I suppose I should have remembered to tell them. I'm so used to it now it didn't cross my mind." She walked over to the door and opened it. "Hi there."

Her feisty little mother stopped squishing through the mud to glare at her. "You could have warned us."

That fired Jo's back up, no matter what she'd just told Claire. "I did. I told you it's been a wet spring. I told you we lived on a farm."

"But this?" Mom waved her manicured hand to encompass the ground around her.

Brad grasped her elbow and all but lifted her across to the

squishy grass. "There you go, Denise."

Mom toddled up the steps, Brad right behind her.

Jo edged backward into the kitchen. "Welcome to Green Acres." If only she weren't lying about the welcome part.

Brad looked around with disdain oozing from every pore. Not that Jo expected anything different from him.

Mom leaned forward and kissed the air beside each of Jo's cheeks in turn. "Oh, Josephine. You don't have to live like this. Just come home. Brad will find you something to do in his company, won't you, darling?"

Brad jerked like he'd been bitten. "Yes, of course. There's always room for one of our own."

Claire, who'd disappeared like a wisp of fog, now floated into the kitchen from the corridor. "Why hello, Mr. and Mrs. Jimmiesin. Good to see you."

Brad looked her up and down as though she were an animal at the zoo.

Mom glanced at Jo.

"This is my friend Claire Halford. She's a chef."

Brad's eyebrows rose so quickly they merged with his bushy hair. "A chef." Statement not question.

Jo took a deep breath. "Yes, she trained in Paris and worked at a great spot in Seattle the past few years."

Jo's mom examined Claire. "I'm sure that's nice, dear. It can't be easy making decent food in a kitchen like this."

Claire smiled. "It's a bit of a challenge, to be sure. But we're starting on our community house in a couple of weeks, and we'll have more space in there."

"It's not coming a moment too soon," Brad said.

"How…lovely." Mom's lip trembled. "You girls plan to keep living together? How big will the new place be?"

Jo opened her mouth to answer, but Mom pushed on. "Why not each build your own? If it's money that's holding you back—"

"About two thousand square feet," Claire cut in. "We'd go smaller if we didn't need room for guests. And a commercial kitchen, of course."

Jo's mother's eyes bugged out. "*Smaller*? But…two thousand? My word, there's no elbow room in that tight a space."

"More than double what we have now." Jo gritted her teeth. Just because Mom had upgraded from an apartment to a huge mansion when she hooked up with Brad didn't mean Jo had appreciated the vast caverns of his California estate.

"We are each planning to build our own cottage later," Claire went on. "Then we'll use the community house as a bed and breakfast for people who want to come and experience life on our farm."

Brad wiped his shoes against the mat.

Jo could just about hear his thoughts. *Like anyone would want this experience.* Little did he know lots of their college friends were jealous. They had a great gig happening here.

Mom turned to Jo. "I was going to offer you money for your own place, but—" She shook her head as she looked around.

Jo only hoped any mice, alive or dead, would stay out of her mother's line of vision.

"—but I really can't condone this kind of lifestyle. I do think you should come back to California."

Had she forgotten Jo hadn't asked for her approval—or her cash? "Why don't you come sit down in the living room?"

Brad glanced at Jo's mom as she took a step toward the adjoining space.

"Won't you stay for dinner, Mr. Jimmiesin?" Claire asked. "We're having chicken stir-fry with kale and wild rice tonight."

Perfect for the caviar man. No surprise when he shook his head. "Thanks anyway." He attempted some sort of smile then leaned down to peck his wife's cheek. "I need to return to Spokane. My first appointment is at eight in the morning. I'll check your bag in at the hotel on my way through, Denise. See you Saturday." Brad reached for the doorknob behind his back.

Jo's mom cast a desperate plea in his direction. "How will I get to town?"

Brad paused. "I'm sure one of the girls won't mind giving you a lift." He looked over Jo's cast arm with disapproval. "Not, perhaps, Josephine."

No duh. Should Jo say something about their mandate and the number of trips to town they made in a week? Nah, no point. Someone would drive Mom in, or she would drive all of them crazy. No discussion required.

Claire felt the same way. "Sure, I can give you a ride after dinner, Mrs. Jimmiesin. It's not a problem."

Brad nodded. "That's settled, then." His disdainful look swept the trailer once more before he disappeared out the door. A moment later the Lexus lurched out of the driveway.

"Come on in the living room, Mom." Jo turned toward the rickety recliner. "Claire will let us know when supper is ready."

"Dinner," Mom corrected on autopilot.

Like it mattered.

"Where is the other one? Sierra, I think her name is?" Mom perched on the edge of one of the loveseats. Maybe she was afraid it would swallow her.

Jo settled into the recliner. "Picking up groceries."

Mom's eyes narrowed. "I thought you said there was only one car between you."

"Oh." Jo waved a hand. "She has the bike trailer."

Mom's face contorted as she leaned forward and lowered her voice. "I raised you better than this. This may be all your friends can afford or aspire to, but you don't need to sink this low. I commend your loyalty to them, but all you need to do is say the word and I'll set things up for you at home."

Jo stared blankly. Her mother thought all this was someone else's dream, not hers? Okay, not the mud so much. Or the mice. Or even the trailer. But the rest? "Uh, thanks. But it's my choice. I want to be here."

"Well, I never." Mom flapped her hand in front of her face. "You had everything money could buy, Jo. Why throw it all away?"

Mom made it sound like she was really trying to understand, but experience told Jo otherwise. She took a deep breath. "Money isn't the most important thing to me."

"Apparently."

And apparently her mother would never understand. No surprise there.

o0o

"Zach, my boy, can I get you to go out on a call when you're done here?" Wally Taubin leaned against the doorframe of Exam Room 2.

"Sure. A couple more sutures and this pup will be as good as new." Zach smiled at the pre-adolescent girl who rubbed her puppy's ears. He completed the stitching and tied it off. "No more letting him run into barbed wire fences, you hear?"

The girl looked up at him with wide eyes. "I'll try, Dr. Nemesek."

Zach resisted the impulse to muss her hair. "Nadine here will tell you what you need to do to help Bandit heal quickly, okay?"

She nodded.

Nadine waved her hands to shoo Zach away, and he followed Doc Taubin into the refrigerated pharmacy at the end of the corridor. "What's up?"

"Problems out at the Waterman farm." Wally stacked boxes of medication into an insulated case. "Several cows coughing. He hopes it's nothing serious, but you know it could be."

Zach's heart sank. Number one reason he wanted to be a city vet? He hated working with large farm animals, especially cows. No other animals were quite so stupid—with the possible exception of sheep, but at least sheep were small enough to manhandle. Cows… He shook his head. His preferences didn't matter today. He'd signed on to cover for Wally and so he would. He picked up one of the packages and read the dosage-to-weight ratio. Looked like he was going to be at the Watermans' for most of the day by the amount of meds Wally was sending along.

His boss turned a pensive frown to Zach. "I wish I could be of help to you, but the hip gives out too easily and I can't risk injuring it now with only a few days until surgery."

"Oh, I'll be fine." Zach hoped he sounded more confident than he felt. "Gary will give me a hand, no doubt."

Wally nodded and proceeded to brief Zach on the procedure. They'd done shots like these in college, but never since.

"You'll need to inoculate the rest of the herd so it doesn't spread."

"How many head?"

"Only thirty-five, plus calves."

Only? Yeah, he knew it wasn't a big farm, but still. There went the day.

Wally put his hand on Zach's arm. "Waterman is worried. Those cows represent his farm profit for the year. Not only that, but Leasks' feedlot is next door to him. What would happen if the disease got into there?"

No doubt the situation was the other way around. That's where Dad had been working, after all. And he was sick. Zach had dug into enough case files to suspect it wasn't a coincidence. He sighed. Nothing like a little pressure. He grabbed his coveralls and boots then snapped the case lid shut. "I'm on my way."

Chapter 17

Claire brought Jo's mom out to the farm the next morning before she and Sierra left for appointments in town. Jo watched the VW pull out of the drive for the second time in half an hour. Too bad she hadn't been scheduled to work, but her mother had somehow timed her visit well, and Jo wasn't due back at the care home until Monday.

To give Mom credit, today she wore slacks and a turtleneck rather than a dress suit. But as soon as she opened her mouth, Jo remembered the same person lived inside the clothes.

"When will you be done in this God-forsaken place and come home where you belong? You know we didn't pay your way through university so you could throw it all away in some hick town on the border."

Jo filled the kettle and turned it on to heat. She pulled out the coffee beans and grinder, one at a time, and set them on the counter. "This place isn't forsaken by God. He made it and poured almost more beauty into it than it can hold."

"Beauty?" Disbelief etched Mom's voice.

"Sure, it's brown and muddy right now. But the fruit trees have already blossomed and the grass will grow."

"But there's no culture."

Jo glanced at her. "Depends on what you mean by that." She buzzed the coffee grinder. Getting the lid off with one arm in a cast was a pain. She dumped the grounds into the French press, barely getting any on the counter.

"But."

"Mom, we've been over this." Like last night. "I appreciate the education, I really do. Do you want me to pay Brad back? Because I can start with payments if you like."

Her mother's eyes narrowed. "Brad has nothing to do with it."

Right. Because her mother had been rolling in dough when she met the guy.

"You could have anything you wanted if you came home to work for Jimmiesin Farms. You could build a mansion right next door to ours." Mom's nose twitched in distaste as she evaluated the little trailer. "Get a cleaning lady."

The kettle whistled and Jo turned to pour the boiling water over the grounds. *Lord, what do I say to her?* "I appreciate the offer. I really do."

Hope infused her mother's voice. "Then you'll come?"

Jo shook her head. "No. I have to do what I believe in."

The perplexed look on her mother's face pained Jo. How had she managed to cling to the values her grandparents had taught her, when they'd so obviously escaped her mother? Must be a gene that skipped generations. Good thing Jo wasn't likely to have kids. She wouldn't want them to take after their grandmother. She pushed the plunger down, separating the liquid from the grounds, then poured the brew into two pottery mugs. "What do you take in your coffee?"

"Just sugar."

Jo closed her eyes for a second. This was going to go over well. "There's honey."

"That's not what I asked for."

"It's what we use for sweetener. Unless you want molasses."

Ouch. She should've bit her tongue instead of adding that.

"Very funny, Josephine Lynn. That would be even more disgusting."

Which wasn't quite an answer on a sugar substitute. Jo set the honey jar on the table, hoping there were no mired toast crumbs.

"You're serious."

"Yep. Do you know how much energy it takes to refine sugar? Plus most of it is genetically modified. Honey is much more natural."

"I don't need a sermon, Josephine." Mom's nose curled as she dipped a spoon in the honey jar and transferred it to her mug. "Do you want some, too?"

Jo set a plate of Claire's muffins on the table. "No, thanks. I drink my coffee plain."

Mom sniffed. "I can sure see why."

No way was Jo going to dignify that with a response.

Mom eyed the muffins suspiciously. "What are those? I suppose they're some kind of health food."

"Pumpkin bran. Claire made them."

"No thanks. I had a large breakfast at the hotel."

For Denise Jimmiesin, that meant a croissant and coffee. Whatever. Mom lifted the mug to her lips, grimacing.

Jo sliced open a muffin and buttered it. Now what? Mom was going to be around for another couple of days. An hour last night had been more than enough. Time to take the initiative. "So, Mom, what have you been up to in California? How's Brad's farm, er, agribusiness doing?" Not that she wanted to know. Jo disapproved of her mother's lifestyle every bit as much as her mother disapproved of hers.

Her mom sniffled. "Business is good, as usual. Brad's considering opening an organic division. People seem to lap up that sort of thing. It should be right up your alley."

What she was really trying to say was that Brad had found another sure moneymaker. "Organic isn't everything."

Mom's eyebrows angled up.

"No, really. Brad will still need to add tons of additives to the soil when he's growing a bazillion acres of carrots in the same fields every year. That's not farming. It's big business."

"Well, yes. It's how he makes money."

"Which isn't as important to me as helping the earth replenish itself."

Her mother shook her head, obviously trying to figure out the difference.

Jo heard a rap at the door. Saved by the bell. Strange, as she hadn't heard a car drive up. Her heart began to triple-beat. Zach? He was one of the few close enough to walk over.

"Come in," Jo called.

Mom's eyes grew huge and her jaw worked back and forth as the door began to open. Mom, afraid? Of what?

"You don't know who it is," she whispered.

Rosemary breezed in carrying a plate covered with a tea towel. "Hi, Jo. It's so hard to tell when you girls are home, with only one car. But I thought I'd take a chance. Didn't think you'd be going out too far these days." She finally noticed Jo's mom, who sat partially hidden behind the open door. "Oh, hello. I didn't know you had company. I can come back later."

"No! Join us for coffee." *And save my hide.* "My mom is visiting from California for a few days. Mom, this is my neighbor Rosemary Nemesek. Rosemary, this is my mom, Denise."

Rosemary set the plate down and extended her hand to Jo's mother. Jo tried to see her neighbor through Mom's eyes. Pretty sure Zach's mother came up lacking. The knees of Rosemary's jeans had met a little garden dirt earlier, and her *#1 Grandma* t-shirt had obviously seen better days.

"Pleased to meet you," Rosemary said. "You must be so proud of your daughter."

Jo nearly choked. "The coffee in the French press is still hot. We just made it a few minutes ago. Can I offer you a cup?"

"If I'm not interrupting."

"Not at all." Jo bounced up and poured a coffee. "Take anything in it?"

Rosemary slid into a vacant chair. "Sugar, thanks."

A squeak came out of Jo's mother that didn't sound all that high class.

Jo ignored her and set a mug and teaspoon in front of her neighbor. "Just honey. Right there on the table."

"Hm." Rosemary opened the jar and dipped a spoon in. "Never tried that in my coffee before. Should be interesting." She pulled the tea towel off the plate she'd set down, revealing chocolate chip cookies, still steaming. "Here, enjoy."

"Thanks." Taking her seat again, Jo picked one up and noticed her mother reaching as well. So much for the large breakfast in the face of normal-looking cookies. Molten chocolate oozed around Jo's mouth. Mmm.

Mom had a dainty nibble and her eyes widened. "You made these? Yourself?"

Oh, come on, Mom. Like you've never tasted homemade before.

Rosemary glanced at Jo, who lifted a shoulder slightly.

"Yes. I'm heading into the city Saturday to see Steve at the medical center. He's been complaining about institutional food so I thought I'd bring a tin of his favorites." She grinned. "But he doesn't need them all."

"Her husband came down with Guillain-Barré," Jo told her mother, then turned back to her neighbor. "How's he doing?"

"He's getting around a bit with the walker now, but everything exhausts him."

Jo shook her head in sympathy. "How much longer will he stay there?"

"It's so hard to know. When the physiotherapist feels he's regained all that he's able to, for now. We're trying to look at every day he's there as something positive."

Jo's mom pursed her lips. "What's that? I've never heard of

it."

"Guillain-Barré is a type of autoimmune disease. They may have traced it back to the feedlot where he worked part-time." Rosemary sipped her coffee. "Mixing farming and big business just isn't good for the land or the people."

Jo's mother stiffened.

Whoa, this conversation better get diverted. "Well, I'm glad he's doing better." Jo hesitated. Not a big enough break. "What's Zach up to?"

As soon as his name came out of her mouth, she regretted it wholeheartedly. Her mom's eyes narrowed and Rosemary's twinkled. Why hadn't Jo asked about the garden? That would have been more logical. Or at least less incriminating.

"He's working for Doc Taubin for the next couple of months. Wally's having hip replacement, you know."

"That's ni—" Jo began, but Mom interrupted.

"Who is this Zach?"

"My son. He recently graduated from veterinary college."

Jo felt her mother's gaze and refused to meet it.

"Is he single? He sounds like a good catch."

Heat flowed up Jo's neck and spread across her cheeks. "Oh, I'm sure he is for somebody. Just not me."

Rosemary raised her eyebrows, and Mom looked back and forth between them.

Jo tried again. "Really. We're simply not compatible personalities." More like their core values didn't match, but there was no point in airing all that in front of both their mothers. She picked up a second cookie—they really were very tasty—as Rosemary opened her mouth.

Whatever she was about to say disappeared in Jo's mother's shriek as she scrambled up onto her chair. "*Mouse!*"

Uh oh. And the creature didn't look that lively, either.

o0o

Zachary pulled into the driveway, every bone in his body aching. Gary Waterman's cows had resisted being corralled, resisted entering the chute, and then resisted being inoculated. At least it was done.

"Want some supper, son?" Mom looked up from her hand-quilting hoop. "There's a plate in the fridge you can zap."

"Thanks." He shrugged out of his jacket and hung it up behind the door. About the only good thing about this gig was not having to fix food for himself after a long day at work. He found the plate, stuck it in the microwave, and leaned against the counter while he waited. "That quilt doesn't look like your usual. Isn't it a bit small for your Romanian orphans?"

She held up the hoop, displaying a small quilt containing yellow ducks and turquoise waves. "I'm donating this one to the hospital auxiliary gift shop. They're raising funds for a new whirlpool tub in the physical therapy department."

"They don't have one?"

"They could use another. Too many people need it."

The microwave pinged. "I hope Dad isn't in there that long. When are you going to see him next?" Zach carried the plate to the table.

"Saturday. I've done some baking for him. I'll take this baby quilt along and get it finished before I leave to come home. Then it's back to the Romanian quilts."

He nodded and dug into the sausage casserole. His favorite.

"Those girls next door still have mice."

Zach stared at his mom, a fork halfway to his mouth. Where had that comment come from?

"And that tiny girl's mother sure can scream."

The train had left the station without him. Zach shook his head. "Back up a minute. Whose mother? What are we talking about here?"

"Josephine's mother is visiting. She's something else."

"That's a surprise." Like mother, like daughter.

Seemed Mom caught the sarcasm in his voice. "What happened? I thought you might be falling for her."

Zach shot a look at his mom, but she had her head bent over the quilting hoop. "It would never work. She's too stubborn. And…" He let his voice trail off.

Mom sighed. "And you're not planning to stay. I know."

If she knew everything, why did she bring it up?

Chapter 18

The next afternoon Rosemary dropped Jo off at The Landing Pad. Mom had flat out refused to come back to the farm again, preferring instead to remain in the mouse-free hotel and hold court there. And Rosemary, bless her heart, had not only offered Mom a ride back to town yesterday, but volunteered to bring Jo with her to town on her grocery trip today. Jo had hated to accept the offer at all, but she was cornered.

Because a day with her mother was what she wanted most out of life.

Jo peered through the truck cab before slamming the door. "No more than two hours. Please."

Rosemary's eyes twinkled and for a brief moment Jo saw a huge resemblance between her and her son. "I'll pray for you, Jo."

Jo trudged up the hotel's wide, carpeted steps to the third floor, then down the corridor to #312.

Her mother opened the door.

Jo stared at her, trying to think when she'd last seen her so haggard. Her hair was not perfectly coifed, and her makeup did not quite hide the saggy lines beneath her eyes. "You okay, Mom?"

She sniffed and turned away. "The bed is very uncomfortable and the room smells funny. This morning the hot water ran out in the middle of my shower, and I had to rinse the conditioner out of my hair with tepid."

Jo edged her way around the end of the bed to the only easy chair in the room and settled into it, the springs shifting beneath her. The Landing Pad had definitely seen better days. "I'm sorry to hear that."

Her mom swung to face Jo. "Why are you punishing me this way, Josephine?"

Jo's jaw dropped. "Pardon me? This isn't my hotel."

"Making me come all this way to the backside of beyond to find out what is going on in my only child's life? I email you, and you choose not to answer. I phone you, and you are too busy to talk. How am I supposed to take that?"

Jo worked her mouth open and closed. Had she really been that obvious?

Her mother nodded. "Exactly. You've been avoiding me, and now that I have seen the, the *hovel*, in which you live, I understand better. You're embarrassed to admit you made a mistake."

No, that wasn't it at all.

"I understand. It's hard to admit one's faults to one's mother." She perched on the edge of the bed and leaned closer to Jo. "I know my own dear mother, may she rest in peace, did not accept my choices at all."

Jo gulped for air. "You ripped me away from my grandparents and the only home I'd ever known. You took me away from them and then they died and I never got the chance to see them again."

"It was for the best."

"It was *not* for the best! I was happy there. You never asked me what I wanted. I was ten years old. I was old enough to be consulted. You just—just *bulldozed* over my feelings and told me it would all be okay." Jo's right hand clenched on the arm of the chair's frayed upholstery. If she had two good arms she'd pull herself out of this deep sinkhole of a chair and stalk out of here. "It wasn't okay. Not even a little bit."

Her mother patted Jo's cast with her manicured hand. "Let it out, baby. Let it out."

"I am twenty-five years old." Jo forced her voice to level. "Don't patronize me."

A frown crossed her mom's face. "How did I fail you? All I wanted was to give you a better life than I had, growing up."

Seriously? "You didn't marry Brad for my sake, Mom. Don't even pretend. I was happy with Grandma and Grandpa."

Mom's eyes narrowed. "You were growing up a tomboy. I only wish I'd met Brad when you were younger. Then maybe I could have saved you from all that turmoil. I know my parents meant well, but…"

Brad, her salvation? Brad, the man who didn't care who he stomped on in his quest for money?

Her mother looked down at the hands she twisted in her lap. "I don't know why you've never appreciated him. He's given you everything a girl could want."

That did it. "With tainted money."

"Tainted?" Her mom rose slowly to her feet, glaring down at Jo. "How dare you!"

The room was too small for them both to stand, but Jo felt like she was suffocating in that chair. She gripped the arm. "What else do you call it when a businessman cuts so many corners that people get sick and die, and all he can think of is how it affects his bottom line?"

"You obviously don't understand business. If you don't make money, the business folds. It is a simple concept."

"On other people's blood? I don't think so." Jo tried to slow her thoughts, to control them, but they zoomed straight from her mouth. "All he cared about was if he still had enough profit to lease a yacht in the Mediterranean that summer. Six people *died* and he dodged lawsuits to protect his vacation."

"Look, it was a bad situation. I'll grant that. But it wasn't really Brad's fault. Not personally."

"He's the head of his company. If he doesn't take responsibility, who will?"

"He did." Her mother's eyes flashed. "Brad's company paid out the lawsuits. He did the right thing."

Only when the media ran with the story and supermarket chains began canceling produce orders. Only when officials threatened to shut down all of Jimmiesin Farms' operations. Only when he and his lawyers had been backed into a corner. Only then.

Jo took a long, shaky breath. Why had she thought for a moment that her mother was ready to face the truth? When the scandal shot to the top of the news during Jo's second year of college, she'd been mortified. Then relieved that Brad had never adopted her and given her his name as Mom had constantly pushed for. Then determined to do her part for a world that didn't depend on huge corporations to feed families.

Mom stared at her from narrowed eyes. "Your high morals didn't stop you from accepting college tuition."

A flush crept up Jo's face. "It's been bothering me, trust me. How much do I owe Brad? I'll figure out a way to repay it."

Her mother lined the TV remote up with the edge of the nightstand. "I keep telling you it wasn't Brad."

"Well, whose else could it be?" A sudden thought pierced Jo's mind. "Have you been gambling?"

"No. I have *not.* Just leave it alone."

"Well, don't say I didn't try. I want to live my life respecting God and making sure I'm doing what He wants."

"I don't know where you got all this talk about God." Mom shot Jo a nasty look.

Interesting day when God was less contentious than other subjects. "I got that from my grandparents, too. I went to Sunday school and learned about the Bible and God's plans for me. Didn't they take you when you were a kid?"

"Free Sunday morning babysitting with entertaining children's stories." She fluttered her hands in dismissal.

Lord, give me words. "There's more to it than that. Sure, kids can believe, but it doesn't do them much good unless they recognize their need for God and ask Him to forgive them. Then it becomes a life-long commitment."

Mom sniffed. "I'm sure I don't know what you're talking about."

"Only the most important aspect of life." Jo tried to gentle her voice. "Grandma told me you loved to learn about God when you were little. What happened?"

"I grew up." Her mother paced the small space. Even here, in this chilly room, she wore a short-sleeved sweater and knee-length skirt with hose and heels.

"What do you mean, Mom?"

"Oh, don't be ridiculous. The Bible is something most people grow out of, like believing in Santa Claus. You can't go back to your childhood, Josephine. This…this *farm* you have isn't like your grandparents'. Times change. People move on. Regression is bad for society."

Jo blinked and gave her head a shake. "You see my choices as regressive? As clinging to my childhood?"

Her mom frowned. "What else can it be? You'll soon learn it's a lot of hard work. You break your fingernails and get dirt wedged behind them. Your hands get callused and your muscles ache. It's a nasty way to make a living. Most can't do it."

Best Mom didn't take a close look at Jo's hands. "I'm not afraid of labor, Mom. We'll have guests paying to come experience our lifestyle."

At Mom's shocked look, Jo grinned. "I'm serious. There's a huge market in it. So we'll hire out what we can afford, and what can be done ethically, but all three of us are willing to get those sore muscles. It's for a good cause."

"Ethically." Mom planted her hands on her hips. "What does that have to do with anything?"

Jo stared at her. "Pardon me? It has everything to do with everything. You think I'm here reliving my childhood? No. We're trying to preserve the earth so that future generations will have a place to live." Back to discussing her mother's husband, then. "That house Brad built for you is completely unsustainable. The two of you don't need a fraction of that space or the expensive furniture and art that's in it. It's just for show."

Mom sank to the edge of the bed. "Well, I never."

"That kind of money could have sheltered dozens and dozens of families in true need."

"Now that's enough out of you, Josephine Lynn. Everyone makes their own future. Those people had their chance. It's not my fault they live under a bridge somewhere. Look at me."

There was nowhere else to look.

"I pulled myself up by my own bootstraps and found myself a wealthy husband. How dare you tell me I don't deserve all the prestige Brad offers me? He's one of the richest men in the country."

"To whom much is given, much will be required."

That seemed to take the wind out of her mother's sails. Mostly because she didn't have a clue what Jo was talking about, judging by her blank expression.

"God doesn't allow us wealth so we can pamper ourselves. He gives it to us to use wisely, to share with those who are less fortunate. To make sure there's still a clean planet for future generations."

Mom shook her head, but said nothing.

How Jo wished the silence would last. Rosemary couldn't return fast enough. But how could Jo convince the people of this town if she couldn't even get her own mother to look at the situation clearly?

That wasn't her job. All God asked was for her to be faithful.

"I don't know why I even came." Her mom's voice dripped with ice. "I should have stayed home in California where I belong."

Jo's words flew out before she could censure them. "So, why did you come?" She clapped a hand over her mouth. Too late.

Mom's face crumpled. "You're my daughter, my only child. I can see you don't think I love you, but you're wrong. I wanted to see for myself what called you so much you threw away everything Brad and I offered you."

"I'm sorry, Mom. I shouldn't have said that." Oh, dear Lord, was it too late now to ever mend things between them? "Please forgive me."

Was that sniffling real or only dramatic?

Jo surged ahead. "What I said was uncalled for. I have to make my own way in life, and follow my beliefs. I know it doesn't look like much right now, but I hope someday you'll be proud of me."

"I hope so, too."

Ouch.

Conversation continued stilted. It seemed forever until Jo's cell phone rang. She thumbed it on. "Rosemary!" She probably hadn't done a good job of covering her glee when she heard her neighbor's voice at the other end, but managed not to make eye contact with her mother.

"Ready to go, or do you want a bit longer? I can go for coffee with a friend if you like."

"Five minutes will be fine." *And please don't make me explain that out loud.*

Brief silence, during which Mom's hands waved in Jo's face.

"Okay then. I'll be right over."

Mom clapped her hands and Jo sighed. "Just a sec," she said into the phone then covered it. "What?"

"That's your neighbor?" At Jo's nod, she went on. "The one

who is going to Coeur d'Alene in the morning to visit her husband?"

Jo nodded again, trying to squelch the hope that rose in her.

"If she'd be willing to drop me off at the Hampton Inn, it would save Brad six hours of driving. I'll pay her for her trouble, of course."

Jo removed her hand from the phone's microphone. "Rosemary? My mom's wondering if you'd be willing to give her a lift to the city tomorrow, if you're still going."

"Oh, she's leaving early?"

"Sounds like it." Hopefully.

"Why don't I pop up, and we can talk about it? Room 312?"

Jo confirmed and thumbed the call off. Faced her mother.

Mom twisted a curl behind her ear. "I hope you're not too disappointed."

"No, I understand. I'm not the best hostess with this broken arm." Guilt poked at Jo. That certainly wasn't the main issue, but it seemed easiest to focus on.

"It may be for the best. It's such a long drive for Brad."

There was a rap at the door. Rosemary must have been in the parking lot when she called.

Mom glided over and peered through the viewfinder before she opened up. "Hello again, Rosemary."

As though they were best friends now. Jo managed not to roll her eyes, instead smiling and waving at Zach's mother.

"Hi, Denise."

"Please do come in for a moment." Her mother backed away, graciousness personified. Then she turned and glared at Jo as though she should jump up and offer the premium seat in the house to company.

Of course it would take five minutes of flailing like a beached whale to get upright with only one usable arm. Either way, she should probably get started on that.

"Jo says you're looking for a ride to Coeur d'Alene

tomorrow?"

Mom nodded. "My husband had planned to come pick me up after his meetings in the morning, but I'd be happy to save him the trouble if it works out."

To say nothing of getting away from her daughter. Her daughter with the big, tactless mouth.

Rosemary smiled. "You're right. It's a long drive, and I'm going anyway. Your company would be welcome."

Jo stifled a grimace. Rosemary wouldn't ever say that again, not once she'd experienced it.

"Of course I'll pay the fuel and get you lunch."

"We can discuss it in the car." Rosemary jingled her keys. "I'd planned to leave about seven. Is that okay with you?"

"I'd prefer a little la—"

Floundering out of the deep chair, Jo bumped into Mom with her cast, perhaps a little harder than necessary.

She glanced at Jo and somehow read her face. "I'm sure I can be ready by seven."

"Well, that's settled, then. I'll see you in the morning." Rosemary peered past her mom at Jo. "You ready?"

Jo couldn't be more ready, but remembered the manners her grandmother had taught her and gave her mom a brief, awkward hug. "Thanks for coming to visit me, Mom. Keep in touch." Preferably by email.

Chapter 19

"Heave *ho!*" Jacob Riehl flipped a straw bale to his dad on the third tier.

Jo watched Sierra's brother and father. Why couldn't she be up on the wall, helping to arrange the bales or drive the metal rods through to pin the layers together? Or maybe join Claire and Sierra, who were fitting a wooden frame into the dining room window gap? Yeah, they kept finding little jobs for her to do, but it wasn't the same.

This was not how she'd imagined the building process to go. She'd meant to be the ringleader. Be indispensable. Not an awkward lump of uselessness.

Sierra mopped sweat off her forehead. "Jo, could you get a jug of water?"

"Right on it." Jo grabbed the two-quart water cooler off a loose bale and headed in to fill it.

When she came back out, Mr. Riehl sat straddling the wall while he waited for Jacob. "Good thing I have more vacation time. This is slower going than I'd thought, but I can stay a few days into next week."

Yeah, the girls had had higher hopes. Ever optimists, they'd assumed they could will the house into being.

Sierra tossed a half-bale at her brother. "I wish you'd find a job doing something else, Dad."

Jo sighed. If she'd been the betting sort, she'd have placed good money Sierra wouldn't be able to resist. How many times had this conversation rerun over the past few years?

Mr. Riehl pushed his baseball cap back on his forehead. "I'm a truck driver, Sierra. I love seeing where the open road takes me. Your mother's career keeps us in the city, and I can't handle that day in, day out."

"You should move out here. Mom could open an optometric clinic in Wynnton."

He wedged the half bale against the back door framework. "Not going to happen, sweetie. We have our home, our church, our lives in Portland."

"You know that's not it, Dad. Just…truck driving. And worst of all, driving for a grocery line. That goes against every cell in my body."

"A job's a job, Sierra. If I don't take it, someone else will. It's not like they'll stop hauling oranges from Florida on my say so. I'm just the delivery man, taking the stores what they've ordered."

He had a point, there. The first issue was to get shoppers to stop demanding food from far off places. Oranges from Florida were bad enough, but what about the mangoes and papayas and bananas being shipped way farther?

Sierra picked up the water jug and took a deep drink. "Every voice helps. Every vote counts. You can't just keep aiding and abetting the system."

"Sweetie, I know how you feel. I respect what you girls are doing here, but you can't change the world. All a person can do is what seems best to them at the time. And what seems best to me is to keep putting your little brother through college so he can take care of Mom and me when we're old and decrepit."

Jacob flipped another bale up to his dad. "You're already ancient and half senile. I don't think I can get educated soon enough to save you from your decline."

"Hey, now." Mr. Riehl jammed the bale into place. "You get on up here and pound the rod through, you strong young thing. Save my muscles for taking a round out of you later."

"Hah, Dad. Nice try." Jacob clambered up the wall while Mr. Riehl scooted over.

Sierra grinned, shaking her head, and handed the sledge and rod up to her little brother.

Jo tried to squash the jealousy that threatened to rear its ugly face at the easy banter between the Riehl family members. Had she ruined any hope of ever having something similar with her mother? But there had never been a time when this might have been normal for them. Had there?

Rosemary hadn't told her what she and Jo's mother had talked about in the three-hour drive last weekend. Jo had only seen Rosemary once since, when she'd come hunting for the escaped Domino, and she'd looked at Jo somewhat speculatively. Jo was pretty sure her mom had filled Rosemary's ears with what an ingrate Jo was, and how superior Denise was to the likes of Rosemary.

Jo's mom would probably like Zach. He was nearly ambitious enough to suit her. Jo tried to shove the thought of him out of her head, but that was like trying to keep mice out of their trailer. Even with the poison down below—and Jo cringed at the thought—a few more had still staggered in somehow. They'd trapped something like twenty-eight before they'd agreed to stop counting. Just a drop in the bucket compared to how many thoughts Jo had of Zach.

A late-model pickup truck turned in the end of the driveway. Jo frowned, not recognizing it as it parked beside the Riehls' motor home. Mr. Graysen swung out the driver's door and took in the building site, waving a hammer in salute.

Jo's heart lifted immediately. She hadn't seen the church elder since their last meeting about the local harvest meal.

"So this is where the house raising is at! Anything an old codger like me can do to help?"

Bless him.

o0o

"Dr. Nemesek? You're wanted on the phone." Nadine poked her head around the door of Exam Room 2. "I buzzed but you mustn't have heard."

Zach looked up from cutting a leg cast off a sedated Labrador retriever. "Who is it? Can I return the call in a few minutes?" Of course, Nadine wouldn't interrupt if she didn't think it sounded urgent.

"It's Gary Waterman. Remember you did the shots on his cows the other day?"

Oh, no. His stomach plummeted. "Don't tell me they're dying."

She shook her head. "No, he said his are doing better, but wondered if Mr. Leask next door had called you."

Zach stared at her. Strangely the fact that the Watermans' cattle had improved wasn't as much comfort as he'd hoped. "Leask?"

Nadine sighed and twisted a long lock of hair behind her ear. "I take that as a no."

"Why would he?" The feedlot owner had little patience for Zach—or his sick dad—for all they attended the same church.

"Gary said a bunch of Leasks' cows were coughing yesterday, too. And right now there's a cattle liner backing into their loading chute."

So Leask was shipping sick cows, hoping to get his cash before they weakened too much. Zach grimaced but shook his head. "I can't stop him, you know. If the cattle are able to walk on, the sale is legal."

"Waterman hoped you could talk some sense into the man."

Nadine tapped a pen against her thigh.

"What would Wally do?" Zach couldn't believe he was asking. It sounded too much like that whole 'what would Jesus do' movement, and he tried hard not to think about that. "I haven't seen the feedlot in our client database. Are they ours?"

"He'd probably go talk to them, but you're right. They're not our clients." Nadine pushed herself away from the doorframe.

"Wait. I'll make a couple phone calls. See what I can do."

Her face lit up. "Need me to finish up here?"

He nodded and headed for the office, where he slumped on the chair and cradled his head in his hands.

It wasn't so much what Jesus or Wally would do. More like what Josephine Shaw would do. She'd stomp right up to the guy and give him a piece of her mind. Siccing her on Leask was a temptation—so he could be a fly on the wall.

o0o

"Never seen this kind of house go up before." Mr. Graysen scratched his head.

"Me neither," Mr. Riehl hollered from across the building, fourth tier. He and Jacob had been working their way across the back wall.

"I'll give you the tour, if you like." It was about the only thing Jo was good at with the stupid broken arm.

Mr. Graysen nodded. "I'd like that. How come it's u-shaped?"

"We figure on a solar room in the center of the south wall with living spaces protecting it from either side. The living and dining rooms are here on the west side. The window next to Sierra's dad is in the back entry. Bathroom's next to it, then the bedrooms down the east wing." Jo pointed across the U.

He glanced at the old trailer. "Be a bit of a step up for you girls."

Jo laughed. "Yeah, we're hoping so, though it's still not big by modern standards."

"I see that." He hefted his hammer. "Not sure if one of these is useful. Can't much pound nails into bales. What about the roof?" He followed Jo in through the gap for the main door.

"We ordered trusses." Much against their will, but even they had to be reasonable sometimes. "They're arriving Monday."

Mr. Graysen nodded, though it looked like the acknowledgment was for the whole project rather than merely the joists. "They putting them up with a crane?"

"That's the plan." Jo only hoped the small crew could keep up. Nothing irritated her more than watching instead of helping. *God, why?* What stupid timing to fall out of Zach's dumb tree house. She still couldn't believe it.

"What about utilities? What have you got planned there?"

"We're going solar on the electrical. Sierra took some classes on wiring at Home Depot. We'll need to have it inspected before we plaster over it. If solar isn't enough, we plan to install a windmill next year. We get a stiff breeze down the valley quite a few days of the year."

"Wind. Yes, we get a lot of that. And sun." Clearly he was trying to latch onto the parts he understood.

"Folks use too much power in general. We're trying to make do with less. A sustainable amount."

He scratched his chin. "That wind you mentioned also brings cold air down the valley. What about heat?"

"Yeah, that trailer doesn't have much insulation. We only moved in last March, but even then there were days we could feel the wind howling through." She patted the nearest straw bale. "This is a good insulator, and the house is sited to make the best use of solar heat. We're figuring on wood backup."

"You sure you won't be attracting mice with all that straw?"

Jo shuddered. "We'll seal both sides, so there will be no way for them to get into the walls." She could hardly wait for the end of rodents. That would be even better than having room to spread out.

Mr. Graysen's eyes narrowed. Jo could practically hear his brain gears grinding as he contemplated the building. "Plumbing? I suppose you're doing something fancy there, too."

Now that was a sore spot. Jo forced a laugh. "Not fancy, so much. We're on a spring here with plenty of good water, but we don't want to waste it, of course." She'd taken the basic plumbing class at Home Depot before she left Seattle. This was supposed to be her department, and look at her. Like she could do any of it with one hand.

"Of course." He shook his head, but a glimmer of a grin played around his lips. "Let me guess. Gray water system and a composting toilet?"

By this time they stood in what would become the kitchen. "Yep. How'd you know?"

"Lucky guess. Where are the wet areas?"

"See, the sink will be here, looking out into the dining room. And the bathroom and laundry are right close by. We tried to group everything to save on pipes and labor."

Mr. Graysen nodded. "Good thinking. Now, this is something I can do. Ever drive past Ed's Plumbing Shop out on the highway? That was mine, before I retired. They just kept the name."

Jo stared at him, unable to believe his offer. "You'd do the plumbing?"

He waved his hand. "I'd love to keep my hand in."

"We'd pay, of course."

"We'll see, we'll see. Now show me your water line. Is it in place yet? Hot water on demand or tank?"

Jo led the way to the back of the trailer where the water line extension would start. She pulled aside the skirting and listened as Mr. Graysen crawled underneath, muttering to himself about the supplies he'd need.

Wow. Huge answer to prayer. Of course, lately most of Jo's requests had been kind of demanding. She wanted God to snap His fingers and heal her arm. She wanted Him to throttle her mother. She wanted Him to smack Zachary Nemesek upside the head. She wanted Him to take away the longing she felt for the guy. Mostly Jo was disgruntled and taking it out on God as well as the humans in her life.

Maybe her roommates had been uttering the prayer that was currently being answered. She sure hadn't been. A pang of remorse angled through her. She didn't even like herself anymore.

Chapter 20

"Thanks for coming with me, son." Zach's mother smiled at him as he opened the car door for her in the church parking lot.

He was here under false pretenses. She thought he'd offered to come this morning because God was working in his life. Well, who knew? She might be right. But the real truth was that he hadn't seen Jo for way too long. He'd been by the nursing home twice last week and hadn't seen her at all. He couldn't muster the courage to go over to the trailer—or the new house site—and talk to her there. He'd tried, but his feet wouldn't take him even though Domino would be more than willing.

He'd parked beside the VW Golf. If Mom noticed, she didn't say anything. Hey, it was the first empty stall. Zach took a deep breath and tugged his sweater hem straight. He'd even worn dress pants.

"Nemesek!" Gabe's voice boomed across the lot.

"Hey, man." Mom might be fooled as to why Zach had come to church, but Gabe wouldn't be.

Gabe clapped him on the back. "Good to see you. Want to sit with me and Bethany?"

"Maybe." Why not? His mother had her own routine, her own preferred pew, anyway.

Gabe held the church door for all of them. Zach shot a quick glance around the foyer. Jo! He forced his gaze on past, but Gabe's elbow had already connected with Zach's ribs. "Yeah, she's here."

Zach focused on his friend. "So how you doing, man?"

A grin played around Gabe's mouth as he reached behind him and pulled Bethany around. "Pretty decent, all things considered."

Zach gave Bethany a quick side-hug. "Hey, you. How's the kiddo?"

"Growing. All is well." She spread her hands across her belly, revealing her increased bulge.

Gabe slid his arm around his wife and looked down at her, eyes alight with pride. "The twelve-hour shifts are proving nasty, though. Ankles swollen and all."

"Oh, you." She shrugged his arm away. "I'll be fine. It's way too early to take maternity leave." Bethany looked up at Zach and batted her eyelashes. "He's just complaining because all I want to do when I'm home is sit around with my feet up, so he's doing the cooking and cleaning."

Her lips still moved but the sound faded away as Jo turned. Sierra caught sight of Zach and grinned, fluttering her fingers. But Jo's gaze locked onto his with all the force of an electrical surge. He took an involuntary step forward.

"We lost him," Gabe said with a laugh, but Zach didn't turn back.

Jo linked arms with Sierra and Claire, all but pulling her friends into the sanctuary. Protecting herself.

Zach could chase her down, but he'd look a fool. That nearly didn't stop him. After church. He'd talk to her then. Patience was a virtue.

oOo

Whatever Pastor Ron said during his sermon was lost on Jo. Her mind was imprinted with Zach's face and the expression when their eyes had locked. Desperation. Regret. Something else she didn't want to see or acknowledge. If her heart were to heal, she'd need to keep away from him, but that might be difficult until he returned to the city.

Like now after church. He'd looked determined to speak with her, but she couldn't locate him to avoid him. Leaving the sanctuary was slow going as everyone felt the need to shake hands with the pastor. It seemed rude to dodge between folks and escape. Besides, her friends seemed content to poke through line.

"You should see what these girls are doing out at the farm." Mr. Graysen's voice boomed across the foyer, diverting Jo's attention. "That's quite a house they have going up. The walls are made of straw bales."

She strained to see whom he was talking to, but all she could make out was the back of an older man's head. He was shorter than Mr. Graysen.

"And when the big bad wolf comes along, it'll blow down." The man snorted. "That's not a civilized way to build a house."

"Mr. Leask?" Sierra whispered from beside Jo's elbow.

"I think so. He never has anything good to say about anyone."

She laughed, but without humor. "Especially not one of us. He's like our archenemy with that feedlot of his."

Jo felt Zach behind her. Might not have been true, but her pulse always seemed to know which direction he was, like a compass pointed north.

"Hey, girl! How's the arm?" Bethany hurried over to the girls, dragging Gabe by the hand.

"Getting better." Jo hoped. Couple weeks down, another month to go. "How are seed sales, Gabe?"

His face brightened as he glanced at Sierra. "Pretty good. Thanks for phoning around, Sierra."

News to Jo. She looked at her friend, eyebrow quirked.

Sierra shrugged. "I called the list of people signed up for the harvest dinner and reminded them Nature's Pantry now carried organic seed."

Gabe grinned. "And they told their neighbors. I mean, that component will never haul my business into the black, but I've sold enough to justify the experiment."

"That's great."

Bethany looked past Jo. "Hi, Zach."

Jo's heart hiccupped, but she didn't turn.

"Good morning, Bethany, Gabe." Zach sounded so serious.

Jo focused on feeling his presence behind her. No turning around. No acknowledging his existence.

"Coming for lunch, man?" Gabe's gaze passed Jo to Zach.

"Yep. Just as soon as I take Mom home."

If she and Zach hadn't had the hamburger fight, would Jo have been included in an invitation like that? Well, the argument had occurred.

Zach hadn't shown any interest in dedicating himself to a sustainable lifestyle like she and her roommates had done. Which was why she wasn't going to see him anymore. No kissing, no hormonal surges, nothing like that.

She closed her eyes and took a deep breath and then realized she couldn't feel Zach behind her any longer even though she hadn't heard him walk away.

Sure enough, a few seconds later she caught sight of him over by the foyer door, talking to Rosemary and Mr. Graysen. Being this in tune with his whereabouts irked her no end.

o0o

Zach wasn't leaving this spot by the outside door until he'd talked to Jo. No way, no how. His mother and Mr. Graysen had meandered out to the parking lot, still chatting, but Mom would be ready to go home soon. She'd have to wait.

Jo and her friends still stood with Gabe and Bethany, talking and laughing. Until Jo glanced up and saw Zach. The flush on her face deepened, and she said something to Sierra, who looked over at Zach and nodded. Whatever all that was about.

Then she edged her way across the foyer, eyes averted. A kid dodged out the door just in front of her and she jerked back, dropping her Bible.

Zach sprang in front of her and caught it before it hit the concrete steps. He held it out to her.

Her wide brown eyes stared up at him, blurred with a little moistness. "Thanks." She clutched the leather book to her chest.

It was all Zach could do not to slide his hands around her back and pull her close, but maybe not with the way her jaw set. Not with the memory of that thwack on the cheek a few weeks back. Not with the memory of the quarrel he'd never been able to explain to his grandmother. His mouth turned dry and his pulse hammered. "Jo? How are you?"

Her eyes narrowed slightly, and a tear squeezed out and began the descent of her right cheek.

He watched it slither down, wanting to wipe it away. "Why tears, Jo?" he asked softly. "Does your arm hurt?"

"I-I'm fine."

But she didn't sound it, not with her voice cracking.

Zach's feet remained rooted to the foyer floor. "I'm sorry I made you angry. Can you forgive me? Can we try again?"

Jo shifted, biting her lip and breaking contact with his eyes.

He forced his hands to drop to his sides.

"Try what again?" she whispered, peering at him through lowered lashes.

Caution flew to the wind. "Try *us* again. I know we have some differences, but can we attempt to work things out?" His heart hammered louder than the truck someone revved in the parking lot.

She hesitated, closing her eyes. After eternity had swung by for the second time, she took a deep breath and met his gaze. "I don't think so, Zach. There's no point."

Zach's balance wavered. A swarm of bees seemed to encircle his head. "But—"

"The things that are vital to me aren't to you. Some things can be compromised on." She hesitated. "And some can't. I'm sorry."

He stared into her eyes, aware that other tears followed the first on its journey down her cheek. His gut twisted into a pretzel. "Deny we share an attraction," he ground out.

Jo swallowed hard and looked away.

"Deny it." Gentler this time.

"I-I can't."

Hope soared. "Then why? Look, I get that I keep messing up, but I can't quite figure out why." So he'd probably do the same again, all unknowing. "Explain it to me. Teach me. I have a high IQ. I can learn."

She wavered on her feet. Maybe in her resolve? "Zach, our lives aren't going the same direction. I'm rooting into the land at Green Acres. You want nothing to do with the farm."

Didn't he? Did he? The bees swarmed again. Maybe if one of them stung him he'd wake up from this quiet nightmare.

"I can't go back to the city, even if you ask—" Her hand clapped over her mouth and her eyes grew huge. She elbowed past him and down the steps.

"Jo, wait!" Zach jumped, landing in front of her. "I'm not talking forever. Not yet. Can't we take things one step at a time? See where it leads?"

Her head jerked back as she stared up at him. "That's another place we're different, Zach. I will never date a man I couldn't see marrying. Why put myself through that? Why build up false hope?"

"But—" What could he say? That he'd stay in Galena Landing? That he'd give up his own dreams? That she was worth everything to him? He didn't know. Couldn't know. Not yet.

Chapter 21

"All hands on deck!" hollered Jo.

The deep rumble from down the road manifested itself into a semi-truck loaded with trusses.

Jo stood back as everyone else swarmed out the door, pulling on work gloves. She'd give nearly anything to be taking her place atop the bale walls, helping fasten down the trusses. Instead, she plunked down on the landing. In an hour someone would have to take a break to drive her to the nursing home.

Behind the heavily loaded semi were several pickup trucks, led by Mr. Graysen. Men in overalls piled out, and Jo's roommates let out a whoop and a cheer. Tears flooded Jo's eyes as she counted out half a dozen men she'd seen at church. This was what Jesus wanted his followers to be like.

Her mind slid to Zach and she tried yet again to convince herself he wasn't her kind of guy. After all, he wasn't here, was he? No. Of course, he wasn't retired like the men Mr. Riehl and Mr. Graysen currently organized into teams. Small detail.

Zach wanted to leave the valley. Jo wasn't going anywhere ever again, except possibly on vacation. This was totally home, or would be once the roof was on, the walls plastered, the cupboards installed, and…okay, the house itself wouldn't be home for a while, but that didn't change anything. Here Jo's heart was at rest.

Or would have been if Zach had never entered it.

Rosemary hiked up the driveway, Domino leashed at her side. She shielded her eyes from the morning sun for a moment, then noticed Jo sitting on the stoop and made her way over. "I heard all the hullabaloo and had to see what was going on." She leaned against the trailer steps next to Jo, and Domino took a quick slurp at Jo's hand.

Jo leaned over to rub the pup's ears. "Big day here today."

"So I see." Rosemary gave Jo an appraising look. "And I'm guessing you're chafing at the bit because you can't be in the thick of things."

Jo blew out a long breath. "Ooh, yeah."

"You need a hobby, girl."

Jo shrugged and slid down to stand beside Rosemary. "No time for one."

The crane lifted the first truss onto the walls, where several of the crew set about securing it in place.

The pup leaned hard against Jo's leg. She'd have toppled over if the side of the steps hadn't braced her body against his weight. He'd been putting on size. "Rosemary, what do you charge for pups like Domino? We're hoping to run some stock starting next year, but either way, a dog is such good company."

Rosemary looked from Jo to Domino and back again thoughtfully. "I don't know that we're going to raise any more. Sadie's getting on. I used to run a decent business breeding and training Border collies, but I'd already been getting out of it when Steve got sick. Now…" Her voice drifted away.

Jo's gut sank. *Too late.* And Rosemary would never part with Domino. He was her dog, even though Jo saw him most often with Zach, or running wild and free on his frequent visits to Green Acres. These days he'd duck under the fence and streak back across the field when he heard Zach or Rosemary whistle for him. Jo guessed she'd have to make do.

A shout rang out from up on the walls, indicating time for another truss.

Jo wrenched her gaze back to Rosemary. "How's Steve doing?" Sure, she cared about Steve and Rosemary, but she'd have been lying if the question didn't really mean, 'how long will Zach be in the valley?'

Rosemary grimaced. "Good and bad. He's getting around some with a walker now. He finds the physical therapy very painful but he's trying to push past it."

"So he's still improving?"

She shook her head. "Not as quickly as we'd like. His age is against him, as is the fact that he'd had the flu not long before. They say twenty percent don't fully recover."

"But eighty percent do." Seemed Jo had to be the optimist here.

Rosemary's gaze met hers through a veil of tears. "Someone has to be in that twenty, Jo. Looks like my husband may be one of them."

"But God can heal him. We just need more faith."

Her neighbor slid her arm around Jo's shoulders and tugged her close. "Yes, God could choose to heal Steve. It's true. But what if He doesn't? It doesn't mean our faith is too weak. We still live here in a world full of sin." She swallowed hard. "Everyone is going to die, Jo. I'm just thankful that now isn't Steve's time."

"Me, too," Jo whispered.

"You're a bit like me, always trying to see how you can fix things."

Shouts rang out from the building site across the yard, and Domino whined.

Jo shook her head. "Not to try seems like it's giving in to the status quo."

"True enough." Rosemary sighed and released Jo. "But sometimes—sometimes we must remember that God is in control. We do our bit, but ultimately, it's up to Him how things turn out. In fact, he's perfectly capable of doing His work without our help. Even yours."

Um, yeah. She agreed with that in theory. In reality, it seemed God often needed a helping hand. Would this planet be in such an environmental mess if God took control? Obviously not.

"I've got advice for you."

Jo raised her eyebrows and looked at Rosemary.

"The fate of the entire world isn't on your young shoulders. Relax a bit, and let God be God."

o0o

Zach leaned on the Watermans' rail fence, watching the calves thunder down the pasture, tails high like little flags, while their mothers placidly chewed their cud. "They're looking good."

Gary Waterman nodded. "Yep. Thanks for the help that day." He pulled off his baseball cap and scratched his head. "Thinking of putting the farm up for sale. You hear of anyone looking to buy, let me know."

"You?" Zach tried to process the information. "You've been farming here forever. Wasn't this your dad's place?"

"Yep. I still wanna farm. Gets in a guy's blood, you know?"

Best ignore that part. "So, why sell?"

Gary's chin jutted to the feedlot next door. "Them. Just not natural, what Leask is doing. Since they moved in there five years ago, my herd has been sick more than ever before. There's all the bawling from them calves being cramped up over there, plus it stinks. Farms don't have to smell so bad, day in, day out." Gary glanced at Zach. "Well, you'd know that. Your dad runs a clean spread. Wasn't his fault he had to work for Leask. There's not much money in farming these days. Leastways not the way we've always done it. Emma and me, we're thinking on options."

"I see. So you're looking for other farmland?" Maybe his folks would sell out to a guy like Gary. Good folks, the

Watermans. Sounded like a win-win to Zach.

The farmer sighed. "If I get a bite on this place, I'll start looking around. Your folks have a great spot. Someone is sure to snap it up faster than mine, what with the feedlot next door here. Might take me years to get out."

He had a point. There was a stark difference between the calves on Watermans' side of the fence versus Leasks'. Zach pulled away from the rails. "I'll pass your name along if I hear anything."

"Thanks." Gary reached out and shook Zach's hand. "It's good to have you back in the valley, boy. I hope you'll give good thought to taking over your dad's place. We need more young farmers around here."

Zach grimaced. "I'm not so keen on the idea, myself. I didn't spend eight years in college so I could muck stalls, no offense meant."

"We're glad to have you back as a vet. Oft times a man with a family needs a job as well as the farm to make a go. Still, there's no life like it."

Was the county's entire population ganging up on him? "Now you sound like my mom." Zach tried to smile. "I've tried to convince them to sell out, too. Especially since my father got sick. But they can't imagine living anywhere else."

"I was real sorry to hear about your dad. Rumor has it they've traced that bug to the feedlot?"

Zach nodded. "I don't know they can prove it, though."

Gary stared at the Leask spread and shook his head. "See why I need to get off this land? Just can't trust that man and how he runs his op." Then he looked back at Zach. "But I hear your dad's getting better?"

"Yes, but not as quickly as his doctors hoped."

Gary shot him a sympathetic look. "Sorry to hear that."

"Yeah, me too." If only Dad hadn't taken ill when he had. Then, by the time Dad was ready to retire, Zach would have been well settled somewhere else and the pressure to take over in Galena Landing wouldn't have been as great. Or even if Dad had contracted the illness a few years later. Remorse flooded Zach. *Oh, man.* He'd never seen himself as selfish before this, but it was hard to push the guilty thought aside.

"Since those Green Acres girls moved to the area, I've been doing more thinking about how farming should be done. Feedlot there is just plain wrong." Gary stared pensively across the fence. "But we were guilty of a lot of wrongdoing, too, Emma and I. Casting a blind eye to where our food was coming from. You'll never believe it, but we raise beef cattle here and still bought all our meat from Super One. Too lazy to keep a calf back every year and grow it out for our family. We'd been selling to the same corporations as Leask."

Had Jo—those girls—infected everyone? Zach swallowed back frustration.

"Emma hadn't grown a garden in years. Too busy. She works at the feed store in town, you know. But she came home from that meeting last month at the church all determined to plant vegetables again." Gary pointed toward the farmhouse. "Things are sprouting up all over her garden. Want to see?"

Not really. The mention of the neighboring women had turned the entire conversation sour in Zach's mouth, but he needed a good escape.

Briiiiing. Saved by the cell.

"Not this time. I've got to get back to the clinic. Full docket this afternoon." Zach reached in his pocket for his phone.

"Thanks for stopping by. You're a busy man." Gary turned away.

Zach checked the caller ID. Yvette? No way was he answering this one, but if the cell kept ringing, Gary would wonder why. Zach thumbed the phone on, then off. He hiked over to the Mustang, climbed in, and pulled out of the farmyard.

Why would she call him? Hadn't she made it clear enough she

was now involved with Garth Draper? It had been obvious how little she cared the night he'd proposed. Thank God she'd turned him down. Not that he wanted to think about God, either.

The list of thoughts to avoid was growing. Didn't want to think about God, or Yvette, or the farm, or his dad, or his grandmother's dementia. Or Jo. Especially not about Jo.

Chapter 22

"There, Mrs. Humbert!" Jo balanced a cafeteria tray across her cast arm as she edged into the room. "I brought you a piece of rhubarb crisp."

The old lady sat in her wheelchair beside the open window. Birds and butterflies flitted amongst tulips in the courtyard just beyond. She turned at Jo's words and smiled a greeting. "Do come in, my dear. Rhubarb. Now that's a treat."

Jo beamed, thrilled to have caught Zach's grandmother on a rare good day. She set the tray on the side table. "It's from your old place. Are you the one who planted it there?"

"My John dug those in. Not so many people in the mountains like the taste. They say it's too tart, but John grew up on the plains where it was much prized. I grew to love it, too, the first fruits of spring."

Jo squeezed Mrs. Humbert's shoulder and sat down around the corner of the table. "I'm so glad he did. We're enjoying it very much, and looking forward to the other fruit, too. What on earth did you do with six long rows of raspberries?"

Mrs. Humbert looked thoughtfully at Jo.

Was she really in there today? She slid in and out of the present seamlessly.

"People came for you-pick," she said at last. "And I froze lots. Rosemary taught me to make the raspberry vinegar."

Raspberry vinegar? Rosemary had served it that day on the veranda. Refreshing. "I'll have to get the recipe from her."

"Sweet is good," Mrs. Humbert mused. "But too much is too much. The vinegar gives it a bit of tang, you know? Both are needed for balance."

Jo laughed. "Like the rhubarb. I can't imagine it without some honey to pull back the tanginess. But some people want only sweet." Did she have too much vinegar for a guy like Zach?

Mrs. Humbert's gaze drifted from Jo to the bowl in front of her, and she startled. Must have forgotten Jo had set it there. She picked up the fork and stabbed into the treat.

Jo resisted the impulse to reach out and steady the trembling fingers. Something caught her eye, or the lack of something. "Where are your rings, Mrs. Humbert?"

The elderly woman held up her hands and looked from one to the other.

Jo squeezed her hands and guided them back to the table. "Your wedding rings. From John."

"Oh." Mrs. Humbert picked up the fork again. "Rosemary took them. They kept sliding off. John said we should get them resized."

Jo nudged the bowl of rhubarb crisp closer, her heart twisting at the thought of Zach's grandmother having to give up her link to her husband. What had happened to her own grandmother's rings?

"I wish I'd known my own grandparents better." The words were out before Jo was aware she'd spoken them.

Mrs. Hubert cast a glance her direction and a clump of fruit, already precariously balanced, landed in her lap.

"Oh, I'm sorry." Jo sprang for a napkin and cleaned up the spot. "I shouldn't have distracted you."

"That's fine, my dear. I'll finish this and you tell me about your grandmother." She eyed the bowl in front of her and zeroed in for another load.

Jo couldn't bear to watch. "My grandparents had a small farm not far north of here in Canada. My mother and I lived with them until I was ten. Then Mom married Brad and we moved to California. About a year later my grandparents' old house caught fire. The wiring or something. Both of them died." She'd tried to keep the words unadorned with emotion, but her voice quivered at the end, much like Mrs. Humbert's fork. "I missed them so much. Mom didn't let me go with her to the funeral. She said I was too young."

Mrs. Humbert chased a piece of rhubarb around the bowl, trying to corral it. "She was trying to do what was best for you."

"That's what she said." Jo sniffled and blinked back tears. "What she keeps saying, actually. She still thinks she ought to run my life, but she's wrong."

The old lady paused in her mission to eye Jo. "You harbor resentment, my dear."

Oh, now that was an understatement. "I shouldn't have burdened you with that, Mrs. Humbert. I'm sorry. Here, let me help you with that bite." She captured the spoonful and helped the old woman grasp the utensil.

Mrs. Humbert swallowed. "Bitterness hurts the bearer more than the recipient. I've found when I hold a grudge I can't find peace with God. Are you a believer, my dear?"

Jo nodded, the words piercing her heart.

"Then God wants you to forgive your mother."

"But she isn't sorry. In fact, today I had an email from her demanding I come back to California and head up my stepfather's new organics division. She's certain, just because I believe in nutrition, I'll run on back there and do what she wants."

Mrs. Humbert's cloudy eyes focused on Jo's face. "Have you prayed about it?" She wiped her shaky hands on the napkin then dropped it.

"I don't need to. I know what God wants of me, and it isn't that." Jo snagged the napkin off the floor, crumpled it, and tossed it in the trash. Then she picked up the bowl.

"Going so soon?"

Jo slumped back into the seat, tears burning her eyes. She'd been so testy lately. "I'm sorry. I have my life mapped out. I know what I need to do."

The old woman nodded slowly. "You like to control things."

"I wouldn't put it that way." But so many other people would—and had. From Sierra to Rosemary. To Zach. Only he'd said so much more. Had she possibly deserved his accusations?

Mrs. Humbert's pale, cool hand covered Jo's, still trembling lightly.

Jo squeezed back.

"I will pray for you, my dear. God loves your zeal, I'm sure, but He wants your heart."

"Thanks." Jo only hoped Mrs. Humbert would stay lucid long enough to make good her promise. She stumbled for the door, needing to clock off work and head home. Needing, at least, some space to think.

Used to be easy to submit to God. The desire to walk lightly on the planet was like a beacon in Jo's soul she knew came from Him. But Zach? That seemed to be a desire with little to no confirmation from the heavens.

That made her angry. Frustrated. And so it went in circles in her head, pressure building up until she felt it would burst, splattering brain cells everywhere.

Moments later she exited the care facility, hoping Sierra had remembered the promise to pick her up. She scanned the parking lot and froze. Sierra was there, all right. She'd parked the Golf right next to Zach's black convertible. She stood behind the vehicles with him. Nudging Zach with her elbow. Tipping her head back in laughter. His deep chuckle mixed with Sierra's light giggle.

Jo choked down the snake of jealousy. Nice they could enjoy each other's company. She stalked over to the hatchback and tossed her bag in the open window.

"Hi, Jo." Zach's voice close behind startled her.

She turned slowly. "Hello." Looked up, afraid to meet his gaze, but finally did. Uncertainty lurked in his deep brown eyes. Yeah, well. She'd seen him with Sierra. She took a deep breath. "Your grandmother is doing very well today. I'm sure she'll be glad to see you." Maybe he'd get the message that she, Jo, wasn't. Whatever. She pulled the car door open and slid inside.

Sierra climbed into the driver's side and leaned across Jo to wave at Zach through Jo's window. "See you later, Zach. I'm so glad I ran into you."

Jo's jaw clenched and she stared straight ahead. *I just bet you are.*

The few seconds before the car pulled away from the curb seemed like eternity. Jo shot a sideways glance at Zach as he turned and headed in Galena Hills' sliding doors.

"What's the matter with you?" demanded Sierra.

"Nothing."

"Nice try. I know you better than that."

Yeah, she did. And she ought to know what was wrong without Jo needing to spell it out. But she would if she had to. "You seem awfully comfy with Zach."

"Jealous, are we?" Sierra's voice held a glint of humor.

"I didn't say that."

"Oh, come on, Jo. Lighten up. You sent the guy packing, which means he's fair game. Not that I have designs on him, mind you. I'm just saying."

She called this game fair? Not a chance.

o0o

If only Zach hadn't been detained by Gary Waterman. Or run into Sierra in the parking lot. He might have made it inside the facility before Jo got off work. Not that he'd have found her with Grandma, of course, though Grandma said Jo had brought her rhubarb crisp minutes earlier. He'd leave the bag of organic chocolates in Grandma's drawer and see if she remembered to offer some to Jo.

Back home at the end of a long day, Zach stepped out of the car and stretched in the late afternoon sun. The sweet scent of apple blossoms wafted over him, soothing away some of his stress. The city never smelled this good. And come summer and autumn, this entire mixed orchard would provide fruit of all kinds. He remembered a berry-stained face and clothes as a youngster, and picking an apple on his way to the school bus. Those were the days.

The back door swung open and his mom appeared on the veranda, wreathed in a huge smile. "Zachary, guess what! Your father is being released on Friday."

Zach pocketed the keys to his car and ruffled Domino's ears. Old Pete, lying on the deck, thumped a greeting with his tail as Zach came up the steps. "That's great. You driving to the city to get him, or do you need me to?"

Mom threw her arms around him. "You couldn't leave until after work. We'll manage."

Whoa, was she crying? Zach patted her back. "Hey, it's okay."

"It is now." She blinked back tears and beamed at him. "It's been such a huge ordeal and I've missed him so much." She pulled out of Zach's arms and opened the screen door.

Zach couldn't help himself. "It's not over yet. It's not like he's the same as he was before he got sick. He can barely get around."

"He's the same inside. You think all the rest of it matters? Not really. He'll be home where he belongs."

Someday he wanted a love like his parents had. A love that

wasn't based on good looks—though his mom was a real cutie in the old photos—but on something more enduring. If he were honest with himself he hadn't been looking in the right places. That's where he'd gone wrong with Yvette. He'd taken on that relationship without thought to the future. Apparently there was still unfinished business or Yvette wouldn't have called him. Was it too much to hope she'd forget to phone again?

Jo's words echoed in his mind. She'd never date someone she couldn't see marrying. He was one of those people, but he couldn't keep her out of his head. She hadn't looked so happy to see him in the Galena Hills parking lot. Why did his subconscious not seem to get the memo there was no future with her?

Why did he even want one? His life would never be comfortable with her. For one thing, he'd probably never get to eat a burger again. Though if they were made out of sick cattle like Leask's, maybe he didn't want to.

Jo wouldn't have let that happen. She wouldn't have settled for a few phone calls and being told there was nothing the authorities could do as the sale was legal. Jo would have gone out there and given Leask a piece of her mind. Probably she'd have stopped the truck even if she'd had to lie in the dirt in front of it. She wouldn't have given up like he had.

But he couldn't do everything. Could he?

"Zach?"

He pulled himself back to the moment and allowed the screen door to smack shut behind him. "Sorry. What was that you said?"

His mother shook her head. "Wow, you were not even here. I asked if you could help me set things up for Dad in the living room. I think stairs are a bit beyond him just yet."

"Um, sure. Want me to do the chores first?"

Mom smiled. "Please do. And take Domino. He's antsy today."

Zach grinned at the pup, who licked his fingers then bounded down the steps beside him. His mom went back in the house and the screen door snapped shut.

His phone rang again, and he pursed his lips as he checked the display. Yvette. At least this was a better time to talk to her. Why couldn't she leave him alone, though?

Finally, on the fifth ring, he answered.

"Zach, how are you?" All breezy and pleasant, like nothing had happened.

He wasn't going to fall for it. "Fine."

"When will you be back in Coeur d'Alene? I've missed you."

Whoa. Where had that come from? Once he'd have done anything to hear those words. "Not sure, why?" He wished he'd bitten the question back, but it was too late. She'd heard.

"Some things have come up." She hesitated.

"What, Draper dump you?"

"Very funny, Zach." But she didn't laugh. "Just thought you might like to know you're going to be a father."

Zach jerked to a halt in the middle of the barnyard, seeing nothing around him. His blood pressure shot sky-high. "That would be a bit tricky, wouldn't it? Being as we never had sex?"

Yvette laughed. "Like anyone would believe that."

"Anyone who knows me would believe me. If you got yourself knocked up, Yvette, blame Draper. Don't drag me into it. I'm innocent as you well know."

"It's hard to *blame Draper*, as you so eloquently put it, when I'm farther along than that."

Zach willed control over himself, over his words. He even caught himself praying. "I seem to recall you were sleeping with some other guy while dating me. Call him." If she'd been standing in front of him, he'd have been hard put not to wring her pretty neck.

"No one would believe that, either."

Yeah, right. Once it had become obvious what kind of girl she was, he should have guessed something like this. "Yvette, I'm not the father of your child. You are the one who kicked me out of your life, not the other way around. Don't come crying to me again. You made the mess, you deal with it."

"If that's all the support I get out of you, I'll have to abort. Sorry, but I can't raise a child on my own."

His heart plummeted. "Yvette, this is not my baby. You know it." No way could he marry her now. He didn't want to, whether or not he could ever smooth things out with Jo. Whether or not he *wanted* to get together with the little spitfire. He'd seen Yvette for what she was—a manipulating opportunist—but this current trick was beyond his understanding. Yet, send an innocent baby to death? She was such a liar. Surely she didn't mean this. But what if she did?

"Zach?"

His hands shook. His whole body shook. "What? Did you say something?"

"I need to talk to you. When are you coming to Coeur d'Alene?"

No. He couldn't. Shouldn't. But Mom was going Friday. He had to work, though. "Not anytime soon. I'm working and can't get away."

"Look, I'll drive out as far as Wynnton. That's halfway, so it's fair. Meet you there tomorrow? What time are you off?"

"Yvette, no. I work late on Thursdays."

"Friday, then."

"No."

Her laugh was harsh. "You want this on your conscience?"

Why did she insist on pushing this onto him? He thought of Bethany, glowing with radiance as her belly swelled. That's how it was meant to be. One baby, two parents who wanted it and loved each other. Not this…this *farce* that Yvette was trying to involve him with. "I don't have anything to say to you, Yvette."

"The park on the edge of Wynnton. Five thirty on Friday. Meet me." Her phone clicked off.

Chapter 23

Domino bounded to meet Jo, cavorting around her legs as she made her way up Nemeseks' driveway the next morning.

Rosemary sat back on her heels in the garden and wiped her gloved hand across her forehead. "Jo! Good to see you." She eyed the flat of tomato seedlings beside her.

"Oh, I didn't mean to distract you." Jo came to a halt at the edge of the dirt. "I should have realized you'd be out here planting on such a nice day." She leaned over to scratch the pup's ears.

"I'm trying to get them all in today as I'm going to pick up Steve from the hospital tomorrow."

"Great! So he's recovered then?"

A shadow seemed to cross her face. "No, not fully. But he can get around again, with a walker."

What to say? "Well, it's good he can come home, anyway."

There was silence as Rosemary finished troweling in a couple more tomato plants. After a bit she clambered to her feet, stripping off her gloves. "Care to have some raspberry vinegar and a muffin?"

How long had Jo been away from the building site? Not that her friends couldn't do anything she could, and five times as fast.

"Sure, I'd like that." Jo mounted the veranda steps behind Rosemary and lowered herself onto the swing. Domino plopped down by her foot, rolling over to bat at it every time she pushed off.

A few minutes later Rosemary came out of the kitchen carrying a tray.

Jo helped herself to a muffin and a glass of juice. "Your garden looks really good."

Her neighbor settled into the wicker rocker. "It's coming along. Feels good to get my hands in the dirt again." She grinned. "Or at least my gloves. Your garden is doing well, too."

She was simply being kind. The girls had been too busy on the house-building site to do more than plant a few seeds yet. Jo had tried to keep up with the weeding, but not all the weeds could be managed with one hand. "You mean for someone who doesn't know what they're doing?"

They laughed together. "Something like that." They sat in companionable silence for a few minutes then Rosemary set her glass down. "Was there something on your mind, Jo?"

Besides Zach? At least she'd timed her visit for when she knew he'd be at work. Once he left the farm at seven, he rarely returned before five. "I'm just a little bored these days." She waved her hand toward the garden. "I should have remembered you'd be too busy this time of year."

Rosemary leaned forward. "I have an idea. Why don't you ride with me to the city tomorrow? You must be due for an excursion. I need to stop by the fabric store and pick up supplies for my next projects. You could help me select some. Maybe once you're out of the cast, you'd like to try your hand at it, too."

Jo shook her head. "I don't think I'd have the patience to quilt." But a trip to the city? Normally that wouldn't be much of a draw, but… " I should probably stay home and help out where I can, anyway."

Her neighbor grinned. "You just finished telling me there

wasn't anything you could do. Come on, you don't have to rationalize everything. Everyone deserves a day off now and then. It's okay to have a little fun."

"Well, I, uh…"

"It's not like we're making an extra trip. I need to pick up Steve."

Rosemary must have heard about the Green Acres' energy conservation mandate. Her face turned pensive, and Jo tried to imagine one's long time spouse being so changed by an illness. "Are you sure I won't be intruding on your reunion?"

"No, it's fine. We'll have lots of time." Her voice caught. "A few weeks ago I thought we might be out, but God gave us a reprieve. I'm thankful for every minute we have together now." She looked Jo square in the face. "It's hard seeing him weak as a newborn kitten."

o0o

An attendant steered Steve's wheelchair across the hospital parking lot, while Rosemary walked alongside. Jo jumped out of the car to help out.

"Steve, I'd like you to meet Josephine. Jo, this is my husband, Steve."

"Josephine! Good to finally meet you." Steve clasped Jo's hand.

No doubt he'd once had a firm grip. Exhaustion wreathed his face, yet he hadn't been out of the hospital for more than five minutes.

"Likewise. I've heard so much about you."

"All of it good, I hope." Steve struggled out of his wheelchair and into the car's front passenger seat with the help of the aide.

Jo exchanged a glance with Rosemary. Her smile looked as feeble as her husband's handshake. Jo clambered into the back seat then patted Steve's shoulder. "Of course. You must be glad to be heading home."

"It'll be good to get back to the farm." He leaned against the headrest as Rosemary thanked the attendant and rounded the car. "So good," he added in little more than a whisper.

"There's no place like it, that's for sure. Galena Landing is a world removed from Kootenai Health Unit. Or Wynnton Hospital, for that matter."

Rosemary returned, started the car and pulled out to navigate the immense parking lot.

Steve twisted toward Jo. "I see you hurt yourself some. Rumor has it you fell out of Zachary's old tree house?"

Heat flushed Jo's face. "Yeah. It was raining and I wasn't being careful. I slipped on the deck and crashed into the railing, which broke. Over I went."

"I should get Zachary to take that tree house down."

"Oh, that's not necessary." She may have answered a bit too hurriedly. "Once I'm out of the cast and have some time, I'll climb up to repair it. I kind of like having it there."

"Your call. It's your property now, after all." His eyelids drooped from the effort of being upright.

Rosemary glanced at Jo in the rearview mirror. All Jo could see were her mischievous eyes. "Perhaps now would be a good time to ask what you think of our son, Jo."

Steve's eyes sprang open as he straightened. "What's this?"

Jo fought to keep her voice casual and even. "Oh, nothing to get excited about. Zach's a nice enough guy, but we don't really have much in common."

Steve's shoulders sagged. "He still wants to be a city boy, does he?"

"As far as I know."

"He might be weakening," Rosemary volunteered.

Jo met her eyes in the mirror, unable to squelch the leap of her heart. "Of course there's more to it than that." Lots more.

Zach's parents exchanged a look Jo couldn't read. Their silent communication spoke of years of practice and reminded Jo of her grandparents. Mom and Brad, on the other hand, spelled everything out. Usually at volume.

"Like what?" asked Steve.

"He doesn't share my environmental values. I'm sure Sierra explained our plans for the farm when you all drew up the papers."

Steve nodded.

"And besides, if I ever get married, the guy needs to be passionate about Jesus."

Rosemary stopped the car at a red light. "Oh, you'll get married. I wouldn't worry about that too much if I were you."

"I'm not *worried*, precisely." Liar. She'd only been kissed once in her life. Zach Nemesek. And she'd slapped him for it and pushed him away every other time he got too close. But what else could she do? The reasons she'd just cited were true. Valid. Not something she was willing to back down on.

Even if it meant Zach walking out of her life forever? Her heart clenched. A man who truly loved her wouldn't ask her to give up the things she valued most. He'd share those passions. A niggling at the back of her mind wondered what compromise *she* was willing to give, but she shoved it back. What she was doing was right, no doubt about it.

"I've been praying much for Zachary," Steve said at last. "I know God is working in his heart. We need to remember that God's plans for Zach might not be the same as what we want."

Jo didn't want to think about that.

Rosemary shot a look at Steve. "Meaning what?"

Steve leaned back into the seat and closed his eyes. "Meaning that the Lord may have a purpose for him in Coeur d'Alene. Or maybe some other city."

"Oh, I don't think so." Rosemary shook her head vehemently.

Jo hoped Rosemary was keeping a close eye on traffic.

"We don't know everything," Steve murmured. "The farm isn't that important in the long run. Being right with God is all that really matters."

Now there was a concept Jo hadn't considered in a long time. How could the farm not be essential? That's what God had called her to do. Didn't he expect her to do everything within her power to make it a success?

A tiny thought pestered at the back of her mind. Maybe He expected her to do everything within *His* power, not hers. Maybe she wasn't as important as she'd like to think.

Chapter 24

Why, oh why was he here? Zach pulled into the opposite end of the parking lot from Yvette's red Corvette. He wrapped his arms around the steering wheel and rested his forehead on them.

"God." He'd been out of the habit of talking to his Heavenly Father for a few years. Somehow, the last forty-eight hours had catapulted praying to the top of his to-do list. Little else had been on his lips the whole drive from Galena Landing. A few curses had tried to bubble up, but Zach's upbringing had kicked in. He'd always believed in God. Never stopped, though he'd been doing his best to ignore that still small voice. "God, help me."

Something tapped on his window.

He ended his prayer with, "please," and looked up.

Yvette retracted her cherry red fingernails from the glass and tilted her head expectantly.

With a sigh he opened the car door and slid out.

She wrapped her arms around him, and he stiffened until she released him. "You said you loved me." Her full lips pulled into a pout.

He'd been stupid. "I once thought so." He shoved his hands deep into his jeans pockets and leaned back against the car door.

Yvette's mascara-laden eyes narrowed. "Well, it doesn't matter. Love is overrated, don't you think?"

No way would Josephine Shaw think such a thing, let alone

say it. And then there was his mom, so excited to be bringing Dad home today. Was their love all a hype? Not a chance. He wanted what they had, somebody to grow comfortably old with. Not that his folks were old. At least they hadn't seemed so before Dad's illness.

Yvette sighed. "Your mind is obviously elsewhere."

"What do you want from me?"

Her eyes widened. How had he once thought that seductive? "I didn't think it was fair to you that everyone but you knew you were going to be a father."

Please, God. "You know, there's no way you can prove that. How can you, when it's clearly untrue?" He kept his gaze on her face, away from her low-cut neckline and the belly that might—or might not—be swelling. "In fact, a paternity test would back me up and you know it."

"I could get Dad to reconsider the job situation."

Zach held his gaze steady and crossed his arms. "And toss Draper out like last week's trash? Not interested." And it was true, to his amazement. She was a viper and the farther away he stayed from this day on, the better off he'd be. "I'm settling in Galena Landing." The words hanging in the air shocked him, but he didn't retract them. She didn't need to know he wasn't sure.

Yvette shifted from one foot to the other. "You've changed."

He nodded curtly. "Just in time, by the sounds of things. So what do you really want? Why are you trying to lure me back? Tired of Draper already? Maybe this is his kid."

She narrowed her gaze. "It's not."

Zach shrugged. "Well, it's not mine, either. If you've been sleeping around and gotten yourself knocked up, that would be your problem, not mine." He levered his body off the side of the car and reached for the handle. "Anything else?"

"I can't believe you're treating me this way." Somehow she managed to squeeze out a couple of tears.

Oh man. He hated when women wept. "Yvette, you made

your choices. All I can say is I'm grateful you turned me down. You have no idea how much."

She reached for him, but he grabbed her wrists and held her at a distance. "No. I'm not falling for your story. I have no idea if you're pregnant or not, but I do know I'm not responsible. Whatever your game is, I'm not playing it. Go back to Coeur d'Alene, go back to the mess you've made, and deal with it."

"I thought you were a man of character."

And what a character he'd been. "Meaning?"

"I can't raise a child on my own, Zach. I dropped out of college to work for Dad, and he won't be impressed. If you don't come back, I'm going to have to abort. There's nothing else I can do."

This wasn't his child. Not his responsibility. And besides, she was likely bluffing. "I'm sorry you've made bad choices, but they're all yours. Find the baby's real dad—if you even know who he is—and get help from there. I'm not getting sucked back in."

Yvette twisted out of his grip and clutched his arms. "It's on your head, then."

He pushed her away, but she dodged in. He averted his face before her lips could meet his then wrenched out of her embrace. "No, Yvette. It's on yours." The problem being, she was now the one leaning against his car door, making it difficult for him to drive away. "There's only one other thing you can do."

She tilted her head and raised her eyebrows.

"Go to church." He and Gabe used to attend together before Gabe returned to the valley and Zach had transferred to the veterinary college in Pullman. "Pray and ask God's forgiveness."

Yvette spat at his shoes. "Now you've gone all religious on me."

Zach shook his head. "I've never not been. I just lost sight of it for a while. Now, if you'll excuse me, I have chores to do back home."

She didn't move. "Farm boy."

And she'd thought to win him over? He pressed his key fob and the car door locked, beeping.

Yvette jumped a little and glared at him.

"I'm going for a walk along the river for a few minutes. When I return, you'd better be on your way back to the city. I'm done with you. Forever."

"Just try and get a job anywhere in North Idaho or Washington. I'll see to it no one will hire you."

She'd already done her worst and Albert Warren had been interested anyway. Zach shrugged. "So be it. The world is bigger than your sphere of influence." He strode away from his car hoping Yvette wouldn't key it or something in her anger. But she couldn't be reasoned with. The thought of all the veterinary clinics in the Pacific Northwest being closed to him didn't bother him as much as it once had. It was all up to God. It always had been.

o0o

Rosemary turned a worship CD on low when Steve dozed off in the front passenger seat. Jo stared out the window, watching the landscape whiz by. Commercial orchards and vineyards lined the rolling hills as they crisscrossed the Galena River. Fruit trees stood festooned with frothy blossoms, like brides awaiting their weddings. Jo tried to snap her brain out of that track, but the beauty mesmerized her. *Thank You, Lord. I live in the most beautiful place on earth.*

They drove through Wynnton, stopping at every traffic light. Steve awoke, grimacing.

Rosemary glanced over and turned down the CD player. "You okay?"

"I need a pit stop."

Jo met Rosemary's gaze in the mirror and nodded. "I could use a stretch, too."

"There's the park here on the outskirts of town. Easy access to the washrooms." Rosemary slowed the car and flipped on her signal light.

Steve straightened. "Looks like Zach's car at the other end."

Jo craned to see, though of course Zach didn't drive the only black Mustang in the world. If anyone would recognize his specific vehicle, though, it would be his dad. A blonde in a skimpy, bulging top and short shorts lounged against the hood like she posed for a hot rod magazine cover. Must not be Zach's car after all.

Rosemary parked near the public washrooms, and Jo climbed out quickly. The blonde flicked a glance their direction then resumed her pose, staring down the trail to the river.

Jo hurried to the ladies' room while Rosemary pulled Steve's walker out of the trunk. Jo grinned. They must look a sight, like escapees from some accident ward. Not that she cared. It wasn't any of the other woman's business. Jo came back out before Rosemary and Steve had made it to the men's room door, so she told Rosemary she'd go down to the river for a few minutes. Rosemary nodded.

The river flowed from the lake at Galena Landing down through Wynnton and continued westward, where it eventually joined the Columbia network. The sign pointed the way to a gorgeous set of rapids here. Jo strode toward the viewpoint ahead.

A man rounded the bend in the curve beside the viewpoint and her heart lurched. *Zach.* What was he doing here? And then…that *was* his car. His car with that, that *female*.

He jerked to a stop when he saw Jo and their eyes met. No point in either of them pretending they hadn't seen or recognized each other. "Jo?" His voice seemed pitched higher than usual.

What to say? Bah, forget the niceties and cut to the chase. "Who is she?"

Panic crossed his face. "Who is who?"

Oh, seriously. What kind of an idiot did he take her for? Jo raised her eyebrows and jabbed her thumb over her shoulder.

He closed his eyes and took a deep breath. "She's still there."

Strange words. But Jo needed to know. "Who is she?"

Zach's eyes focused on hers and he stepped closer, hands outspread. "Jo, it's not what you think."

How could he possibly know what she was thinking? She hadn't a clue, herself. "That's not answering my question."

"That's Yvette, a girl I used to date. We broke things off months ago." His eyes pleaded for understanding.

"So that's why you're meeting her in Wynnton. Because you broke up." That made some kind of sense in what universe? But Jo's heart had sunk down to her toes. Why, oh why, did she keep fantasizing about this man who was clearly not worth her efforts?

"She…" He licked his lips. "She had something she wanted to talk about."

Jo raised her eyebrows. *So tell me what, buddy. Not that it will help.*

He glanced past Jo then focused on her face again. "I told her to leave, but she's still there."

Genius. He'd noticed.

"Listen, are my parents here, too? Mom said you were going to Coeur d'Alene with her to get Dad?"

She nodded. "They're in the washrooms."

He closed his eyes and took a deep, shuddering breath. Even looked like he might be praying. Probably a good idea, although too late.

"I take it your parents never met your *girlfriend*." Couldn't help the emphasis on that last word. If that was the kind of female he was interested in, obviously he'd been toying with Jo out of boredom. The two women couldn't possibly have been more opposite. Jo hoped.

"No. And now's not a good time. Honestly, Jo, you have to believe me."

Believe what? Why the desperation? Something was going on, but she didn't trust him. She searched his face for clues.

A car door shut behind her. Jo swiveled on the path and marched toward the parking lot, no longer interested in the river. She could feel Zach at her heels. Could feel some sort of impending doom.

"Zachary!" Steve's voice.

"Hey, Dad. Good to see you."

Didn't sound like it to Jo. She glanced up as the woman unfolded from the Mustang, a look of interest on her face, as she seemed to notice Zach's parents for the first time. Then her eyes found Jo's and narrowed. Like she had anything to worry about.

Rosemary took in the girl's stance and frowned. Hadn't she noticed her when the car pulled in? Or maybe she'd been convinced it was someone else's vehicle after all.

The girl slinked toward them. "Zachary. Someone I should meet?" She cut between Jo and Zach, turning her back on Jo as she reached for Zach's arm and snuggled against him.

Jo debated ramming the girl's artificially tanned elbow with her cast. Accidentally, of course. But Yvette shifted out of easy reach before Jo could wrestle her conscience down.

Zach disengaged her hand from his arm. "Yvette, go back to Coeur d'Alene. You're not part of my life. There's no one here for you to meet."

Yeah, take *that*.

They stood in the space between Rosemary's car and the Mustang, an awkward group, nobody sure what to do or say next, curiosity alive on every face except for Zach's.

Yvette smiled sweetly at Rosemary. "You're Zach's mother?"

Rosemary nodded cautiously.

"Then you'll be interested to know that Zach and I are expecting a baby."

Chapter 25

Seconds had never moved slower. Zach had time to register the expressions on everyone's face: the triumph on Yvette's as she linked arms with him, the shock on his dad's, and the disappointment on his mom's. He wasn't prepared for the blazing hatred on Jo's.

"She's lying." Zach shook Yvette's hand away. The words were meant for everyone, yet no one but Jo. He took a step closer to her, but she pivoted and strode down the trail toward the river. "You have to believe me. I never had sex with Yvette." Jo kept going, so Zach raised his voice. "Never once."

He stared after her helplessly, not daring to leave Yvette alone with his parents, even to follow Jo. She hated him anyway. Had from the beginning. She'd never done a thing to encourage him. Not really.

Zach glared at Yvette's mocking face. "I don't know why you're doing this to me. You know I thought I loved you." He turned to his parents. "I told you that. Told you I wanted to marry her, that I wouldn't dishonor her before our wedding, no matter how much she pressured me."

To his relief, Mom nodded, albeit cautiously. Dad, however, looked downright gray. The poor man was barely off his hospital bed and Yvette's shocking tale wasn't doing him any good. Zach crossed the asphalt and slid his arm around his father. "Dad, let me get you back in the car. I'll explain everything when we're home. For now, please just believe that she's lying." Without turning to see Yvette's response, Zach all but carried Dad to the passenger side of the car while his mom hurried ahead and opened the door.

"I believe you, son," Mom whispered as she pulled the seatbelt around his dad. "You coming home now?"

Zach nodded, aware of Yvette's presence…and Jo's absence.

Mom straightened. "Zachary, you need to talk to Josephine. This impasse between the two of you is ridiculous."

She must have been reading his mind. Zach closed his eyes. "She hates me. She did before. Why would that change now?"

"Men," Mom muttered and shut the passenger door with a little extra force. "I need to get your father home. Where did Jo go?"

Zach jutted his chin toward the river. There weren't too many ways this day could get worse, unless he followed her and she blistered his ears off again.

Mom rounded the trunk of the car and glanced through the windows at Dad, who leaned against the headrest with his eyes closed. She looked at Zach and pursed her lips. "You find Jo and bring her home. Your father is all done in." She reached for the driver's side door handle.

"You're the one who offered her the ride." He heard the panic in his voice. "You can't leave her with me. She won't get in my car." Yvette's car remained parked a few spaces down. Without her in it. That meant she was still behind him somewhere. No way did he need to be left here alone with those two women.

His mother pulled her hand away from him. "Look at your dad. My first priority is getting him home. You find Jo and talk to her. Pray. I don't understand what all is going on, but if you say you didn't sleep with that…that *female*, I'll give you the benefit of the doubt. I do remember the vows you took in high school, and I've always known you to be a boy—a man—of your word."

She opened the car door, settled herself, and slid down the window. "I'll see you at home." The car purred to life and began to back away.

Why couldn't he say *no* to his mother? He turned to deal with the problems that faced him, but the parking lot was empty. Zach smashed his fist against the Mustang's hood. Didn't take a genius to figure out Yvette had targeted Jo.

Oh, God. Are you there? I've screwed up, big time. I thought I'd backed away before I'd gotten burned, but the flames reached farther than I guessed. Please help me. He thought for a moment about his mom's words and some of the things Gabe had said. Once it had given him great peace and joy to be right with God. *Help me find my way back.*

o0o

Jo stared down at the river rapids but couldn't see a thing through the burning tears that blurred her vision. Her arm ached, her head throbbed, and her limbs trembled, both from the speed at which she'd run the forest trail and from fury.

How had she ever fallen for this stupid guy? She should follow her mom's advice and go back to California. Possibly she should also become a nun or something. Just block off her heart so no man could ever break down the walls.

Yeah, nice try. Too late. In all Sierra's casual talk on men over the years, her friend had failed to mention how much heartbreak there could be. She'd been smart enough not to let things get this far. Just far enough to flirt with a guy like Zach.

The thought mocked Jo. This far, indeed. Hadn't she been fighting it tooth and nail the whole time she'd known Zachary Nemesek? He wasn't right for her. He just wasn't. Evidence aplenty, and this escapade only proved it. He had no redeeming qualities. Other than great parents. And Gabe. Gabe wouldn't have an imbecile for a best friend, would he? But…

Footsteps crunched on the path behind Jo and she stiffened. Four options. Well, no. It couldn't be Steve. With any luck, it would be Rosemary. They'd cry together about what a wretch her son had turned out to be and then go home. Zach would leave for Coeur d'Alene to raise his baby with that floozy, and Jo could recover. Sure, he said he was innocent, but who made stuff like that up?

"That must have been a shock to you." The worst of the three remaining possibilities. The woman with the sweet, biting tone.

"No, why?" Lying through her teeth, but Jo wasn't about to give Yvette any satisfaction.

She came up beside Jo and leaned on the railing at the edge of the viewpoint, bosom bulging over her crossed arms. She glanced over at Jo, finely plucked eyebrows raised.

Jo wanted to claw the superior smirk right off her face but managed to maintain control. No point in dignifying the situation with conversation. There was nothing to talk about. Jo turned for the parking lot. If *she* was at the viewpoint, then Jo wouldn't be.

"Just so you know, he's not that great a guy."

Jo froze two steps down the trail, her back to the city girl.

"He basically told me to get out of his life. Guess that means I'll be aborting the embryo, since I can't really raise a child on my own. You can have him. He's old news."

Jo's mind didn't know which part of that to latch onto. Zach said Yvette was lying, but why would she hold the facade over his head when she'd failed to get her way? Jo chose to focus on the other. "Don't want him, so it doesn't matter." *Liar.*

Yvette laughed. "Yeah, right."

Jo's ears burned. Was she really that transparent?

In the distant parking lot, a car engine started. Her ears perked. Sounded like Rosemary's. Jo broke into a jog, intent on getting away from Yvette and to her ride, but even as she did so, the gears shifted and the motor's sound dwindled. Must have been someone else, but who? Zach? No, his car sounded different.

Panicking, Jo picked up speed. She broke into the parking lot to see Zach leaning against the Mustang, hands clasped on its roof. Praying? Nice try. Didn't he think it was a little late for that? Jo tore her gaze away and took in the asphalt space. Only the black Mustang and the red Corvette remained.

Rosemary had abandoned her.

o0o

A sharp intake of breath pierced Zach's prayer and he glanced up.

Jo, eyes wide, trembled at the edge of the parking lot, with Yvette nowhere to be seen.

He tried to smile, tried to mask the writhing turmoil inside. "There you are! Dad was at the limit of what he could handle, so Mom headed home and asked me to bring you."

Rosemary wouldn't do this to her. She must have pulled around the other side of the parking lot. Only there wasn't another side.

A distance behind her, Yvette appeared on the trail. From the smirk on her face, the girls had had a little chat. What he really didn't need was for all three of them to get into it some more.

"Jo? You ready? Let's get going."

She hesitated.

Zach pulled the passenger door open. "Please."

Jo cast another desperate look around the parking lot then hurried forward.

He felt her pain. She wanted to spend the next hour with him as much as he wanted to spend it with her. Perhaps less. Because his heart kicked up a notch at her nearness, and it was clearly apparent that hers did nothing of the sort by the scowl she cast his way. Still, she jumped into the car and he shut the door behind her. As Yvette hit the asphalt, Zach yanked the driver's door open and climbed in.

"See you, Zach!" Yvette called out with a wave. "I'll be in touch."

Over his dead body. He started the car and backed out of the parking spot, then squealed onto the highway.

Silence reigned in the car. Better than recriminations, maybe, but it wasn't a pleasant quiet. He glanced at Jo. She'd turned to stare out the window, her back to him as completely as possible with her seatbelt on. Her narrow shoulders slumped. And trembled.

Crying? His gut clenched. He wasn't prepared to deal with that. He was ready for yelling. He could argue with feisty, but this?

"Jo?" He cleared his throat.

She stiffened but didn't turn.

"Jo, I'm sorry."

A sniffle. "It's true, then."

"What? No! Yvette lied through her teeth."

"Then what're you sorry for?" Bitterness laced her words.

Where to start? "I'm sorry you ever had to meet her. I'm sorry you heard her accusations."

Jo shifted. "She must have based them on something."

"Desperation."

She shot a furious look at him.

"What? No. Not for me, at least I don't think so. I think she probably really is pregnant, but I have no idea who the father is. I promise you I'm telling the truth. I never had sex with her. Not once." He took a deep, shuddering breath. Man, this was hard. He'd never really talked about this kind of stuff with a girl before. Not one he cared about. "Gabe and I made a pledge when we were in high school. A bunch of kids in our youth group did. We promised to save ourselves for our future spouse."

At that revelation, Jo's jaw twitched but her eyes remained focused on the road ahead.

His anger flared. "What, you want to see the results of paternity tests? Guaranteed beyond a shadow of doubt they will prove my innocence. I've kept my vow."

What more could he say to her? She was set against believing him. Why this, now, when he'd just begun to sort himself out?

Chapter 26

"Whoa." Sierra glanced out the trailer window at Zach's departing car. "How did that happen?"

Jo glared at her. "It's a long story. A really, *really* long story."

"I've got time." Sierra flopped into the loveseat.

Jo would rather forget Zach even existed. She wanted to believe him, but seriously, why would that scantily-clad woman create stories like that one? And did it matter, anyway? Jo just needed to get him out of her head, once and for all.

Did she have to give Sierra the complete low-down? Yeah. The girls had promised to be there for each other, and the weight was more than she could handle on her own. She was such a mess inside. If Sierra and Zach were meant to be together, she'd have to get used to it.

"I'm waiting." Sierra looked at Jo expectantly. "Did you two kiss and make up?"

Nice try. Jo lowered herself into the big chair. "He's just a jerk, anyway. It doesn't matter."

Sierra laughed. "Now who's being silly? I think you really care about him."

"I thought *you* did," Jo shot back.

"And you said you weren't jealous." Sierra leaned forward. "He's a really nice guy. Quite a catch. You should try harder. Meet him halfway."

"Halfway to Coeur d'Alene? Not a chance."

"Not what I meant, Jo. Though as cities go, it's small and pretty nice."

Jo glared at Sierra. "It hasn't come up, thank you. I suppose you'd ditch us all for some guy and move back to the bright lights?" The appropriate answer would be "of course not."

Sierra winked. "For the right guy, you never know. A shot at happiness doesn't come along every day. Now take Zach, for instance—" She pointed her pinkie at Jo as her cell phone rang. Sierra rolled her eyes, swiped it on, and said, "Hello." A few seconds later, her face blanched and she surged to her feet. "No! Is he okay? What happened?"

There was a pause while Jo searched Sierra's face for clues, but she turned away. Her voice broke. "No. Oh, no. He'll never be able to live with himself."

Claire entered the room, her eyebrows raised as she looked from Sierra to Jo. Jo shook her head and shrugged.

"Can you get a flight into Spokane? … I'll leave right away. Call me when you have details. … Love you, Mom. See you soon." Sierra turned slowly around as she set the cell down.

Claire wrapped her arms around her friend. "What happened?"

Sierra sagged against Claire. "My dad. He crashed the grocery truck."

Claire and Jo exchanged glances. "How bad?" Jo asked.

"He's been rushed to Coeur d'Alene."

Claire frowned. "So it happened somewhere near here?"

Sierra nodded into Claire's shoulder. "This side of Wynnton."

There hadn't been an accident anywhere Jo had seen. No sirens, flashing lights. Surely she'd have noticed. She blinked the thought aside. "Is he stable?"

Sierra took a long, shuddering breath. "Mom talked to him.

They're not sure if there's internal bleeding. He's pretty banged up."

Claire rubbed Sierra's back. "If you're heading to the city tonight, you'll need somebody. I'll drive."

"There's more." Sierra's voice was muffled.

The girls waited.

"It was a head-on. The woman in the car wasn't so lucky." Sierra broke down in full-blown crying.

Jo's heart sank. "Oh, no." She tried to imagine the grieving family and how awful they must feel.

"There were deer on the road." Sierra managed to get the words out. "Mom said the woman swerved to avoid them and ran right into Dad's truck."

"So it wasn't exactly his fault." That was a relief, anyway. Jo patted Sierra's back. "I'm glad he'll be okay."

"But I need to see him." Sierra pulled out of Claire's arms.

Claire nodded. "I'll go pack a bag for both of us. Do you want to come, too, Jo? Or stay home alone? If you need something, you could call Nemeseks."

Like that would happen. "I'll stay here." She stood in the middle of the living room while Sierra and Claire rushed around. In just a few minutes, the VW's taillights disappeared down the drive.

Jo headed down the hall and into the bedroom. Threw herself down across her bed and prayed for Tim Riehl and the family, for the unknown woman's family. For Zach. For herself.

o0o

Zach faced his mother over cups of Earl Grey at the kitchen table. Dad, loaded up on painkillers, was already asleep on the twin bed Zach had set up in the corner of the living room.

"How'd it go with Jo?"

Zach sighed. "Not very good. She doesn't believe me."

"She told you that?" Mom had a sip of tea.

"As good as." Zach twisted his mug around on the table. "Mom, I'm sorry. I've made a huge mess of stuff over the past couple of years. I don't know where I went so wrong."

She clasped his hand across the table. "By ignoring God?"

Zach thought back. Why had he quit going to church and hanging out with the gang from the college-and-careers group? It'd seemed so reasonable at the time. He'd been busy, tired. Just needed to get a bit of extra sleep Sunday mornings. To finish his homework Friday nights. To hit the library during the prayer group that met Tuesday noon.

It wasn't that he'd stopped believing. He'd just sort of let his faith slide into a back corner of his life. He could retrieve it any time with no consequences. He hadn't become evil.

Right. Look where that had gotten him. Flirting with disaster.

He met his mother's gaze. "That was the start, for sure."

"You don't need me to tell you that God is waiting for you to offer your life back to Him, do you?"

He shook his head. "I've already started. I didn't know how far I'd drifted until Yvette called me."

"You had a near miss."

"Not that easy." He whooshed his breath out. "If I don't 'own up' to the baby, she'll terminate."

"She can't hold you responsible."

Zach lifted a shoulder. "It feels like she can."

"Son." Mom waited until he finally met her gaze. "You know I'm not for abortion. No doubt about it. But if you're not responsible for this pregnancy, then going along with her isn't the right thing to do, either."

"I know, but..."

"There isn't a but."

He stared at her. "I'll be responsible for the death of an innocent child."

"No, son. Yvette is the one making this choice. Not you.

What does she expect you to *do*?"

"She wants…" Zach scowled, thinking hard, as his words trailed off. Yvette hadn't said she'd changed her mind about marrying him. Not that the offer was still on. Had she been looking for money? That seemed silly. Jeff Hammond had more cash than a hundred Zachary Nemeseks, and it was highly unlikely he'd turn a pregnant daughter out onto the streets. "I don't know what she wants."

Mom nodded slowly. "Call her bluff."

He already had, just by walking away. But the sensation she wasn't done with him lingered. Mom was right, though. He couldn't take responsibility for Yvette's choices—past or future.

"So, about Jo." Mom's eyes gleamed.

The phone on the kitchen wall rang shrilly.

Zach lunged, hoping to catch it before it went off a second time. Dad needed his rest. "Hello?"

"Zachary?"

"Speaking." He glanced at his mom and shrugged. Didn't know who it was.

"It's Pastor Ron." The man hesitated. "I have some bad news for you."

Zach frowned. "Hi, Pastor. What's that?"

"Can you come over to Gabe's apartment? He needs you."

Had Bethany lost the baby? What irony, after Yvette's flippant talk. But how could he help Gabe with that? He cleared his throat. "Can you tell me what happened?"

"There's been a terrible accident." The older man's voice caught. "Beth…Bethany…her car…she's dead."

"Bethany?" Zach's world reeled for the second time that day. Bethany's laughing face and rounding belly floated through his memory. That was someone who deserved to be pregnant. Not Yvette. "That can't be right."

"Gabe has to drive to Wynnton to identify her body. He can't do this alone, Zach." The pastor choked on his words. "He needs his best friend. You."

o0o

Zach pulled the Mustang into the parking lot of the Wynnton Hospital. A few vehicles dotted the space, well lit by streetlights.

Beside him, Gabe rubbed bloodshot eyes and stared through the windshield at the emergency room doors. His jaw twitched.

Zach put his hand on his friend's shoulder. "Ready, man? I'll come in with you if you want."

A tear glistened on Gabe's cheek as he slowly shook his head. "I can't believe it."

The drive to Wynnton had been quiet. Zach tried to break it a couple of times, but Gabe didn't respond. Zach had failed his pal. He couldn't begin to imagine what Gabe was going through.

"Hang on to God, man. I know it's rough, but He's got your back." Rough? Who was he kidding? The kick he'd felt in his gut when Jo rejected him could only be a minor hiccup compared to losing a beloved wife of several years, a best chum since childhood. Bethany had been Zach's friend, too. *Had been.* How did a guy start thinking of a friend in past tense?

"He's got a strange way of showing it." Gabe's Adam's apple bobbed as he swallowed. He shot a look at Zach. "And since when did you start believing that?"

"I've been doing some thinking. I'm finding my way back."

Gabe's jaw twitched. "Yeah, that's great, man." He shoved the car door open with unnecessary force and climbed out. He leaned back in. "Nice that God loves you, cause He sure as hell doesn't love me." The door slammed.

Zach's mouth dropped open.

His best bud, shoulders drooping, hands shoved deep into his pockets, wove across the sidewalk to the hospital doors. They parted automatically, the garish light beaming all around him. Two women ran toward Gabe and embraced him, but he shook them off. The trio remained framed in the doorway.

Everyone here knew Bethany: nurses, doctors, lab techs, cleaning staff. She'd been working here, what, three years? Four? But they were Bethany's friends, not Gabe's. And even though Gabe clearly did not know it, he needed Zach at his side. The guy was hurting. He couldn't have meant what he said.

Zach locked up the Mustang and followed Gabe into the building. He nodded at the two nurses. "I'm his best friend. Name's Zachary."

Gabe shifted away from him. Only slightly, but noticeably.

"Dr. Seeley said to call him when you got here." The nurse's lips trembled. "He'll take you d-downstairs."

Gabe nodded curtly.

Zach caught the young woman's eyes. "Thanks."

She cast a sidelong glance at Gabe and hurried behind a windowed wall, where she lifted a phone. Zach watched her lips move but couldn't hear.

Gabe jammed his hands back in his jeans' pockets and hunched over to the window.

Was the doc going to be long? Zach didn't know how much of this he could handle. But it wasn't about him. It was about Gabe. Gabe, who spurned Zach's help. Who doubted God.

Well, Zach had doubted God aplenty, too, and for less reason. He leaned back against the nearest wall and closed his eyes. *God, Gabe doesn't want to talk to You right now. He's hurting.* Man, Zach was, too. He blinked back hot tears. *We like to think we're in control, but I'm learning—the hard way—that's not so. Please, God, comfort Gabe. He needs you so much.*

The statue of Gabe stood at the window, and the nurses had retreated to the safety of their zone. Zach went back to the business of praying.

o0o

Jo blinked her eyes open against the early morning light streaming in the window. She must've fallen asleep at some point, but all she remembered was tossing and turning, her thoughts all a-jumble. Zach. Sierra's dad's accident. Zach. Yvette. Zach.

She'd almost blurted everything out to Sierra, almost asked her friend for advice. Would have, had the phone not rung. What would Sierra have told her?

Probably that she was pig-headed, and it might be true. At least that's the conclusion she'd come to sometime in the wee hours. The accident—the death of some unknown woman—had taunted Jo. If it had been her life cut short, would her attitude and her posturing have been worth it? Maybe she'd been too hard on Zach. He'd tried to talk to her and she'd shut him down.

Jo stared at the ceiling.

She'd put on a porcupine's armor, making sure no one could get close to her. How would she even know if Zach changed? He'd never get a chance to say so.

Life was grayer than it used to be. Not as black and white. But she'd been so busy trying to keep all the compartments in her life separate she hadn't been watching for God's leading. Maybe He was trying to tell her something. Maybe she ought to apologize to Zach. Let him explain. Then if he didn't profess his undying love to her—and why would he?—she'd know she'd given him the opportunity. Maybe then she could move on.

Decision made, Jo rolled out of bed and shrugged on some clothes. Still too early to go next door. She took a bowl of granola out onto the front step.

Domino ducked under the barbed wire fence and careened up the trailer steps, practically wiggling right into Jo's lap. He'd grown over the past few months and must be near his full size by now.

Jo burrowed her face into his silky hair and told him all about the mess with Zach, all the dreams and hopes that lay shattered, even the ones she'd had that didn't include love. The June morning sparkled around her yet everything seemed drab.

"Heel, Domino. I'll walk you home." Handy to have an excuse, should the discussion not go so well. As Jo walked, she prayed, but her thoughts were so disjointed she could only hope God understood her better than she understood herself.

Rosemary sat in the wicker rocker on the veranda, hunched over her open Bible. She glanced up when the pup barked a greeting. "Domino! How…?" Her gaze flew to Jo's face and she took a deep breath. "Jo. I'm sorry he keeps bothering you." Dark circles hung under the older woman's eyes, and her cheeks looked moist with tears.

"It's okay, Rosemary." Jo hesitated for an instant. "Are you all right?" She climbed up the few steps.

Rosemary managed a wan smile. "I'm okay, Jo. Hanging onto the fact that God is God and He's in control. We're not. I don't know why we even try."

"Is it Steve?" Or Zach. Was this about Yvette? Had he owned up?

"He'll be fine. We did have some bad news last night, though."

Bad news must have been roaming the neighborhood like a pack of wolves. "What happened?"

"You know Gabe and Bethany Rubachuk? From church?"

Jo nodded, relief flooding her that the problem wasn't Zach. "Health food store." Zach's best friend.

Rosemary took a deep breath. "Bethany was killed in a head-on crash last night. Zach's been gone all night with Gabe to identify her body."

Jo's brain garbled. "Bethany?" *Oh, God, no!* A head-on. What were the odds? "W-what kind of an accident?"

"She swerved to miss a deer and a semi-truck ran right over her little car. They say she probably didn't even see it coming."

Chapter 27

Zach huddled under his rain slicker, not that it did much good. He'd tracked Gabe this far and wasn't giving up now. His buddy hadn't been at church this morning, nor at the apartment or store—no surprise there—nor any other logical place Zach had been able to think of until…

The tree house.

Why it had come to mind, he didn't know, but when he'd followed the road on past his folks' place, past the trailer, and around the corner, he'd been rewarded by a glimpse of Gabe's beater car in amongst the trees.

Now Zach stood under the golden willow and peered up. The knotted rope was not dangling. So, that's where Gabe was. "Rubachuk!"

Silence. Well, not really. Even here in the forest the rain beat on everything, including the platforms above Zach's head.

"I know you're up there, man. Drop the rope for me."

He hadn't been up that thing in years, but memories flooded back. All the times he and Gabe had hung out here. Young boys, reading comic books and eating candy bars. Teenagers, talking about girls. About Zach playing the field, and Gabe's intense crush on Bethany.

"Go away, Nemesek. I don't want to talk."

Zach cocked his head. "Can I come up if I keep my trap shut?"

"Never happened yet."

"I'll do my best. I just want to be with you, man."

A scrape on the wet planks above, then the knotted rope tumbled within reach. Zach took a deep breath, asked God to zip his mouth, and climbed up.

Gabe slumped against the trunk. The overhang of the upper deck and the long, drooping branches kept the rain from blasting him directly. At least he wore a jacket and wouldn't catch his death of a cold. He made no move to acknowledge Zach's presence.

Zach plopped down beside his buddy, drawing his knees up and wrapping his arms around them. He glanced sidelong at Gabe. What could he say that would make a difference? Anything? Right. He'd promised to keep quiet. That took the pressure off. Kind of.

Across the platform, the railing had splintered off where Jo crashed through in weather very like today's. He should fix that. Zach grimaced. Or not. The tree house was on Green Acres property. By all rights, both he and Gabe were trespassing.

He could do it for Jo. He'd come in the roundabout way like he had today, and she'd never know he'd been there unless she wandered out by chance and caught him. Would she recognize the repair for what it was?

The thought stilled his heart. Time to admit something to himself, perhaps? He'd do it because he loved her. Because it might be one of the few things left that drew them together instead of wedged them apart. Because his life wasn't complete without her.

He inhaled deeply of the sweet, damp, willow-laden air and blew it out again in a long breath. In and out again. Like a cleansing. Time to stop running from God, from the farm, from

Jo. Time to change direction and run toward them. Were they connected? What if he committed to stay and she rejected him again? What if he was never good enough for her, never environmental enough? Never green enough?

Gabe's voice interrupted his reverie. "I don't suppose you can give me a good answer why God killed Bethany." His voice broke. "And our baby."

Please God. Give me words. But there didn't seem to be an answer. "Not really." Zach's mind slid to Yvette's pregnancy. *Let it go, man. It's not yours. You know it.*

"I didn't think so." Gabe heaved a huge, shuddering sigh.

Zach had tried so hard to control his own life. What had it got him? Nothing but a false paternity suit and a lost job opportunity. It was time—past time—to let God have the reins.

Gabe's voice broke through Zach's thoughts. "I've spent my life serving God. But it's not good enough. He's thrown away my gift and trampled it in the mud."

Zach had heard all the pat answers. People offered them to him and Mom when Dad contracted Guillain-Barré. But at least Dad lived. Zach opened his mouth, ready to repeat some of the wise axioms. Shut it again.

"What does God really want, anyway? He doesn't care about us. We're just game pieces on His stupid chessboard. 'Oops, had to sacrifice a pawn. Too bad.'" Gabe rammed his fist on the wooden planks, causing the raindrops to splatter.

It sounded like there were a few holes in Gabe's thought process, but Zach had nothing to plug them with. It wouldn't accomplish anything to stick up for God. If God couldn't prove Himself to Gabe—well, Gabe was right. God wasn't worth serving.

Gabe's elbow jabbed Zach in the ribs. "What, you're not going to spout some nonsense to me about how she's an angel in heaven, and God needed her more there than I needed her here?"

Zach met his buddy's eyes and shook his head. For

someone who'd demanded silence for his company, Gabe sure had a lot of questions.

"And don't tell me I'm in some league with Job. That I'm important enough for Satan to test my faith. That's garbage."

Hadn't even crossed Zach's mind. Best not to remind Gabe that God had restored everything that had been taken from Job. A new family down the road would not be the same thing as having Bethany and their baby back.

"I hate the truck driver that killed her, you know that? If he hadn't been there, Beth could have avoided the deer. And he'll be fine. Just a few bumps and bruises."

Zach hadn't given much thought to the other guy in all the time he'd been focused on pulling Gabe through this. "I'm sure he's really sorry."

Gabe jerked away, shaking. "Big lot of good that will do. It won't bring Bethany back." His voice broke. "I never even got to meet my baby girl."

Once again, Zach shoved thoughts of Yvette's pregnancy out of his mind and pulled his focus back to Gabe.

"You're not going to offer to take me down to the pub and drown my sorrows?"

That did it. "Gabe, I never turned into a drunk just because I quit going to church and reading my Bible. Sure, I'd have a few beers at a party, but that's a long way from drowning in alcohol. If you're going to push me for a reaction, stay above the belt."

Gabe's jaw trembled and tears sprang to his eyes. Or it could be the rain getting to him at last. He leaned back against the trunk and closed his eyes. "I don't know what I'm going to do. How I'm going to survive."

Zach leaned closer, wedging his shoulder tight against his buddy's. "I know, man. It's awful."

"My soul has been ripped out."

Please, dear God. Help Gabe. Help me. We need you here. "I know." Zach's own throat caught. "I know."

Chapter 28

On Wednesday Claire drove Jo to Wynnton to have her cast removed. Jo averted her eyes as they passed the riverside park on the way into town. Horrible place, for all that it displayed God's beauty. It also reminded Jo of Zach and words she wished she could take back.

Across the highway a wrecking yard drew her attention through its chain link fencing. Two men in coveralls stood beside a little red car, hood accordion-folded clear to the doors. Jo knew that car. She stared, her gut rolling.

"Claire." Jo's voice came out faint.

Claire glanced at her. "What?"

But they were already past. "That was Bethany's car in that lot. I'm sure of it."

Claire glanced in her mirrors and hit the brakes, swerving to the side of the road.

A truck blasted by, horn blaring.

Claire backed up until the girls could see into the yard again. "Looks like it to me. It's a Corolla about the same year as hers, anyway. And would match what we heard about the damage."

Jo stared at the crumpled car, trying to imagine being in the vehicle when it happened. "No wonder she didn't make it through."

One of the men glanced up, noticing their car, as Claire pulled back out onto the highway. "Does anyone in town know it was Sierra's dad that hit her?"

Jo shook her head, tears burning. "Not from me. It's not that I've been trying to keep it a secret, exactly. It just never seemed like the right time."

"Yeah, me neither. I don't think Sierra has told anyone, either."

"It'll come out sometime." Jo shifted in the passenger seat, trying to get comfortable. "I mean, in the end Mr. Riehl only had a few bruises. It doesn't seem fair that Bethany died. I wouldn't want her mom or Gabe to blame us."

Claire shot Jo a look. "That'd be crazy. Why would they?"

How could Jo explain to her that she'd been blamed for zillions of things growing up, most of them way out of her control? "People look for a target."

"I don't really know Doreen, but Gabe's our friend."

Jo's gut said otherwise.

o0o

"Who was that, son?" Dad's voice, stronger than it had been a few days ago, called from the living room.

Zach stared at the cell in his hand, his mouth twisting as he mulled over the conversation he'd just ended. Not long ago he'd pushed his dad's counsel aside, but this time he felt like he needed it. He shoved the phone into his pocket, walked through the archway, and plopped down into the recliner. "Albert Warren."

Dad's eyebrows drew together. "Should I know that name?"

Zach shrugged. "He owns East Spokane Vet Clinic. He's the guy who offered me a job a couple of months ago."

His dad nodded, dark eyes obviously trying to read Zach's mind.

"The guy he hired then wants to take a leave of absence to go backpacking in South America. Doc Warren wants to know if I'm ready to come work for him now."

"Just to fill in? For how long?"

Zach shook his head. "Nope. Permanent. He told the guy he wouldn't be able to hold the position open for the six months he wants to be gone."

Dad's voice flattened. "So you're leaving us."

If only it were that easy. "It was my dream come true."

"Was?" A lilt of hope.

Of course Dad would catch that. Zach leaned forward, elbows on his knees, and met his father's gaze. "I don't know what to do."

Dad nodded and relaxed against the sofa armrest. "Pros and cons?"

Zach hesitated. "Well, the pro is that it's the job I've wanted for years. Albert Warren respects me and wants me to work for him."

"Anything else in favor?"

The museums and movie theaters flitted through Zach's mind, followed by the city's ethnic restaurants and specialty shops. He tried to hunt for more solid memories, like the church he'd attended with Gabe when they'd been in college together the first few years. It had been a big city church, running like a well-oiled social club. Nothing like Galena Gospel Church.

"I need a job. Wally Taubin expects to be back in the saddle next week. Though how the man ever managed the workload on his own beats me. He's way older than me and I could barely handle the hours."

"He might be willing to sell out."

Zach shook his head. "He's not even sixty yet. He's never said a thing to me about retiring early."

"A partnership?"

"There's been no indication that he's thinking any such thing."

Dad appeared to contemplate. "Well, then. What are the cons?"

Zach took a deep breath. "You're not ready to start farming again yet, are you?"

Dad swept a hand to indicate his body. "I wish."

"Yeah, that's what I thought. So the timing, while better than last time, is still a negative." But that wasn't all that prevented him from jumping at Doc Warren's offer. Since the day he and Gabe had sat in the tree house, he'd been praying about Jo and how he could mend the rift between them. Was this God's answer? That Jo wasn't the right girl for him? Zach raised his gaze to meet his dad's.

"So. Anything else a negative for accepting the offer?"

Besides Jo? Nearly everything. The smell of rain in the orchard and of fresh-mown grass. He'd miss Domino, Sadie, and Old Pete. He'd even miss the stupid sheep. The timing was still all wrong. He couldn't leave unless he knew things wouldn't work out with Jo. That God specifically wanted him at Warren's clinic.

Dad grinned. "Wouldn't have anything to do with a cute snip of a girl from next door, would it?"

When had Dad learned to read him again? "She seems pretty special, all right. But she won't give me the time of day. Well, you saw."

"Those weren't exactly the best of circumstances," Dad said mildly.

A sharp laugh came out of Zach. "True. But you'd be amazed. Any time Jo and I get together there are sparks. Not sparks in a good way, either. Sparks that are just shy of exploding the known universe."

His father chuckled. "Your mother used to be like that. Never me, of course." He winked. "She was a ball of fire."

"Watch who you're talking about in past tense," Mom hollered from the kitchen.

Zach hadn't heard her come in. Had she been listening for long?

"I like Josephine." Mom leaned in the archway. "You better make an all-out effort to win that girl over, Zachary John, or I'll never forgive you. She's a wonderful young woman."

"When did you tell that veterinarian you'd have an answer for him?" Dad asked.

"A couple of days."

Mom nodded briskly. "Better get off your backside and onto your knees. Make a plan, and start implementing it. You don't have long."

Zach shook his head. "You're both crazy." But as for the praying, he'd already started in on that. "Something like this takes longer than a few days."

Dad grinned. "Not necessarily. Let's start with this. You need a place to live after you're married, right?"

Zach choked. *"What?"*

"I'm guessing you don't want to live in Grandma's trailer with all those girls, or in here with your old parents hanging around." Dad's eyes twinkled. "And Galena Landing is a fair commute from your apartment in the city."

Zach stared at his dad as heat rose in his cheeks. Did he have to answer this nonsensical question? And besides, it was a long way from a done deal. "I've given notice on the apartment anyway."

"Better tell him what we're thinking, Rosemary."

Mom crossed the room and sat down beside Dad, who took her hand. Both looked serious.

Zach glanced from one to the other. Were they actually going to put the farm on the market? His heart sank. Not that. Please. Not when he'd just started to fall in love with it all over again.

Mom spoke first. "Daniel and Arlene are flying into Spokane

today to be here in time for the funeral."

Zach nodded. Gabe had mentioned his folks were on their way.

"They've been after us to come see the work they're doing in Romania at that orphanage. We've never been able to take the time."

Dad took over. "So, when they go back in September, we want to go, too. They say a gimped guy like me can do plenty to help. Those little kids need someone to be a human jungle gym. Somebody to spend time with them and read them stories." Dad inhaled sharply. "I can still do that."

"What?" Zach stared in disbelief. "You're going to Romania in two and a half months? How come you never mentioned that you were considering this?"

"We just finalized things." Mom patted Dad's leg. "Or, I should say, almost finalized them. There's still the question of what to do with the farm while we're gone."

Here it came. He'd been half waiting for the other shoe to drop. He jerked to his feet.

"Gary Waterman wants to lease the land." Dad's voice came like a knife to his back.

Zach pivoted and stared at his parents. "What? Gary *Waterman*?"

Mom raised an eyebrow. "You've made it clear you didn't want it. Things aren't settled yet, but that's the direction we're leaning."

"We thought you and Jo could live in the house, though." His dad's voice faltered. "At least until we get back next year. Unless you don't want to."

Conflicting emotions ricocheted around Zach's brain. He'd been wishing something would happen to break his folks out of this deadlock with the farm, only… Had he been too late? "Can I-can I think about this for a bit?"

o0o

Zach hauled an armload of boards through the wet woods. It would have been better to wait until things dried off a bit, but time pressed in around him. This evening he needed to be at Gabe's side in the funeral chapel, and he'd set the timer on his cell so he wouldn't be late.

Even with his parents back in town, Gabe needed Zach. Tomorrow Bethany would be laid to rest. It seemed almost sacrilege to seek his own happiness when his best friend faced anguish and loneliness.

Of course, Zach didn't know if Jo would be willing to talk to him or not, willing to hear him out. That chat with his folks had infused him with hope, though he couldn't have said why. It wasn't like Jo had tossed him a bone of encouragement.

Zach looped a rope over a high branch and began hoisting boards up to the platform. Besides fixing the railing, he'd had a couple of other thoughts on the drive to the lumberyard. It wouldn't be that hard to add a proper roof over the lower platform. Maybe—if all went well—later in the season he could screen in the area so it would be welcoming even once the mosquitoes made their appearance.

Whistling, he measured out the length of a needed board and began to saw. He blocked out the passage of time and immersed himself in the project.

"I wondered if it was you making all that racket. What are you doing on our property?"

The hammer slipped out of Zach's hand and dropped from the tree house deck to the forest floor. He stared down at Claire, who'd appeared from nowhere. Thankfully the hammer had missed her by a mile.

He had no words. Surely she could see what he was doing. He held out his hands to indicate the treehouse.

Claire stared up at him, hands planted on her hips and a

frown on her face. Didn't look like she was buying his attempt at the silent sell.

Zach worked his way down the knotted rope. That needed a more elegant solution, as well. Maybe a rope ladder like they sold for fire escapes. But first, Claire.

"When are you moving back to Coeur d'Alene, Zach? When will you get out of Jo's life?"

He opened his mouth, closed it again. He'd known she didn't much like him, but where had this much bitterness come from? "Claire, I-uh. What if I don't want to get out of her life? What if I…want to be in it forever?"

She laughed, a short, sharp bark. "Then I guess you've got some changing to do, buster. Because you're not the kind of guy she's looking for. The kind of guy that can make her happy."

Zach grabbed his hammer and tossed it up to the platform. "What makes you an expert in what is best for her?"

Claire raised her eyebrows. "Maybe I got it from Jo herself?"

Please, God. Help me out here. "I'm not sure what I ever did to make you dislike me so much, but I'd like to point out that it's not so much a guy that can make her happy."

At her look of protest, he held up a hand. "Hear me out, please." A couple months ago, he'd never have believed God words would come out of his mouth again. Whew. He'd had a close call.

She pulled her lips into a sullen line and crossed her arms over her chest. "Fine. Talk."

"When I came home, I didn't want to be here. I wanted to stay in Coeur d'Alene and live the easy life. I only came back because I was between jobs and my dad was sick."

Claire gave a crisp nod.

"But, you know, God brought me back here for a bigger reason."

Her eyebrows went back up, and Zach grinned. "I don't know if that bigger reason includes Jo, I really don't. But one thing I'm certain of. I needed to be here to get pulled back into a right relationship with God."

"Then what're you doing about it?"

He frowned. "What do you mean?"

"If you're walking all nice with God now, how is that changing your life?"

Didn't look much like she believed him. Fair enough. "God isn't changing me like a tsunami, Claire." Zach held out his palm and droplets splashed into it. "He's working in me like gentle rain." Except for… He grimaced. "Gentle rain with some thunderstorms, like Bethany's death."

Claire studied his face, and Zach stood there, hands at his sides, waiting for the examination to be complete. She leaned in close. "Zachary Nemesek, if you hurt her, I will never forgive you. Not as long as I live."

He rocked back. How could she even think that? And yet he *had* hurt Jo already. More than once. He managed to keep his voice steady. "I have no intention of it. But Claire? What have I done to offend *you*?"

She glowered at him. "We came here as a team, the three of us. We need Jo. If she left us for the city, everything would go wrong."

"I didn't say anything about taking her away." Just how would it work, anyway, if he remained in the valley? Would next door be close enough for Jo? Would he feel like he'd married a girl with too many sisters? Not that anything was sure. "Do me a favor, Claire?"

"What?"

"This may surprise you, but I want God's will in my life. Also in Jo's. Even in yours. I've tried to control my own life. That didn't work out so well." And oh, how it hadn't. But if Jo hadn't told Claire about Yvette, he wasn't going to bring it up now. "I'm done trying to manipulate things the way I want them. My plan is to pray, to do my best, and to trust God for the outcome He wants, even if it's different than the one I thought I wanted."

Was her face softening any? "What do you want from me?"

He set his hand on her shoulder, and she didn't shrug it away. "I just want you to pray, too. Not with me, not for me, unless you want to. But for God's will to be done. For all of us."

Claire stared at him a moment longer, then gave a sharp nod. "Fair enough."

Chapter 29

After the funeral, Doreen sat in a corner of the church basement near the stairs, twisting a tissue and refusing the plates of food people offered her. When she was alone for a moment, Jo slipped into an adjacent chair.

Not that she had a clue what to say. She didn't know Bethany's mother well. Hadn't even known Bethany well. "I'm so sorry."

Doreen glanced at Jo from red-rimmed eyes then focused again on the crumpled tissue in her lap.

Mrs. Humbert's words came back to Jo's mind. Words about forgiveness, acceptance. "I-I hope you and Bethany were close." Jo's voice trembled. How painful for Doreen if her last memory with her daughter was of angry words.

Bethany's mother looked at Jo strangely, her jaw quivering. "She was my sunshine," she whispered.

Jo nodded. Would fewer regrets make it easier? Or harder?

"The last thing she said to me was that she hoped she could be as good a mom to her baby as I was to her."

Words that would never come out of Jo's mouth. Did that say anything about her as a daughter, or only about her mom's parenting skills?

"Th-that means the world to me." Doreen blew her nose into her sodden tissue.

Jo snagged a fresh one from a nearby box and handed it over.

"Thanks." Doreen dabbed her eyes. "Tell your mom how much you love her. Don't let the opportunity be lost."

"She drives me crazy. We have nothing in common. All we do is argue. Fight."

The grieving mother grasped Jo's hands with surprising strength. "Talk to her, Josephine. Don't let one of you d-die with this between you."

Jo blinked back tears. "That's what I've been thinking the past few days. I'd hate myself forever."

"And if the unthinkable happened—" Doreen buried her face into her hands for a moment. "If you should go, she wouldn't be able to bear it. There's something about mothers that daughters don't understand." She blew her nose and searched for a fresh tissue.

The holy grail of motherhood seemed open before Jo. "What's that?"

"Your child grows within you for nine months. She's completely a part of you, truly part of your body, of your being."

Jo nodded her understanding.

"But for the daughter, it's different. The mother is never part of the child. Not like the child is part of the mother."

Could her mom ever have had these intense feelings for her? It didn't seem possible.

Doreen wiped her cheeks. "We never expect our children to die before us. When my mother passed, she was old and ready to go. I was ready to let her, but now I see that willingness stemmed partially from who is part of whom." She took a ragged breath. "Having Bethany gone is like having a piece of my soul torn out and stomped in the dirt."

Jo became aware of someone close, someone listening, and she glanced up to see Sierra, whose bloodshot eyes matched

Doreen's. Sierra knelt in front of the older woman and took both hands in hers.

No, Sierra. Don't. This isn't the time or the place. There will never be the time or the place. Not that telepathy had ever worked between them before, and it didn't now.

"I feel so awful, Doreen. Can you ever forgive me?"

Doreen's brows pulled together. "Forgive you what?"

And as fate—or God—would have it, the ebb of conversation in the basement retreated just as Sierra spoke. "My father drove the truck that hit Bethany."

For one shocked instant, the silence was complete.

o0o

Gabe's hand clenched Zach's forearm with a grip so tight it snatched his breath, but he couldn't tear his gaze away from Jo. Somehow in that one second of panic, a miracle happened. Without thought, he'd looked for Jo. The marvel was, Jo had found him. His heart sang. This was what he'd envied in his parents, or the beginning of it, anyway. Her subconscious knew they were meant for each other, even if she wouldn't admit it yet.

Gabe jerked Zach forward. "Did you hear that?"

Yeah, he had. Zach held his ground and put a hand in front of Gabe. "Don't, man."

Not that it helped. Gabe shoved past him and stalked toward the women in the corner. Zach hurried to catch up. "Gabe, no."

Gabe towered over them, face red and twisting as a battle fought within him. "What did you say?"

Sierra, cheeks pale, stood and stared at the floor by Gabe's feet.

No doubt every eye in the room was focused in on her, but Zach wasn't about to check.

She lifted her chin slightly, revealing blotchy eyes. "My dad." She took a deep breath. "My dad drove the truck that hit

Bethany."

"That's no excuse."

Zach slipped his arm around Gabe's shoulders and his eyes met Jo's again briefly. "Man, she's not making excuses. She's giving facts."

Gabe shrugged Zach off. "He took everything I have."

Doreen stumbled to her feet. "Oh, Gabriel. Don't. Don't take it out on this poor girl. It's not her fault."

Gabe sagged inward. He shook his head and turned away.

Zach took his arm. "Hey, man. It's okay. It's all so raw."

"It is *not* okay. Nothing is okay. Leave me alone." Gabe stumbled for the stairs.

Zach stared after him. Should he follow? Reason with him? Didn't seem appropriate. He had to respect Gabe's right to some privacy, but it was a fine line to toe. The old Ford roared to life outside a moment later, then sputtered out of the parking lot.

Doreen sagged back into her seat, pulling Sierra down with her. The two women wrapped their arms around each other and cried. Jo bit her lip, eyeing them, then glanced up and caught Zach still watching her. She averted her gaze, her cheeks flushing.

"Well, if that don't beat all." Mr. Leask slung his arm over Zach's shoulder.

Smelled like a bit of alcohol on that breath. Zach edged out of the embrace and faced the older man.

"Sounds like some kind of irony to me. That Rubachuk boy's been putting on airs about how all his organic stuff is better than anyone else's food. But just a regular old grocery truck wiped out his family." The man took a bite out of a raspberry tart.

Zach stiffened. If the guy couldn't help having such nasty thoughts, he should learn to keep his trap shut. "So you're saying it's justice?"

Mr. Leask's gaze ranged as though gauging the bystanders. "Well, no, I wouldn't go so far as that. Just sayin' there's some kind of quirk of fate, don't you think?"

"There's no point in rubbing salt in deep wounds." Mr. Graysen put his hand on Mr. Leask's arm. "Maybe some of us look at this situation in just the opposite way."

Mr. Leask shifted away. "How's that, Ed? Didn't know there was another way."

Zach shot a look at Jo. Sure enough, she was tuned in, like most everyone else in the church basement. Doreen's face was buried in her hands.

"Is that a good tart, Nolan?"

Mr. Leask's shocked gaze took in the pastry he held. "What has that to do with anything?"

A glimmer of Mr. Graysen's train of thought trickled into Zach's mind.

"Now, let's look at this thing logically." Mr. Graysen now seemed to address everyone in the room. "There's been a terrible tragedy. I don't want to undercut the loss felt by the Klimpton and Rubachuk families. It's real, Nolan. Very real."

Mr. Leask shifted uncomfortably, nodding.

"Nor do I wish to burden young Sierra here. Her family, too, has been deeply affected. But the fact is, like you pointed out, it was a reefer truck. Eighteen-wheelers crisscross our nation, Nolan, bringing California tomatoes to Florida and Florida tomatoes to California, seems like. Big trucks are everywhere." He poked his chin toward Sierra. "No offense."

Sierra nodded. Beside her, Jo leaned forward, intent on Mr. Graysen's impromptu speech.

"Saying Sierra is at fault because her dad drove the truck is ridiculous. Saying her dad is at fault is closer."

Sierra stiffened, and Jo reached out to her.

Mr. Graysen went on. "The deer was more at fault, but that's not the whole story either. I'm sure the man needs a job to feed his family like we all do. What's wrong with the system is that we require so many of those blinking trucks to start with. And you know what?" He paused, looking around the room.

"We can do something about that."

"What's that?" Mr. Leask shoved the rest of the tart into his mouth.

Mr. Graysen grinned. "Good tart, Nolan? Wonder what's in it?"

"Berries. Whatever." He wiped a red smear off his mustache with a napkin.

Zach bit back a laugh. The feedlot owner caught in his own trap. A glance at Jo revealed she'd figured it out, too.

Mr. Graysen turned around, searching the crowd for someone. "Claire Halford? Come over here a minute, please."

Zach stepped to one side as Claire, wiping her hands on an apron, approached. Her gaze flicked around. Probably not used to so many people staring at her. "Yes?"

Mr. Graysen picked up a large platter with two raspberry tarts left on it. Zach had eaten a few of the dozens that weighed it down earlier.

"I'm sorry." Claire reached for the tray. "There aren't any more."

"Oh, I wasn't asking you to refill it," Mr. Graysen said. "I saw you bring this in earlier today. You made these, right?"

Claire nodded, still obviously unsure what the church elder's point was. Zach knew, though, and a glance at Jo confirmed she was enjoying the show, too.

"Would you mind telling folks where you got these ingredients from?"

"Well, the raspberries are from Green Acres, and the honey is from that beekeeper over on Jordan Road. The eggs and butter are from Stedmans." Claire frowned. "I wasn't able to source local wheat."

Mr. Graysen clapped Mr. Leask on the shoulder. "See, Nolan? If more people thought like Claire here, trucks hauling cattle or groceries wouldn't have so much business, would they?"

The other man looked confused. "I don't get what you

mean."

"It's all up to us." Mr. Graysen looked around the room. "We make choices, and businesses rise to meet them. I suggest we start making choices like Claire has done." He poked his chin toward Jo and Sierra. "And her friends. Like Gabe, too. We're going to have a local meal here in a few months. If the food is half as good as Claire's raspberry tarts, it'll be a feast."

Mr. Leask eyed those last two tarts. "Mighty good, ma'am," he said to Claire, and reached for one of them.

o0o

Jo heaved a sigh of relief. Still hated that Gabe was angry, but grief didn't look at logic. Surely he'd come around when he had time to heal. Still troubled that every time she found Zach, though, he was looking at her like they conspired together.

"What a good man," Doreen whispered. "Sierra, child, don't fret about your father. It wasn't his fault. He didn't mean to."

Conversation picked up in the room again, and some of the older women pressed close to Doreen, offering their condolences.

Jo looked up, wanting to thank Mr. Graysen for his support. If only Zach, his back to her, wasn't talking to the church elder at the moment. Maybe Zach would move on, leaving Mr. Graysen free, if she waited long enough.

The older man's voice traveled across the room. "I hear you've got a good job offer back in the city."

Zach's words were clearly audible. "Yes, East Spokane Veterinary Clinic called back to offer me the job I interviewed for a couple of months ago. The guy they hired then has itchy feet and wants to do some traveling."

Mr. Graysen whistled. "My daughter takes her pets there. She says Albert Warren runs a tight clinic."

"He's an all around great guy. It's hard to imagine a better place to start my career."

Bile rose in Jo's throat. So much for reading anything into those looks they'd shared. Any relaxation she might have sensed in Zach came from an obvious source. He was headed back to Coeur d'Alene and the life he loved. Maybe even Yvette.

Good thing the stairway was right behind her. She could slip out without being seen.

Chapter 30

Wally Taubin had been back in the clinic full time for only a few days, but Zach already couldn't remember how he'd managed on his own for six weeks. Should make it easier for his boss to agree to Zach's plan. Maybe.

Zach grabbed a can of pop from the staff room fridge as Wally came in for his lunch break. "I've got a question for you, if you have a minute." He gauged the older man's expression from the corner of his eye and took a deep breath.

Wally sagged into a chair, rubbing his hip. "It's been crazy busy, hasn't it? Does every animal in the county need something major this exact week?"

Zach pulled the tab and tipped back the can, letting the sweet carbonation pour down his throat. "Seems so. How's the leg holding up?"

"Hanging in there. Was that your big question?" The older man's eyes twinkled. "If it was, then it's my turn. I have one for you, too."

Zach laughed. Could his boss hear the nervousness in it? "No, that wasn't it." He hesitated. "I've been thinking. Wondering. Any chance you might be interested in hiring someone full time?"

"Have you been snooping around my ledgers?"

Zach backed up a step. "No, sir. I wouldn't do such a thing."

The gleam hadn't left his boss's eyes, though. "I've had my bookkeeper going through everything in the past few days, trying to figure something out."

"Sir?" Zach's brain buzzed. He knew he was above board. Had Nadine been stealing from the company? He couldn't imagine it. She'd been here almost as long as Taubin had been a vet. "I'm not following."

"I'm pulling your leg, boy. But not about assessing my bottom line." Wally ran his hand along his hip. "I might be interested in hiring the right person temporarily."

Zach schooled his face against showing his disappointment. "Oh. I see." Maybe it was a good thing he hadn't turned down Albert Warren yet. "I'm in need of something more permanent than that." But would he lose Jo? No, he wouldn't think that. For starters, he didn't already have her. And for seconders, he'd given it all to God. There it would rest, no matter what.

Wally held up his hand. "Not so fast, young man. I do have a bit of a dilemma. Some of the farmers have talked to me about your work." He scrutinized Zach's face.

Oh no. Zach wracked his brain. What had he done wrong? No one's animals had died under his care. No one seemed offended by him, other than a few comments about his youth and inexperience. "I see. May I ask what they're saying?" If he were going to be released again, he'd need a good reference. *Please, God, don't let it be so bad.*

"Three different clients have approached me individually to ask me if you were planning to stay on in the valley, son."

Zach leaned back against the counter, daring to breathe.

"Once upon a time you told me you were only back short term. Didn't even want to work for me, isn't that right?"

Caught. "I hate to say it, but I needed a solid reference as badly as you needed a temp. Hammond refused to give me one on account of my breakup with his daughter."

Wally frowned. "Yvette?"

"Yeah, why?"

"That's strange. I just got an invitation to an intimate gathering, I think they called it." The vet rummaged along the counter behind him, pulled a white envelope with gold edging out of a stack, and handed it over.

Zach scanned it quickly, his head whirling. Yvette was marrying Garth Draper two weeks from Friday? Wow, no grass had time to grow under *her* feet. This had to mean she'd given up trying to pin her pregnancy on Zach.

He handed the paper back to Wally and nodded sharply.

"No response?"

What was he supposed to say? "Narrow escape is all."

Wally leaned back in his chair. "Tell me."

"We dated a few months. I—" How to say it? "I figured I knew better than God what kind of woman was right for me. I knew I was playing with fire, but I didn't think I'd get burned. I kept the relationship pure, though it wasn't easy." He thought back. God had certainly protected him. "That's what led to our breakup."

"That's it?"

Their gazes locked and Zach shrugged. "That's it. I'm just glad she found someone else." Some of the stress from the past few weeks lifted off his shoulders.

"Alrighty then. You've had a change of heart, but I still don't want to hire you permanently."

Zach stared at his boss. Those words weren't lining up right, somehow.

Wally grinned. "What I really need around here is a business partner. I don't suppose you're up for buying in at this stage, are you?"

He *what*? Zach snagged a chair closer with his foot and dropped into it heavily. "Let me get this straight. I can work for you for now, and maybe in a few years, when I'm established a bit, I can buy in?"

"Yes, son. That's what I'm saying. I'd hoped all along you'd stay, but you seemed dead set on getting back to the city."

Zach forced his thoughts and emotions into order. "Albert Warren has offered me a position at East Spokane."

Wally's eyes narrowed. "And yet you asked for a job here."

"Yes, sir." Would he regret it? Settling in the Galena Valley looked more and more appealing, but not if Jo wouldn't have him. She'd disappeared from the funeral luncheon when he wasn't looking, after he'd hoped to have a word with her. If they remained at loggerheads—or worse, she married some other guy—he'd regret promising to stay. Once he bought in, he'd be committed for sure.

"You look like you still aren't certain." Doc Taubin tipped back his chair. "I thought a stint of fresh air and open space would be all you'd need to remind you of the joys of country living."

Zach grinned. "Fresh air like out at Watermans' with all that cow manure?"

"Smell of money, son. Smell of money. You did good out there. Gary spoke highly of how you handled things that day. No complaints."

"Thanks. I guess I have some decisions to make." Zach rose.

Wally's eyebrows shot up. "You ask me for a job, I offer you one, and you say you need to think about it?"

Zach met Wally's gaze and nodded. "On my knees."

"Fair enough. I'll join you in that."

As Zach stepped into the hallway, Wally's voice followed him. "Wouldn't have anything to do with that girl, would it?"

Zach kept going.

o0o

Domino had been spending nearly as much time at Green Acres as he did at home. After all, there were more people outside much of the time. Once Rosemary understood that the girls didn't mind having him around—and when he proved he'd zip back home when called—she'd let him be.

Jo picked off a small basket of raspberries and called the pup from his nap under the tree. Her roommates were in town and the weeding caught up, so she'd spare a few minutes to visit with Rosemary. The pup—young dog, really—seemed sedate and grown up for once as they made their way down the road.

Rosemary sat on her back veranda, hand-stitching a lap quilt. She looked up and smiled. "Jo! Good to see you. How have you girls been keeping?"

"Pretty well. I brought you some berries."

Her face lit up. "Oh, thank you. I'll just put them inside and grab something cool to drink, if you've got a few minutes?"

Jo nodded and, as Rosemary went in the house, climbed the few steps and sank into the porch swing. Domino flopped by her foot.

Shuffles came from inside and the screen door opened. Jo glanced up to see Steve trembling over his walker. "Company!" he said, smiling.

Jo popped up to help him with the door then he settled into a wicker chair. Even though she'd recently been an invalid herself, she found it hard to know what to say to him. She hadn't known him before his illness. What had been his interests besides the farm?

Besides his son?

Rosemary bumped the door open with a tray of sparkling red glasses, clinking with ice cubes. Jo thanked her as she helped herself, and took a sip. The raspberry vinegar was as awesome as always.

"You'll have to teach me how to make this. There are more berries ripening than I've ever seen in my life, let alone at one time."

Rosemary looked pleased. "It's the perfect balance, isn't it? Sweet with a bit of tart."

Hadn't Mrs. Humbert said almost the same thing? "Like life," mused Jo.

"So what brings you here today?" Rosemary settled back into her chair and picked up the quilt.

Jo leaned closer to have a look. She'd seen that heritage seed packet fabric the day she'd gone shopping with Rosemary. Rosemary had bought material for several pieces for the Romanian orphans. This didn't seem like her usual fare, trimmed out in pea green and carrot orange. Stunning.

Jo wasn't about to tell the truth—fishing for news of Zachary. She hadn't seen him since the funeral last week, and he hadn't been in church for all his talk of renewing his spiritual life. What she'd overheard about the job offer in Spokane must have been true. Jo shrugged. "Just a pleasant day for visiting the neighbors."

Steve leaned back in the chair, face pale and drawn. "Good to have you."

"That's a beautiful quilt." Jo fingered the edges. On the verge of asking if she could buy it, she hesitated. The orphans needed every stitch of warmth they could get.

Rosemary snipped a thread. "I'm thrilled I'll be able to deliver the next batch of quilts from the guild myself. Or *we* will." She shot a glance at Steve, who nodded though he didn't open his eyes.

"Oh? You're going to Romania?" And how come Jo was always the last to know?

"In September." She hesitated. "We're going for the better part of a year."

Jo's head reeled.

"Steve's doctor has provided a letter for Nolan Leask saying that he needs at least that much time to recuperate before he can go back to work. We've cashed in some savings bonds and, well, we're going."

"Wow. That's great. Really." But it didn't feel like it. She'd never imagined 'next-door' without Rosemary. The rumor about Zach must be true. There'd be no reason for him to stay if his parents weren't here. "What about the farm?"

Steve grinned—or possibly grimaced. "Gary Waterman has approached us about leasing the land."

Thud. The sound of Jo's heart bottoming out. She tested a dozen different ways to ask about Zach as Rosemary turned the quilt and started stitching another section. But there didn't seem to be any way to broach the topic without making her interest obvious. "What about Domino? And Sadie and Old Pete?"

Rosemary set the quilt on her lap. "A rancher from Montana has asked to buy Domino." She gazed fondly at the pup.

Jo's foot nudged the dog every time she pushed the swing off, but he was sound asleep. She couldn't imagine Green Acres without Domino's frequent visits. "If you're selling him, would you consider me?" Tears sprang to her eyes. "I probably can't afford him, though."

Hands trembling, Steve grasped his glass and took a sip. "I don't want to sell him. I want to come home to him."

Hope surged.

Rosemary grinned. "Would you be willing to foster him while we're gone? He half thinks he belongs to you anyway."

Jo breathed again. "I'm sure the girls won't mind. We'll be into the bigger house by fall, so Claire won't trip over him every step she takes."

"Oh, he doesn't need to be inside all the time. Zach can move the dog run next door." She picked up the quilt. "Now that we've discovered the hole Domino dug under the fence between the bushes, we're wiser to his canine ways."

"So that's how he's been getting out." Having Zach move the run would give Jo one last chance to see him. Her gut cramped, but she nodded. "That could work, but we don't mind him inside."

"He's not feeling well right now, though." Rosemary's needle whipped in and out of the fabric, outlining a tomato. "Have you noticed he's got a bit of a cough?"

"He's had less energy, for sure. I just thought he was growing up."

Rosemary shook her head. "There's more to it than that. Zach's started some tests today."

The opening she'd been looking for. "I heard Zach got offered a job in Spokane."

Steve's eyes remained shut, but his lips twitched.

Jo might have imagined that.

"He has," Rosemary confirmed, not looking up. "He's met Albert Warren before and was really impressed with the man's ethics and practice."

There was a short pause while Jo struggled to process this information.

Rosemary glanced at Jo. "It's what Zach's always wanted. Or so he says."

The day didn't seem as bright or as warm as it had. Even Jo's arm seemed to hurt more than earlier. But what else had she expected to learn?

She'd have to settle for having Domino live with her. Sure, the dog adored her, but it was a far cry from the love of the man she'd fallen for. Hard.

o0o

Zach peeked around the open door. "Grandma?"

She lay on the bed, her hair spread like a halo against her floral pillowcase.

"Grandma?" He came nearer, set his package on the table, and touched the hands that lay folded across her chest.

"John?" Her eyes blinked and tried to focus on his face, but didn't quite manage.

He hooked a chair closer to the bedside with his foot and sat, caressing her hands between his. "Zachary, Grandma. Rosemary's boy."

"Zachary John," she whispered.

"Yes." Maybe it wouldn't be as difficult a visit as he'd first suspected. "I brought you something."

"Oh?" She struggled slightly to sit, then caved back against the pillow.

"Here, let me tilt the bed for you." He reached for the button, increased the angle of the bed's head, and helped her adjust.

"Thank you." Her voice seemed weak today, reminding Zach that her time on earth was drawing toward an end.

"I brought you something, Grandma."

"Oh?" She strained to see.

Zach grinned, reaching behind him. "Do you remember Josephine?" He brought the brown paper bag closer.

Grandma looked puzzled.

"Jo. She works here and sometimes brings you treats." Not the kind he'd brought, of course, but Grandma had always liked fruit, too. He slipped a small heart-shaped box out of the bag. "Jo told me that Grandpa used to give you chocolates in a heart."

"Grandpa?" Her fingers caressed the embossed top of the cardboard heart. "John."

Zach grinned. "Yes, John. I ordered this from the Internet for you. Would you like a chocolate?" He opened the box and tilted it toward her.

Her hand trembled but managed to get a piece of candy to her mouth.

Zach selected one and closed the lid. "Here, I'll set it on your bedside stand so you can see it, Grandma. And you can get one whenever you want."

She watched him arrange the box on the little table. "Jo."

He grinned. "This time you can offer a treat to her. The box says it contains organic dark chocolate. Perfect for my two favorite girls." And he could only admit that out loud because this one confused so many things no one would believe it if she told on him.

Grandma nodded as she savored the candy in her mouth.

But there was something else, too. Zach pulled a small jewelry box out of his pocket. "Mom—Rosemary—got your wedding rings cleaned and the prongs tightened." He opened the box and showed her.

Emotion flitted across her face. "John's gone."

Zach squeezed her hands. "Yes, Grandma. He is."

His grandmother closed her eyes for a long moment, and a tear trickled down her cheek. "A good man. Like you."

Zach's heart contracted. For once she'd remembered there were two of them. "Thank you. It means a lot to me, to hear you say that."

"Heaven. Soon I'll see him there."

He held her hands. "Not too soon, I hope." If there was a wedding, he wanted her to come. But it was still a big if.

"Soon." Grandma touched the rings, nestled in the satin lining. Her lips moved but no words came out. Then she pushed on the lid.

Zach obliged her and snapped it shut. "I'll put it in your drawer."

She shook her head and pushed the box against his palm. "For you. Josephine."

"Really? You want Jo to have these?"

Grandma sagged against her pillows. "Marry her."

He'd try. But not just because his grandmother asked him to.

Chapter 31

Zach turned the riding lawn mower in a tight curve beside the end of the driveway. How would he approach Jo with his declaration of love? Would it be best to sweep her off her feet, literally, and kiss her? That had only been partially successful last time. So maybe he should lay down all his cards in order. That he could work here. That his parents' house—

"Hi, Zach!"

Startled, he geared the mower down and pulled off his earmuffs.

Sierra stood a few feet away, straddling her bike. "Sorry to disturb you. You looked deep in thought. I was just wondering if your mom was home. I wanted to ask her something on the quilt."

"No, they're at Dad's PT appointment."

"Okay. I'll catch her another time." She put a foot on her pedal.

"Wait!" Zach turned off the mower and walked closer. "Can I ask you something?"

"Sure." Her forehead creased in a slight frown. "What's up?"

Now or never. "Well, it's about Jo. You see, I-I'm pretty sure I love her." More than pretty sure. Certain.

Sierra shrieked, reached over, and grabbed his hands. "Really? She's convinced you can't stand her."

Zach pulled back. "We've had some problems. Some misunderstandings. So much has changed in my life in the past three months. It's crazy. Hers, too, what with you guys moving here and getting settled in and all."

Sierra nodded, her eyes gleaming.

"I don't know. Do you think I stand a chance? I don't even know if she'll talk to me, but I just can't go on this way." Plus there was the box containing his grandmother's rings burning a hole in his pocket.

"What are your plans, Zach? Because I don't think she'll be leaving here for the city."

He hung his head. "No, I know. I couldn't ask her that. And honestly, I don't really want to go back either. It pulls me in some ways, but it's been good to be back here surrounded by nature. Working outside and seeing things grow."

Sierra raised a quizzical eyebrow. "All well and good, Zach, but you're a veterinarian. Jo said you'd been offered the job of your dreams in Spokane."

Zach met her gaze. "I turned it down today. Wally Taubin offered me a permanent position right here, with the option of buying him out when he's ready to retire." He spread his hands out. "So...Galena Landing is my new home."

Sierra hopped off the bike faster than he'd have thought possible and flung herself in his arms. "Oh, that's terrific news. She'll be so happy!" She twirled him around.

Zach pulled back, trying to catch his balance. Movement down the road snagged his attention. Jo! She stood at the end of the Green Acres driveway, probably out of earshot, but definitely within visual distance. Even from here he could make out the shocked expression on her face as she pivoted and marched back up the driveway.

"Jo!" he called, but she didn't slow her pace. He turned to Sierra, heart sinking. "See? She won't talk to me."

"I'll make her see reason." Sierra bent down and grabbed her handlebars. "Don't worry. She gets a little jealous, but she'll come around." She biked off, hollering Jo's name.

Zach stared after the two of them. He hoped Sierra knew Jo better than he did, because his experience told him that Jo's mind was not that easy to change. He'd have to pray that she'd accept him. He'd been giving it all to God the past few days—and it wasn't over yet.

o0o

Well, that was her answer then. Jo had been trying to catch Zach for two days, hoping to apologize and wish him well at his new job in Spokane. Give him a chance to change his mind about severing their relationship. Bah. There was no relationship.

There he was twirling around the driveway with Sierra. Her best friend. Who said Zach was a great guy. Who said Zach might even be worth moving to the city for. Well, Sierra could have him if that's what she wanted, and good riddance to the both of them.

Zach called her name. Like she would trot over now and ask what he wanted. Indeed. Sierra, too, but her former best friend would be harder to avoid. Well, Jo would do the best she could. She blinked back burning tears and forced herself to keep from running all the way back to the ugly old trailer.

Wheels ground on the gravel behind her. Jo lifted her chin. No way was she giving Sierra the satisfaction of knowing how much seeing them together hurt. Her mind raced over every time she'd noticed their interaction over the past months.

"Jo! Slow down. Listen to me."

She kept going. Almost to the steps now.

The bike crashed to the ground, wheels chirring, and a hand grabbed at Jo's arm. She yanked away.

"Josephine Lynn Shaw. Don't be so stupid."

Stupid, was she? Jo stomped up two steps so she could look down on Sierra, then turned to glare at her. "What?"

Sierra's eyes sparkled. "Whoa, what's got your knickers in a knot? A wee bit of envy going on here?"

Jo shot her a look that ought to freeze over the Amazon then wrenched the trailer door open. In she went, down the hall, and into her bedroom. Sierra shoved at the other side of the door. Jo rammed her hip against it and turned the lock.

"Jo, you're crazy! If this is about me hugging Zach, it isn't what you think. Not at all."

Right. And Jo had been born yesterday.

"Would you just listen to me?"

Jo leaned against the door, her arm throbbing. "Fine, then. Why were you hugging Zach?" How it cost to even say the words.

Sierra hesitated.

Jo's temper flared. "Thanks. Thanks a *lot*."

"Don't be such a baby. I can't tell you what it was all about, but it's not what you think. You have to believe me."

"I don't have to believe anything." Jo crossed to her iPod and cranked the volume to maximum. Rock music thundered into the air, surely loud enough to cover her sobs. She flung herself on the bed but tears wouldn't come.

The nerve of both of them. Zach, leading Jo on while eyeing Sierra. Sierra, telling Jo not to be jealous while making moves on Zach herself. The double-crossers. Oh, what a fool she'd been. They'd probably be getting married soon, and with any luck Sierra would leave for the city. It was more her element, anyway, for all her talk. But weddings took months to plan, and there was no stinking way Jo was going to sit here, smiling and nodding, and help Sierra pick a wedding dress or flowers. Sierra's maid of honor? So not happening.

She needed out. *Now*. In the worst way.

With what for options? She'd find a job at some other health care facility, though she'd miss Mrs. Humbert. Unless…unless she swallowed her pride—as if she had any left—and phoned her mother. Phoned Brad. Asked if that organics department job was still open. Even a lifetime of Brad had to be better than watching Zach and Sierra raise a cute family of tow-headed little boys just like Zach.

o0o

"Hey, Rubachuk." Zach let the door to Nature's Pantry shut behind him.

Gabe stood behind the counter, looking like remaining in one spot took every bit of self-control he could summon.

"I saw you'd opened back up. Thought I'd say hi."

"You and half the town."

Zach rested his hands on the counter between them. "It means people care about you, man."

"Doesn't make things better. It's just a reminder." Gabe raked a shaky hand through his hair. His eyes had sunk back into his head. Guy didn't look like he was getting enough sleep. Then again, could Zach blame him?

"Can I take you to dinner? Someone once told me the food at The Sizzling Skillet was excellent."

Gabe's tortured eyes met his. "Thanks. No."

"That same person wouldn't take no for an answer when I didn't want to go."

"Sorry. No thanks."

"What have you been eating, Rubachuk? Not much by the looks of you. I'll wait right here while you close up. It's almost five thirty. You're not going anywhere without me."

Gabe's shoulders sagged. "I don't want to talk about her."

Zach had a vague clue how Gabe felt. He didn't want to talk about *her*, either. Could Jo possibly have misunderstood? But Sierra had promised to explain. Was Zach counting too much on someone else to fix things? The box in his pocket dug against his skin.

"Nemesek? You're making a big mistake. Life is short, man." Gabe winced even as he spoke. "Don't waste time playing silly games. Get in front of Jo and tell her how you feel. You may not have as many chances as you think."

Zach fixed a light smile in place. "It's probably too late already. Don't worry about me. I'm here for you, for what *you* need."

"No." Gabe grabbed his arm. "Bethany's gone. Sh-she's dead. Nothing I can say or do will bring her back. Jo's alive. Fight for her."

"You don't understand. I've all but worn my heart on my sleeve, and she's rejected me. Time and again. I need to move on." She hadn't even been to see Grandma and found he'd left dark chocolate for her, organic, at that. Surely Grandma would have remembered, even with her fragile hold on reality.

"All but?" Gabe's fingers tightened. "*All but?* Are you crazy? Lay it out. Leave no room for misunderstanding. Tell her how you feel."

He closed his eyes, opened them again. Looked at Gabe. "I'll try one more time. For you. Now, you coming to dinner or aren't you?"

Chapter 32

Jo fingered her cell phone late the next afternoon. Her mother had been on her mind since she'd spoken with Doreen. She really didn't want to talk to Mom. But if something happened to her while Jo held this grudge, she'd never forgive herself. Had Jo been showing Christian love, or had she been too busy trying to push her opinions down her mother's throat? Maybe that's what all this had been about. A chance to spend time with her family and try to make things right.

So it might be God's leading. If so, He had a nasty sense of humor, dragging Jo's heart through all this emotional turmoil to reunite her with her mom and stepdad. Still, in the eternal scheme of things, maybe He considered it all worthwhile.

Jo's contact list was open, but her finger hovered over her mom's name. *Please, God. Give me words.* Jo tapped the screen. Listened to the ringing way off in California. With each buzz her stomach fluttered. What if her mom didn't have her cell on her? Maybe sh—

"Hello?"

Jo cleared her throat. "Hi, Mom. It's me. Jo."

A brief hesitation. "Josephine?"

"Yes."

"I didn't know you knew my number."

Ouch. She probably deserved that. Maybe she should try for a light tone. "Yep, got it here in my phone, right next to your name."

"So, is something wrong? I can't remember the last time you phoned me." Her voice brightened. "Are you coming back to California?"

"About that." Jo swallowed hard. "You said something a few weeks ago about a position in the organics department. Is that still open?"

Silence for a few seconds. "Don't toy with me, Josephine."

Jo paced to the window and stared out. "I'm not."

"You'd come home? Really?" Mom's voice rose in excitement.

How had Jo never seen that beneath Mom's harsh exterior, she really did care about her daughter? Maybe this would be for the best. Maybe things would work out.

But without Zach? Without Claire and backstabbing Sierra? Jo stared at the orchard, the garden, and the straw bale house, finally to lock-up. Was she crazier to leave or to stay? "If you'll have me."

"How soon can you get here?"

Domino rounded the corner of the trailer, head down. A shudder ran through his body, and he staggered then toppled over. Rosemary had mentioned he wasn't feeling well, but this? Something was wrong. Terribly wrong.

Jo launched herself toward the door. "Mom, I gotta go. I'll call you back." She thumbed the phone off. Car. Keys. Thank heaven the girls had biked. Jo turned and grabbed the keys off their hook by the door. No time to lose. She sprinted for the car and opened the hatchback.

Domino drooped against the ground, trying to wag his tail for her as she scooped him up and laid him in the car. "I'll get help for you, buddy. Hang in there."

She jumped into the driver's seat and revved the engine. In seconds she was careening down the road toward the veterinary clinic. With any luck Zach had already left for his new job in the city. She couldn't bear to face him with his dog gravely ill. But there was no choice. No time to stop and see if Rosemary was home, no time to talk to anyone. She stomped on the accelerator as Domino coughed weakly from the back. The dashboard clock gave the time as 4:55 PM. If only she'd get there before the clinic closed.

Jo swerved into the parking lot and laid on the horn as she screeched to a halt right in front of the clinic doors. *Please, God, let Domino be okay.*

o0o

Zach made his final patient rounds of the day, talking to the dog he'd neutered and then the tabby that had endured an attack from a vicious tom. At the front of the clinic he heard blaring, then high, excited female voices. Nadine had been shutting down the computers last he'd seen. There must be an emergency.

He sighed. No wonder Doc Taubin wanted another vet here. The practice really was busy enough for two of them. He'd hoped to finish up the repairs to the tree house tonight, but by the sounds of hurried footsteps coming down the corridor, that wasn't likely.

"Zach?" Nadine's head poked into the recovery room, her eyes wide. "Come quick."

He followed her, frowning. She'd seen nearly everything in her years with Taubin. It'd take something dramatic to rattle her. She flung open the door to Exam Room 2 and urgently beckoned him in.

A black-and-white dog lay on the table. *Domino.* Zach surged forward. The pup hadn't been well this morning, but now seemed to be barely hanging onto life. Zach mentally combed through the tests he'd run and compared them to the dog in front of him. "Oxygen. Stat."

Nadine reached for the equipment to give the pup desperately needed air.

For the first time Zach noticed the person crying in the corner, back to him. Short. Petite. Brown hair escaping one long, thick braid.

Jo.

"Where did you find him?" His voice broke as he swiveled to disinfect his hands. *Oh, God, no. Not Domino.*

"He came to our place, but he could barely walk." Jo clutched her keys with white-knuckled fingers. "Will he be okay?"

Zach met Nadine's eyes and poked his chin toward Jo. "Get her out of here and call Wally."

Nadine put her arm around Jo's shoulders. "Come, hon. Have a seat out front. Dr. Nemesek will do everything he can."

She squared her shoulders. "I'll stay."

Oh, no she wouldn't. Zach couldn't focus with her in the room. And he had to. He could barely concentrate anyway. Nadine led Jo out, still protesting, while Zach prepped a blood transfusion. He only hoped he was guessing wrong.

o0o

Jo paced the waiting room, straining to hear anything from down the hall. Preferably a bark. She twisted her hands, peered down the hall, retraced her steps. Should she stay? Zach would come talk to her. Maybe he'd send Nadine. Then Jo wouldn't have to look at him or hear his voice while her mind replayed the enthusiastic hug she'd seen between him and Sierra.

She couldn't leave. Not if there was anything she could do for Domino. Which there probably wasn't. But still.

Why didn't Zach come out? Or his assistant? Surely one of them would tell Jo if Domino died.

Tears burned her eyes. She dropped to her knees in front of one of the reception chairs and buried her face in her hands. *Oh, God. Please help Zach. Please save Domino.*

But God hadn't saved Bethany, so why would he care about a dog? Was it even right to ask? Yes, the Bible talked about God caring for the sparrows. That He counted them and knew when they fell. Domino was bigger than a sparrow. Smarter.

"Josephine?" A man's voice, but not Zach's.

She raised her tear-stained face to the older vet. "Y-yes?" She stumbled to her feet. "Please tell me he'll be okay."

"I hope so." The lines on his face spoke of worry. "Zach's a good vet, and he has an excellent reason to try his hardest."

"But?"

Doc Taubin shook his head. "It's tight. You're doing the right thing there, praying. God's in the business of answering prayer."

Jo couldn't think of many He'd answered favorably recently. Not since they'd bought the land.

Her disbelief must have shown, because Doc Taubin smiled as he sat down beside her. "Not only is the young man a good veterinarian, but he's an answer to my prayers. If it weren't for him, I'd still be hobbling around needing hip surgery. But as it is, I'm feeling better than I have for years." He patted Jo's hand. "I'm going into Spokane on Monday to see my surgeon, and I expect a clear bill of health."

Jo had once thought Zach might be an answer to her prayers, too, but anymore it didn't seem like it. She tried to smile at the vet but it took more courage than she could muster.

Raised voices sounded from down the corridor.

Doc Taubin surged to his feet, Jo right beside him.

Zach rounded the corner, fatigue plastered across his face. He stopped dead when his gaze landed on Jo. "You still here?"

That hadn't sounded very welcoming. Jo took a shaky breath. "How is he?" Domino couldn't be dead, could he?

He looked from Jo to his boss and back. He practically spit

out the words. "Mouse poison. We've looked at his chest x-rays. Pumped his stomach and run the blood work. There's no doubt."

Jo's world spun. She stumbled back and fell into the chair. Closed her eyes.

When she opened them again an instant later, Zach glared at her from across the room. "Know anyone who uses mouse poison, Josephine Shaw?"

She'd only put it under the trailer, making sure the skirting was snugly back in place. But then… She gaped at Zach. But then she'd moved a piece to show Mr. Graysen the water line. Had she gotten it back tightly, with one arm in the cast? Domino's condition was more her fault than she'd dreamed.

"Your face tells the whole story." His eyes blazed. "We may not be as good as you in other ways, but we don't use poison on vermin at *our* farm. Dad won't have the stuff on the property, so I know good and well Domino didn't get into it at our place. You're the only people I know who have an out-of-control mouse problem. If he didn't find the poison at Green Acres, where did he?"

Her eyes riveted to his, and she could barely breathe. The whole waiting room wavered.

"Bah! It's as I thought. You may preach a good green sermon about fertilizer and water systems, but you don't practice what you preach. Doesn't every package of poison clearly state to keep it well away from pets? Doesn't it?"

She nodded slowly. "I'm sorry. So sorry."

"Sorry won't save Domino. You and your high and mighty ways, all that environmental stuff, and you poisoned my dog!"

Chapter 33

Jo turned in the driveway to see her roommates mixing cob plaster beside the straw bale house. Claire and Sierra stomped in a circle, hands on each other's shoulders, with mud oozing between their bare toes and laughing like fools. Jo stared at them through tear-blurred eyes. They'd obviously be fine without her when she was gone. She hadn't been pulling her own weight since she broke her stupid arm. They were used to doing things without her. She shoved the car door open.

Claire dropped her hands. "Jo, where have you been?"

They'd *want* her to leave once they knew what she'd done. What she'd forgotten to do. "It's Domino." Jo's voice cracked. "H-he got into mouse poison."

Sierra's arms fell to her sides and her face blanched. "No." She swung on her heel and stared at the trailer skirting, but of course the piece Jo had moved was on the back. Sierra strode around the end with Claire at her heels. Jo trailed along behind.

Sure enough, fresh dirt mounded beside a hole that led under a bent corner of the skirting. Not that Jo needed to see it to know it had happened. Zach's accusation had stabbed her heart with the resonance of truth.

Claire and Sierra examined the situation, murmuring to each

other. They could discuss it until the cows came home, but it wouldn't bring Domino back. Only God could do that. He might if He still loved Jo. Not that there was a lot of evidence.

"You didn't answer me." Sierra turned around and rested her hand on Jo's arm. "Is Domino okay?"

Jo hadn't heard her. "Zach had to pump his stomach and give him blood and some kind of antidote. I don't know if he'll make it or not."

"Zach was on duty?" Sierra's eyes brightened.

Of course she'd care about that, but did she have to be so obvious? "Yes." Jo pulled her arm from Sierra's touch and headed around the trailer.

"Did he tell you?" Her voice was eager. Too eager.

Jo stopped but didn't look back. "Tell me what?"

"If he didn't say, I'm not sure I should."

Her worst fears realized. "Look, I wish the two of you very happy together." Liar. "All he told me is what a moron I was to let his precious dog into mouse poison." She wouldn't be able to hold the tears back much longer. Her shoulders trembled from the effort already. "And he's right, of course."

"Wish *us* very happy?" Sierra grabbed Jo's arm and yanked her around. "What on earth are you talking about? It's not me he loves. Open your eyes, Josephine Lynn Shaw!"

That's what had gotten Jo into this mess to begin with. Open eyes. The tears would not be held back any longer. "In my dreams, Sierra. Not in real life. My eyes *are* open. He doesn't care about me."

"He does." Sierra shook Jo until Jo's teeth rattled. "He told me it was all about you."

Jo pulled herself out of Sierra's grasp, backing up slowly, staring at Sierra. "You lie."

"I do not."

"Well, it's too late, now." Jo ran for the steps.

"It's never too late unless one of you is dead," Sierra shouted just as Jo slammed the door then locked it. Their keys might be inside, with any luck. She'd have a few minutes to herself.

In the living room, Jo fumbled with her laptop, willing the airline page to load quickly from sleep mode. She'd looked at the best flights to California. How soon could she leave? A blackout period over the weekend for some stupid reason. Monday. That was the soonest? Three days she had to hang around here and live with the mess she'd made? It couldn't be. But it was.

The girls pounded on the door, demanding to be let in.

Jo ignored them as she entered her charge card number. She could ask one of them to drive her to the airport, but in the mood they were in, they'd deny her for sure. So, how else could she get there?

Doc Taubin. *Providence.* He'd said he had an appointment with his surgeon that day. Surely he'd give her a ride. The airport wasn't that far out of the city. She hunted for his phone number.

o0o

"Zachary? Looks like he's more alert now." Wally Taubin rested his hand on Zach's shoulder.

Zach lifted his heavy head and ran fingers through already tousled hair. He'd sat by the pup's oxygen tent day and night all weekend. He barely dared to doze off for fear Domino would need him.

But Wally was right. Domino's ears had perked and his eyes looked brighter, though his breathing still labored.

He was going to make it. Zach slid his hand in and ruffled Domino's head. The pup gave a half-hearted attempt to lick his hand.

"Take the day off, son. You need some rest. I asked Nadine to call today's appointments and postpone them. She can keep an eye on the lad."

Zach stared at his boss, the words barely registering. "Take the day off?"

"It's Monday. I've got a checkup with my surgeon at two." Wally glanced at his watch. "And you're in no shape to look after the clinic. Go home." He headed for the door then glanced back. "Look, you know Josephine didn't mean to poison Domino."

Zach rubbed his burning eyes. "I know. She really likes the dog a lot. It's just—"

"Everyone makes mistakes."

And he'd made a big one Friday, yelling at her as he'd done. It had been chewing at his gut all weekend, but he'd pushed the guilt away and focused on monitoring Domino.

"It's maybe none of my business, but I think you should talk to her before she leaves."

Zach squinted. "Leaves?" He tried to make sense of the word and failed. "Who's going where?"

"Jo. She's flying out to California this afternoon."

Zach shot out of his chair, Domino momentarily forgotten. "California? To see her mom? But they don't get along." What was going on? She'd been really distraught when she left the clinic the other day. He'd yelled at her. Said unthinkably hurtful things. Regret slammed into him like a bull at full speed. He'd had no business treating her that way.

"So she said." Wally watched Zach closely. "Don't know when she'll be back."

"But—"

"Listen to me, son. Listen real good. She's a fine girl. She and her friends are shaking things up in this community. And I think you've fallen for her. Don't let her go without telling her that." Wally leaned closer, his nose inches from Zach's. "You'll regret it the rest of your life."

Chapter 34

Jo's tears had dried up, but her resolve stood firm. Sierra and Claire had, individually and together, done their best to dissuade her from leaving Green Acres all weekend, but she had no ears for their entreaties. Finally the two of them had taken the car and left for town this morning. As though lack of a vehicle would keep her at the farm.

Her bags stood packed by the trailer door. Wally Taubin would be here in an hour to pick her up. She hated leaving without knowing Domino's fate, but the vet would be able to tell her in the car. No way was she calling Zach, not after that earful he'd given her. No way was she calling Rosemary, either.

She ran her hand over the straw bale walls, partially cobbed in, and tears started to flow again. This house was her dream. This garden. This orchard. This farm. Everything here.

She looked around, walking the property, trying to say goodbye. California was the opposite end of her universe. Brad couldn't fool her with his organics division. It was all for profit, but maybe she could make a real difference there anyway. She could build her own house—adobe, perhaps, to suit the climate. Her friends wouldn't be there, though.

Nor would Zach.

But she'd get over him. She had to.

Her steps migrated to the foot of the willow at the edge of the property. Time to say goodbye to the tree house, the place that had become a symbol to her, representing the Zachary Nemesek who loved the land. That might, someday, have loved her.

She looked up and blinked. The undersides of the platform's floorboards looked brighter somehow. But the knotted rope did not hang down. Jo bit her lip. *Why?* Her last chance to pour her emotions and prayers out to God in that beloved place, and she was denied.

Jo leaned her forehead against the trunk. *Oh, God, please give me your peace. I'm so torn.*

In the distance, a dog yelped. The reminder of Domino was too much to bear. She broke down and poured her tears into the willow's rough bark.

Again the dog barked, closer this time. Faint hope fluttered in her chest. Domino? But it couldn't be. Just a few days ago he was dying. Dying from her carelessness.

"Jo?" Strong arms tugged her from the tree, wrapped around her, and pulled her close. "Jo? Don't cry. I'm sorry."

He was tall like Zach, he smelled like Zach, and he sounded like Zach. But it couldn't be him, because Zach didn't care. Jo pushed away, and through tear-blurred eyes, caught a glimpse of black and white by her feet.

"Domino!" She collapsed on the ground and threw her arms around the dog. The face lick was welcome, but not as enthusiastic as she would have liked. She blinked hard and looked closer.

"It's Sadie," came Zach's voice. "But Domino's going to be okay." He knelt down beside her in the scraggly grass. Touched her shoulder.

She looked up. It really was him. "Is he truly all right? I'm sorry, so sorry. I didn't get the paneling tight again under the trailer after Mr. Graysen was here. And you're right. Such a double standard—using the poison. I'd never forgive myself if Domino d-died."

"He'll be fine. He's looking much better today. It will take a while before he's got his energy back, but he's past the critical stage." He looked into her eyes for a long moment. "I forgive you, Jo. But can you forgive me? I said so many things I regret."

Jo wedged her hand underneath her to prevent it from reaching out and soothing the worry lines from his face. He didn't look like he'd slept for a week. She turned away. "I deserved everything you said."

"No. Never that."

She didn't dare meet his gaze, but the silence hung for a long moment. Finally she managed the words, "Thanks for telling me." The knowledge should help ease her transition as she left.

"Jo? I came to find you." Like a magnet his eyes drew hers. "I have something to show you. Something to tell you."

Her breath hitched, and she swallowed hard. "Like what?"

Zach's hand reached for hers and he pulled her to her feet. "Come up to the tree house?"

"But there's no rope." Not that she'd be able to find the coordination to shimmy up, anyway.

A glimmer shone in his eyes and Jo's heart turned over. "There's something safer." He pulled on a narrow cord she hadn't seen, and a fire escape ladder tumbled down in front of them. He gestured. "After you."

Jo wasn't sure she could climb even this with rubbery legs, but somehow she managed. Hope seemed determined to bubble up, no matter how she tried to submerge it.

Zach appeared on the platform before she had a chance to do more than glimpse a new, sturdy railing. What had he done? Why?

He must have read the questions on her face. "I've been working on this for awhile. At first, I meant it as a gesture of friendship, something you could remember me by when I returned to the city."

Her breath froze. The hope sank. She'd been right all along. "It's me. I'm leaving."

Zach's hand brushed her cheek. "I don't want you to go anywhere."

"But—"

She couldn't have torn her gaze from his for anything in the world. He leaned closer, closer, and his arms began to reach around her. Then a grin quirked up the corners of his mustache. "Perhaps I should ask permission. May I kiss you, Jo?"

She really ought to say no. They had no future together. Instead, she took one step closer and felt his hands tighten around her back. But no. There were questions that needed answers. Jo pushed back and gained enough space to look up into his eyes. "What about Yvette?"

Zach's forehead pulled into a frown. "It turns out she was bluffing. She's engaged to somebody else now. Don't worry about her."

He bent his head to hers, but she pulled away, needing to know. "I thought you and Sierra…"

A finger tucked under her chin forced her to look up. "It was never about Sierra. She's great. I like her as a friend. But she's not you." Zach's eyes questioned Jo as he leaned closer, his lips touching hers hesitantly at first, then with growing passion.

This kiss was everything she'd dreamed of since the day by the tractor. A final tribute to what might have been. She shifted in Zach's arms. "I need to get going," she whispered against his face.

He tightened his grip. "There's nowhere else you need to be right now. Nowhere more than here. We have so much to talk about."

So many regrets. Jo shook her head. "I have my plane ticket. I have a job waiting for me in California."

"California?"

His fingers slid down her cheek and ran across her lip. "Please don't go. Cancel your flight. I need you to stay."

She trembled at his touch. Could he possibly mean those words?

"You complete me in a way I never thought possible. I love you, Jo. I love you because you know what you want, and you'll do what it takes to get it. I hope you're willing to put up with me for the rest of our lives."

Words she'd never expected to hear. Jo's knees threatened to give way.

Zach cradled her against his chest and kissed her gently. "Please, Jo. I love you," he whispered against her lips. "Will you marry me? I'll never be whole without you."

The word "yes" nearly burst from her lips. She wanted him more than anything in the world. *Almost* anything, that is. But trade Green Acres for Spokane? She'd been willing to escape Green Acres *because* of Zach. Wouldn't it be so much better to escape it *with* him? They'd come back often to visit at the farm. His parents lived right next door, or would again when they returned from Romania. She'd find things to do in the city. Local food movements existed everywhere, and if not in Spokane, she could start one. She'd be giving up everything for Zach, but true love didn't come by more than once a lifetime.

She reached up and traced the short hair along his jaw.

He caught her finger between his lips.

"Yes, Zach. I'll marry you."

o0o

The answer had taken longer than Zach had hoped, but her passionate response against his mouth wiped away any doubts. For a long moment he reveled in the knowledge that she loved him back, that their lives would be twined together forever.

She pulled away, breaking the kiss with a startled gasp.

"What is it?" He brushed the hair from her forehead with one hand and cradled her against his chest with the other.

"My flight. D-Doc Taubin must be waiting."

"Taubin? What has he got to do with anything?" But the answer rushed in. The fact that his boss knew Jo was leaving. That today was his hip checkup in Spokane.

"He's giving me a ride." Jo strained to see her watch.

"Let me call him and tell him you're not going. Cancel your flight, Jo. Don't leave me. Not now, when we're just beginning to plan for our life."

"But when do you start your new job?"

Zach pulled his eyebrows together in a frown. "My new job?" He'd thought to surprise her with it, but she already knew. "Did Doc Taubin tell you?"

Her forehead furrowed. "Why would he?"

Okay, he was officially confused. "Because he's my boss?"

Jo shook her head as though trying to clear the cobwebs. "But when do you start the *new* position? You told Mr. Graysen it was your dream."

It still took him a second. "With Albert Warren at East Spokane?"

She nodded, biting her lip.

Zach grabbed Jo around the waist and twirled her around. "You thought I was asking you to move to the city with me?"

"Yes?" What else was she supposed to think? It was all he'd ever talked about. The only dream he had.

"Oh, Jo!" He kissed her firmly, passionately. "Thank you!"

Her lips trembled, but she smiled, blinking back tears.

Zach set her down and took her face between his hands. "Listen to me. Yes, Albert Warren offered me a job. A good job. But I turned him down—"

She gasped, eyes wide.

"—because Wally Taubin offered me a better one. Right here

in Galena Landing. I'm not asking you to leave, Jo. I want us to stay. Right here."

She closed her eyes, and he couldn't resist teasing her eyelids with his lips. "My parents are leaving for Romania on September first. What do you say to a late August wedding? Then we can live in their house while they're gone. It will give us time to find a place of our own. Or maybe build?"

"Really?" Her eyes flew open at that. Those sparkling brown orbs he'd grown to love.

"Really." He grinned. "So you see, there's no time for you to go visiting anyone in California. We've only got two months to put a wedding together. Are you up for it?"

Jo let out a long breath and offered him a tremulous smile. "I am *so* up for that."

"Let me call Wally and cancel your ride." Zach dug his cell phone out of his pocket. "And then, can we do some more kissing?"

Chapter 35

The wedding rehearsal was over, and Jo had changed back into her comfy clothes. This was the last night she'd spend in the dumpy old trailer. In a couple of months her friends would move into the straw bale house, but not her. Tomorrow she'd be at a fancy hotel in Spokane, then off on a two-week honeymoon. With Zach. Every day from then on she'd wake up beside the love of her life. Bliss.

Holding a glass of raspberry vinegar, Jo leaned into the tire swing and dangled her feet against the ground. She'd trade this in for the porch swing on the veranda next door. Not a bad swap, all things considered. Like Zach. She eyed the veggie-patterned quilt that Rosemary had given her for a shower gift, now spread out on the picnic table. Not only was she getting the husband of her dreams, but the coolest in-laws on the planet.

Her mom, dressed in a tan suit, settled on the picnic bench. "I want you to know I'm very proud of you, Josephine."

Whoa. Words Jo never expected out of her mother. "Really? How come?"

"For sticking to what you believe." Her mom ran her fingers along the quilt's hand stitching. "I'm sorry you didn't come back home after all. But, well, you have a very nice young man. Brad and I wish you both the best."

Jo reached for her mother. When was the last time she'd wanted to hug her? "Thanks. And thanks for the trip. To visit Hawaii for their green living expo is more than I dreamed of."

"About that." Her mother's brown leather shoe stroked across the lawn. "That's not really from Brad and me. No more than your college fees were."

Jo frowned. "I don't understand."

"Your grandparents." Her mom bit her lip. "When I went back for their funeral and to handle their affairs, I listed the farmland with a real estate broker. It was snapped up by a golf course development. Then there was the house insurance money. I've been spending the proceeds on you."

"I-I don't know what to say." The thought of her childhood places manicured into greens and sand traps was just absurd. But she had to let it go. Her life was full here. She was rich in what mattered most. "Thank you." *And thank you, Grandma and Grandpa.*

"The wedding, though—that's Brad. He insisted. I'd always thought we'd do more for my only daughter's special day. But you refused the prestigious guest list—"

"No need for all Brad's business contacts to come clear out to Idaho, Mom. I don't know them."

"—and the catered reception."

The church had kicked in, moving the date of the locally grown potluck forward to celebrate the wedding.

"But the cake is awesome," Jo pointed out. It had come from the finest caterer in Spokane. Slathered in real butter cream frosting, of course, and covered with fondant vegetables. The bride and groom on the topper wore overalls and floppy straw hats, and a Border collie leaned against the bride's leg.

Her mother sighed. "I'll just stop by and see if Rosemary needs help with anything before we go back to the hotel. I'll see you in the morning."

Zach ambled up the driveway, Domino at his side. The pup broke away and ran to Jo.

Jo's mom edged away from him. "I can't believe you're having a…a flower *dog*. Whoever heard of such a thing?"

Jo slid out of the tire swing and knelt by Domino's side. "It's all his fault we got together, isn't it, you big puppy?" She grinned up at her mom. "He'll look great with a floral wreath around his neck."

"What if he runs off with the rings?"

Zach came closer. "He won't do that, Denise. No need to worry."

"It's a mother's prerogative to think of everything." Mom sniffed. "Is that friend of yours going to hold up for the day?"

"Gabe?" Zach took a deep breath. "Yeah, he'll be okay."

Jo caught Zach's gaze. Gabe was undoubtedly still hurting, but who could blame him? He'd insisted on standing up for Zach, though. Told them both that's what friends were for.

Mom took a few steps toward the rental car, pointy heels sinking into the ground with every step. "Now don't you keep her too long, Zachary. You hear? She needs a good night's rest for tomorrow. It's a big day."

"Yes, ma'am." Zach winked. "I remember."

Brad, in the driver's seat, lifted a hand to acknowledge Jo.

She waved back and watched the Lexus purr out of the driveway.

Zach swept her up in his arms and gave her a whirl. "Domino knows better than to run off with the family heirlooms, anyway. Grandma's happy you have her set, Jo. Even if she thought I was John."

"She's a sweetheart." Jo twisted the old-fashioned engagement ring on the third finger of her left hand. She kissed the tip of Zach's nose. He'd had the set sized to fit her. "Wearing her diamond makes me happy."

He wrinkled his nose and pulled back. "Of course. Rings don't grow in gardens. We have to recycle where we can."

The End

Recipe for Raspberry Vinegar

A refreshing summer drink
with a tingle like a carbonated punch.

To make your own Raspberry Vinegar concentrate:

- 6 cups fresh or frozen raspberries
- 1 cup white vinegar

Pour vinegar over the berries, cover, and let brine for 2-3 days at room temperature.

Strain out juice and discard the pulp.

Measure the juice and add an equal amount sugar or honey, heating to dissolve.

This will make about 1 quart concentrate. Pour a small amount in the bottom of a glass and fill with water. You'll soon see what strength you enjoy! The quart of concentrate will make about 8 gallons of beverage but stores perfectly fine in a covered jar in the fridge for a long time.

If you're making a mega-batch (I often do 4-5 gallons of frozen berries at a time), you can preserve the concentrate by hot water bath canning quart jars for 15 minutes.

Enjoy a taste of summer year 'round!

Dear Reader

Do you share my passion for locally grown real food? No, I'm not as fanatical as Jo is, but farming, gardening, and food processing comprise a large part of my non-writing life.

Whether you're new to the concept or a long-time advocate, I invite you to my website and blog at www.valeriecomer.com to explore God's thoughts on the junction of food and faith.

Please sign up for my monthly newsletter while you're there! It's the best way to keep tabs on my food/farm life as well as contests, cover reveals, deals, and information about upcoming books. I welcome you.

Enjoy this Book?

Please leave a review at any online retailer or reader site. Letting other readers know what you think about *Raspberries and Vinegar: A Farm Fresh Romance* helps them make a decision and means a lot to me. Thank you!

Keep reading for the first chapter of Claire's story, *Wild Mint Tea: A Farm Fresh Romance.* Following that is the first chapter of *More Than a Tiara,* my novella in a Christmas duo entitled *Snowflake Tiara.* Both are available from most online retailers in ebook and print.

Wild Mint Tea
A Farm Fresh Romance
Valerie Comer

Chapter 1

"Do I have kale stuck in my teeth?" Claire Halford twisted in the VW's passenger seat and bared her teeth at her friend.

Sierra Riehl grimaced and plugged her nose. "We haven't had kale all week. Are you telling me you haven't brushed that long?" She fluttered her fingers in front of her face.

To wave away Claire's bad breath? "Of course I brushed." But in all the unaccustomed staring in the mirror that morning, had she truly examined her teeth? She'd taken a dollop of mousse to her short hair and dug makeup nearing its expiration date from her drawer. Once she wouldn't have left the house without either, but the rototiller didn't care.

She'd even allowed Sierra to slather her nails with polish. Of course it was only to cover up the fact she hadn't been able to scrub all the garden dirt from underneath them.

Claire stared at the small-town hotel at the end of the parking lot. It had seen better days. Probably before she'd been born. Somewhere in there a gray-haired dude had set up a temporary office to hire a chef. Well, maybe he was only middle-aged. Forestry contractors couldn't be too ancient and still hike the nearby mountains every day. Could they?

She puffed out her breath. She needed this contract. Needed to do her part in making the payments on Green Acres Farm. She smoothed her gray slacks. Even for an interview she couldn't do a skirt and heels.

"Look, you're totally going to rock this. Relax." Sierra reached across and turned Claire's necklace.

What if the clasp came around during her interview? "Thanks. It keeps slipping."

"Not a biggie. It's not like you'll lose points for it." Sierra stuck her nose in the air and affected a British accent. "We were going to hire you, my dear, but your necklace clasp shows your true personality is lacking."

Claire couldn't stifle a snicker.

Sierra grinned back. "That's better. Really, how bad can it be? You're applying to cook for a reforestation crew. This is not some swanky restaurant on the pier."

"But I need this job. There isn't another 5-star a block down the waterfront to try next." Though Michel's invitation to operate his newest Seattle restaurant was a temptation. No, it wasn't. Working with him had been inspiring and challenging. Living on Puget Sound was great, but not a place for her to put down roots. Not like she could at Green Acres, at least if she could pay her portion of the mortgage.

"Don't worry. We can manage without it."

Claire stiffened and checked her watch. Five minutes to show time. "Easy for you to say."

Sierra had just come back from three weeks in Mexico with her parents and siblings, for crying out loud. Must be nice to have enough money in the bank to lounge around in the sun, even though Claire had no desire to go anywhere on vacation. This was home. And home was enough.

That didn't mean she could take advantage of Sierra and assume the bills would all get paid on the farm. Claire had to do her part.

"Seriously. It's a nice idea, but cooking for thirty people day in and day out for three months will take a lot of time and energy, and we've just started getting word out that Green Acres is a destination worth coming to."

"Are you trying to talk me out of it? Because it's not working."

"No, of course not." Sierra's eyes belied her quick words.

"Just it isn't the only game in town. We can pour our resources directly into the farm instead."

"By resources, you mean cash. And I don't have any." Claire was barely paying her own share of basic expenses out of her wages from The Sizzling Skillet. With the contract from Enterprising Reforestation, she'd be able to quit her job—whew—and get ahead to regroup.

"Earth to Claire. Not just money. You've done a great job on the Green Acres website. It looks totally pro. Any day now we'll start seeing results from it. We just need to get that search engine optimization stuff working in our favor."

Claire shoved the car door open with probably more effort than required and climbed out. "Thanks. I appreciate that." And she did. But what did Sierra know about scraping to make ends meet?

Her friend leaned across the center console to meet Claire's gaze. "Knock 'em dead, girl. I've got your back."

Claire nodded. "Thanks. Say a prayer." She tucked her folder and purse under her arm and flicked a wave back at Sierra.

She marched forward into The Landing Pad, Galena Landing's premiere—well, only—hotel. It was hard to imagine a town more off the beaten track, even for northern Idaho. Which meant that a tree-planting crew was her best bet at raking in some cash this year.

The front desk attendant sent her to a suite of rooms down the corridor. A hand-scrawled sign stuck to an open door. Enterprising Reforestation.

Please, God. You know I need this job.

Claire pasted on a bright smile and breezed into the room. "Hi, I'm Claire Halford. I have an interview at ten."

A petite woman with a boyish haircut glanced up from her iPad. "Noel will be right with you."

As if on cue, a side door opened and a plump middle-aged woman came out. "Thank you so much, Mr. Kenzie," wafted back over her shoulder. She nodded at the receptionist and took Claire in with narrowed eyes as she swished past.

"Noel will see you now, Ms. Halford."

"Thank you." Claire offered the woman a smile, wishing she could wipe her sweaty hands. Was Sierra serious when she said it might leave stains on her pants? Best not to risk it. She paced to the now-open door, entered the temporary office, and stilled.

Who had she expected to see? Not a guy of about thirty, his slightly messy brown hair longer than her own, with a hint of stubble on his cheeks and chin.

He looked up and his brown eyes widened.

He had no right to be this cute.

"Noel Kenzie." He got to his feet behind the folding table and reached his hand across to shake hers, giving her a good view of a tan t-shirt stretched across a muscular chest and covering the top of a pair of faded blue jeans. A lethal combination.

Better keep some distance from this one. "Hello, Mr. Kenzie. I'm Claire Halford here about the contract for feeding your tree planting crew." Marks on her pants, nothing. If only she weren't leaving stained creases on the folder she clutched.

He took his time looking her over.

Could he tell this wasn't her style? She didn't do ruffles, but Sierra had insisted.

"Just call me Noel." Through her lashes she could see him watching her, a speculative gleam in his eye. A gleam that better be about the good food she could feed his employees, buster. He sat down and motioned her to the straight chair across from him.

Claire complied, laying her proposal on the edge of the table.

He picked up the papers and glanced through the top few. "Tell me what you can offer that's within our budget, Claire. It looks like you downloaded all the pertinent information regarding crew size and dietary needs."

"Yes. The crew runs about thirty people, with five vegetarians and two celiacs." Hopefully he wasn't one of the vegetarians. Not that it mattered, of course. "The menu details are on the next pages."

Noel's eyebrows arched as he scanned the sheets. "This doesn't look very exotic."

He wanted haute cuisine? For tree planters? Claire's shoulder muscles tightened. "More like good, healthy meals made from local ingredients wherever possible."

Noel shuffled the papers to glance over a new one. "I don't mind telling you my crew is expecting a bit more flair." He frowned, still reading. "The résumé you sent in said you'd trained in Paris and worked with a French chef in Seattle for several years?"

That had been enough traveling to do her a lifetime. "I did."

He laid the papers down and folded strong, tanned hands over them. "I'm not seeing that influence in your menu, and I must admit those credentials are what led to this interview."

"I don't have easy access to those ingredients here." She met his gaze.

Noel's head was already shaking. "Food service trucks come to northern Idaho. Where do you think the local restaurants get their stuff? I would have thought you'd be aware of that."

Claire forced her jaw to unclench. At least enough to answer him, hopefully civilly. "I'm aware, Mr. Kenzie." Too bad if he didn't want to be called that. She needed the distance. "I've worked as the night chef at The Sizzling Skillet for the past year and have placed many of the orders. It's really not the same as getting fresh ingredients at Pike's Place Market."

"Then, why. . .?" He raised his palms and tilted his head to one side. His wavy locks slid over one eye, and he didn't bother brushing them out.

It was all Claire could do not to reach across the table and do it for him. Focus. Not on the guy, but on the contract. The contract she was about to lose before she even had a real shot at it, if she wasn't careful.

And then she probably would never see Noel Kenzie again. That would be a good thing. Except she needed the money.

Claire straightened her shoulders and looked him in the eye—the one not hidden. "Your crew puts in long hours of hard physical labor. They need the best possible fuel their chef can provide." She tapped the papers in front of him. "This menu represents a tasty, well-balanced diet to maximize their metabolism."

He pursed his lips. "Thanks for coming in. I'll consider it, and if I have any questions, I'll let you know. Your contact info is in here?" He riffled through the stack.

His body language said he wasn't going to hire her. "Yes, my cell number is on the cover page."

He found the right sheet and slid it on top of the others. "All right then. Unless there's something more you wanted to add?"

Like she'd sell out to the food service industry? Not hardly. "I'm a good chef, Mr. Kenzie. My entrees got starred reviews in the Seattle newspaper, and I pride myself on finding the best, freshest food I can to work with. You and your crew will be delighted with the menu."

A glimmer of humor peeked out of his eyes and twitched at the edges of his mouth as he got to his feet. "I'll keep that in mind as I make my decision over the next few days." His gaze swept her body. "Don't worry, Claire. I'll be calling you. Either way."

Yeah, right. She clenched her teeth into the best smile she could. "Thank you, Mr. Kenzie." She gave him a stiff nod as she rose.

Men. Couldn't he keep his personal life out of his business interviews? All she wanted from him was a chance to prove she could earn a decent living here in the boondocks. Not in Seattle. That wasn't the dream she and Jo and Sierra had been building toward for years.

If Claire couldn't work for Enterprising Reforestation, she'd find some other way to pay her share of the farm. There'd be one. She just had to find it.

o0o

Noel raked his hands through his hair. No doubt the whole mass stood on end by now, but even those zillion antennae sticking straight up weren't bringing in the signal he needed to make his choice.

Not that there was one. Polly Solomon's bid offered everything his crew was used to eating, right on budget. The vegetarian items were heavy on tofu, but whatever. They fit the parameters.

No, the problem lay with stinkin' cute Claire Halford. Only once had she almost smiled. That hint of a gorgeous woman becoming animated was going to haunt him. Almost enough to invite her back, just so he could feast his eyes on her when she relaxed. But while Noel wasn't opposed to a few months' worth of flirting, he couldn't let it get in the way of his crew's culinary needs.

He flipped through her bid again, her earnest brown eyes seeming to beg him for the chance. Noel frowned and turned the papers over then got to his feet and headed into the adjoining room.

"Any other interviews lined up today?" he asked his foreman.

Jess swiped off her iPad and glanced up. "The guy from Wynnton couldn't make it today. He'll be down tomorrow."

Then he wasn't all that dependable to start with. Noel was stuck with choosing between Polly and Claire. He sure knew which woman he'd rather look at over meals, but that was no way to decide.

"Neither applicant suitable?" Concern lined Jess's voice. Or maybe only curiosity.

Noel grimaced. "No clear winner." He crossed to look out the window into the hotel parking lot. Beyond the pot-hole-ridden concrete marched a band of trees. Long, narrow Galena Lake lay beyond, glistening in the morning light with tree-covered hills watching over it from the eastern shore.

A guy hardly needed food with a view like that. Couldn't even see the clearcuts from town. Clearcuts he'd come to replant with new trees, new life for the future.

"Oh, come on. That Claire Halford doesn't look like a loser."

"Give it up, Jess. She's too serious. It doesn't look like she's cracked a real smile in years." It would be fun to see if he could get laughter out of her. She wouldn't be one of those girls who flirted and giggled all the time. Her laugh would be quiet but genuine, more like a chuckle. What would it take to make that erupt?

Jess's sharp elbow to his ribs brought him back into the hotel room. "A sense of humor isn't required in a chef, you know. Maybe she's a great cook."

He glanced down at the spunky gal who'd been his foreman the past four seasons. "Not required, perhaps, but it helps. You know how Simon keeps the crew entertained with his one-liners." Too bad his regular chef needed this contract off for a family emergency.

"There's only one Simon."

Did he imagine her wistfulness?

Jess quirked her eyebrows at him. "And Polly has a sense of humor? Somehow I hadn't picked up on that."

"Whatever."

Jess jerked her chin toward the door. "If we're done here, let's check out that farm on Thompson Road."

"Yeah, Elmer's place. It would be a handy to set up the rigs and tents right at the base of the access road."

"Not only that, but Claire Halford lives down that way. Mighty handy for her getting to work on time."

He shot Jess an irritated glare to cover the flicker of interest she'd evoked. "Not a good enough reason. I don't know that she can pull it off. She doesn't have experience with this type of work."

"Only one way to get it. It's not like she's new to the cooking world.

Noel narrowed his gaze. "Whose side are you on, anyway?"

"Yours." She grinned. "She got your attention, didn't she? You could use a stabilizing influence in your life."

Noel choked back a snort. "Grab your bike, girl. Elmer's is only about five miles out of town. Maybe some wind in your face will scourge those thoughts right out of your head."

And maybe out of his.

1889
Snowflake Tiara
Angela Breidenbach
Valerie Comer
2014

Snowflake Tiara

September 2014

A Christmas Romance Novella Duo
Angela Breidenbach
Valerie Comer

What if someone sees you doing good?

The Debutante Queen by Angela Breidenbach

Helena, MT, 1889: Calista Blythe enters the first Miss Snowflake Pageant celebrating Montana statehood to expose the plight of street urchins. But if her hidden indentured orphan is discovered, Calista's reputation and her budding romance with pageant organizer, Albert Shanahan, could both unravel. Will love or law prevail?

More Than a Tiara by Valerie Comer

Helena, MT, 2014: Marisa Hiller's interest in competing in Miss Snowflake Pageant for the city of Helena's 150th anniversary is at zip zero zilch when she discovers the official photographer is Jase Mackie. Can Jase make amends for past mistakes and offer her, not only a tiara, but a partner in her crusade to help needy children and families?

Chapter 1

Just ahead of her, a group of at least a dozen people drifted into The Parrot Confectionery, talking and laughing. Marisa Hiller growled in frustration. First a large delivery truck blocked the alley so she couldn't drop her box of fresh rosemary at the back door, and now the front of the candy shop was clogged with customers. So much for agreeing to Brian's late-afternoon request for the herb.

She shifted the large box to her other hip and peered in the wide glass windows. Yup. It would be a few minutes before she could edge her way through to the back of the business.

Her gaze caught on the wooden notice board sheltered beside the door with dozens of posters in various degrees of tatter. Homemade ads with photos offered puppies, while tear off strips provided the kennel's phone number. Pampered Chef parties, the Helena Symphony, a new daycare in town. A person could live their whole life off a board like this.

A larger poster in the top corner begged attention. Miss Snowflake Pageant? She narrowed her gaze and stepped closer to see the details. Back in the day, she'd have been the first in line to sign up for this kind of competition. Now? Not so much. Not after. . .

"Marisa? Marisa Hiller?"

For an instant she thought her imagination was simply too vivid if she could hear that voice so clearly, right when her memory of him had surfaced. She'd slipped back in time, maybe. But no. The voice had been real. She pivoted.

Jase Mackie.

Her gut lurched. What was he doing in Montana? She hadn't seen him since JFK airport. Since. . .

For a second he looked like the old Jase. The shock of red hair she'd once run her hands through. The blue-green eyes that once looked adoringly into her own. She'd kissed those freckles on his nose.

But then his eyebrows pulled together and his gaze grew wary. "It is you. I thought I must be imagining things."

"Real and in the flesh." Marisa did her best to tamp any feelings out of her voice. It'd been twenty-seven months and nine days since they'd flung hostile words at each other beside the luggage carousel. She'd grabbed her bags and run for a taxi, blocking out not only Jase's words but Terry's. Yeah, that had gotten her fired. She was supposed to keep personal matters out of her work.

She yanked her gaze free of Jase's and glanced through the confectionery door beside her. Maybe she could squeeze past the late-season tourists peering into the candy case if she lifted the box above her head. "Been nice seeing you." *Liar.*

"You look good."

In jeans with a ripped knee? A tank top with tomato stains? Not precisely the runway model apparel he'd last seen on her. Marisa's gaze locked back on his.

He looked surprised to have let the words out then his chin jerked toward the notice behind her. "Going to enter that pageant? It looks right up your alley."

"I just noticed the poster, so I don't exactly have any plans. Never heard of it before." Not in this century, anyway.

"Oh." His gaze slid away, then back.

She'd missed him. Missed everything she'd dreamed might happen in those heady days.

Before he'd ruined everything.

Marisa took a deep breath. He'd never come after her. Never apologized. Her conscience pricked. Not that she'd left a forwarding address with Terry. No, she'd left everything behind in one go. She'd returned to the apartment she'd shared with two Broadway actresses, packed up her stuff, rented a truck, and driven across the country. Mom needed her, she'd told herself. It'd been true. Still was. The farm wasn't huge, but it was theirs, and needed them both to make it work.

She shoved her hands into her jeans pockets. Cropped, unpolished fingernails wasn't how Jase remembered her.

"Marisa, I—"

She shook her head and backed up a step. "I've got to go."

He reached past her and tapped the poster.

Every fiber of her being stretched toward the heat from his arm. She shifted away. Wished she could shift nearer instead.

"You should consider entering. I can totally see you doing something like that."

She blew out a breath. The nerve. "You lost any chance to give me advice."

"It's not advice." A shadow crossed his face, and his lips tightened. "I'm a friend drawing attention to something you may not have noticed."

"You lost the right to call me your friend, too. What are you doing here, anyway? Go back to New York. Just get out of my life and stay there."

"This is home."

"Since when?" East coast city boy, born and bred. Helena, Montana, might not be the Wild West anymore, but it wasn't big enough to hold the likes of Jase Mackie.

"My folks bought a resort west of town last year, planning to semi-retire, and I moved my studio here a few months ago." He pointed up the walking mall that'd been created along historic Last Chance Gulch.

She could make a snide comment about following mommy and daddy, but who was she to call the kettle black? She slept in her old bed, with Mom's room down the hall.

"How about you?"

Marisa lifted a shoulder. "This is where I grew up. On a farm."

His face brightened. "I'd love to do a piece on a local farm. Could I—?"

Their eyes collided for an instant, then the light went out of his and his shoulders slumped. "Never mind."

"I'd rather not." It would never do to be seen as eager. She wasn't. Not really. She'd been doing her best to forget him. Seeing him again created a pothole in her road, but she'd get back up to speed in a minute. But—what if he still cared? What if he was so awkward here, right now, for the same reasons she was? Attracted but burned. Oh man. Had she just admitted her infatuation, even to herself? Was there any hope?

She took a step back. "If you want to do a farmer story, get in touch with the Tomah CSA. There are more than a dozen member farms. Maybe someone will be happy to work with you."

"CSA?"

"Community supported agriculture. People in the Helena area can pay a monthly subscription fee and get a box of produce delivered every week."

"Oh. I've heard of that sort of thing."

Well good for him. It was her life. Her chosen life, she reminded herself. A worthy calling providing real food to people. She'd been trying to do that in Kenya, too.

Stay clear of Jase Mackie. He's a dream smasher.

She pivoted and yanked the door to The Parrot open. She'd edge her way to the back one way or another.

"Marisa!"

She'd walked away in JFK, and she could do it again.

~*~

Jase pulled into the parking lot at Grizzly Gulch Inn. He rested his forehead against the Jetta's steering wheel. Man, he'd bungled that. For over two years he dreamed of what he'd say, how he'd apologize — if he ever found her again. How she'd throw herself in his arms and forgive him for being an idiot.

Um, right. Hadn't happened. But still, he'd seen her. She looked as good as always, even with minimal makeup and her long brown hair pulled back into a lopsided ponytail. The casual look of someone who worked for a living and got her hands dirty, like that day in Kenya.

He'd tried to convince himself he was over Marisa. After all, he'd been seeing Avalon for several months. Did she even have a down-to-earth side?

She definitely couldn't hold a candle to Marisa.

He groaned and thumped his head on the wheel a couple more times for good measure. Maybe he'd knock some sense into himself.

A tap sounded on the car window. "Jase?"

He glanced up at his sister's concerned face. With a sigh he pulled the handle and opened the car door.

Kristen stepped out of the way as he exited. "You okay, little brother? You look like you just had a nightmare."

"I'm fine."

"You don't look it."

"Thanks. I think." He glanced around the parking lot and spotted her rental car. "I didn't know you were coming up this weekend. Did you bring the kids?"

"Yes, they're around back in the playground with Dad. Todd had to work, and you know how much the kids love it here. So much more room to go wild than the apartment."

Jase fell into step beside her as they headed toward the side door that led to their parents' penthouse suite. "Why did you come?"

She turned laughing eyes and pouting lips his way. "At least pretend you're happy to see me." Her elbow caught his side.

"Why wouldn't I be? You're my favorite sister."

"The only one." Kristen sighed dramatically. "Good thing I gave you a niece and nephew, or you wouldn't even notice my existence."

"Not so." He grinned down at her. "But it does help."

"You need to get married and have a family, Jase. Seriously. The kids adore you. And besides, they need cousins. You wait too much longer and Charlotte will be old enough to babysit instead of play with them."

Images of Marisa flooded his mind. She wore a strappy gown and crazy tall heels, shorts and beachwear as she had in Kenya, jeans—

"Earth to Jase?" Kristen's voice mocked his thoughts. "Your brain headed over to—what's her name—Avalon, isn't it? When do I get to meet her and see if she's worthy of my little brother?"

He gave his head a quick shake. "Oh, she won't be." In his mind, Avalon frowned, her lips pulling into a pout as though tempting him to kiss her displeasure away. But it was true. Kristen would see through Avalon in a heartbeat. Why hadn't he? Why had it taken a chance encounter with—?

"Right." Kristen studied him as he reached past her to open the door to their parents' penthouse suite. "Well, I can solve your problem."

"My problem?" A wave of irritation sloshed over him. "It's none of your business. Sweet sister."

Kristen went on as if he hadn't interrupted. "The pageant is drawing in all these beautiful, poised women. You might meet somebody new."

Or someone from his past.

"Hi, you two." Mom floated over. "Dinner's ready, so you're just in time. Grandpa will be up in a minute with Charlotte and Liam."

"Sounds good." Kristen dropped her briefcase on the marble kitchen island. "Guess what I found out." She opened the latches and pulled out her laptop.

Jase leaned his elbows on the counter and faked a bright, interested smile. "The sun sets in the west?"

"Oh, you." She swatted at him, and he shied away with years of practice. "No, really. Mom and I were talking last weekend about how registrations for the pageant have been kind of slow."

He'd been in Wyoming, shooting a fall wedding on a leaf-studded ranch. "There's still lots of time."

"Yes and no. The businessmen are loath to sink their money into it if we don't get a big name or two on the list. Somebody who will pull in some attention for the pageant among all the other events going on for Helena's 150th birthday. We may not need a full docket for another month, but we do need the right woman or two to make sure people take the event seriously."

Jase angled his head and nodded. "Makes sense."

"And I found someone. I mean, not that I've asked her yet, but it's why I'm here this weekend." Kristen's green eyes glowed with excitement.

The door flung open and a four-year-old locomotive slammed into Jase's leg. "Uncle Jase! Uncle Jase! I comed to see you!"

Jase squatted and pulled his nephew into a hug. "Hey, Liam. Good to see you, buddy." He reached out his other hand, and Charlotte placed hers in it with a little curtsy. "Princess Charlotte." He pressed a kiss on her palm. He knew how mere subjects presented themselves to royalty.

"Sir Uncle Jase, I am pleased to see you." Then the princess dissolved into little-girl giggles and snuggled against him.

"See? Jase needs kids of his own."

He looked up at his sister, whose hands waved as she talked to their parents. Sure, he wanted a family, but at the right time. With the right woman. He blocked Marisa's image and plunked on the floor to tickle the stuffing out of these two.

"It wasn't as difficult as I thought," Kristen went on. "There weren't many descendants along the way, but you'll never guess what I found."

All tickling aside for the moment, Jase leaned against the base of the leather love seat. "What are you talking about, Kris? I'm completely lost."

"Oh. Mom and I talked about how cool it would be if we could find a descendant of Calista, the first pageant winner in 1889, the year Montana became a state. If there happened to be a woman of suitable age, etcetera, and she could be persuaded to run, we'd easily get all the backers we need for the whole pageant."

"Sounds like a long shot."

Liam tackled him again, stubby fingers inflicting more pain than pleasure.

"It seemed like it." Kristen nodded. "But it turned out to be a fabulous idea. There is one person who has the perfect credentials, more than we'd dreamed of."

"Tell us already." Mom apparently felt like Jase did. Kristen always dragged everything out for the most dramatic effect.

"Okay. So you know Calista married Albert, who'd been the owner of the original Tomah House. The family sold it in the 30s and bought a small farm on the other side of Helena. And they still live on that farm."

"It would help if Miss Snowflake is a local girl." Mom sounded excited, especially for someone who wasn't so local herself.

"Right. But it's even better than that."

The laptop creaked open, but Jase couldn't see the screen from his spot on the floor.

"She's actually modeled in New York. She's drop-dead gorgeous. See? She's done a bunch of work for Juicy Couture. Tory Burch. Michael Kors." Kristen glanced over at Jase. "You might even know her. You've shot sessions for some of those designers, haven't you?"

Jase's jaw clenched and the room tilted a little. Good thing he was already on the floor. He held Liam off at arm's length. "What's her name?" But he knew.

Author Biography

Valerie Comer lives where food meets faith in her real life, her fiction, and on her blog and website. She and her husband of over 30 years farm, garden, and keep bees on a small farm in Western Canada, where they grow and preserve much of their own food.

Valerie has always been interested in real food from scratch, but her conviction has increased dramatically since God blessed her with three delightful granddaughters. In this world of rampant disease and pollution, she is compelled to do what she can to make these little girls' lives the best she can. She helps supply healthy food—local food, organic food, seasonal food—to grow strong bodies and minds.

Her experience has planted seeds for many stories rooted in the local-food movement. *Raspberries and Vinegar* and *Wild Mint Tea* will be followed by more books in the Farm Fresh Romance series including *Sweetened with Honey* (November 2014) and three additional tales set on Green Acres Farm in 2015-2016.

To find out more, visit her website at www.valeriecomer.com, where you can read her blog, explore her many links, and sign up for her email newsletter. You can also use this QR code to access the newsletter sign-up.